storm

gathering
rene gu

teridge

Tyndale House Publishers, Inc., Wheaton, Illinois

Visit Tyndale's exciting Web site at www.tyndale.com

TYNDALE is a registered trademark of Tyndale House Publishers, Inc.

Tyndale's quill logo is a trademark of Tyndale House Publishers, Inc.

Edited by Lorie Popp

Designed by Dean H. Renninger

This novel is a work of fiction. Names, characters, places, and incidents are either the product of the author's imagination or are used fictitiously. Any resemblance to actual events, locales, organizations, or persons, living or dead, is entirely coincidental and beyond the intent of either the author or the publisher.

Library of Congress Cataloging-in-Publication Data

Gutteridge, Rene.
   Storm gathering : prequel to The splitting storm / Rene Gutteridge.
     p. cm.
   ISBN 0-8423-8765-X (pbk.)
   1. Football coaches—Fiction. 2. Self-destructive behavior—Fiction. 3. Brothers—
Fiction. 4. Texas—Fiction. I. Title.
   PS3557.U887S76 2005
   813′.6—dc22   2004023860

Printed in the United States of America

10 09 08 07 06 05
7   6   5   4   3   2   1

For Don and Sonja And Don Sr. and Helen

prologue

Innocence was drowning in the blood of this jungle. All around him the sickening sound of small explosions, like the delicate and steady tap of a snare drum, shattered nature's tranquility. He hoped he wouldn't have to shoot a kid. Back home in Texas he never thought life was that interesting or wonderful. So why was he fighting so hard to survive?

A bullet screamed past his ear and he fell to the ground, clawing the dirt to get a grip so he could scoot under some brush. Gasping for air, he trembled underneath the brush, trying not to make a sound. He prayed. He didn't even know whom he was praying to. *Please, please, please.* Whatever held his life, he begged mercy of it.

Words . . . shouting . . . nothing he could understand. But he knew what they meant: Kill them. Kill all of them. He fingered the trigger of his weapon. His mother's face smiled in his mind.

Either he was going to live or die. He could hear them walking. Talking. It sounded like the language of the devil.

Lowering his head, he put his cheek into the dirt. A tear rolled across his nose, but he didn't dare move to wipe it. And he didn't dare acknowledge it. He had no training for this, only simple human instinct. The part of him that still felt human wanted to curl up and cry.

They were only yards away, hacking at the shrubs and the trees. He could stand up and go out in a blaze of glory, killing as many of the maggots as he could, or he could try his luck and hide. If captured, he would enter into a hell he couldn't even fathom.

Another tear trickled around his nostril, and he could faintly smell his mother's perfume.

Ten feet away. Crunching. Walking. Talking. He wanted to shut his eyes, but he could only stare forward. All he could see was a tangled mess of limbs and leaves.

And then a sandal. Black and dirty. It was in front of him now, hardly visible through the shrubbery. It had stopped and turned slightly. The shouting seemed far away. Yet one man lingered, waiting, sensing his enemy was near.

A few seconds passed, and the sandal moved away. Random machine-gun fire echoed against distant hills. Minutes ticked by, but Sammy didn't move.

Finally, rolling over onto his back, he released the grip on his gun and carefully wiped the sweat off his brow. Mud trickled into his eyes, burning them.

Sammy started to sit up. On the other side of the shrubbery he'd hidden under, he could see someone about eight yards away. He'd been found. He jostled for an angle to shoot.

But it was too late. Gunfire filled his ears, and Sammy reached up and covered them, curling into a ball and falling back into the bushes. His fingers climbed up and down his torso. He stared at his hands, expecting to find blood dripping off his palms. He looked through the shrubbery and saw the bottoms of two boots, mud caked in the crevices of the soles.

He scrambled to his knees. "Matty?" he cried. Crawling toward the body as fast as he could, he could see blood trickling out of his best friend's mouth. His baby blue eyes stared at the sky of the same color. "Matty!"

Matty's eyes moved slightly, acknowledging that his name had been called. He focused on Sammy and Sammy took his hand, his eyes roaming down Matty's gaping and bloody chest.

One more breath would be his last, and Matty's face froze out the life that had been there just seconds before. An anguished scream threatened to crawl out of Sammy's throat.

A noise from behind caused him to turn around. Ten yards away in the shadows stood an American soldier with a trail of smoke twirling up toward the treetops from the barrel of his gun.

chapter one

taylor Franks stood behind the Delta ticket counter, her feet swollen from a day's worth of stress. She slipped off one of her shoes and crunched her toes toward her heel, trying to relieve the pain. She'd been on since 6 a.m.

Twisting at the waist, she popped the vertebrae in her spine while staring out the large pane of glass that gave a nice view of the planes rolling to their gates but also allowed the late-afternoon sun to make the gate area too warm.

"Hey, there." Her fellow gate agent, Liz Lane, logged on to the computer next to hers. Liz glanced up. "Looks like we got a full boat today."

Taylor nodded. A busy crowd swarmed in front of them.

Liz smiled and said, "Saw those roses in the break room."

Taylor typed in her password for the tenth time today.

"From?" Liz asked.

"Who do you think?"

"No way." Concern swept over Liz's jovial expression.

Taylor didn't want to say anything more. She couldn't. The thought of it made her stomach wilt with dread for so many more reasons than she could say. "You're a great friend, Liz."

Liz looked at her with surprise. "Well, thanks. Why do you say that?"

Taylor concentrated on the computer screen. "You should just know that. I don't think I've ever met a lovelier person."

A dazzling grin spread across Liz's face. "Thanks."

The red phone at the counter rang. Taylor's heart sank, and Liz seemed to hold in a curse. "Please tell me this isn't what I think it is," Liz said. She snatched up the phone and listened to the voice on the other end, glancing at Taylor and mouthing *flight operations desk*.

Liz hung up the phone. "Flight 1565 is canceled. Flight attendant got sick and they don't have a replacement." It meant they were about to handle a riot.

Taylor studied the oblivious crowd. A family in the corner was dressed in Hawaiian shirts. Three businessmen stood together, each holding their golf-club cases. A father tried to juggle two suitcases and a rambunctious toddler. Two kids, barely over sixteen, kissed as they sat between two elderly people with equally disapproving expressions on their faces. Taylor rubbed her fingers across her forehead.

"You okay?" Liz was looking curiously at her.

"I'm . . . um . . ."

"You're white as a ghost!" Liz said. "Are you feeling all right?"

"This is going to be a nightmare."

"I know, but remember our motto!"

"One passenger at a time." Taylor checked the clock in front of her. Thirty more minutes and she would've been gone. Thirty more minutes.

"I'm switching the sign," Liz said, grabbing the Delayed sign from underneath the counter.

In a few seconds, the two hundred people in front of her would all make a mad dash for the counter. Taylor wasn't sure she could handle it. Not today. She keyed the microphone. "Ladies and gentlemen, Flight 1565, service from Dallas/Fort Worth to Los Angeles, has been delayed."

The crowd roared like a stadium full of fans just witnessing a fumble.

She kept her eyes forward, not looking at anyone directly. "A flight attendant has fallen sick, and we do not have a replacement for this flight. Another attendant is on her way, but because of regulations on how many hours a flight attendant can fly, we cannot board the plane for two hours."

Another angry groan.

"We have another flight coming in from LA, which will be here in one and a half hours. Please approach the counter to have your tickets reissued if you do not have baggage checked. If you do have baggage checked, please go to the front ticket counters at the entrance of the airport. Thank you for your understanding and patience."

Liz eyed her. It wasn't normal for them to send passengers back to the front ticket counter. But it was a way to manage the crowd.

A mob of bickering people shoved its way forward, businessmen pushing elderly people, women screaming at children.

A sharp line of pain traced itself over the top of Taylor's head and down her neck. And then it kicked in. Survivor mode. It always did. Her fingers flew over the keyboard while she handled each passenger swiftly and easily, hardly regarding their faces, just trying to get them to their destinations.

After she helped a family of six, a man approached the ticket counter and handed her his ticket. "What are my options?" he said gruffly.

Taylor didn't look up but instead entered his number into the computer.

"I said, what are my options?"

"One moment, sir. I'm checking."

"I have to get to Los Angeles by seven o'clock."

Taylor typed in the codes. "Sir, I'm sorry. That doesn't look poss—"

"Make it happen!" the man demanded.

Liz glanced over as Taylor jumped. "Please, settle down. I am trying to help you."

"I don't care if you have to put me on another airline; I want out of here. Now."

Taylor continued to type quickly despite her shaking hands. After a few moments she swallowed down her nervousness and looked the man in the eyes. "All that's available is a flight on American Airlines, but it won't get there until seven thirty. Will that work?"

"That's no good!" the man yelled.

"Sir!" Taylor gasped. "Control yourself!"

The line behind the man, at least a hundred people long, seemed oblivious to his rage. She could tell that Liz was watching his every move.

"I don't expect you to understand," the man said through clenched teeth, "but it is vital that I get there by seven."

"Sir, there is nothing I can do here. You can wait and I can try to put you on the other flight coming in from LA, or you can board the one that will leave in two hours, and that will get you there by eight thirty. Or I can put you on American. All the other flights that would get you there by seven are completely booked."

"*No!*" The man pounded his fist on the counter.

The people behind him hushed their conversations.

Taylor pressed her shoulders back and stared hard at the man. "Sir, I'm going to tell you this one time. Step back and lower your voice. Now."

"Why you whiny little piece of trash," the man seethed. "What kind of moron does it take to do this job? It's not my fault this flight was canceled! I deserve to get on another flight! Do you hear me! I *deserve* it!"

"Step back, sir," Taylor said, but her voice trembled.

"*Get me on another flight!*" the man shouted, sticking his finger into Taylor's face.

Beside her, Liz picked up the phone. "We need assistance at Gate 12. We have an irate." That was the word they used for a passenger out of control. It seemed to be an understatement today.

The man's red face whipped toward Liz. "What do you think you're doing, lady? Calling the cops?!" His voice had risen to a high-pitched shrill.

In the distance the pattering footsteps of the police neared.

The man drop-kicked his carry-on bag toward the gate window. It nearly hit an old man observing the scene.

Taylor backed up to the wall. She wanted to get in this man's face. Stand up for herself. But she couldn't. In fact, Liz was the one who called security. Shame made her knees weak. She had never been able to stand up for herself. Not to her alcoholic father. Not to her dominating supervisor. Not to her whacked-out boyfriend.

But that was all about to change.

Suddenly Taylor lunged forward. "Get out of my face, you loser!" she screamed.

The man froze. The line behind him moved back. Liz's mouth hung open. But before Taylor could say anything else, the police seized the man and threw him to the floor. Quickly handcuffing him, they picked him up and dragged him away. He was hollering obscenities all the way out of sight.

Taylor shut her eyes, took a deep breath, and stepped

forward, trying to smile at the next passenger, an older businessman.

"Whatever flight you can get me on is fine," he said meekly.

Taylor typed in his passenger number, then felt a hand on her shoulder. "You better come with me," Edward Foster, her supervisor, said. Behind him, Roger, another agent, was waiting to take her place.

"I'm fine," Taylor said, brushing the hair out of her face. "It's over."

"Come with me, Miss Franks," he said, taking her arm and forcing her toward the Jetway.

Taylor glanced at the crowd. A few sympathetic faces scattered among the mostly annoyed ones told her she might as well have been the sick flight attendant.

Inside the Jetway, Edward stopped and stood in front of her. "What was that back there?" he said in his usual demeaning tone.

"The guy went nuts."

"So did you."

"I just stood up for myself." Taylor knew perfectly well that Edward couldn't possibly understand the power she drew from this one small incident.

"That isn't protocol, Taylor," he said in his squeaky little voice that made her want to set a mousetrap.

Taylor bit her lip, not sure what was more maddening: Edward Foster and his dreamworld of authority or half-insane passengers with airport rage. "It's 1995, Edward. People do crazy things these days. How was I to know that guy didn't have a knife or something worse? I was just defending myself."

"First of all, he's already been checked through security, so he wouldn't have a weapon. Secondly, screaming at him and calling him a loser wasn't even close to appropriate. I'm going to have to write you up. I hate to do that, but what you did back there was unacceptable." His white blond eyebrows elevated halfway up his forehead. "Go ahead and go on home. I'll see you tomorrow." He turned and exited the Jetway.

Taylor was trembling from head to toe. Little did Edward know she'd just been stepped on one too many times.

The skin on Aaron's cheek burned and tingled as if someone had struck a match against his jawbone. He panted underneath the heavy hand that was clasped over his nose and mouth. His body twisted and writhed against his brother's. If he could only get his knee loose . . . there!

Cusswords mingled with spit spattered across Aaron's face, but now his brother was on the ground and beneath him in one quick maneuver. Mick had always cussed like a sailor, and today was no exception. Years of anger bubbled just beneath the surface, hot lava about to spew.

"Settle down!" Aaron yelled at him.

Pinned against the ground, Mick stared hard into Aaron's eyes, trying to catch his breath. "Don't tell me to settle down."

The gaping wound across Mick's left eyebrow shimmered like the fiery indignation in his eyes. Aaron had caught him with a left hook only moments before. He had not meant to split the skin, but it had been his first instinct when Mick swung at him.

"I'm going to stand up, Mick. If you try anything again, though, I'll put your face in the dirt and knock you unconscious."

"I'd like to see you try that."

"Make a move and you'll be licking dirt in your sleep." Aaron rose, cautiously backing away from him.

Mick sat up, touching the back of his wrist to the wound above his brow while looking at his brother.

"You're going to need stitches," Aaron said.

Mick cursed again under his breath and scooted a few feet away so his back was against a large maple tree.

"My goodness, you have a mouth on you."

"Shut up," Mick said. "I'm so sick of your holier-than-thou act." He stood, causing Aaron to take guard. He hobbled toward his house. "It was stupid of you to come here today. What did you think was going to happen? I'd throw my arms around you? pat you on the back? beg to be your best man?"

"I didn't have any expectations," Aaron said. "I just thought you should know."

"Ah. A warning."

"I didn't expect you'd jump up and down. I didn't expect you to swing at me either."

Mick shrugged and stared at the horizon barely visible through the crowd of homes in front of him. "So you told me. What are you sticking around for? Want to go another round?"

"I'm not here to fight with you. Why are you so upset about this? You weren't in love with her!"

Mick's chuckle was low and deep, mixed with a groan. "Is that your justification? I wasn't in love with her? How could I know that? You stole her three weeks into the relationship!"

"I didn't steal her, Mick. She didn't want to be with you."

"Did she tell you that?"

Aaron looked away. His brother's wrath seemed incurable. It had been four months, and he was as angry as the day it happened. "You would've dumped her like every other girl you use and dump. Jenny is too special for that."

"You don't have to tell me she's special. I know that. I knew it the day I met her."

"You need to get your life together, little brother. What's it going to take with you? You've already wrecked your car, nearly killed yourself, drunk out of your mind. You can't hold a steady job, a steady relationship. You alienate almost everyone who tries to help you."

"So I need to be more like you, is that it? Elite law enforcer. Perfect lover. Best son. Child of God."

"Why do you always make this about us? It isn't a competition, Mick. Can't you see your life is spinning out of control?"

"Maybe by your standards. But the problem is, nobody can live by your standards. Have you mentioned them to Jenny yet? Have you let her know you expect her to be perfect?"

"Unbelievable!" Aaron shouted and then turned away, ripping his fingers through his hair. "You drive me crazy! I'm going to be burying my little brother someday! My only brother! Because you're so *stubborn*!"

"You have the solution to everything, don't you?" Mick murmured, sweeping past him in the backyard and heading to his back porch. "Go to church. Be good. Be nice. Accept the fact that my brother stole the one woman that I—" He stopped and wiped his mouth. "You can let yourself out the back gate. And don't expect an appearance at the wedding. Frankly, I never want to see you again." Mick opened the screen door and slammed it shut on his way in.

Mick's temper knew how to coax Aaron into doing things he shouldn't. How Aaron wanted to kick down that door and choke some sense into that boy!

Instead he checked his watch. He was supposed to

meet Jenny in an hour for their regular Tuesday night dinner. He opened the gate, latched it back, and limped to his truck.

He was getting too old for these kinds of fights.

"What happened to you?" Jenny's mouth hung open as she stood in greeting at their favorite restaurant. Aaron kissed her on the cheek and sat down. "Are you okay? Did something happen at work?"

Two bruises on either side of his left eye and a scrape across his chin and jaw were evidence enough of a doomed attempt at talking with his brother.

"I'm fine. It looks worse than it is."

"Yeah, right. What happened?"

"I went to see Mick today."

"You told him?"

"Yeah."

"He hit you?"

"He didn't take it well."

Her eyes brimmed with tears, which they often did because of an overly tender heart that had won his affection almost immediately. "I'm sorry," she said.

"Mick's a loose cannon. He's still angry. He's been angry for a long time, way before you came along. It just all came out today."

"I guess."

"I think Mick had stronger feelings for you than we realized," Aaron said, pausing as the waiter took their drink orders.

"Why do you say that?"

"Just some things he said."

"Oh."

"It'll be okay."

Jenny stared at the table, her arms folded loosely in her lap, her lips puffed with sadness.

The waiter returned and Aaron ordered for both of them. When the waiter left, Aaron couldn't contain the question any longer. "Were you ever in love with Mick?"

"What kind of question is that?"

"It's a simple one."

"Who am I sitting here with? Who am I going to marry?"

Aaron tried to smile, but her expression told him things he didn't want to hear. "You were in love with him."

"He was completely wrong for me. You know that. We've talked about it."

"We talked about how wrong he was for you. That doesn't mean you weren't in love with him."

"Why are you asking now?"

"Because I want to know."

"What does it change?"

"Nothing. On my end. But maybe it will help me understand Mick a little better," Aaron said. "When I told him today, he was so crushed. I thought you two had a casual relationship. That's how it seemed when I met you."

"It was a casual relationship. I knew the moment Mick and I met that he was trouble."

"So why did you date him?"

"I was tempted; I admit it. I'd been a good girl all my life, gone to church, dated the good, Christian guy. And then I met Mick. And he was . . ." She looked unsure if she should go on.

"I know, I know. Strikingly handsome."

"That's not what I was going to say."

"Come on," Aaron said. "It's been that way our whole lives. I was always the mature, good son with high ambitions. Mick always had the looks."

11

"You're handsome and you know it."

"You were saying?"

"I don't know if I should go on."

"I didn't mean to interrupt."

"Maybe you did. Maybe you don't want to hear this. And maybe you shouldn't. What good is it going to do now? I'm in love with *you*. I'm going to marry *you*, Aaron. You're the one who I've waited my whole life for. You're the one who saved me from marrying a guy like Mick."

"Mick thinks he was in love with you."

"I can't speak for Mick." She stared at the straw in her drink. "It was an intense relationship. Only three weeks. But intense. I was nearly willing to throw away all my convictions for that guy. And then I met you." She smiled. "And I knew you were the right one for me."

Aaron propped his head up with his hand and scratched at his forehead with his fingers. "You know, I always wanted to be Mick when we were younger. I always wanted to be that guy who could have any woman I wanted. By God's grace I ended up with the *only* woman I ever wanted." His grin faded with thoughts of Mick. "I'm so scared for Mick. I don't want to see him throw his life away. All he wants to do is chase storms and women—with a shot of tequila, or whatever it is he drinks."

"He'll find his way," Jenny said. "God won't let him slip away without a fight."

chapter two

the swarthy, soulful harmony of Seal's "Kiss From a Rose" pumped through the bar's stereo system. For a Wednesday night, the dance floor was crowded with attentive couples.

"Another scotch," Mick told Jimmy.

Jimmy shot him the familiar just-this-last-time look and took his glass. Soon another glass slid toward him. "You okay?"

"Yeah," Mick said. "My brother's getting married."

"Aaron, right? The cop?"

"Yeah."

"Well, tell him congratulations. And whatever you do, don't lose the ring, like I did at my brother's wedding. It was a nightmare."

Mick turned on his barstool to watch the crowd again, scanning the room for the kind of woman that might want to marry him. It was an amusing game he liked to play after his third scotch. Near the door a tall, sophisticated, way-too-young blonde engaged in a lively chat with girl-friends. Near the bathrooms a professional woman, maybe an attorney, stood with two friends, looking out of place and ready to go home.

He imagined a conversation.

"And what do you do for a living, Mick?"

"Well, Miss Professional Woman, I'm a part-time football

coach and just got fired from my accounting job that I have to work because I can't make enough money coaching football. Oh, you have to leave so soon?"

Another woman, a redheaded giggler broke his concentration. She glanced up at Mick once, shot him a smile, and went back to whatever was so stinkin' funny.

The cumbersome Band-Aid above his brow reminded him he probably should've gone to get stitches, but why not have a scar as a token of brotherly love? His fingers retreated as his day-old wound shouted out its protest with a surge of pain.

Across the bar on the other side, he spotted a beautiful, petite brunette. Her hair was cut short, right below her ears, wispy and modern. Was she gazing into a scotch? He watched her for a few moments, wondering if someone would join her. But her only companion seemed to be formidable thoughts. Bryan Adams's "Have You Ever Really Loved a Woman" cleared the bar and crowded the dance floor again.

Mick stood, making his way around to the other side of the bar, flashing Jimmy a smile as he noticed his intention. Mick took the seat next to her. "Hi."

The woman looked up, gloom brushing annoyance over her face. "Please do yourself a favor, save yourself some time, and go away. I'm not here to get picked up."

Mick smiled. Feisty. "I don't find many women who drink scotch."

"Good for you. Now go away."

"Come on. At least let me buy you another drink. Looks like you could use a little more liquid to drown your sorrows in. I've been watching you. You look depressed."

"Why don't you just leave me alone, okay? I'm not interested in spilling my guts to a guy who looks like he's been in one too many bar fights."

"Who says I want you to spill your guts? I was hoping I could spill mine."

She looked at him sideways, and amusement softened her expression. "Got it bad, do you? What, did some beautiful woman dump you for a better man?"

"Something like that."

"Well, there are certainly many women around here who would be willing to be your rebound. I'm not one of them." She sipped her scotch and studied him. "You are a handsome one, aren't you?"

"But never the good son. That's my brother's job."

"Oh, poor thing. Handsome and rebellious. What a combination. I think I dated you in high school."

Mick grinned. "I wish."

"Look," she said, "I'm flattered you're over here. You're just as adorable as you can be, even with scotch on your breath. But I need to think. And I can't do that while you're whispering sweet nothings into my ear."

"What are you thinking about?"

"And apparently not the smart son either. Aren't you getting the message here? I want to be alone."

"Maybe you don't need to be alone. Maybe you need an ear."

"I have two of them. Thanks."

"Come on. I'll tell you my sob story; you tell me yours."

She laughed. "Is that seriously the pickup line you use on all the ladies?"

"Only the ones who look sad."

Her thumbs traced the rim of her glass. "Okay, maybe on any other night I might entertain the thought of sharing a dance and a drink with you. Those eyes of yours are tantalizing, to say the least. But not tonight. This isn't a good night." Her eyes darkened.

"All right." Mick touched her shoulder and she startled.

"But whatever's bothering you, you shouldn't keep it inside. Believe me. Keeping it inside makes you do crazy things, like clobbering your only brother and telling him you hate him."

She looked at his Band-Aid and then at him. "I'll keep that in mind. Thanks."

Mick slid off the barstool and turned to head to the bathroom.

But she said, "She must've been something special."

"Who?"

"Whoever you lost."

"Why do you say that?"

"Because of the way you're looking at me. You're over here to pick up on me, but in your eyes I see someone else's heart in the way."

"Yeah, well, she's out of the picture now, so I guess it's time to move on."

"She broke your heart?"

"I broke my own heart. I was too stupid to see what I had in front of me. I didn't realize it until she was gone into the arms of my brother."

Her eyes registered surprise. "Interesting."

"Yeah. Well, enjoy your evening."

Mick went to the bathroom, splashed water on his face, and then leaned against a stall door, trying to make the right decision for once in his life. He should go home. He'd had enough to drink. Staying around the bar would only get him in trouble. There was nothing here for him but a bad hangover. Swinging the stall door open, he tripped and fell against a small brick alcove, his right cheek scraping against the rough surface.

"Go home for once in your miserable life, you moron!" he growled, rubbing his cheek and checking for blood. No blood. "Learn something from your brother."

Mick agreed with himself and left the bathroom. He pulled out a twenty to pay Jimmy, then turned.

Standing behind him was the woman he'd just spoken with. She offered a gentle smile, holding out her hand. "My name is Taylor."

He shook it. Firm grip, silky skin. "Mick Kline."

"Maybe I'm up for a sad story after all," she said, sliding onto a barstool.

Mick sat next to her and looked at Jimmy. "Two scotches, please."

Shep Crawford's fingers rolled across the ten pencils whose tips were still dull and blunt while the clear buzzing sound of the pencil sharpener filled the office. He pulled the second pencil out of the sharpener and examined the flawless point. He pressed his finger into it and drew blood. Perfect. The pencils were a rarity. One could hardly find a pencil at a police station, only black ballpoint pens, which was why the majority of his were locked in the bottom-left desk drawer.

He placed the pencil into the silver holder that sat three inches from the right corner of his desk, next to the stamp dispenser and the stack of envelopes ready to go out in tomorrow's mail, laid out in order of importance. Each stamp was flush against the white corner of the paper.

He picked up the third pencil and let the sharpener blades saw at its wooden flesh. The sound filtered out the murmuring coming from behind other cubicles. Computers, machines, lights, people. Sometimes he wished they would all just shut up.

Detective Randy Prescott, with his fancy hair and his fancy shirt, strolled up beside Shep's desk, setting his coffee mug on a stack of folders, which he eyed curiously. "How long did it take you to stack these?"

"If you leave a coffee ring on that folder, you're going to be wearing it, not drinking it."

Randy sighed and picked up his mug, glancing at the top of the folder to make sure there was no evidence of a coffee ring.

Shep nodded in the direction of Randy's desk, which looked like a pile of garbage. A real stink in the midst of the homicide division. "Five seconds of extra effort to not live like a pig."

Randy smirked off the comment and sipped his coffee. Shep put pencil number four in the sharpener.

"They have mechanical pencils you never have to sharpen," Randy said.

Randy was probably just trying to be helpful. He was new to the division and hadn't picked up on Shep's "idiosyncracies," as his captain, Fred Bellows, liked to put it.

Idiosyncracies. He'd heard a fellow detective call it idiot-syncracies once. He paid for it; he was now working the desk in some small town. Everyone paid for things eventually.

He sharpened pencil number five.

Randy still stood by Shep's desk and suddenly picked up the small framed picture that sat at the edge. "Who is this? Your dad?"

"I don't expect you to know who that is, but for the betterment of your measly little life, I'll tell you. Thomas Juggerson."

"Who?"

Shep snatched the frame out of Randy's hand and placed it back on his desk after wiping Randy's fat thumbprint off the glass. "They were going to throw this away. They're redoing the entryway, making it more 'modern.' Thomas was going to be thrown out with the trash."

"He a relative?"

"No, Randy, he is not a relative. He happens to be one of the bravest men around. Back in 1960, this man gave his life and saved five of his fellow officers in a shoot-out. You don't see that kind of bravery these days. Nobody cares about the guy who gives everything. Out with the trash." Shep stared at Juggerson's haunting gray eyes.

"Well, I'm going home," Randy said, checking his watch. "You know it's after nine, right?"

The whirling sound of the sharpener was the only reply Randy got. He shrugged and walked back to his messy desk, shuffling papers around before he was able to put his coffee mug down.

Pig.

Shep stole glances at Randy. Perhaps Randy thought his wardrobe made up for his incompetence. The man had yet to solve a crime on his own. He wore the detective badge like a piece of women's jewelry.

"See you tomorrow," Randy said as he passed Shep's desk, carrying a soft leather bag stuffed with Cheetos and files and who knew what else. It bulged at its center.

Irritation picked at Shep. His fingers twitched, and an anxious foot bounced his knee up and down. "Tomorrow." He smiled. "Gonna catch me a bad man tomorrow."

Randy turned to him. "There hasn't even been a crime committed."

"There are always crimes being committed," Shep said. "Always men wronging other men. And they think they're not going to get caught. Always. They go on with their lives. And think they'll never get caught." He picked up pencil number six.

Randy Prescott should be selling insurance somewhere. He didn't belong in homicide. But Captain Bellows always did like a suck-up. The sharpener's sound rose in pitch as Shep pressed the pencil down harder.

Randy moved on.

Taking the pencil out, he examined it. Poked his finger into it. Picked up pencil number seven.

Five minutes later, Shep had twelve perfectly sharpened, No. 2 pencils. He pulled them together in the pencil holder so all the erasers touched one another. He swept his hand across his desk. Everything was in its place. Even Randy, whose place was somewhere outside this office. Probably with his homey little wife and bratty little kid.

"Gonna catch me a bad man," he said in a singsong. The alarm on his watch beeped.

Now it was time to leave.

chapter three

Something soft poked into Mick's cheek when he tried to move and pry open his right eye. A bright patch of light stung his vision. Nausea swirled in his stomach with his tiniest movement, and his head roared with pain.

Hangover. Go figure.

But where was he?

He tried not to focus on the physical ailments that were giving him few clues as to the mystery of his surroundings but on his memory, which was foggy at best.

His fingers came to life suddenly, and as he patted his way around his body he realized he was on . . . carpet?

Not a good sign.

He rolled his forehead so it was facing down and opened his eyes. Yes. He was staring at beige carpet.

A disgruntled groan fled his throat when he lifted himself up off the carpet into a kneeling position. His stomach lurched and his head spun. Taking deep breaths, he managed to recover enough so he could open his eyes again. In front of him was a multicolored, pastel couch. Next to it were a recliner, light blue, and a TV and a stand, decorated with picture frames and ivy real enough looking to be fake. A quaint, brick fireplace was against one wall, and there was a small kitchen and dining area. He gazed outside through sheer white curtains. He could see a railing. He was in an apartment.

Whose apartment?

He stood, steadied himself three times, and walked to the kitchen, turning on the water and splashing his face, then spitting out the vile taste in his mouth. He grabbed a glass from the cabinet next to the sink and drank half a glass of water. A horrible uneasiness settled into his emotions, causing him to hold his breath.

Was that a shower running? No. The treetops swishing in the wind outside. A window was slightly open, and the screen was hanging off. His ears tuned in to the sounds outside. Busy streets.

He slowly made his way back toward the living room, looking around, shielding his bloodshot eyes from the light coming in through the windows. As he neared the couch, an image of a woman shot through his mind.

Taylor. He remembered sitting on the couch with her. She was at one end; he was at the other. Had she been crying? He couldn't remember. But now he knew where he was.

Had he passed out in the middle of her living-room floor? fallen off the couch? A groan left his lips, and he covered his mouth in embarrassment.

He picked up a picture of Taylor and a friend from the top of her TV. Her brown hair was longer, held back with a clip at the back of her head. Her friend, a blonde with sunglasses on, hung her arm around Taylor's neck.

Mick walked toward the back bedroom, carefully listening for anything. But the apartment was quiet.

"Taylor?" he managed, his voice scratchy and accompanied by a burning sensation in his throat. "Taylor? It's Mick."

Nobody was home. Had she left him passed out in her living room? Mick sighed. He patted his back jeans pocket, glad to know his wallet and keys were still there. He wandered around the apartment, trying to get a better idea of the woman who'd taken him to her home last night. He was fully dressed and relieved to know he'd not done something incredibly stupid . . . other than pass out on her living-room floor. That was embarrassingly stupid.

Her house smelled like a florist's shop, but there were no fresh flowers around. Lots of candles, though. And a lot of mementos indicating she liked to travel.

Mick forced an imaginary conversation with Aaron and what would surely be accusations out of his mind and decided he'd better find out what time it was.

He looked at the microwave clock: 7:30 a.m.

Panic raced him across the room toward the door. He was supposed to be at the school in fifteen minutes to help in the weight room. He decided to leave Taylor a note. He found a notepad, scratched down his phone number, and put it on the kitchen counter.

Outside, the sun's bright rays assaulted his eyes. He stumbled down three flights of stairs, barely dodging an older woman who was coming up with a sackful of groceries.

"Excuse me," he said, holding on to the rail and finishing off the last ten steps. At the bottom, he walked toward the parking lot, where at least two dozen cars were lined up. But after three minutes of looking, he realized his green Toyota Camry was nowhere in sight.

Had he ridden in her car?

Where in the world was he, anyway? The tall sign above him read Greenview Apartments. They were the kind that looked nice on the outside and were cozy on the inside. He'd priced apartments like this once but couldn't afford them.

As he stood there wondering what to do, he was reminded of Taylor's scent. He'd thought she smelled amazing, even against the various and unpleasant smells of the bar.

"*I let her slip away.*" Those were the words he'd spoken to her sometime last night. Talking about Jenny to another woman. But she'd seemed concerned, willing to listen beyond whatever sad story she was living. Did he ever hear hers? The hangover blocked any further inquiries from last night. At least for the moment. Hopefully the fog would lift later. Right now he had to get to the school.

He still had no idea exactly where in Irving he was. He hoped he *was* still in Irving. He could see himself hopping a plane and landing in Kentucky. He decided to walk to the apartment offices.

Inside, a young, scholarly looking woman smiled a greeting.

"Can you tell me the address here?" Mick asked.

She handed him a business card. "It's on there. Are you looking to rent an apartment?"

"No. I'm lost." Mick looked at the card. "Can I borrow your phone?"

"Dial 9."

Mick dialed his perpetually unemployed buddy, whom he always called when he was too drunk to get home.

It was early September, and even in the morning, the heat of the day was already arriving. He looked at his crinkled shirt and pants as he waited by the curb, then swept his hand through his hair. He hoped his eyes didn't look too puffy. They felt like they were about to explode out of his head.

━━━━━━━

Jarrod requested they drive by the 7-Eleven. They'd been on their shift since six, but Jarrod hadn't managed to shake off whatever wild and crazy party he'd attended the night before. Aaron got out of the cruiser, glancing back to watch

Jarrod slowly pull himself out by gripping the car-door window.

"Good morning, Officer Kline," Martha said as they walked in.

"Hi, Martha." Aaron smiled and went to the coffee counter. He was stirring in cream and sugar when Jarrod came up beside him, a coffeeless Styrofoam cup in his hand.

"She's here!" Jarrod whispered.

"Who?"

"Kelly, I think is her name."

Aaron looked over his shoulder to see a tall blonde grabbing a newspaper. He rolled his eyes.

"She's so hot!"

"You didn't really want the coffee, did you?" Aaron asked. "You just thought 'hot babe' would be here."

Jarrod grinned but dispensed coffee into his cup for effect, ferociously blowing the steam off the top as he watched the woman pay for her newspaper.

"Why do they have to make this coffee so hot?" Jarrod complained.

It always amused Aaron how Jarrod couldn't stand hot coffee. Or his hamburgers with too much ketchup. Or his shoes tied the wrong way. For a man who wanted everything right in his world, Aaron thought he might be in the wrong profession.

"Come on, let's get out of here," Aaron said. He walked by Martha, gave her a wave, and dropped a few cents into the MS box that sat on the counter.

Walking out behind him, Jarrod said, "Why do you always do that?"

"Do what?"

"Give money to the charity of the week?"

"I don't know. I mean, we get free coffee, so why not?"

"Exactly. We get free coffee. It's one of the very few

perks of this job, and then you have to go and make it not a
perk by putting change in the box." Jarrod stopped. "Wait;
I think I left my sunglasses in there."

Aaron eyed him. "Did you just see another good-looking
woman go in?"

"No, I swear it."

Aaron walked back in with Jarrod, hoping to catch at
least the headlines of the newspaper while he waited. As
Jarrod roamed to the back of the store, Aaron noticed a
woman, seemingly upset, talking with Martha. He stared
at the newspaper and listened.

"Well, have you called?"

"Yes, several of us have." The woman sniffled. "I hope
something bad hasn't happened."

Aaron glanced over his shoulder, and Martha motioned
for him to approach. "Officer Kline, this is Liz. She usually
comes in about twenty minutes after you fellows."

Aaron smiled at the teary-eyed woman. "Hi, Liz."

"Liz Lane," the woman said, offering a hand.

Martha said, "Liz feels as if something might have
happened to one of her coworkers."

"Why is that?" Aaron asked as Jarrod came alongside
him, flipping his sunglasses on top of his head.

"I've called her several times and there's no answer. She
didn't come to work yesterday. This is the second shift she's
missed," Liz explained. "I'm having to cover for her again, and
I was supposed to have two days off. It's just that she's not that
kind of person, you know? She always shows up for work. Or
at least calls when she can't come in, which is really rare."

"Where is work?" Jarrod asked.

"We're both gate agents for Delta." The woman shook
her head, worry crossing over her features. "I've worked
with Taylor for two years—"

"Her last name?" Jarrod interrupted.

"Franks."

Aaron gave Jarrod the I'll-handle-this look. "Sorry, go ahead," he said.

"Anyway, she's very responsible. Taylor comes to work even if she's sick because she knows how crazy it gets when we're shorthanded. I've called every hospital around to see if there was a car wreck, but she's not there. And supposedly we can't even file a report until tonight."

"How well do you know Miss Franks?" Aaron asked.

"Pretty well. We know each other some socially, beyond work. Taylor has me on this exercise kick, and I joined Gold's Gym where she works out. I just started last week. She wasn't there last night."

"I'm sure Miss Franks is fine," Aaron said. "It's probably just a misunderstanding."

"I've called her house. Her cell phone. I didn't want to call her mother, make her worry. She doesn't talk to her mom much anyway."

"You have that number?" Aaron asked.

Liz nodded and took his pad and pencil. "This is her address, all her contact numbers. Plus my home phone." She handed it back.

"Does Taylor use drugs or alcohol that you're aware of?"

"Absolutely not," Liz said. She looked down at the carton of cigarettes she'd purchased from Martha. "Maybe a few drinks at a bar, but nothing more. She's not an addict or anything like that. Just social drinking. Mostly."

"Okay . . ." Aaron was jotting down notes, studying Liz's body language. "You're . . . um . . . you're sure, Miss Lane?"

"Yeah, I mean . . . yeah." She sighed. "She's been on antidepressants," she said in nearly a whisper.

"For?" Aaron guided her out of the way of an approaching customer and to the sidewalk outside, with Jarrod following.

"Losing hope in life," Liz said. "Just like the rest of us. She's not a freak. She just had a few bad years."

"Boyfriends? Lovers? Ex-husbands involved?"

"There's an ex-boyfriend. They haven't been serious for a while. It's an on-again/off-again dysfunctional thing. I don't know much about it, really. She's pretty private. Last week, though, she mentioned going on a couple of dates, so I figured it was over with this guy. But Tuesday she got this big bouquet of flowers from him."

"*Him* have a name?" Jarrod asked.

Liz ignored Jarrod and looked at Aaron. "I don't know his full name. Sammy is all I know. She doesn't talk about him much, to tell you the truth. That's why it was surprising when she got the flowers. Over the past couple of years, he's only sent a few things to work and always signed them using what I guess are his initials. SAE. Once some flowers. Well, like three measly roses. Once a candy-gram or some ridiculous thing. Usually after they've had a fight or something."

"Any indications of what the relationship was like?"

"I don't know. I mean, I don't think it was a good relationship. I guess Sammy's just your regular stupid guy." She glanced at Jarrod with those words.

"Anything else you can think of?"

Liz took a lighter from her purse. "We had an incident at the airport Tuesday."

"An incident?"

"Guy went nuts on us when his flight was canceled. Had to be dragged away. Made some threats to Taylor, really shook her up. But that sort of thing happens. It's just part of our job. I can't imagine Taylor not coming to work because of it. But . . . there was something strange about her. Usually she can handle something like that. This time it seemed to really bother her."

"Know the guy's name?"

"Airport security will have it."

"We'll go see what we can find out for you. I'm sure Taylor's fine. Okay?" Aaron handed her his card and said they'd be in touch.

"Let's go find out why this young woman didn't make it to work today," Aaron said to Jarrod, who was staring at a woman pumping gas into her car.

chapter four

C oach Kline." Owen Gruber, the athletic director for the high school, said his name with the kind of enthusiasm one uses when talking about a mouse problem in the home. Mick was trying to smooth down one side of his hair, which he hadn't realized until now was sticking straight up. Owen didn't fail to notice. "Looks like you had a productive evening last night."

Mick bit his lip, trying to hold in the string of slander that wanted to rip Owen from the top of his small head, down his pencil neck, through his flat chest to his size-8 shoes. A not-so-kind smile replaced the words. How Owen Gruber, who hadn't played a sport in his life, managed to become athletic director was still a mystery. It was rumored to have something to do with how much money his grand-mother gave to the private Catholic school.

With the religion came the code of ethics that was continually stated and hardly ever followed. Last year, the head basketball coach was caught partying with the players after they won conference. He was reprimanded with a slap on the hand and continued congratulations for his success. There were some things ethics simply couldn't control—the heart of a man driven by power and sports politics.

Mick tried to nod, realizing that Owen was right in the middle of giving him the speech about his tardiness. Just one nod would get Owen off his back. But he couldn't seem

31

to give the guy respect. So he simply sat there, his hands
folded in his lap, staring at the gold carpet under his feet
because it was more interesting than Owen's beady, judgmental eyes.

"Don't you want to make something of yourself,
Kline?" Owen said.

*No, Owen, I want to be a loser for the rest of my life. That's
what I've wanted to be ever since I was a little kid and my dad
had dreams of me being just like my brother.*

"You're still working on your bachelor's, right?" Owen
asked.

"Of course," Mick said.

His second bachelor's. He had his first in accounting,
which he found out he hated. He'd been working on the
second for four years. Money was the first problem. Lack of
drive was the second. He didn't want to teach kids math.
He wanted to teach them football, in hopes of one day
climbing that almighty educative ladder to a Big Twelve
school. It was a pipe dream, really. At the age of
twenty-eight, he was still assisting at the high school level,
albeit a large high school.

Mick was well-known around Irving. Everybody had had
such high hopes for him when he was quarterbacking over a
decade ago—his family still did. He wished he had those
same hopes for himself, but as far as he was concerned, he
was a has-been. He'd dropped out this semester. That was
before he knew he was going to have extra time since he got
fired from his accounting job for being perpetually late.

Outside, thunder rolled over the flat roof of the athletic
building. Owen barely noticed. Mick could hardly stay in
his seat. He loved the weather. Just like his dad. He and his
brother and his dad would pass the spring watching storms
roll over the plains of Texas, analyzing the direction, the
wind . . . the feel of them.

When a big one came, which it always did in a Texas spring, it was unmistakable. The air seemed to swallow itself. The sky looked as if it were lowering. The birds would fluster in the trees. The animals would pace their dwellings.

But Owen Gruber would never be able to appreciate—or even notice—what Mick considered to be glorious. Owen Gruber never looked up. He always looked at himself—which was exactly what he was doing now. Picking balls off his fancy knit sweater that he thought made him somebody.

"Stop being late," Owen finally said, flicking the lint away. "You know Coach Rynde hates it, and so do I. Rynde thinks you have coaching talent. I don't know that I agree with him, but as long as he sees it, why don't you take advantage of it? Breaks hardly ever come in life, Kline. Especially for people like you, who seem to abuse any break you get."

"Are we finished here?" Mick asked.

"Yeah, fine. We're finished. In one ear, out the other."

"Mom used to say that," Mick said, standing and walking out the office door. Rain pelted the skylight of the athletic lobby. Mick stood at the front glass doors, watching the rain wash the parking-lot concrete.

His mind drifted to Taylor. He could see her face clearly. The hangover was starting to free his thoughts, one by one, through the pounding pain in his head. How many drinks had he downed last night?

"Kline," Coach Rynde called, "let's go pump some iron."

"On my way," Mick said. He tucked in his shirt, still trying to smooth out his hair. He needed a haircut. He needed a life makeover. He needed a purpose.

While he stared into the rain, another woman's face filled his thoughts. Jenny Arlington's. Why couldn't he erase his mind as easily as Coach Rynde erased the black-board after practice? A swipe of the eraser and the plays were gone. Now Aaron always appeared at Jenny's side. Why couldn't he just let go of her? Why must he battle his feelings? He saw Aaron's and Jenny's hands inter-twined at the dinner table . . . that first night the family had tried to come together and behave as if nothing out of the ordinary was going on. As if, not two months earlier, Mick had not sat at the same dinner table with her by his side.

"Taylor," he said aloud. He hoped she would call.

Aaron drank his coffee as he drove against the Irving traffic. The mixed odor of jet fuel and bus exhaust caused him to turn the cruiser's air to circulate.

"Okay, I've held my tongue long enough," Jarrod said. "I'm dying to know. What's up with your face?"

His young, hypercurious partner hardly ever let anything go. "Got in a fight with my brother." Aaron shot him a look. "Don't ask."

"Okay . . . ," Jarrod said, still blowing the steam off his coffee. After a few moments of silence, he asked, "So what'd he do?"

"What'd who do?"

"Mick. Driving drunk? Bar fight?"

"What makes you think he did something?"

"Isn't he always doing something?"

"He didn't do anything. We just had a disagreement."

"It's always like that, you know. Pastors' kids go party. Firemen's kids burn down the school. Principals' kids flunk out. And then . . . well, you're not his dad, but you get my point."

Jarrod needed a good smack. "It's not what you think."

"What do you mean? Mick's always in trouble."

"He's just . . . he's . . . he's . . ." When was he going to stop making excuses for Mick? Jarrod was right. Mick was always in trouble. It'd been like that since Aaron and Mick were kids. Early on, Aaron realized making the right choices would make his life better. Mick always liked to see what would happen if he made the wrong ones. And at twenty-eight, he still hadn't stopped.

Aaron glanced at Jarrod, who was staring at him. He realized he hadn't finished the sentence. "Mick's going to come around. I pray for him every night."

Jarrod gave a half laugh. "There it is," he said, pointing to the apartment complex. He put his cup on the dashboard and said, "You got a mint?"

"A mint? What for?" Aaron pulled to the curb, trying to find his notepad.

"I've been drinking coffee. And we all know how attractive ticket agents can be. It's practically a job requirement, you know."

"First of all, you haven't been drinking coffee. All you've been doing is blowing on it. Second, we're on the clock. No flirting." But it was hopeless. He'd once witnessed Jarrod flirt with a car-crash victim while waiting for the ambulance and fire trucks to arrive. The woman wasn't seriously hurt, but she had been stuck in her car, and Jarrod had volunteered to hold her hand. It was shameless.

"Taylor," Jarrod whispered as they walked up the stairs toward her apartment. "That's such a great name. I mean, when have you ever met an unattractive chick named Taylor? Huh?"

Jarrod actually expected an answer back.

"This is it," Aaron said, standing in front of apartment

345. He knocked three times. "Miss Franks? It's the police. Are you okay?"

"Doesn't sound like anyone's home," Jarrod said.

"Hello? Miss Franks?" Aaron tried the doorknob, and to his surprise, the door opened. He looked at Jarrod, who was equally surprised. "Let's go in," he said quietly. "Carefully."

Jarrod nodded, his eyes widening. The men stepped inside. "Miss Franks? It's the police. Are you okay?"

There was no answer. Jarrod moved toward the kitchen, and Aaron looked toward the living room. Near the corner was a window, the cut screen flapping in the wind. Aaron snapped his fingers to get Jarrod's attention, then pointed at the window. Aaron indicated he was going down the hallway toward the bedroom. Both men's hands settled on their guns.

"Miss Franks? It's the police." Aaron stepped in a few more paces and called out her name again. The air conditioner kicked on. "Hello?" Apprehension slugged at his heart.

He turned and walked down the hallway. "Miss Franks?" He called her name loudly, hoping to not startle her too badly if she was caught unaware. The bathroom faucet dripped steadily. The bedroom was a little messy, the bed unmade, laundry sitting out. But there was no sign of a struggle.

Nobody was home.

Aaron returned to the living room. "Go get the apartment manager," he instructed Jarrod, then studied the window more closely. The screen was torn, probably cut. Apartment buildings in general were not known to have superior maintenance. A trained eye was going to have to check it out. He looked to the other buildings and saw half a dozen windows open. It was that season when people were often careless about open windows and unlocked doors.

"Is everything okay?"

Aaron turned to find a middle-aged man standing in the doorway, gazing around the room. "Taylor Franks. Do you know her?"

"Not well," said the apartment manager. He held out his hand and introduced himself as Chuck. "But she's been a great tenant. Always on time with her rent."

Jarrod walked in behind Chuck. "Halloway and Martin are on their way."

"What's happened?" Chuck asked.

"We're not sure. Coworker reported her missing this morning. Her apartment was unlocked and she's not here. Do you know what kind of car she drives?"

"No. But I can look it up in our files. She has a designated parking space. I'll be right back."

Aaron squatted in front of the small table that was beside the open window, where two picture frames had fallen over.

Jarrod was behind him observing the room and the window. "This doesn't look good."

"It's an odd scene," Aaron said, standing. "No sign of a struggle, but signs that she left in an unusual manner. Look over there. Her purse is still on the chair."

Sergeant Halloway and Detective Martin walked in the door. "What do we have?"

Aaron filled them in. Halloway was staring at the open window when Jarrod called, "Hey! Found something!"

The others turned. Jarrod was in the kitchen, pointing to the counter. As they walked over, Jarrod said, "It's a phone number on a scrap piece of paper. Next to this glass."

"Don't touch anything," Halloway said. "Let's run this number, see who it belongs to."

Aaron managed to say, "Don't bother."

Everyone turned to him. "What do you mean, don't bother?" Halloway asked.

"I know who that number belongs to."

—————

Shep Crawford drank green tea and gazed out the top window of his home, an old firehouse he'd refurbished himself. He loved it here. The walls seemed to speak of the mightiness of man, the courage that it takes to give up one's life for a person who is probably not worthy of it. He still kept some of the portraits of the old firefighters on the wall, most likely dead and gone by now. Forgotten heroes. He swallowed the scorching hot tea.

He was on duty in about ten minutes. In the bathroom he quickly shaved, then brushed his teeth. He pulled a decent-looking shirt over his white undershirt, stained from years of sweat and hard work. He hated buying new undershirts. A man's undershirt should tell the story of his life. All those men with their prissy white shirts bleached to perfection. All the stories ironed out. Didn't they understand that's what makes them men?

A pole offered an alternative to the stairs, but Shep opted for the stairs this morning. He blazed down them, humming "The Star-Spangled Banner," touching the American flag hung on the wall as he trotted past.

Outside, the large garage seemed to swallow his sedan.

"I'm going to catch me a bad man today," he sang, taking a white rag and buffing the side mirrors and taillights on his car. "Gonna catch me a bad man today."

chapter five

halloway and Martin were trying to calm Aaron down, who was condemning and defending his brother in one breath. "I don't know what this means," he said as he paced outside the apartment on the cement walkway. "This is crazy."

Halloway said, "Aaron, listen; let's just get ahold of your brother, okay? He can probably clear all this up. He's probably with the woman right now."

Aaron nodded, but his mind continued to field one anxious thought after another.

The apartment manager, Chuck, walked up the steps. "Her car is here. That white Rodeo. See it down there?"

Aaron looked. Covered parking. There it sat. He quickly scanned the parking lot for any sign of his brother's car, but there was none.

"Oh no," Halloway said.

"What?" Aaron asked.

"Look." Halloway pointed below. "Who called Homicide, for crying out loud?" Nobody responded, and Halloway growled under his breath. "This is just great. Crawford of all people. I hate that man. I truly, truly, truly hate him."

Aaron watched Shep Crawford step out of his sedan. He was a tall man with shadowy eyes, who hardly ever smiled. Deep craters weathered his skin. And when he walked, he always looked as if he were walking against the wind.

Aaron gripped the iron railing in front of him. "This is not a homicide."

Halloway shook his head. "Crawford's going to come in here and start running the show."

A forensics truck pulled up.

"Looks like he already is," Aaron said.

"We need to establish that Taylor is or is not with your brother, Aaron," Halloway said. "Can you get in touch with him?"

"He's at school today, coaching."

Halloway watched as Crawford began climbing the three flights of stairs. "We have six homicide detectives on the force. Why did it have to be this loon?"

Martin whispered, "I heard the guy marks everything he owns with his own blood so it can always be identified as his through DNA."

"You're kidding," Halloway said.

"I swear I heard it."

"Marks everything he owns with his own blood. Now that's a control freak for you," Halloway said as Crawford walked toward them.

Even though Aaron had dealt with Shep Crawford on only one other case, he knew the man had a reputation among other officers as being as crazy as some of the criminals he pursued. But nobody could dispute his effectiveness. He was practically a legend. Years ago he'd solved a serial rape case by piecing together the fact that each victim had a faint smell of pine on her clothing. That led him to a registered sex offender who lived in a camper in the woods.

Still, there was something off about the guy that nobody could put a finger on. Most of the time he looked like a disheveled mess, yet everything around him was in perfect order. Aaron guessed he was in his fifties. His gray and white hair hung in strings over the tips of his ears and was thinner on top.

"This is ridiculous," Halloway said and walked back into the apartment, apparently to guard his territory. He looked back at Aaron. "What are you waiting for? Go find Mick."

Aaron's feet felt like lead. Part of him wanted to stay here to find out everything that was going on, any piece of evidence they might uncover. But he thought the sooner he could clear Mick's name, the better. The high school was about fifteen minutes away. Telling Jarrod he'd be right back, he left.

"Come on, Jerrings, you woman! Push it!" Mick stood over the two-hundred-and-fifty-pound linebacker and barked out the order. Jerrings's face was turning red and his large, white teeth bore down like a clamp. "Come on!" Jerrings's muscles shook, but he finally got the bar up. Mick helped him move it to the rack. "Good job."

Jerrings sat up, trying to catch his breath.

"Kline!" Coach Rynde called.

Mick looked up, and Rynde was pointing to the doorway of the weight room. He saw his brother standing there in full uniform. Mick rolled his eyes. He thought better of causing a scene by telling his brother off. He walked toward the doorway, shoulders back and eyes hard. "What do you want?" he said, still fifteen feet away.

Aaron's normally kind eyes were equally cold. "We need to talk outside."

"I need you to get out of here. I said I don't want to see you again."

"This isn't about us. You know a woman named Taylor Franks?"

Mick shook his head but then stopped. Taylor. The woman he'd left the bar with? The woman whose apartment he'd woken up in? He stuffed his hands into the pockets of his sweats but couldn't stuff the expression away that told Aaron everything he needed to know.

"I don't know her," Mick said. "I met her. Once. Last night. At a bar." He fought another urge to punch the judgmental look off Aaron's face. "It's none of your business!" Mick roared. "What are you doing now? Following me?"

"You don't know where she is?" Aaron guided him out into the hallway.

"Where she is? No! She wasn't even in the apartment when I woke up—"

"You went to her apartment last night?" Aaron whispered harshly.

"It's not what you think. I don't even remember half of it."

"What's that supposed to mean?"

"What do you think it means?"

Aaron rubbed his face. "Brother, this is not a game. You better tell me what you know and tell me fast."

"Why?" Mick demanded.

"Because Taylor Franks is missing, and your phone number, along with what I'm assuming are going to be your prints on a glass, is on the kitchen counter."

―――――

"This is absurd," Mick grumbled as he rode across town in his brother's cruiser.

"You better take this seriously," Aaron said, glancing at Mick, who was staring out the passenger's window.

"She took me to her apartment last night. We had a few drinks, talked. That's it. I left this morning." Mick's fingernails scraped against the side of the door. He let out a huge sigh. "Nothing happened," he said, looking at Aaron. "Despite what you think."

"I don't know what to think," Aaron said, slowing for a stoplight.

"I just left my number there. I didn't even talk to her this morning. She was already gone."

"You met her at a bar?"

"Yes, Aaron. A bar. A big, bad, horrible, sinful bar."

Aaron glared at Mick while the car was stopped. "Shut up. Just stop that mouth from running, would you? A woman is missing and you were the last person to see her. Do you understand how serious this is?"

"I understand that you would love nothing more than to see me go down."

"Not for this." Aaron turned left and headed toward the apartment complex. He turned into the parking lot. "Where's your car?"

"Back at the bar, I guess."

"Which bar?"

"Tony's, I think."

"Back to old habits, eh?"

"I was just unwinding," Mick said, getting out of the car. Then he noticed the police cars and the forensics truck. "How do they know she's missing?"

"She didn't show up for work yesterday. Coworker says she never does that."

"Maybe she's out driving around."

"Her car's still here. There was a screen cut and a window open in her apartment."

Mick glanced up at the third floor, where officers were moving in and out of the apartment.

Aaron caught his arm. "You need to tell me right now exactly what happened. I can't help you if you don't tell me."

"Who says I need your help?"

"Your pride is going to be your downfall." Aaron tried to look him in the eyes, but Mick only stared at the ground, muttering something under his breath. "Come on," he said, leading him toward the apartment. "Go in there, tell them everything you know. Be helpful. We want them looking at you as a witness, not a suspect, okay?"

Mick followed him. "Which do you think I am?"

"Don't make this personal."

"You think I did it?"

Aaron stopped and faced him, pointing a finger at his chest. "I think you decided a long time ago that you're not worth much. You bought into that lie, Mick, and you're living your life like you couldn't care less if you are alive or dead. You're worth a whole lot more than you know, and I pray you someday realize this."

Mick shook his head and shoved him away. "Nice sermon."

Aaron grabbed his arm and with a heavy hand guided him toward the stairs. "Let's go."

Inside the apartment, the buzz stopped when Mick and Aaron walked in.

Halloway greeted them and growled, "This is ludicrous. Crawford is treating this like a crime scene, and we've hardly established that the woman is missing! Look—" he extended his arm behind him—"the forensics guys are here! Crawford is out of his everlasting mind!"

"Maybe it's a slow homicide day," Aaron said, trying to spot Crawford over Halloway's shoulder. He couldn't see him.

"So, you know where this Franks woman is?" Halloway asked Mick.

"He doesn't know," Aaron said.

"I can speak, Aaron." Addressing Halloway, Mick said, "I left my number for her. That's all."

Suddenly a booming voice echoed behind them, and Aaron and Mick looked up just in time to see Crawford cross the living room, his face stern and authoritative. He hadn't even noticed Aaron and Mick near the door yet. He was handing out commands like candy to children.

Halloway moved aside and Aaron walked forward, Mick behind him. "Lieutenant Crawford, this is Mick, my brother."

Crawford's intense eyes narrowed at Mick. "You were here last night?"

"Yeah."

"Why?"

"Taylor invited me home from the bar where we met."

Aaron was trying to read Crawford's perplexing expression. Disappointment? Is that what he was seeing? Like Mick had spoken about Crawford's own daughter. While Aaron watched him carefully, Crawford's eyes roamed the room, noting the corner where the open window was and then down the hallway, his hands pressed into the lower part of his hips.

Mick glanced at Aaron with uncertainty. Aaron could only shrug.

Crawford faced the officers. "Reported missing from work, what, twenty-four hours? thirty-six hours?"

Aaron nodded.

"You say you met her at a bar last night. What time?" Crawford asked Mick.

"I'm not sure. Maybe at nine. We talked at the bar for about an hour. Then I rode home with her." Mick cleared his throat. "And then I guess I passed out."

"Why do you say you guess?" Crawford asked.

"I woke up this morning with my face in the carpet," Mick said with a half laugh, nodding toward the living room.

Nobody else was laughing, and Aaron thought he was going to throw up. What in the world had Mick gotten himself into now? They were going to take him to the station, interrogate him, and if Taylor Franks showed up dead, probably charge him with murder. And all Mick could do was laugh about being drunk.

"So this was just a one-night fling?" Crawford asked.

"Not even that," Mick said. "Nothing happened. We were just talking. You see, my brother here stole my girlfriend and is now marrying her, so we shared sob stories. That's all."

This seemed to agitate Crawford, who stepped a couple of inches closer to Mick. "Sob stories? What'd she say?"

Mick shrugged, staring at his feet. "Nothing, really. She looked sad when I saw her. That's what drew me to her. Pretty woman sitting alone, drinking scotch. At first she wanted me to bug off. But then she said we could talk. We just talked about relationships." Mick glanced at Aaron with hot eyes.

"Did she say anything about a relationship? a boyfriend?"

"Not really. She mostly spoke in general terms. I got the feeling she'd had her share of loser boyfriends."

Crawford took out a notepad. "Loser boyfriends. She didn't name any names?"

"I don't remember any."

"Because you were drunk."

"Or she didn't say any," Mick said forcefully.

Crawford was not deterred. "Was she drunk?"

"No, not really. Had a couple of scotches. But she drove. Got back here alive, didn't I?"

"Can the humor," Aaron said to Mick, which wiped the smile off his face.

"Did she say anything about going anywhere? leaving?"

Mick scratched the back of his head in recall. "I don't remember too much of the conversation. I'm sorry."

"I'd suggest you remember all you can." Crawford observed the Band-Aid over his eye. "What happened to your face?"

Mick fumbled his words, while everyone shifted uncomfortably. Finally he said, "Just a fight. The day before yesterday. Aaron can confirm it," Mick said, touching the Band-Aid.

Aaron stared at the strange scratch across Mick's cheek, which he was sure had not come from the fight. He swallowed and looked at Crawford's amused eyes. "Yeah. It was the day before yesterday."

"Okay." Crawford shrugged. Then without warning he turned back to the living room, suddenly seeming uninterested.

Mick looked at Aaron and Aaron looked at Halloway.

Halloway seemed perplexed. "Crawford, you want us to take him in?"

"Naw," Crawford said and began walking back toward the bedroom.

Halloway appeared stunned when he turned back to Aaron and Mick. "Looks like you're free to go," he said.

"Crawford's done?" Aaron asked.

"Stay around the city," Halloway told Mick.

Aaron said, "Mick, go wait by the car. I'll be there in a second." He watched his brother drag his feet out the door and down the stairs like an eight-year-old boy on his way to his room.

"What do you think?" Aaron asked Halloway.

"I'm surprised Crawford didn't bring him in. He's always itching to get his hands on a criminal, you know."

"Mick's no criminal. He makes a lot of bad judgment calls, but he would never harm a woman."

Halloway's nod was not full of confidence. "We've contacted her mother, who hasn't heard from her, and a couple of acquaintances, who also haven't heard from her. We'll interview neighbors as soon as we can find them. The fact that her car is here isn't a good sign. And the fact that your brother was drunk and hardly remembers a thing isn't going to go over well."

"Then why is Crawford letting Mick go?"

"Who knows with that guy. Probably playing some sort of mind game. He's got some of the strangest methods. Sometimes I think if he weren't playing detective he'd be in a mental hospital somewhere. Have you seen the way he organizes his desk?"

"He was in the military, wasn't he? The discipline probably came from that."

"I don't know. Seems more obsessive-compulsive to me, but I'm no shrink."

"Well, he always gets the bad guy, doesn't he?" Aaron said with a small smile.

"Yeah. Let's just hope it's not your brother."

mick and Aaron rode in silence back to Tony's to get his car, except when Aaron asked about the scratch. The explanation of falling into the bathroom wall at the bar seemed like a lame excuse, evident by Aaron's unemotional stare out the windshield.

At Tony's, Mick got out and unlocked his car, pretending like he was going to get in. He watched his brother's patrol car peel out of the parking lot. When he was out of sight, Mick walked into Tony's, but not before momentarily observing the dark clouds swirling overhead. Storms would develop later on with the afternoon heat.

At noon, scarcely a soul was around except a bartender named Lisa, a hard-looking woman with white spiky hair and a dark mole on her chin. Her bright pink lips flashed a smile as he walked in. "A little early, aren't you, tiger?"

"Scotch."

"What else is there, right?" Lisa fixed his drink.

Above him, ESPN was showing highlights of foreign soccer. Mick wouldn't need to be back at the school until three. He was going to have to come up with something to tell Coach Rynde. All he'd said earlier was there was an emergency.

An emergency was a bit of an understatement.

Lisa scooted the glass toward him. "You okay?"

49

"Um . . . yeah. Fine. Hey, what time does Jimmy get here?"

"Afternoon usually. Four or so."

"Thanks." Mick avoided her eyes and stared into the drink that last night had erased his memory. Images and conversations floated near the edge, threatening to fall into darkness, wanting to be rescued. But they were too far away, like paper floating on the wind, darting and dashing but always elusive.

Taylor had not mentioned a boyfriend that he could remember, but he had sensed great turmoil in her life.

The smell of the scotch was foul in his nostrils. It reminded him of everything that went wrong last night . . . everything that was going wrong in his life. His body, nearly trembling with the desire to drink it, also forecasted the result of indulging.

Licking his lips and looking at the drink as if it were a raging bull ready to gore him, Mick tried to be reasonable, tried to think like the rational man he thought lived deep inside him. "I can't do this," he whispered to himself.

Lisa was at the other end of the bar mopping up a mess on the counter.

He nudged the glass away from him a little, scratching at his brows with a fidgety finger. But his body nearly moaned in protest. With just one drink, he could be a little less on edge. His thumbnail tapped the side of the glass, flicking at it over and over again. His head screamed no! His body screamed yes! If someone could just saw him in half.

"Here, let me help," Lisa said suddenly. She took the glass and dumped the scotch in the sink. Her half smile and warm eyes told him she understood. "Now, get outta here, okay?"

Relief flooded Mick's body. "Thank you," he said and

slid off the barstool. He wasn't sure what he was going to do for the rest of the day. But boredom always seemed to get him in trouble.

There wasn't a person in Taylor's apartment standing around. Everybody had been assigned a task. So nobody noticed Shep examining pictures of Taylor Franks. But he did. And with great attention. He looked at every picture, every setting, every scene. He studied the picture of her mother, plump and matronly. Shep immediately noticed there were no pictures of a father around. It didn't surprise him.

He stared at the fallen pictures by the window, facedown and on the carpet. He addressed one of the crime-scene technicians, remembering the days before they were all mostly civilians. Times were changing. But he didn't need any of it to bring about justice. "What do you make of those pictures?"

"Definitely a result of someone climbing in through the window," the technician said, pointing to them with fingers spread. "Just the way they are lying indicates it. We've gotten plenty of photos." He knelt down to pick one up. After examining it, he showed it to Shep. "See this guy? Looks kind of old to be a boyfriend."

Shep scrutinized the picture. Taylor's arms were wrapped around the man's waist affectionately. Her eyes were bright. His eyes were dim. He studied his face. "A man with secrets."

The technician smiled. "Guess you'll be finding out who this guy is. We're going to bag these photos."

Shep nodded and turned to survey the room.

Randy Prescott was walking down the hallway toward him. "Nothing out of order in the bedroom. Bed unmade, that's all we noticed. We'll need to find out if she makes her bed every morning."

"Her mother's on the way," Shep said, staring at the hallway walls as Randy approached. "Look." He pointed out several pictures that were slightly tilted. Shep dragged his hand along the wall, and as he did, he showed how each picture would have tilted if a hand had hit it. "Get a picture of this. There may have been a struggle down this hall."

Randy went to get the photo tech.

Shep walked back to the bedroom. He'd been in there earlier, but people had bustled around him, and he liked to work alone. He scanned the room, but the only face in his mind was Mick Kline's. What kind of loser was he? And why would a classy woman like Taylor invite him back to her apartment? Weren't women smart these days? savvy? Didn't they understand what made them vulnerable?

He'd fought off anger through the morning and now realized he had an immense challenge ahead of him, but he always liked a challenge. He was just going to have to control his anger. For a man who always liked to be in control, his anger was certainly a thorn. Behind him, he heard Randy walk in.

Shep's gaze went to her bedside table. The phone receiver and base were at an odd angle. He smiled and glanced back at Randy, who seemed like he didn't really know what to do other than stand there. "Look at the phone."

Randy looked at it, shrugged a little. "Yeah. What about it? I think they already ran her phone records. Nothing unusual showed up that they saw right away, anyway."

Shep walked over to it and picked it up. "Let's see who Miss Franks called last."

"It'll be on her phone records." Randy sighed as if he couldn't imagine anything more boring.

Shep pushed redial without turning the phone on. After reading the numbers on the display panel, he handed the phone to Randy.

Randy's eyes widened. "Nine and one. This didn't show up on her phone records."

"That's because the call never went through. She didn't get a chance to turn the phone on or apparently finish dialing 911," Shep said. He headed back down the hallway toward the living room.

Someone called out his name. He turned and saw Halloway leaving the bathroom. "Come look at this."

Shep walked back to the bathroom. Halloway had flipped on the light and was pointing to the tile floor.

Crawford squatted and saw it immediately. Six droplets of blood, each about the size of half a dime, made a short trail ending next to the bathtub. "Tell the techs to get in here and see if we have blood down this drain."

Halloway nodded and vanished.

Shep returned to the living room and announced, "We officially have a criminal investigation, folks."

Mick swallowed the feeling that told him this was the last place he should be. Sitting in his car across the street from the elementary school, he glanced in his rearview mirror, half expecting to be followed. But it seemed when the detective said to let him go, they really let him go. Aaron appeared as shocked as anybody, but that was his brother. Perpetually skeptical.

Sour bile swam in his stomach, reminding him that his not-so-noble decline of the drink earlier was costing him now. This was the stupidest thing he'd done in a while, but desperation made people do stupid things. If only he still had that accounting job, he would have somewhere else to go other than here.

He checked his rearview mirror one more time, then his watch. Getting out of his car, he crossed the street and walked toward the school. Above him, a few straggling, heavy, gray clouds were joining the large thunderhead out west, casting random shadows that cooled his sweaty skin. The atmosphere warned that things could get violent very soon. All the right ingredients were there.

He stood for a moment and observed the clouds. His dad still liked to think of himself as an amateur meteorologist. And he supposed those were the days when the family had been tight, when brotherly rivalry extended only to treasured toys and T-ball.

Mick walked inside the school. At the front desk, he signed in and then waited alone in the designated area. He passed the minutes he sat there trying to paste together his shredded memory from last night. But as hard as he tried, he simply couldn't remember anything.

"What are you doing here?" Jenny stood above him.

He stood and tried to casually fold his hands together. But just like when he first met her, she still made him tremble. "Do . . . um . . . do you have time to talk?"

She glanced behind her shoulder and sighed, but those gorgeous brown eyes of hers were liquid compassion. "Come on. Not here." She took his elbow and guided him out a side door.

They stood under the overhang of the building. A brownish green haze hovered over the schoolyard. It was definitely going to storm. Jenny looked up at the sky. "Good call not to have recess outside today." She wrapped her arms around herself. "Why are you here?"

"I just wanted to . . . I'm not sure. I just needed to see you."

"Why?"

Mick stared at his tennis shoes. Words were hard to come by.

"Aaron told me he told you," she said softly. The wind blew her blonde hair back from her face. "Said you didn't take it too well."

"I didn't."

"You shouldn't be angry with him, you know," Jenny said. "He loves you. I wish you knew how much."

"I'm not here to talk about Aaron," Mick finally said. He was at least a foot taller than she, and he'd liked the idea of how easily he could protect her. Glancing up, he noticed a few curious eyeballs staring from a classroom window. One little girl stuck her tongue out.

Jenny was now staring at her own feet. "Then why are you here? I don't understand."

"To . . . to, uh . . . to see if you would . . ."

"Would what?"

"Give me a second chance."

A surprised laugh escaped her lips, and her eyes formed perfect circles. "Oh, Mick. Please, don't—"

"Just hear me out, okay? Please hear me out."

Jenny pressed her lips together but didn't look at him. Instead she engaged her hands. For the first time, Mick noticed the ring. It was a diamond solitaire. A large one. He could never afford anything that nice.

She stuck her hands in her pockets. "I'm listening."

"Just . . . just give me another chance."

"Mick, what are you—?"

"I'm not the better man. I know that. But you didn't give me a chance. I could've proved to you, shown you—"

She held up her hands. "Wait. Don't insinuate that I

didn't give you a chance. One, we were all wrong for each other. Two, you hadn't called me in a week when your brother called."

"I know," Mick said, swiping at the sweat that dampened his hairline. "That was an awful mistake. I was just playing that stupid game everybody plays. I mean, it wasn't even a game, really. It was just stupidity. I had feelings for you, and I thought I wasn't good enough for you, and then I realized that I wanted to try to be good enough for you."

"Aaron and I are meant to be together," Jenny said, the firmness in her voice straightening her posture. She looked him in the eye. "You and I are not."

"But wasn't there something there? I mean, can you deny that?"

"I won't deny it. There was attraction. Maybe even deeper than that."

"A lot deeper than that!"

"But I should've never dated you in the first place. Our lifestyle choices are at different ends of the spectrum. I compromised my beliefs for you, and that scared me."

Angry words wanted their chance at attention, but Mick held his tongue. Getting angry at Jenny was not going to help matters. "I was going to change."

Jenny closed her eyes at the statement. "That's absurd. People don't change for other people."

"I would've. You just didn't give me a chance. I'm trying to get my life under control."

"I know," she said, touching his arm lightly. "I know that. You're a good man. You don't give yourself enough credit. You make poor choices, but I think it's because of how you see yourself. You're always comparing yourself to Aaron. Be who God created you to be."

Mick swallowed, her touch still lingering on his skin. "Look, Jen. Please don't marry Aaron. At least not without giving me another chance. That's all I'm asking for. Just another chance."

"How could I do that to your brother? I've committed my life to him."

"I know. But if you'll just—"

"No. No, Mick. I won't let you come between us. I'm marrying Aaron, and I wish—I pray—that you would support that. You're breaking Aaron's heart."

"So my heart doesn't matter?"

"You're being unfair. To say that, and to ask me to give you a second chance."

Mick's nostrils flared as he let out a defeating sigh. Rain dropped to the sidewalk. But he already felt cold and wet.

"Don't let this destroy your family. Be happy for us and know that the right woman is out there for you. Get your life together, believe in yourself, *forgive* yourself. Let God help you."

Mick chewed on his lip, trying to keep his emotions at bay. "All Aaron wants to do is point out my flaws. That's probably how he won your heart, huh? Pointing out how bad I am?"

"No."

Lightning spidered across the sky. Soft thunder followed. Jenny checked her watch.

"Aaron's going to come home tonight and tell you who-knows-what about me, but I hope you, of all people, will at least give me the benefit of the doubt."

"What are you talking about?"

"You seem to be the only person who has any hope for me."

"I don't understand. What is Aaron going to tell me?"

"I've made mistakes in my life. The biggest one was letting you go. But I have a moral compass. I'm not sure Aaron believes that anymore."

Mick began walking off, but Jenny followed him. "What happened?"

He waved her off and kept walking. Now he knew for sure he'd lost her, and he couldn't bear to look into her eyes anymore.

"Mick!" she called, but he opened the gate to the schoolyard, slamming it behind him, his first chance to blow off some steam. "Mick!"

Across the parking lot, his green car was shiny with rain. Fumbling with his keys, he tried to steady his hand so he could get the car unlocked.

"Please! Please! Wake up! You have to leave!"

Mick stared into the rain. Taylor's voice whispered a plea. Was he imagining it?

"Please. Wake up, you moron! What have I done?"

Rain poured over his face, but Mick didn't move an inch. He was remembering something from last night!

"Please, please, please. You can't be here. You can't. Please."

One blink and her voice was gone. Mick wiped the rain from his face. He ducked into his car, his clothes damp against his skin.

chapter seven

Stephen Fiscall's reflection told lies, but he didn't mind, because nobody knew—or cared—what was on the inside anyway. Though he'd been in the southern part of the country for a little over three years, he was a Yankee at heart. Not a popular flag to wave here, but he waved it on occasion. Just to be tacky.

Tacky didn't even begin to describe the dress code for attorneys in Texas. Dusty cowboy boots worn by men who'd never touched a horse in their life. Slicked-back hair held in place by their oily personalities. Shirts that looked like their owners were going to the ranch, not the courtroom. Around their waists were belt buckles to match the size of their egos.

Fiscall was a small man in stature. But it didn't deter him. His mother had always taught him to hold his head high. No one ever explained that he shouldn't take it literally. It didn't matter. He was sort of known for the way he looked when he walked in the courtroom—nose in the air, hair combed without a speck of gel, and a tie, not a bolo. *Not* a bolo! It enraged him to think of some of the wack-job defense attorneys he'd come up against. The poor defendants hardly understood that the trial wasn't about them.

Fiscall straightened his tie and washed his hands, relieved to have his afternoon grande mocha out of his system. The chief of police, Sandy Howard, called it a "chick drink," which Fiscall always found amusing coming from a two-hundred-and-fifty-pound guy named Sandy. Fiscall imagined he could've pulled off the name Kathy just as well. It was simply the kind of guy he was.

Fiscall, on the other hand, knew he was regarded by many a redneck as having feminine qualities, only because he showered daily and groomed himself. He shined his shoes. Shaved his face. Common hygiene courtesies were taken for granted here, he was learning.

Fiscall stared at himself in mock confidence, pressing his shoulders back and raising his chin a nudge. He walked out of the bathroom and straight to his office. The secretary indicated with a nod that he would be greeted when he went in.

Sure enough, Detective Randy Prescott, one of the better dressed detectives he knew, was staring out the second-story window of Fiscall's office. Turning, his Southern good-ole-boy grin sliced right across his face. "Stephen, good to see you! How's our favorite assistant DA today?"

Charmed. "Hello, Detective."

"Thanks for staying a little late. Sure you're ready to get home to the wife and kids."

Stephen Fiscall stepped around to the other side of his desk. Yes. His wife and kids. Who'd left him and now lived in Florida, hardly acknowledging he existed. He hated the small talk of this town. Small talk was cheap and often filthy with hidden agendas.

"So we have a kidnapping?" Fiscall waited for Randy to sit, stood above him for a moment, then also took a seat.

"Yep. Looks that way. We got a cut screen, open window, an attempted 911 call, a missing lady who is a responsible type by all accounts, and a fellow who we can place at the scene. Oh, and blood."

Fiscall was jotting down notes. "Where's Detective

Crawford, anyway?" The man made him nervous, Fiscall admitted. Crawford had an edge to him that was not easy to miss.

"I don't know. Said he'd be here. Went to run an errand or something."

"Go on. How thoroughly do we have the guy placed there?"

"Left his phone number on the counter. Neighbor saw him this morning leaving the residence in a hurry. Fingerprints on a glass. And has admitted to being there."

"Admitted being there. Classic. Of course he knows that will justify his fingerprints being there." Fiscall sighed. "I'll keep the admission in mind anyhow. It may be an arguable point in closing if this ever goes to trial. Big *if* right now."

"The guy also has scratches on his face."

Fiscall heard Crawford's heavy footsteps before he even rounded the corner into his office. Decidedly, Fiscall resisted the temptation to look up. Instead he kept his eyes focused on the paper until he'd made Crawford stand there without acknowledgment for several seconds. Then he nonchalantly glanced up. "Lieutenant Crawford."

"Prescott fill you in?" he asked.

"Working on it."

"Look, Fiscall, here's the deal. This thing is going to get dicey, and you should know that from the beginning."

"Why?"

"This suspect, Kline, he's Aaron Kline's brother. Aaron Kline of the Irving PD."

"Okay."

"He's an assistant high school football coach. Over at the Catholic school."

"And now a psychopathic killer, eh?"

"I'm not sure we have a homicide."

"You have a lot of women show up alive after their homes have been broken into and they've tried to call 911? What else?"

"Reportedly the guy was very intoxicated last night as well," Prescott said. "And the bartender said he'd heard that Taylor had been yelling at someone in the parking lot, but he can't give an exact time."

"So why'd the guy come back to the scene?"

"He didn't. His brother brought him back," Prescott said. "We had the obvious evidence he'd been there, so he couldn't deny it."

Crawford growled, "There's nothing obvious about this case."

"Any signs of struggle?"

"A few," Crawford said.

"What'd he say during interrogation?"

Prescott cleared his throat. "Lieutenant Crawford made the call not to bring him in."

Fiscall couldn't hide his surprise. He looked at Crawford. "Is that true?"

"The guy came to the scene. There wasn't much more we were going to be able to do at the station. Besides, sometimes making a suspect think he's out of the woods lends itself in our favor."

"Fine. Your call. This Kline looks dirty."

Crawford said, "I want some time to investigate further."

Fiscall tossed his pen on the desk. "That's nice, Crawford. But I'm not your boss, and I don't have time for this kind of circus. What are you doing here?" He leaned back in his chair and threw his hands out in question. "You don't need me to tell you that I need more evidence. I always need more evidence. You're not going to hear any arguments from me." Fiscall scratched his chin as he studied Crawford's eyes—dark and glimmering but without his trademark self-assuredness.

Crawford looked at him. "I'm telling you, we arrest the brother of a cop and it turns out not to be him, the fallout is coming down on your office. As I'm sure you've figured out, Texans enjoy a good fallout."

Fiscall swallowed underneath the tight collar of his heavily starched shirt. "Sounds to me like the captain is eager to get this guy."

"An attractive young woman is missing, probably kidnapped. Yeah, the public is going to want a mug shot." Crawford stepped forward. "And you could finally get your high-profile case, right, Fiscall?"

Fiscall faced Detective Prescott, whose eyes were round with uncertainty. "What do you think?"

Randy shrugged, glancing at Crawford. "I don't know. I mean, I think Shep's got a point."

Fiscall groaned and pushed his chair back. "Crawford, for heaven's sake, can't anything go normally when you're involved? Fine, go get your evidence." He stared at his notes. "Get me a smoking gun. A body would be nice."

Crawford started to leave, signaling Prescott to stand.

Fiscall said, "What's that tune you're always humming, Shep?"

Crawford turned, shaking his head slightly.

"I know. Gonna get me a bad guy today. That's it, right? Or catch me a bad man? Something like that."

Crawford's smile didn't give any hint of pleasure.

"Just get the bad guy, okay? Or the fallout's going to be worse than if we get the wrong one."

Crawford wasn't looking at him. His focus was on Fiscall's file cabinet—on a framed picture of the governor standing in front of the American flag.

Crawford's eyes met Fiscall's, but he said nothing.

Fiscall sighed as Crawford exited. He looked at the governor, who had cut the police budget last year by 25 percent. Fiscall smiled. Crawford could never understand political ambition.

On what he was very sure was one of the worst days of his life, Mick Kline could not get Tylenol to kick the headache that rolled against the back of his skull like a loose marble. He'd managed to skirt most of Coach Rynde's questions. Luckily Rynde had hardly anything else but football on his mind, and Owen Gruber was at a local news station giving an interview about how great a team he'd made.

Practice had been a mess. The dark skies had cleared enough to let sunlight through, but the field was nothing but soggy turf. Mud was speckled throughout his hair, and the bottoms of his tennis shoes were caked clods.

At home, he briefly examined the small yard that needed to be mowed. When he'd rented the house, the guy assured him it would be taken care of, but so far Mick had mowed it every time. Unluckily for him, his neighbors took care of theirs, so at three inches tall, his grass was becoming a nuisance.

Of course, he should have more important things on his mind.

But this is what he'd done his whole life. Crisis meant refocus. And why not refocus on things that hardly mattered in the world? If the ground hadn't been wet, he'd probably start up the mower and mow the entire neighborhood.

Kicking off his sneakers onto the front porch, Mick ran his fingers through his hair, specks of dirt falling onto his shoulders. A shower was in immediate order.

He felt for his keys in his pocket, found them, and

unlocked the door. When he didn't hear the usual click, he tried again. Still no click. Pulling his key out, Mick blinked and hesitated, then turned the knob and swung the front door open.

Standing on his porch, he tried to pedal his thoughts backward, beyond the bar, beyond Taylor's, to yesterday afternoon when Aaron had come over to tell him the "good news." Afterward, he'd left angrily. He remembered slamming the front door as he walked out. But had he locked it?

Mick stepped inside, scanning what he could see of his small living room. TV and stereo were untouched. He threw his keys on the small table by the wall and shut the door.

Switching on the light, he took one more good look around and decided he'd left the door unlocked. Wasn't something he would normally do, but neither was slugging his brother, so there was not much he could count on about that day. Not much at all.

Mick threw off his Windbreaker and went to the bathroom to shower. He opened the window above the tub. To him, there was nothing better than the smell after a hard rain. It soothed him as much as a long, hot shower.

Steam filled the bathroom as Mick dumped his muddy clothes in the hamper in his bedroom and threw on his robe. Fatigue was setting in, and it wasn't even evening. A quick shot of orange juice could do more than just about any other drink.

Heading toward the kitchen, the steam of the shower dampened his forehead as he passed the bathroon. He stopped in the middle of the hallway and returned to his bedroom.

His pajama bottoms were not at the bottom edge of his bed. They were near his hamper. Mick stood in thought. His pajama bottoms, without fail, were always at the end corner of his bed, because every morning he left them there when he sat on the edge to get dressed. It was one of those things that he knew would drive a future wife crazy.

But that was two nights ago. Last night he had not come home. Had he kicked them out of the way inadvertently the day before? Not likely. He was more accustomed to stepping over all his clothing. Nobody would believe there was a science behind all those clothing piles.

He scanned the rest of the bedroom. Dresser drawers were closed, but he opened each one anyway, trying to find something out of place.

He moved to his closet, looking carefully at each section. Hangers had been moved. He sensed it. He knelt, trying to get an idea if anything was missing. In the back corner, he had a safe, filled only with baseball cards, but a thief would investigate it.

Pushing the clothes aside, he saw the red metal, always flush against the back corner wall. It had been pulled out at least three inches.

Mick scrambled to his feet, backing out of the closet and whipping around, trying to take in the whole room at once. He backed down the hallway and into the living room.

There. His CD and VHS collection. Usually in a neat pile—nearly the only thing neat in his entire house—it was pushed sideways, leaning against the side of the stereo casing.

The photo album under his coffee table that was always open to a picture of him and his mother and father on vacation in the Bahamas was now open to an old photo of him and Aaron at a baseball game, chummy arms around each other.

Mick glanced at the entryway tile and bent over for a closer look. There—light brown footprints. From the mud.

He followed the prints back to the kitchen. On the kitchen tile, the prints were barely visible, but he could feel them with his fingertips. Nothing else seemed out of order.

His tongue stuck to the roof of his mouth, and he was panting like he'd just finished practice. The after-rain humidity crowded his lungs. Opening a cabinet, he grabbed a glass, slamming it to the counter from sheer adrenaline.

He swung open the refrigerator door and snatched the orange juice container. Mick held it up and stared at it. Completely empty. Somebody drank his orange juice? Clenching his jaw, he threw the container across the room.

Whoever had been here wanted to make sure Mick knew it.

Stomping down the hall , Mick flipped the dead bolt on the front door, then went to the bathroom. He threw off his robe and stepped into the shower. His skin stung as the ice-cold water hit it.

He didn't care. Right now his blood was running cold anyway.

chapter eight

Sammy Earle sighed. A long, exhausting, indifferent sigh.

His secretary, JoAnne, stared at him from the doorway of his office. "Did you hear me? You're late?"

"I heard you," Sammy said, pushing three pieces of Juicy Fruit into his mouth. He was trying to quit smoking. Trying for five years. He'd stopped drinking and using pot, so the other vice didn't seem so urgent. Except he couldn't run a mile anymore. There had been a day when he could run ten. "You keep yapping like a dog and you're going to turn into one."

JoAnne's heavily lined eyes lit with surprise, and she scowled at him as she turned on her heel and left.

If JoAnne could manage an ounce of class, Sammy would probably give her a bit more respect. But her bright pink fingernails and her bobby-pinned bushel of hair did little to make her the least bit attractive. He supposed she dressed trashy to offset her other physical disasters, but it ended up creating a package straight out of the '80s. The woman still wore leggings under her fluffy skirts and hoop earrings that nearly touched her shoulders. Sammy wanted to pin a sign to her forehead that read Wake Up! It's 1995!

Sammy grabbed his briefcase and jacket, smoothing out his hair and trying to pull the crease out of his tie. He didn't feel like defending a rapist today. He hardly ever did.

"Even lowlifes need defense. It's part of being American," his father had once told him. Ambulance Chaser Al was what they called his dad. He died when one of his own defendants shot him to death outside the courtroom.

Sammy did indeed defend lowlifes. Rich and famous lowlifes, though, who paid him a lot of money to try to reverse the mistakes they made when they thought nobody was watching.

Sammy stood by the window of his office and studied the McDonald's Monopoly game he'd been playing. It was laid out neatly on a small table in front of him, all the game pieces he'd won in their proper places. He was not a gambling man. But there were no risks here—other than a fact that eating at the fast-food chain could indeed be an intestinal risk in and of itself—and occasionally it came with certain perks like free fries or a sundae.

"You're late!" JoAnne called again from her desk around the corner. "Judge Greer hates your guts. Why do you egg him on by being late all the time?"

Sammy smiled. *Because Judge Greer hates my guts, that's why.*

He walked out of his office without regard to JoAnne, who was apparently wanting some sort of thank-you for her persistence. Kellan Johannsen was his defendant today. Famous sports star, womanizer, rich kid who didn't know what to do with all he had. For the right price, Sammy was supposed to wash the blood from his hands.

He was the antibacterial soap of the stars. Today he would march into the courtroom with a particular, practiced posture—the one that said, "You're targeting him because he's rich and famous." Then he'd make the woman out to be some sort of high-priced prostitute. And then he'd lift Kellan high up the moral ladder and make everyone doubt their first instincts about the man.

In the elevator, he cleaned the grime underneath his fingernails. The tangible grime anyway.

By 8:30 a.m. Aaron had finished the last of the paperwork from yesterday. Normally Jarrod would do most of it, but Aaron wanted to make sure it was done right. Across from him, Jarrod was on the phone and taking notes.

His stomach grumbled. Jenny had come over early and brought him bagels on her way to work. He'd taken a couple of bites to satisfy her but thrown the rest away when she left.

The hot coffee seemed to be eating away at his stomach lining. Acid burned at his esophagus. He was about to get up for a glass of water when Jarrod hung up the phone.

"That was the airport police," Jarrod said, handing him the paper. "This is the name of the passenger that went nuts Tuesday."

Aaron took the paper. *Timothy R. Marcus. From Grapevine.*

"Said they released him a couple of hours after the incident. Guess the guy was drunk."

"Any charges?"

"They're not sure yet. He didn't do too much except yell. Bad mannered and impatient."

"Do we know what his business was in LA?"

"Job interview. Dinner with some bigwig that was going to make him a millionaire. Left on a flight the next afternoon."

Aaron said, "Okay, let me fill his address out here, and then you can take this information over to Lieutenant Crawford."

Jarrod groaned. "Do I have to?"

"Just set it on his desk. It doesn't have to be a big deal."

"The guy creeps me out. Always humming that stupid song."

"Keep your voice down," Aaron said, shooting him a look. "Just roll with him. Stay out of his way."

"If everyone hates him so much, why is he still here?" Jarrod asked.

"He's good at what he does."

"Is it true he marks stuff with his blood?"

"It's probably a crazy rumor."

"You don't seem to have a problem with him like everyone else does."

Aaron looked up at Jarrod's expectant eyes. The kid probably wouldn't understand why. "Look, the problem with this place is ego. Everyone wants to be in charge; everyone wants to one-up the next guy. That sort of thing doesn't bother me. I figure when it's my time to shine, God will let me know."

Jarrod was grinning with half his mouth. "What does that mean?"

Aaron shook his head. "It means that I don't always have to be number one." By the perplexed look on Jarrod's face, he knew there was no comprehension.

"Aaron."

Aaron turned around to his name being called. Standing in the doorway of his office was Captain Bellows. Aaron stood. "Yes, sir?"

"Need to see you for a second." The captain disappeared into his own office. Inside, he asked Aaron to shut the door. "Thanks for coming in, Aaron."

"Sure." Aaron sat down. "Let me guess. You want me to stay out of the way."

Fred Bellows's deep-set eyes reflected an equal measure of compassion and staunchness. Tall and husky, Bellows was as good a boss as anybody could ask for, but he was always driven by ambitions that on occasion contradicted each other. He said he'd retire next year, but he'd been saying that for eight years.

After a mild heart attack last year, Bellows had finally taken Aaron up on his many invitations to visit his church. He and his wife, Gladys, had come three times.

"It's my Catholic upbringing," he'd told Aaron as an excuse for why he couldn't return to the "protestant" church.

Aaron pointed out a great Catholic church three miles from the captain's house. And that was the end of it.

Fred folded his fingers and rested his hands on his small potbelly. "Chief thought it best."

Chief Sandy Howard, formally from Detroit, was a Navy Seal back in the '70s and ran the department like a drill sergeant from one of his academy days. But Aaron respected him.

"I understand. It'll be cleared up soon. Mick, I mean."

Fred's thick lips pursed in thought. "Doesn't have an alibi."

"I know." Aaron fiddled with the metal on his belt. "They're certain it is a kidnapping?"

"Evidence looks that way."

"Mick didn't do this," Aaron said. "I want you to know that. I don't know what Crawford and his team are going to do here, but I'm telling you Mick is not the person responsible if this woman was indeed kidnapped."

"I know this is tough," Fred said, staring at his desk. He looked up at Aaron. "It's a criminal investigation now. So I just want you to be aware of that."

"Are they going to arrest Mick?"

"Can't say."

"Or won't say?"

Fred sighed and leaned forward on his desk. "Aaron, just make sure that Mick doesn't do anything stupid. That's the only control you have in this situation. He could make things a whole lot worse for himself. You and I both know that. Tell that kid to sit and do nothing."

Aaron bit his lip. He knew one thing for sure. He had no control over Mick and never had. If Mick did something foolish, things would get risky for him very quickly. As if they weren't risky enough already.

"Since Homicide will be handling this, your duties will resume as normal. How's Jarrod working out for you, by the way?" Fred smiled, trying to shift the conversation to small talk.

Aaron obliged. "He's okay. Has a lot of impressions of the world that will quickly be skewed."

"Well, he's got a good man to teach him. This is a tough life, ain't it?"

Aaron nodded and stood. "Anything else, Captain?"

"No. I'll keep you updated as I can."

But Aaron saw in his eyes that any information he was going to get would be after decisions had already been made. Aaron felt his stomach churn but managed a courteous smile.

Down the hall, he noticed a group of officers gathered in front of the television.

Jarrod looked around as Aaron approached. "It's breaking news this morning," Jarrod said.

The officers, eyes averting, parted so Aaron could see the TV, just as a boxed picture of Mick coaching football came up next to the news anchor's face.

"They're calling him a person of interest," the coifed woman said into the camera.

Mick's sleep had been fitful at best. He woke unusually early, tangled in his covers, and knocked over a glass on his bedside table. When he finally managed to get out of bed, he went to the bathroom and splashed cold water on his face three times before one eye would pry open. He ran a toothbrush over his teeth and gargled with mouthwash before going to the kitchen, hoping to find at least a couple of eggs. The clock read 10:12 a.m.

A knock at the front door chased the grogginess away. Mick made his way to the door. "Who is it?"

"Aaron. Let me in."

"Go away!"

"Mick, let me in. Now."

Mick cracked open the door. Aaron was in uniform. Mick had always thought he looked good in it. As if he needed anything else stoic about him. "Is this official police business?"

Aaron shoved past him and into the house, looking around before turning back to him. "No. I'm officially off the case. And it's officially a homicide investigation, if you didn't know that already."

"So what's going on? Are they coming to arrest me this morning? Should I change into something else?" Mick pointed to his pajama bottoms.

Aaron followed Mick into the kitchen, where Mick poured a glass of milk without sniffing the container first. One sip and he spit it into the sink, dumping the rest down the drain.

"I hope you know this isn't a joke."

"Do I look like I'm joking?"

"I just want to talk, Mick. I want to get as much information from you as I can."

"You're not on the case. What does it matter?"

"Because I'm on the police force still, and the more I know, the more I can help you."

Mick leaned against the cabinets and studied his

brother, aware that his own defensiveness tended to blind him to his brother's intentions. Aaron's normally intense eyes did seem less so. The disapproving look that often crossed Aaron's expression was replaced by concern.

"You need to get a lawyer," Aaron said.

Mick tried not to flinch.

"I don't know if they're going to make an arrest, but you need to be prepared if they do."

"I'm not getting a lawyer. It'll only make me look guilty. You already think I'm guilty."

Aaron wiped his face with his hand, and his countenance changed nearly immediately. He stepped closer to Mick. "Guilt has nothing to do with it. You need someone on your side who knows the system and how it works. I've told everybody I know that you didn't do this."

Mick looked away. "What's *this*? Is she dead? Have they found anything indicating she's been murdered?"

"No. But she apparently tried to dial 911."

Mick left the kitchen to pace the living-room floor. "That's insane. I was there. Passed out. But there. I mean, wouldn't I know if something bad had happened? This doesn't make sense."

"You don't remember anything?"

"Bits and pieces of conversation. I think she tried to wake me up at one point." Mick fell into the cushions of his run-down couch. Aaron joined him. "This'll teach me, eh?"

"What?"

"Not to go home with women. Not to drink. Not to go to bars. See what can happen? You can be charged with murder."

Aaron stared at him and then looked away. "I'm not going to lecture you."

"At least I had enough sense to not drive home drunk. That's what got me in trouble in the first place."

"So you had her drive you."

"We'd been having a pretty good conversation as I recall."

"About?"

Mick's head throbbed. He needed food. "Things that don't go right in your life."

"What kind of woman was she? By all accounts, she's a responsible citizen."

"Responsible citizens do frequent bars, you know."

"Mick, drop the defensiveness. You're twisting my words."

Mick sighed. "Fine. She was great. I mean, we just sat and talked. There was this . . . I don't know . . . this sadness to her."

"Sadness?"

"Yeah, I noticed it right away. But she didn't talk about anything specific. Just generalizations, really. Who knows? Maybe her sister ran off with the man of her dreams."

Aaron hung his head like that was the last thing he wanted to talk about, and Mick wished he hadn't said it. It was the last thing he wanted to talk about too. Even the mention of it caused walls to rise.

"Jenny told me you came to see her yesterday at the school."

Mick stood, wanting so badly to leave the room, to leave this mess completely. Was he the biggest fool around? Did he really think he could go over and talk Jenny out of marrying Aaron? Was he losing his mind? or at least his self-control? But maybe it was because he'd never felt like he had with anybody but Jenny. It caused him to swallow his pride and beg. The thought of it made him squeeze his eyes shut, trying to black out the image.

He needed to shift the topic—and fast. "Were you here yesterday?"

"What do you mean?"

"Rummaging around my house?"

"What in the world are you talking about?"

"Were you?"

"No!" Aaron said.

"Where were you?" Mick asked. Aaron wasn't getting out of it that easily. Besides, if it was Aaron it would make that strange, creepy feeling he'd had all night go away. Surely it was just Aaron butting into his business, which wasn't anything new.

"You want to know where I was last night?"

"Yeah, I do."

"I was at church."

"They have church on Thursday nights? Don't you religious people ever take a break?"

"I was there praying for you, Mick. Praying for this situation. Jenny was there too."

An inexplicable anger seized Mick and he turned from Aaron, clenching his fists. Great, Saint Aaron at it again. That sort of thing was the reason Jenny fell for him in the first place. He clutched his chest, sure his heart was about to beat straight out of his chest cavity. How many times he'd heard Aaron say, *I'm praying for you.* It made him want to puke.

After a moment Aaron said, "I prayed that God would reveal the truth. God knows what happened last night. He's our best chance at finding the truth. Doesn't that comfort you in the least?"

"What? That you're praying for me?" Mick asked, turning to him.

"No. That God knows the truth."

Mick stared at Aaron. For most of his life, that was not a comforting thought. It meant God knew everything about him, all his dirty deeds, all his wicked motivations. But now, oddly, it did bring a little surge of hope. Even if he couldn't remember what happened last night, God knew.

"Why did you think I was here last night?" Aaron asked him.

Mick blinked, trying to decide what he should tell Aaron. "No reason."

"I don't believe that." Aaron glanced around the room. "Were you being tailed?"

"Tailed?"

"Yeah. I thought the detectives might want to keep an eye on you."

"Not that I'm aware of," Mick said, resisting the urge to look out the front window. "Just seemed like someone had been here last night."

"Really?"

"I don't know." Mick returned to the kitchen for some water. "Some things were out of place. The front door was unlocked."

"Possibility you could've left it unlocked?"

"Sure. Whatever. I'm probably just imagining it." Mick stared at the picture album he knew had been looked through.

Aaron didn't seem to have anything else to say. Mick couldn't read whether he was sympathetic or skeptical.

Aaron then pulled out a card from his pocket and handed to him. "Here."

"What's this?"

"Guy's name is Bill Cassavo. He's an attorney who goes to our church. I know him and can personally vouch for him."

"I'm not getting an attorney." Mick threw the card on the coffee table.

"Fine," Aaron growled. "Do what you want. You always have." He headed to the door just as Mick's phone rang. Aaron said, "By the way, the news broke the story this morning. Had a picture of you, said you were a person of interest. You might want to call Mom and Dad before they get wind of it."

After the fourth ring, Mick's answering machine picked up. He wished Aaron would go, but he stood there while Mick's greeting rolled through. After the beep, he heard, "Mick. Owen Gruber. You're officially on leave while this . . . thing . . . gets sorted out. Coach wants to talk to you as soon as you can get in, and so do I. I don't know what's going on, but you have a lot of explaining to do. I'm assuming you'll get this message, and they haven't taken you to jail yet."

Aaron walked out, shutting the door firmly.

Five seconds later the answering machine flew across the room.

chapter nine

mick really didn't care if Owen Gruber thought he was the equivalent of pig slop, but to see the look in Coach Rynde's eyes made him ill. Gary Rynde was the golden scepter of high school football. He motivated players, made everyone feel important, and took kids who would normally end up in trouble and turned them into people everyone wanted to be around.

Mick supposed Gary also saw him as a project who could use some motivation now and then. On more than one occasion, Gary had talked with Mick about his drinking and the problem it could turn into someday. He'd also lectured him on his immense coaching talent, but said that his lack of focus and his undisciplined nature lent themselves toward unsuccessfulness.

Mick knew all this. But something kept him from changing. It seemed even a motivational speech from the great Gary Rynde couldn't muster up self-conviction that would stay any longer than a week.

Mick slumped in the chair in Rynde's office, staring at the carpet, wondering how many minutes or hours it would be before his life would officially be over. Of course, according to Aaron, it was over every day he walked without God. He was not about to concur that Aaron Kline had all the answers in the world. Surely Mick could find some answers himself.

Mick glanced up. Gary was chewing his lip and looking into the air. Owen, on the other hand, was studying Mick with an intense smirk trembling at the edges of his lips, waiting to break into a full-force sneer.

"You don't know what's going to happen next?" Gary was studying him.

Mick shook his head. "No idea. I mean, they haven't arrested me yet, so that tells me there are some other angles being looked at. Thank goodness." He propped his tired head onto his hand, closing his eyes at the exhausting thoughts and the men's skeptical expressions.

"You look like you could use a bed to rest that conscience of yours on," Owen said under his breath.

Gary shot him a look that kept his mouth shut for several more minutes.

"Look, Coach, I didn't do this," Mick said. "I was in the wrong place at the wrong time. It's as big a mystery to me as it is to anybody what happened to this lady."

Mick hated the term *this lady*. He'd known Taylor for only a short time, but she wasn't a total stranger. Unfortunately, much of her identity was lost in the fog of his mind.

Gary glanced at Owen. "Give us a minute, will you?"

Owen flinched at the idea, his nostrils flaring in protest. But without another word, he left the room.

Gary rose and shut the door behind him, then turned and leaned against it, crossing his arms together in the same manner he did at football games while watching one of his many plays unfold on the field.

Mick hung his head. Gary seemed to be everything Mick wanted in his life. In his late forties, he was still a good-looking, athletic guy, with a lot of charm, wit, and character. It takes a special personality to relate to kids who think they own the world, and Gary had it. But today, Gary's normally sparkling eyes were sterile.

"So, what are you going to do here?" Gary asked, adjusting the sun visor he always wore.

"Do?"

"You have a game plan?"

Mick swallowed. Well, no. But he didn't really see this as a game that needed a strategy. His perplexed look caused Gary to chuckle a little bit.

Gary strolled over to the large chalkboard he kept in his office, eyeing the Split V-3 play he'd constructed last week. They'd run it a few times in practice, and it seemed to work well. Gary seemed to be a genius at everything he did. But Mick could tell that, though Coach stared at the board, his mind, for once, wasn't on football.

"So you're just going to sit there and take it? Is that it?"

He wasn't sure what Gary was trying to say.

Gary smiled as he went to his desk. He stared at Mick with openly candid eyes. "Mick, you're not a murderer or a kidnapper or anything of that sort. Gruber would love for you to go down for this. But Gruber is an insecure guy who loves to try and squash anybody that might threaten his little throne of power."

"I don't think I'm a threat to Owen."

"Everybody is a threat to Owen." Gary scratched his head and said, "Back in 1984 I was coaching at a small middle school out in Plano. We had a winning team two years in a row, and it really picked the school up. But along came Ricardo Martinez."

"Ricardo Martinez?"

"Two-hundred-pound linebacker with a body that could crush a car."

"Really?"

"Yeah. At fourteen too. Problem was, Ricardo was no good. But his parents didn't see it that way. And his parents were psychopaths."

Mick laughed.

"You know the type, yelling at the Little League games, cursing at small children, threatening to kill their parents. Every time I put Ricardo in, however, he'd mess up and end up costing us a lot. I worked with the kid—or tried to—but at the end of the day, Ric thought he knew it all and was unteachable. He wouldn't even try to implement what I showed him. So I yanked him from the lineup and refused to start him."

"Good for you." Mick smiled.

"Yeah. Until they accused me of sexual abuse."

"What?"

"Yep. Said it happened in the showers when all the other kids were gone. I got suspended, of course, and they began a criminal investigation on me. I'd been married three weeks when all this went down."

Mick's mouth fell open. "I had no idea!"

"That's because I never talk about it. They were some of the worst days of my life. I didn't do it, but how can you prove it?"

"So what happened?"

Gary grinned, stretching his arms over his head and clasping them behind his neck. "The only thing I could do. Fight for myself. And so I did."

"How?"

He shrugged nonchalantly. "Snuck into the family's house while they were gone, hid in a living-room closet behind some coats. Waited. When they returned, my wife called and pretended to be a reporter asking questions, which got the topic started once they hung up the phone. And so I tape-recorded them talking about their plan to bring me down. For thirty minutes they gave me everything I wanted. I stayed in the closet all night until they left the next morning. Then I took the tape to the police before they even brought it to the DA. Since it was still at the investigation stage, the tape was used to prove I was set up. It never went to trial."

"Wow!" Mick shook his head. "That's an incredible story."

The fervor of the storytelling faded, though, as Gary leaned forward on his desk. "Mick, I don't know what happened here, but you better find out. You don't know who you can trust. Doesn't seem like anybody is looking out for your best interest. They're out to find a kidnapped woman and someone they can nail for it. It's either going to be you or the person who did this."

"But how do I—?"

Gary held up his hands. "You're a smart guy. Half the time you don't tap into what's up here. But this is a serious thing, and you're going to have to figure it out fast."

Mick couldn't fathom how he might do that.

Gary stood, holding out his hand.

Mick stood too, shaking Gary's hand firmly. "You've always believed in me, Coach."

Gary smiled. "There's something holding you back. I hope you find out what it is soon." Gary walked him to the door a few feet away. "I'm going to try to persuade the board to make this a paid leave. I'm not sure how I'll fare, but I'll try."

Mick hadn't thought of the financial implications. He tried to keep a steady smile on his face, though. "Thanks."

"Touch base with me on this, okay? I want to remain updated."

"I will." Mick walked down the long hallway that led out to the gymnasium and then the east parking lot. His stomach burned from stress and hunger, so he decided to go to the grocery store.

He'd always lived a bachelor's life, in need of not much

more than milk, orange juice, eggs, and cold cereal. Was there really anything else in life? On occasion, he had been known to go to the trouble of fixing a ham-and-cheese sandwich or a PBJ. And he even liked cucumber sand-wiches, especially when his mom used to bring over fresh cucumbers from her garden before their parents moved away.

He hadn't called their parents yet. He knew Aaron would, anyway. The fact of the matter was he didn't have a clue how to explain this. He didn't much understand it himself.

Mick strolled down the cereal aisle, parking in front of the ones that cost twice as much and were loaded with sugar. He picked up a couple of boxes and threw them into his cart.

"I've found men are all the same."
"Do you think that's fair?"
"Are you trying to tell me you disagree? Here you are,
*   stumbling into my apartment with a woman you*
*   hardly know, expecting who knows what."*
"I'm not that kind of person."
"Then why are you here?"

Mick blinked and the conversation faded. But he saw the scene in his head. They were at Taylor's apartment, sitting on the couch together. Mick's head was buzzing, and the store was swirling. He'd been trying to concentrate. Mick pushed his cart forward.

"You seem genuinely concerned about me."
"I am concerned. I want to help you, but you haven't told
*   me what's wrong."*
"You shouldn't be here. I'm a moron for bringing you

*back here. Why do I always make the same mistakes
with the same kind of men?"*

"What kind of men?"

*"The kind that think of women as pawns in a wicked
game of power."*

"Sir? Sir. Hello? Fifteen dollars and seventy-two cents."

Mick stared at the woman in front of him. He was at the
checkout and hardly remembered getting there. "I'm . . .
I'm sorry. Fifteen and?"

"Seventy-two cents, for the fourth time."

"Right." Mick grabbed his wallet out of his back pocket.
But when he opened it, his money was gone. "What the—?"

The woman at the cash register had her hands on her
hips, as did the mother of four behind him. "Problem?"

"My money's gone!" Mick's mind raced. He'd had his
wallet with him since Wednesday night, and it had been
with him even when he thought somebody might have been
in his house.

"Yeah, it just spends itself, doesn't it?" the cashier said,
popping her gum.

His maxed-out credit card was still there, and he didn't
have his checkbook.

"What's the problem here?" the store manager asked.
His chin was tilted up with authority.

"No money," the woman said.

"My money has been stolen," Mick explained. "I had at
least sixty bucks in here." He knew he'd started Wednesday
night off with eighty or more. But even buying Taylor's
drinks, he wouldn't have spent more than twenty or
twenty-five dollars.

"Sorry to hear that. How are you going to pay for
these?" the manager asked, pointing to the sacked groceries.

Mick stuttered. "I-I can't."

The matronly woman behind him sighed loudly as one of her kids belched in the other kid's face, inducing hysterical giggles.

Mick folded his wallet and walked out, the gnawing hunger in his stomach completely gone.

———

Shep Crawford eyed Captain Fred Bellows, who was standing near the two-way mirror staring openly at the woman in the interrogation room.

"Life has beaten her to a bloody pulp," Fred remarked.

Mrs. MaryLou Franks looked eighty to her fifty-four years. Kind, hollow eyes stared across the room, and in her face years of pain had etched deep, scarlike wrinkles into her skin. She was nervously tapping her fingers against the metal table, waiting.

"You sent Prescott to interview Sammy Earle?" Fred asked, keeping his eyes forward but raising an eyebrow. "I thought he could handle it."

"You hardly ever think Randy can handle anything."

Shep looked through the window. "I think Mrs. Franks will be invaluable. Besides, clues are rarely where you think they should be."

"So you say. Rumor has it you think Kline isn't our man." Fred stepped away from the mirror and to the watercooler. "I don't like being underhanded, Shep."

"All that stuff we found in the victim's apartment seemed a little too convenient to be attached to this Kline guy. I need some extra time. Prescott will give me some good information on Earle, the ex-boyfriend, and then we'll go from there."

"The chief isn't happy. We're all coming under heat for this, including Fiscall. It's a high-profile kidnapping case."

"All Fiscall cares about is the election in eighteen months. He could use a case like this, couldn't he?"

"I don't care about Fiscall. Just get back to me and soon. I want a decision by tomorrow."

"Who's pushing you on this?" Crawford asked.

"Irving is pushing. The story broke this morning and people are going to want to know something, especially with a very viable subject running around town. A viable subject who is coaching their children."

"I think we're going to find Sammy Earle very interesting."

"He's a prominent attorney. Whichever one ends up being our man, we're going to be taking a lot of heat. We better make sure we get it right." Fred rubbed his eyes.

Shep said, "Let's see what this young woman's mother has to say about the man her daughter once loved."

Shep stepped around Fred and went into the room where Mrs. Franks sat, clutching her purse and bouncing her knee.

She stood as Shep entered. "Any word on Taylor?"

"I'm Shep Crawford, head of the Criminal Investigation Unit here in Irving. Please sit down, ma'am."

Mrs. Franks sat back down. "Anything at all?"

"Not yet. We're working every angle on this case, Mrs. Franks, which is why I need you to tell me everything you know."

Mrs. Franks shook her head. "Not much, I'm afraid. Taylor and I have been estranged for a year or so now."

"Estranged?"

"We had a fight. A lousy fight," she managed through soft sobs.

"Over?"

She didn't look up as she spoke. "I'm not proud of it. But I just wanted Taylor to have a better life than me. We were always so poor. White trash, I guess you'd call us. We lived in a trailer most of our lives and hardly ever had enough of anything that was good—plenty of things that were bad, though."

"What was the fight about?"

"She was dating this man, Sam Earle. The attorney I told the other man about. Have you seen him? He's always on the television. Real nice-looking gentleman."

"About my age, isn't he?" Shep asked.

Mrs. Franks nodded. "Yeah. He was an older man, much older than my Taylor. Taylor has never had a problem with men. She just has this class in her, you know? Like she was born to be better than she started out to be. She's so pretty, has the face of an angel; I swear it. When she left home and went to work, she started dressing real nice too."

"And?"

"She began dating Sam Earle a few years back. Maybe three. She bought a new car. Lived in that nice apartment. Was just a class act. And those two, they looked like they belonged together."

"He's old enough to be her father, ma'am."

"Who's counting years? She finally found a man who could give her the world!" Mrs. Franks said. "Maybe you don't know what it's like to have nothin', but it's a rotten life, I tell you."

"So Mr. Earle gave her the world, did he?"

"Would take her to fancy restaurants, big parties. They drove around in a limo a lot. Everyone said they were such a handsome couple, and they were."

"What happened?"

Mrs. Franks diverted her eyes, staring at the window that reflected her homely, dejected image. "Taylor, she's always been so dramatic."

"How so?"

"She blows a lot of things out of proportion, that's all. She used to be a shy girl, back when she was younger. Didn't say much. She grew out of that, though. Anyway, she came home with this story about how Sam wasn't treating her right."

"Treating her how?"

"My goodness, how could he not be treating her right? He was the best thing to happen to her. I'm sure he would've bought her anything if she'd asked."

"What were her claims against him?"

"Claims? Oh, I don't know. The girl rambled about everything, but I guess she might've said something about him hitting her."

"So he hit her."

"That's what she said. And some psychobabble about verbal abuse." Mrs. Franks shook her head and laughed loosely.

Shep leaned forward. "Are you saying that your daughter at one point claimed that Sammy Earle was abusing her, both physically and emotionally?"

Mrs. Franks's sour eyes turned to Shep. "Look, she didn't know what she had. Nothing was good enough for her!"

"You told her to stay with this man?"

"I told her that sometimes you just gotta live with some things. I mean, she wasn't living in a trailer and she had a lot of money. Sam was treating her real good. I guess he had some sort of temper, but Taylor couldn't live with that."

"So they broke up?"

"'Bout a year ago. A little over a year maybe. I told her that was ridiculous. I told her to toughen up. But she wouldn't listen to me. And she stopped talking to me because I told her she should rethink herself. Said I was a weak woman." Mrs. Franks's words sizzled with disdain. "You probably think I'm some sort of bad mother."

Shep carefully wrote down his notes. "Mrs. Franks, we're just trying to find out what happened to your daughter. Have you ever met Mr. Earle?"

"No. Didn't want to. Didn't want him to see our roots. She was better off hiding that part of her life."

"Tell me about your husband, Taylor's father."

Mrs. Franks's body seemed to wilt against the chair. "Why?"

"Simply background information, ma'am. Might be helpful."

"Don't see how. He's been dead a decade or more."

"How'd he die?"

"Liver."

"Liver?"

"That nasty whiskey. Got his liver."

"He was an alcoholic?"

Mrs. Franks's lips tightened into a thin line. "Whatever you want to call it."

"Did he ever abuse you or your daughter?"

"Why's that matter?"

"Did he?"

Mrs. Franks laughed off his question and stared at her purse.

"We're almost finished, Mrs. Franks. Do you think Mr. Earle might've done something to Taylor?"

Mrs. Franks thought out the question. "I don't honestly know," she finally said in a very soft voice.

"Do you know of anyone else Taylor was involved with? Anybody who might want to hurt her?"

"Don't know. She's a sweet girl, sir," she said, her tissue catching falling tears. "The other detective yesterday said there's evidence that she was taken."

"I'm sorry. It does appear that way."

Mrs. Franks's sobs reverberated off the cold, concrete walls. "I just can't believe it."

"Thank you for your time, ma'am. We'll have a detective call you as soon as we find anything else out."

Mrs. Franks stood. "What about that man who's on the news? The football coach. Aren't you going to arrest him? Wasn't he with her the night she disappeared?"

"We'll be in touch," Shep said and walked out of the room.

chapter ten

When the door of the courtroom swung open, Sammy was greeted by a horde of reporters as he accompanied the now vindicated Kellan Johannsen down to the waiting luxury SUV. At six foot seven, Johannsen was a majestic skyscraper among lowly office buildings. The basketball star fastened the top button of his fancy suit and smiled enthusiastically, then shot two victorious thumbs into the air.

It had taken the jury only two hours to deliberate and come back with a not guilty verdict.

Dallas news anchors and reporters shoved their way toward Johannsen as he took to the makeshift podium set up at the sidewalk below. Sammy followed, positioning himself between Johannsen's manager and his publicist, who, thanks to him, still had their jobs. They would not have been able to spin much off a convicted rapist.

Glancing around, Sammy could see a Geo Metro waiting by the side entrance of the courtroom. The prosecuting attorney was escorting the plaintiff to the car, her hand pressed into the young woman's elbow. At the sound of the crowd, they both looked over. The attorney caught Sammy's eye, and even at twenty-five yards away, he could see her contempt.

Sammy offered a wide, belligerent grin, then turned toward the press, whose microphones were spread in front of Kellan Johannsen like a giant bouquet of flowers.

"I'd like to thank everyone for their support," Johannsen mumbled, shifting from one foot to the other.

How Sammy wished someone would teach public-speaking skills to these athletes who always seemed to do so much speaking in public.

"My family, my lovely wife, my children, and everyone else who believed in my innocence from the beginning . . ."

Sammy stared forward, noticing, of course, that Johannsen didn't thank him and his brilliant defense. That was okay. He'd thank him with his wallet.

"Now, please, respect my privacy and the privacy of my family as we heal from this terrible time in our lives." Johannsen backed up and walked toward the SUV.

His defense team followed, including Sammy. As they each crowded into the SUV, Sammy walked around the front to get in on the other side. But he suddenly found himself stopped by a man with dark red hair, and dressed in a blue silk shirt and khakis. "No questions now," Sammy said, trying to step around him to get into the backseat of the vehicle. Reporters were relentless.

"This isn't about the trial," the man said, flashing an Irving Police Department detective's badge.

Sammy looked up at him. "What's this about? A client?"

"I just need to ask you a few questions, sir."

"About what?" Sammy frowned, glancing into the SUV. Johannsen shot him an anxious look, ready to leave the chaos of cameras and microphones. "Can't this wait?"

"It's about a woman named Taylor Franks."

Sammy could not help but swallow. But he steadied his gaze and did not blink. "What about her?"

"We can either do this in front of everyone here or somewhere else."

Sammy swept his bangs off his forehead and turned back to the SUV. "Go on without me. I'll catch—"

The SUV sped off as the door was quickly pulled shut.

The detective was introducing himself as Randy Prescott.

As Sammy turned to him, he noticed someone across the street standing in the shadow of two large trees. The man was leaning casually against the trunk, hands in his pockets, watching. But Sammy could not see his face.

"Why don't we go to my office?" Sammy said, gesturing toward the sidewalk. "It's about eight blocks away."

Aaron had convinced his supervisor to let him take half the day off. He knew he wasn't going to be able to concentrate or drive around the city with blabbing Jarrod by his side.

Mick's stubbornness wasn't helping matters. His pride was going to be his downfall. Why couldn't Aaron reach him? Why did Mick always think his brother was out to get him? Didn't he understand Aaron wasn't the one coming after him?

Accompanied by a quiet security guard, Aaron walked toward the Delta employee break room at the airport, behind the front ticket counters. His stride was as swift as the bustling passengers around him. But his mind was as far away as all of their destinations. He was nine years old, with four-year-old Mick trotting behind him along the riverbed, shadowing his every move.

"Hold my hand, Aaron!"
He took his brother's hand, their fingers entwining.
"Are we going to see some fish today?"
"I don't know, buddy. Don't get in the mud. Mom'll kill me."
The squish next to him indicated Mick's boot had found a

nice muddy hole in which to plant itself. Mick grinned
up at him, his eyes sparkling a strong-willed defiance.
"Come on. We'll wash it off in the stream."

The security guard turned down a small hallway and
pointed to the white door at the end. "That's it."

"Okay."

"Just check out with me before you go."

"Thanks." Aaron walked toward the break room alone.

"Aaron, don't leave me!"

"I'm not. I'm just going to cross over here, see what's up
the creek."

"No! Don't leave me!"

"Buddy, I'm not. I'll be right back. You stay here."

"No! I'm going with you. I don't want to stay alone."

"All right. Come on. Don't get wet, though. Stay on those
rocks."

Aaron adjusted his belt and badge and walked in. Five
or six people were standing around, three of them huddled
together near the refrigerator.

Liz, the woman who'd reported Taylor missing, recognized Aaron. "Officer! Do you have any news?"

Aaron shook his head. He wanted to say as little as
possible. He was breaking protocol by being in uniform and
coming in as if he were on duty. But he figured nobody here
would even understand that homicide was now in charge of
the investigation.

Immediately Aaron noticed the bouquet of flowers on a
nearby counter. Liz and the two men standing by her
followed his gaze. The roses were drooping to the side. He
figured they would still be here. The evidence warehouse

was full already, and they didn't really need the card since the flowers were delivered.

"I haven't watered them," Liz said. "I didn't want to touch them."

A white-haired man with a young face stepped forward. "I'm Edward Foster, Taylor's supervisor. And this is Roger, another coworker."

Aaron shook their hands.

"So nothing new? No arrests?"

"No. Not yet." Aaron walked to the flowers. He carefully picked up the card and turned it over. But when he tried to open it, it stuck. Had it not been opened? Aaron looked at Liz. "You said these were from her ex-boyfriend?"

"That's what Taylor said. Or implied."

"Implied?"

"I said something like, 'Who are the flowers from?' And she said, 'Who do you think?'"

"And you took that to mean?"

"Sammy. Don't know his last name."

Aaron tore open the envelope and took out the small card. It was typed.

```
I'm sorry for everything. I love you.
Sammy
```

"You said he always signed with his initials?"

Liz nodded.

Aaron placed the card back in the envelope. He turned to the three, who were practically leaning over his shoulder. "Have any detectives been here to question you?"

They shook their heads.

"Okay. Listen, some detectives might come by, ask some questions. Just answer them the best you can. I don't know if these flowers are significant or not."

"She hated him and loved him at the same time," Liz said. "She was very conflicted. But also very private, so she didn't say a whole lot about it. I could just tell."

"But they think it's a football coach or somebody like that, don't they?" Edward said. "Isn't that what the news said?"

"They're still figuring a lot of things out," Aaron said. "And of course call if you hear from her."

They all nodded and Aaron left, his heart galloping inside his chest. He was being stupid, but the more he knew independent of the prosecutor, the better. What bothered him most, though, was that the detectives didn't seem to be interested in this Sammy.

They wanted Mick.

After Shep Crawford barged into Stephen Fiscall's office unannounced, Fiscall watched him round the chair he thought he was going to sit down in. Instead, the giant, beastly, frowsy man circled it as if it were prey. Fiscall shifted in his chair.

"So you're saying you didn't leak this to the media."

"You said you needed time. That's what you said." Fiscall sat motionless, resisting the urge to scratch the arms of his chair like a fidgety cat. "I'm always one for building a good case, Crawford. Leaking it to the media wouldn't help that."

"Then why was there a story on the news this morning with Kline's picture?"

Fiscall rubbed an eyebrow. "I have no idea. You know what kind of crazy investigative reporters we have around here. Look, you don't know that Kline isn't our man, do you? I mean, you're just investigating other angles. So what does it hurt that Kline knows he's being watched? See what he does. That can't hurt."

"Your job, as I understand it, is to prosecute the man *we* find to be the criminal."

Crawford's condescending tone urged Fiscall to fight back. Instead, he folded his hands together in front of him, rocking back and forth casually in his chair.

"You have ambitions, don't you, Stephen?" Crawford said, his steely mouth inching into a cheerless smile. "Major ambitions about eighteen months from now when we'll elect a new district attorney."

Fiscall grinned. "I want to get the right man, just like you."

"Are you going to be talking to the media any time soon?"

"Not until an affidavit of probable cause is filed and the judge grants you an arrest warrant."

"By the book, right, Fiscall? That's how you operate. Step by careful step."

Fiscall's jaw jutted forward and he stared hard at Crawford. "Why are you so sure Mick Kline isn't our man?"

Crawford traced the vinyl on the edge of the chair with his finger. "I've seen a lot of criminals in my life, Fiscall. A lot of low-life scum."

"And?"

"And you can't tell simply by the way a man lives. What they have displayed for everyone to see. What they have in their refrigerator. What kinds of pencils they use." Fiscall noticed Crawford glancing at his chewed-up No. 2. "It takes more than that."

Fiscall shook his head. The man spoke in ridiculous riddles. "I'm sure your vast experience in profiling could probably catch all your criminals without a single shred of evidence, but in the court of law I'm going to need a little bit more than a personality profile."

"Have you prosecuted a case without a body before, Fiscall?"

Fiscall stopped rocking. No, he hadn't. "You feel you won't be able to locate a body?"

"I'm just wondering."

"I can prosecute anybody if I have good evidence. So why are you in here talking to me when you should be out there gathering some additional evidence for me? I can't walk into the courtroom with my charm alone."

Crawford shook his head, snorting through his nostrils. "You jump when I say so. Until then, let me do my job."

Crawford walked out, slamming Fiscall's door.

Fiscall shoved his chair back from his desk, banging it into the bookcase behind him. He refused to be bullied by a psychotic homicide detective.

No, indeed, he would not be jumping on command. Smiling, he thought of all the glory that would come along after successfully prosecuting a despised kidnapper and possible murderer.

And putting the brother of a cop behind bars could look very good on a résumé.

n o calls," Sammy instructed JoAnne, whisking the detective into his office before she could ask questions. He shut his door and offered Randy Prescott a seat. Instead of sitting behind his own desk, though, he joined him in the adjacent chair.

He didn't want to appear to be hiding anything.

By the time they'd arrived back at his office, Sammy had learned from Prescott that Taylor had been reported missing, and by the looks of her apartment, the police thought somebody had abducted her. It had apparently been on the news this morning, but Sammy had been in court by eight and hardly ever turned on the TV anyway.

Prescott, droopy eyed and freckle faced, talked slowly enough that time nearly seemed to stop. "When's the last time you saw Taylor, Mr. Earle?"

"Am I a suspect?" Sammy asked confidently, offering a small smile. "It's a logical question, considering my profession."

"Not at this time. I just need some information from you because of your past relationship with Miss Franks." Prescott talked as if he were reading from a manual. He flipped open his small notepad, obviously eager to write down whatever fell out of Sammy's mouth. The problem was, nothing ever *fell* out. Every word that came from his mouth was buffed, waxed, and shined before ever leaving his tongue.

"Detective Prescott . . . it is detective, right?"

Prescott smiled. "Yes."

Sammy scratched his chin. They sent a midlevel officer. That was a good sign. He tried to remember who the supervisor at the Irving Homicide Division was. He couldn't recall ever being in a trial that used an Irving police officer. He relaxed, settling his shoulders into the wingback, crossing his legs, and giving Prescott his full attention. "So Taylor was abducted?"

"That's the angle we're working. When was the last time you saw Miss Franks?"

Sammy shrugged. "I don't know. Saw her a year ago or so. Have talked to her once or twice on the phone since then, but the relationship was pretty much over."

"You dated how long?"

"Twelve, fourteen, maybe sixteen months."

"So it was serious?"

"Sure."

"Why did you two break up?"

Sammy gazed out the window. This was not going to be an easy question. "You know, Detective, things get complicated."

"Complicated how?"

"People see things differently. I mean, Taylor was young. She wanted a life that I couldn't give her."

"So it just didn't work out between you two?"

Sammy had spent six months studying body language in a jury-selection class, so he knew how crucial it was in the law-enforcement universe. Forcing himself not to swallow, he answered, "I can't say it was one thing or another. We fought a lot. In the end, I realized it wasn't going to work."

"So you broke it off?"

"We both did." The tip of his nose begged to be scratched.

"And you say you've spoken a couple of times since then?"

"Yes."

"About?"

"You know, you always second-guess the decision."

"Right."

He watched Prescott scribble down notes. He clutched his fingers together until his knuckles were white. *Right.* Said with a bit of skepticism.

"I can't imagine anyone wanting to hurt Taylor," Sammy said, causing Prescott to look up from his notes. "She's as nice as can be."

"So you're on good terms with her?"

"No, not really. I mean, it wasn't a nice breakup. But still, she's a sweet woman."

Prescott frowned, sizing him up.

Sammy looked out the window.

"And you were at home last night?"

Sammy nodded.

Prescott stood, walking to the door.

Sammy rose, offered a firm handshake, and opened the door for him. "Whatever I can do to help."

"We'll be in touch."

Sammy resisted the urge to ask about suspects. Instead, he smiled gently as the detective left, then glanced at JoAnne, who was watching with interest.

Sammy turned, wanting to slam the door shut, but knowing the detective was still within earshot. He leaned on his desk, his shaking hands hardly able to steady his trembling body. Closing his eyes, he tried to get a grip. But he couldn't. There was nothing stable about this situation. He flipped through his Rolodex, trying to find Harlow Bruer's number.

"Congratulations!"

Sammy whirled around.

JoAnne smiled at him. "I heard the news."

Sammy gripped the edge of his desk as he stared at her.

She frowned. "Are you okay?"

His stomach was thick with uneasiness.

JoAnne said, "I thought you'd be out celebrating with Kellan and the gang."

That case. Sammy said, "Too much work. I need you to get Harlow Bruer on the line."

Her eyes pinched, obviously annoyed that he had not regarded her kind comments. "Who?"

"*Harlow Bruer,*" Sammy said, firing off an intense glare.

"Who is that?"

Sammy tried to muster any ounce of patience that was left in his body. "The publicist, JoAnne. Hollywood's greatest spin doctor." He threw up his arms, punctuating her incompetence. "Get him on the line."

"I thought of all days, today you would be in a good mood." She shut the door firmly.

Sammy made his way around his desk, falling into his office chair and lunging forward, resting his head on his desk, entranced by the expensive carpet underneath his feet, the only thing he hadn't picked out in his office decor.

A nightmare lurked. And this was going to be one long and dark night.

Mick strolled the cement path that led to the Water Gardens, one of his favorite places in Fort Worth. Everything around him smelled aquatic, the air dense with humidity from the leaping fountains. The wind whipped the water out of its place, and it splashed his face and body, cooling him. With damp skin, he turned toward the west, where the fiery sun melted toward the horizon, shooting out fantastical sprays of purple and red light across towering thunderheads. A storm was gathering, drawing energy from every place it could, creating a vortex that would remain hidden in the depths of the clouds until it was ordained to be released.

By the way the thunderhead's cap toppled, Mick knew it would bring rain—a thunderstorm even—but nothing severe. The atmosphere, though unstable, wasn't humid enough to generate the kind of supercells that produced tornadoes or straight-line winds. If he got lucky, there would be a grand display of lightning. He loved this time of year, when evening often brought some sort of storm.

Since childhood, Mick had often been able to predict the weather as accurately as the meteorologists with all their high-tech computers. In midmorning, he would look west or south or northwest and know whether it would storm by evening or not. His parents and their friends even placed bets on him. He'd predict where the storms would form, how fast they would move, and what time it would rain in Irving. He ended up having a 67 percent accuracy rate.

It was the air around him. He was sensitive to it, the way it felt against his skin, how hard his lungs had to work to inhale it. Depending on the temperature outside and the amount of moisture in the air, he could tell whether the atmosphere would conceive a storm.

It was a gift.

But not one with much use.

His parents had encouraged him to follow his other gift, which was math. And so he did what everyone else was doing—got an accounting degree. He couldn't think of anything more boring, and it seemed a graver mistake than his indiscretions, because it was this kind of boredom that landed him in trouble all the time. Thankfully, the football job had opened up, but being the assistant coach, though somewhat fulfilling, still didn't scratch the itch that tickled his adventurous side.

He'd been unsettled his whole life, feeling displaced. He'd had a loving family, grew up happy, possessed great childhood memories. But he never felt satisfied. He still didn't.

Mick walked down stone steps into the shadows of one of the man-made cliffs that formed a spraying waterfall. Suddenly cool, he stuck his hands in his pockets and found a bench to sit on. He was about forty feet below street level, and the noise of the busy city traffic drowned in the twenty thousand gallons of water that flowed through the fountains, the falls, and the delicate rivulets that snaked through the park.

He'd been ten when the park had been completed, and he remembered coming down here with his brother and parents, marveling at the cascading waterfall that fell seven hundred and ten feet down the stone wall. Aaron had nearly pushed him in but caught him at the last second. He had gotten in trouble for it, but Mick thought it was kind of funny. He'd have done the same thing had he thought of it.

A halfhearted rumble of thunder came from the west. Mick figured he had about an hour before rain fell. He closed his eyes, trying to find the peace that these waterfalls had brought him before. The pure sound of falling water desensitized the ugly world around him. If only for a few moments, he felt centered and well and whole. It never lasted, though. And of course his mind couldn't be convinced he was in some exotic and beautiful jungle. It was a manufactured park in the middle of a busy, chaotic city.

But even in his misty and serene surroundings, Mick couldn't stop his mind from racing, from playing out a hundred different scenarios, including being charged with murder.

Mick cursed the day he'd touched a drop of alcohol. He stared through the waterfall, watching the scene with Taylor unfold inside his head. The sound that now filled his ears was that of water slapping stone.

"I like white-water rafting."

"Really? I love women who are adventurous."

"You seem to love women in general."

"I am a fan of the species."

"But you're not a jerk."

"That's perceptive."

"I can tell. You've treated me with respect tonight, even though you're nearly drunk out of your mind."

"I'm drunk?"

"Very funny."

"I had a little bit too much."

"You're slurring every other word."

"It's just my southern accent."

"I like you, Mick. You're very funny."

"But you're not smiling."

"I don't have a lot to smile about."

"Why don't you tell me? You've been mysterious all evening. Hinting at a lonely heart."

"I'm not lonely."

"Then what are you?"

"Nothing."

"Scared? You look scared to me."

"You're drunk. How many of 'me' are you seeing, anyway?"

"Don't change the subject."

"You have to leave, okay?"

"But I don't want to. Aren't you enjoying my charming personalities?"

> *"More than you know. Especially the one that keeps winking at me."*
> *"Then why do you want me to leave?"*
> *"You just have to leave."*

Mick stood, his clothes damp and his hair tossed about his head like he'd overslept for a day. Even his fingers couldn't comb it into place. A couple of young women giggled as they passed him. Mick couldn't even begin to look back at them. He'd normally offer a quick grin, but today there wasn't any flirtatious energy in him. He mostly just felt sick.

After dragging his weary body back to his car, he fought Fort Worth traffic all the way into Irving. The sun was not down, but the storm was darkening the skies early.

Driving down Claremore Street, on the shiftier side of Irving, he watched a neighbor kick his dog back into the chain-link fence that also housed an old pickup with only one tire. He hated this street, but right now this area was all he could afford. Jenny definitely deserved more than this. One day . . . one day he'd make it big.

Mick watched an obese woman in pajamas sweep off a porch surrounded by three-foot-high weeds. He turned down the next street, where everyone mowed.

Nebulous daylight held its own against the darkening sky, creating an almost perfect platform for the timid storm to move above. He always loved the way daylight willed to hang on, the starless sky capping its warm energy against the earth, just for a few more minutes.

A few droplets of rain pelted the sidewalk as he parked his car and walked toward his house. But before he even reached the small porch, he noticed the door. Open ever so slightly.

Though his knees wobbled, his gut told him to kick in

the door and surprise whoever was in there with a nice, precise left hook.

Then he thought better of making all the racket. He gripped the knob, listened, and pushed the door open, gazing into his living room. His furniture was lit by what little light filtered through the windows. Other than that, everything was dark and quiet.

But not settled.

He couldn't believe the scene his eyes were adjusting to. His television had been knocked on the floor, his stereo system next to it. Every drawer in his kitchen was pulled out. Mick fumbled for the light switch on the wall, trying to register what he was seeing. His coffee table was turned over, photo albums strewn everywhere.

He scratched against the wall, grasping at the light switch, his palms slick with sweat.

A shadowy figure appeared from the hallway. Mick lunged for the lamp, toppled on its side next to the table that sat beside the couch. The shade was three feet away. From his baseball days, he knew one good swing would plant this monster on the ground, probably crush his skull too.

He grabbed the lamp and swung it behind his shoulder like a bat, ready for the momentum to kick in and power up this weapon.

"Wait!"

Mick froze. The voice sounded familiar. He stumbled backward, not sure what to do. But before he could think too much about it, the figure was over by the light, switching it on.

"Easy," the voice said.

"Detective . . . Crawford?" Mick pulled the name out of the vast collection of information that had piled into his brain over the past forty-eight hours.

"Shep." The detective walked forward, a good four inches taller than Mick, who was a pretty tall guy himself.

Not letting his guard down, Mick kept his hands squeezed around the metal base of the lamp. He took one step backward.

The detective scanned the room. "Looks like you got a mess here."

chapter twelve

W hat are you doing here?" Mick's words flew out of his mouth with the speed of a cue ball shooting across a pool table.

"I came here to talk to you. Your door was open, and I noticed the whole place had been sacked."

Mick glanced around, still trying to comprehend what was going on. "You found it like this?"

"Yeah. The bedroom and bathroom aren't much better."

Mick dropped the lamp and let out a frustrated sigh. "This is insane. I can't believe I got robbed."

"Robbed?" The detective looked at the TV. "This is no robbery."

Mick swallowed and stared at the detective. "Then what is it?"

"Looks like someone was searching for something."

Mick left Detective Crawford and walked briskly to his bedroom. Hangers were bare, the clothes left in jumbled piles everywhere. Drawers hung on their hinges. Mick couldn't begin to fathom what he was seeing. "What's going on?" he breathed.

He turned to find the detective observing him from the doorway. "Somebody got some motivation against you to do this?"

Mick shoved past the detective and stalked to the

kitchen. He pulled open the drawer where he kept emergency cash. It was still there. He held it up to show the detective. "This is unbelievable." Mick threw the cash on the counter and walked to the living room, falling into the cushions of the couch. "Somebody was here yesterday too."

Detective Crawford joined him, sitting in the chair across from the couch.

Mick immediately knew he didn't like this guy, and it wasn't just because he questioned him the other day. There was something spooky about the detective, the way his narrow eyes cut back and forth like a snake's.

"Where's your police car?" Mick held his pounding head in his hands. He needed a stiff drink. Bad habits were hard to break.

"I drive an unmarked car."

Mick glanced out the window and saw an unfamiliar sedan parked on the street a few yards from his driveway. Everyone parked on the street, so it had hardly stood out when he arrived home.

"You said somebody came by yesterday?"

"They didn't do this," Mick said, gesturing toward the TV, "but somebody was definitely here."

"How do you know?"

"I just know." Mick sat back in the couch. "They wanted me to know."

"Who do you think would do this?"

"I have no idea." Mick grunted. "This whole thing is such a mess."

"You think this is connected to yesterday?"

"I don't know," Mick said. "Are you here to arrest me?"

"No. I just wanted to clear something up."

"Where's your partner?"

"I work alone." Crawford stood, finding interest in something on the carpet. He stooped, looked at it, picked it up gingerly and studied it, then set it back down. "Besides, this isn't official police business."

"Then what is it?"

"I have a feeling about you, Kline."

Mick couldn't imagine what that feeling was. Everyone else seemed to have the wrong impression of him, including his own brother.

"I don't think you did it."

Apprehension, not relief, flooded Mick's body. One leg bounced up and down nervously, but it was the only thing keeping him glued to his seat. "I didn't do it."

"I'm about the only one who believes that, you see. Everyone wants to nail you to the prison wall, son."

"Why don't you think I did it?"

"There are many reasons. Some detectives see the clues they want to see. But sometimes it's what I *don't* see that tells me more. Plus, I have a gut instinct. Solved a lot a crimes over the years listening to my gut. It tells me you didn't kill this woman."

"You found her . . . her body?"

Shep stepped over the stereo and went back to his chair. "No. No body. But 90 percent of these cases turn out . . . poorly. We may never find a body, but that doesn't mean she's not dead." He eased himself back into the chair. "That's a hard thing for the family. Torture."

Mick looked at his hands. "I wish I could remember more about that night."

"Pretty drunk, weren't you?"

"Yeah."

"What *do* you remember?"

"Just snatches of conversation. But nothing significant. I can't imagine that I didn't hear something, though. I mean, that seems so crazy to me, not hearing someone being kidnapped."

Shep shrugged. "Bartender—Jimmy, is it?—said you had a lot to drink that night."

"You talked to Jimmy?"

Crawford's eyes never stopped scanning the room. "He also said Taylor was seen arguing with someone in the parking lot that night. Was that you?"

"I'm still not sure why you're here."

"I want to find out that one thing that proves you didn't do it. One thing is all I need."

"Do you know who did?"

Crawford didn't answer, but his eyes glowed intensely.

"I don't know what else I can tell you, Detective. I hardly remember anything. My car was at the bar, so if I did take her, I didn't do it in my car."

"Good point. But we already thought of that. Could've used her car, then parked it back there that same night."

"Yeah, I guess. Did you check her car for blood? The trunk?"

"It's being processed right now."

"If she was kidnapped, why didn't she scream? I would've heard her scream."

"Could've been gagged. Or could've been blackmailed out of the apartment. Could've left with someone she knew."

Mick couldn't sit any longer. He rose and went to the kitchen, leaning against the breakfast bar. "Looks like a storm blew through here."

Crawford followed him. "I'm going to need your brother to stay out of this investigation, Kline."

"Excuse me?"

"The last thing I need is for him to be nosing around, sniffing up clues."

"I thought he was taken off the case."

"He was. Probably get suspended if he doesn't back off.

I don't want him messing things up. He's going to be hearing things on the news, probably through the department as well. But the fact of the matter is, I'm in control."

Mick shook his head, not completely understanding. Was Aaron investigating on his own time?

Mick walked to the front door, examined it. "Wasn't kicked in. Wasn't yesterday either."

Crawford joined him, amusement crossing his face. "Good detective work." He bent down to look at it. "Lock's been picked. See these scratch marks?" He pointed to the knob. "Amateur. The good ones can do it and nobody will ever know." Crawford straightened and gave him his card. "Don't tell anyone I was here. Do you understand?"

Mick didn't understand. But he took the card.

"I've got the DA's office itching for a suspect, and I've got the media sure it's you. I'm swimming upstream here, and I need time to investigate some things. You're not off the hook, Kline. And if I find your fingernail somewhere it shouldn't be, I'll nail you. Got it?"

Mick laughed a little. "Yeah. But I was already somewhere I shouldn't have been."

Crawford gazed around the room one more time and said, "I'd watch your back. I don't know who has got it in for you, but it looks like they're serious." And then he left, walking across the grass toward his vehicle.

Mick shut the door, leaned against it, and let out a sigh. He shut his eyes, trying to get himself to stop shaking, trying to stop his heart from beating so fast.

He wasn't going to stay here tonight. He couldn't imagine what they were looking for. Evidence? A body? Something else? He rubbed the back of his aching neck.

He couldn't afford a motel room, not even a bad one, for more than a couple of nights. He doubted any of his friends would take him in, being a murder suspect. And sleeping in his car wasn't really an option. Mick walked to his bedroom, grabbed a bag, and threw some clothes into it, going to the bathroom next for some toiletries. Back in the kitchen, he stuffed his emergency money into his pocket.

Then he left out the front door, not even bothering to lock it.

"I know you're not hungry but eat anyway," Jenny said, handing Aaron a plate. Working in his kitchen, she'd made spaghetti with her special meat sauce and topped it with sauteed mushrooms. She added a piece of garlic toast next to the spaghetti on his plate and set down a glass of water.

Aaron smiled at her, though his stomach, with all its worry, had little room for food. "Thanks."

She joined him at the table and began twirling the spaghetti around her fork. "Talked to a Realtor today about selling my house. She seemed confident. Said my neighborhood is selling well." She grinned. "Can't wait to put my decorating touch on this place."

Aaron laughed. "It needs it!"

"I love this place. It's a beautiful house. The backyard is spacious, perfect for a horde of kids, huh?"

Aaron smiled at her, picturing a darling little girl with blonde, curly hair and a splash of freckles across her nose. "Horde is a little optimistic, isn't it?"

Jenny giggled. "Well, at least three, wouldn't you say?"

"Two?"

"Two and a half!"

"A German shepherd would be nice."

The phone rang and Aaron hopped up to get it. "Hello? . . . Yeah. Really? . . . That's odd. Uh-huh . . . okay, thanks."

"Who was that?" Jenny asked.

"Bryan Worell from the church."

"Yeah, works over at the Dallas PD, right?"

Aaron nodded, returning to the table. "He found out the credit card used to purchase the flowers Taylor Franks received at work before she disappeared belongs to a man named Peter Walker. Apparently lives in Maine." He pushed his plate away and grabbed a notepad from the edge of the table.

"You're off the case, aren't you?" Jenny inquired.

Aaron scribbled something in the notepad. "I just wanted to see what these flowers meant. I figured I'd trace the credit card back to this guy who she was supposedly dating." He rubbed his brow. "I don't know what to do with this information. I don't even know if the detectives have sought more evidence from this angle."

"Who is the guy in Maine?"

"Don't know. I have his contact info. But I have to be careful. Like you said, I'm not on the case. If Bellows finds out I've been snooping around . . ."

"So you can't find out who this Peter fellow is, because if the detectives follow the same angle, they'll find out you were there first."

Aaron nodded. "I'll sit on it, I guess. Maybe try to find out what the detectives are doing with the flower angle. If I can. Crawford's going to keep it zipped up, though."

"Who's Crawford?"

"Lieutenant Crawford. He's in charge of Homicide. With the cuts lately, his division also handles kidnappings, where a homicide may or may not have occurred. Kind of a weird guy, but he's known for solving tough cases."

The doorbell rang.

"You expecting anyone?" Jenny asked.

Aaron shook his head, going to the door and opening it. His brother stood there with a duffel bag. "Hey."

"Mick. Hi. Are you okay?"

"Can I come in?"

"Sure, of course." Aaron stepped aside.

Mick walked in, noticed Jenny, and looked away.

"Hi, Mick," Jenny offered. "You want something to eat? I made spaghetti."

He declined, hardly looking her in the eye.

"Okay, well, I've got some laundry to do back at my house, so I'll leave you two alone. Call me later, Aaron," she said before going out the garage door.

"Somebody ransacked my house," Mick said as he threw his duffel bag into a corner, then walked into the kitchen.

"Ransacked your house?" Aaron followed him into the kitchen. "What do you mean?"

"The place is a mess. Everything's been turned inside out." Mick stared at the plates of food on the table but didn't say anything.

"And you said somebody was there yesterday too," Aaron said. "This isn't a police search warrant; I can guarantee you that. We have to let you know."

"It didn't look like the police had been there. But I doubt it was a robbery. TV, stereo, money—it was all still there. The lock had been picked."

"Did you call the police?"

"Not sure police are friend or foe right now, if you know what I mean."

Aaron bit his lip, trying to sort through options. "It needs to be known you've had someone in your house twice. Could mean something in the case."

"You think it's related?" Mick asked.

"Could be. I have no idea. But it's weird."

"Can I stay here tonight?"

Aaron watched his brother's eyes plead, though his expression remained emotionless. "Sure, of course."

"I'm not scared. But I don't want to be there if they come back."

"I understand. You hungry?" he asked, pointing to the bowl of spaghetti on the counter.

Mick smiled. "Beyond belief."

Prescott got off the phone. "Verified that a deliveryman brought the flowers to the airport break room before noon on Tuesday. They were purchased by credit card, but the woman wasn't that helpful giving the info over. Said she'd already been through that once."

Shep looked up. "What?"

Prescott shrugged. "Said someone else called about it already and that she had a flower shop to run, so leave her alone. Not exactly a charming woman."

"Somebody else already inquired about the flowers?"

"That's what she said. Anyway, I have someone running the number; should get something back soon."

"Send it directly to me," Shep said.

"All my notes on the Earle interview are there on your desk. I didn't mention the flowers being sent, like you asked, and he didn't mention them either, which I thought was odd."

"I'll look over everything."

"Okay." Prescott glanced at the clock. "Anything else, boss?"

Shep shook his head. "Get outta here."

Randy grabbed his jacket and was gone.

Shep closed the case folder and leaned back in his chair. His pencils were sharpened. His desk was tidy and dusted. His phone was disinfected. Now all he had to do was solve this crime. Methodically, he sifted through every piece of evidence they had against Kline. He wrote each one on a stenopad.

All they had against Sammy Earle were a bouquet of flowers and a past relationship with the victim.

Things might've been so much different if Kline had not been there that night. Different clues would've presented themselves. Every police eye would have seen things in a different way.

Too bad for Kline. He should've stayed home.

"What's it looking like?" Captain Fred Bellows walked in, his perpetually tired eyes peering over Shep's desk. "I got a call from Fiscall."

"The boyfriend sent flowers the day before the woman disappeared. The *estranged* boyfriend."

"I know. But that doesn't mean too much, does it? In light of the fact that we have a suspect whom we can place in the apartment."

Shep threw up his hands. "What do you want from me, Fred?"

"I don't like the fact that it's Aaron Kline's brother, but if we don't arrest the guy who was there in her apartment the night she was kidnapped, we've got a lot of explaining to do. All the evidence supports him as being our number-one suspect. It'll look like we're trying to cover up for a police officer. It'll ruin us." Fred rounded Shep's desk and looked at him head-on. "Looks to me like this Kline guy is hardly a man of character."

"Neither is Sam Earle. Taylor Franks' mother claims he was an abusive boyfriend, as you know."

"Who wasn't at her apartment that night."

"I'm not finished with the evidence, Fred."

"We'll meet with Fiscall Sunday night to discuss the arrest warrant," Fred said before he walked out.

Shep punched on the TV in the corner of the squad room. The news was coming on, and, no surprise, the Franks case led the headlines. Kline's picture was the first thing up. The press already nailed him. No mention of Sammy Earle.

But things were complicated. And getting more so by the minute. Nothing was as it seemed. He just hoped nobody got in his way.

chapter thirteen

Saturday was spent lazily. When Mick awoke, Aaron told him he'd already been out taking pictures of his house for documentation, and had begun to file a police report, though he'd need Mick to talk to the officer later. Said he'd locked the door but otherwise left everything as it was.

Aaron had made Mick phone their parents, who were worried beyond belief and wanted to fly in from Kansas City where they lived. Mick assured them everything was going to be fine, not to worry.

Mick and Aaron spent the afternoon watching a golf tournament on TV, eating pretzels, acting as if there wasn't an investigation looming over Mick's head. Mick flipped through Aaron's album of pictures and articles of his favorite baseball player, Tug McGraw.

Aaron received a call that the police had a search warrant for Mick's house. From the living room, Mick could hear Aaron explaining what had happened at Mick's house the night before. Mick cringed. It made him look even more guilty. Except Crawford knew. Mick had to rely on that. He figured he'd better not spill the beans that Crawford had been there, since he seemed to be one of very few allies at the moment.

Mick had to admit, it had been a good call that Aaron had filed the report. It helped prove he wasn't covering up something, which was the last thing Mick needed.

Saturday evening Aaron began reminiscing about their days fishing at a family friend's pond. For once, the first time since Thursday morning, Mick forgot about his troubles, because memories of those days were enough to sweep everything else away. He found himself laughing with his brother, something he hadn't done in quite a while. Enjoying his company. Forgetting about Jenny.

Mick went to bed early for lack of anything else to do, but did not slept well. His dreams ranged from thoughts of what might have happened to Taylor to a jail cell he could spend the rest of his life in.

He knew if Taylor turned up dead, his life was going to be a miserable journey of proving his innocence, which would be nearly impossible considering the evidence against him—almost all circumstantial, except for the fact that he was in her apartment and was seen leaving in the morning. Other than that, nobody, including himself, knew what had happened in those wee hours of the morning.

Though fragments of the conversation he had with Taylor were being drawn out of his mind, they made little sense to him, other than confirming that he had been with her that night, and they had talked.

Along with the images of the night came a feeling of deep guilt in the morning. The lifestyle he'd chosen had ended up causing him great grief and possibly contributing to the disappearance of a woman. If he hadn't been drunk, maybe he could've stopped what happened.

Early Sunday morning, Mick rolled out of bed and out of his subconscious nightmare. The house was quiet, and he hoped some coffee was going. In the kitchen, he was glad to see the pot was full, with a mug sitting beside it, along with cream and sugar. To top off his superiority, Aaron was always the organized one. Mick poured himself a cup and, while stirring in cream and sugar, looked around to see if there were any signs that Aaron was awake.

Mick spotted him out the back window, standing on the new deck he'd built over the summer, sipping coffee and observing the sunrise. The deck was fabulous. Large and spacious, decorated with plenty of deck accessories, including a large patio set with six chairs and an umbrella. A humongous grill sat near the edge, looking like it could hold eight steaks easy.

Mick smiled. Aaron always was the suburban man. When not cooking out with fellow officers, he'd throw a neighborhood party "just to get to know people." Aaron had always enjoyed people his whole life, and they enjoyed him. Mick, on the other hand, seemed to need the help of alcohol to be around others.

He went to the window and studied his brother. Deep inside, he knew Aaron mourned for their relationship. As children, they couldn't be separated. But somehow Mick had lost his way. Aaron had been involved in the church and with youth groups. Mick had become a football star and decided that's what he wanted to matter most in his life. Now it hardly meant a thing, and Aaron still had his faith.

Aaron nursed his coffee, with a hand stuck casually in his pocket. Mick wished he knew that kind of peace, the kind that seemed to come so easily for Aaron. Instead, inside he felt scrambled. Everything was upside down. His life was on a downward spiral over which he had little control.

Aaron turned suddenly, apparently aware he was being watched, and waved at Mick.

Mick stepped outside onto the deck. The morning was warm, a slight breeze tickling the treetops. Two large oaks stretched toward the sky, creating the perfect amount of shade for the backyard. Mick noticed that Aaron was probably the only person on earth who could grow such lush grass in the shade.

"How are you feeling this morning?" Aaron asked.

"Okay. You're up early."

"I've been praying, asking God to help us."

"Us? This isn't about you," Mick said.

"You're my brother. It is about me."

Mick shrugged and sipped his coffee. "I love those oaks."

"I'm going to build a tree house in that one," he said, pointing to the left, "someday."

"Looks like that big oak was grown just for one."

"Remember Luke's tree house?"

"All I remember is that you guys would never let me up there." Mick laughed.

Aaron laughed too. "That's not true. You were finally inducted into it."

"Yeah, after eating three worms."

They chuckled and stood in silence for a little while. Then Aaron said, "You going to church with me this morning?"

Mick glanced at him, noticing he already had his slacks and dress shirt on. "Nah."

"Come on," Aaron urged.

"Wouldn't it tarnish your image to have your murder-suspect brother there at church with you?"

"You're not a murder suspect yet."

"If I'm being watched by the police and media alike, wouldn't it seem a little odd that the only time I show up for church is this Sunday?"

Aaron laughed. "You're not the first person to show up at church under desperate circumstances."

"I hardly think an hour in Sunday school is going to solve all my problems. In case you haven't noticed, I've already messed up, and it looks like I'm going to pay for it too."

"Mick, in all of your troubles, don't you want God on your side?"

"I don't think God wants me on His side. I'm not exactly an asset."

"He forgives. He wants to help you."

Mick couldn't think of much to say, so he sipped his coffee and watched the sun move up in the sky.

"Let's go," Aaron said, patting him on the back. "We have free donuts."

Mick smiled but shook his head. "I don't have anything to wear."

"That's never stopped you before."

Mick fidgeted through most of the service. For one, he could smell Jenny's perfume on the other side of Aaron. He'd loved the perfume when they dated. Thankfully, Jenny had been kind enough to meet them at church instead of riding with them, which would've been torture. Mick figured they were just trying to get him used to the idea of their being engaged. But he was thankful they didn't hold hands or do anything that made them look like a couple. Mick respected that about Aaron. He wasn't trying to throw it in his face.

The pastor preached on forgiveness, but Mick hardly paid attention. His heart told him to listen to the words, but the subject wasn't what he wanted to hear. It was too painful to think about. Though he wasn't in a constant shouting match with Aaron, he certainly wasn't feeling the urge to bond with him like they had before. And bonding with him meant bonding with Jenny . . . his soon-to-be sister-in-law. It all seemed so surreal.

Besides that, Aaron had never asked for his forgiveness and in fact had really never admitted to doing anything wrong. Maybe he hadn't technically done anything wrong, but he'd certainly been responsible for breaking the bonds.

Not that their bonds had been that strong before. In their late teens and early adult years, Aaron had always disapproved of Mick's lifestyle, continually harping on him to clean up his act. Mick had rebelled, tired of hearing it from his parents too. Everyone thought he was going down a destructive path. In reality, he'd just wanted some fun.

But admittedly, fun was hard to find in the midst of guilt, and he always felt guilty. Something gnawed at him, and he was never able to resolve in himself a freedom to do as he pleased.

Even when he had a companion, emptiness followed him home every night.

After the service, Aaron discussed going out to eat. "Jenny and I love that Mexican grill down the street. Does that sound good? I'm buying."

Mick glanced at Jenny, whose bright, expectant face suggested that was the best idea in the universe. "Um . . . no thanks. You two go on. You can ride with Jenny, and I'll drive your truck back to your house. I was going to stop by and check on my house anyway."

"You're going to stay with me tonight, right? I think it's a good idea."

"Sure," Mick lied. He had no intention of staying there another night. Where he might stay he didn't know, but he didn't want Aaron controlling his life. "I'll touch base with you later."

Aaron looked apprehensive and was about to say something else, when Jenny smiled at Mick and said, "Mick needs some time, right, Mick?"

Mick nodded, avoiding her eyes. Instead, he caught the

eyes of some churchgoers stealing glances at him. He tried to look casual . . . nonthreatening . . . like a non-kidnapper. He looked at Aaron. "I can use your truck?"

"Sure."

"Okay. I'll see you later." Mick walked through the crowded foyer and out the front doors of the church, bypassing the line that formed to shake the pastor's hand. But as he made his way down the steps, he felt a hand on his shoulder.

"Mick?"

He turned to see the pastor's gleeful face looking eagerly at him. "Yes?"

"I've been Aaron's pastor for several years now. He called me a couple of days ago to tell me what happened, and I've been praying ever since."

Mick didn't know what to say.

"I'm glad you're here today. Is there anything I can do for you?"

The pastor held out his hand, and Mick instinctively shook it. "Thank you," was all Mick could manage, and then he took off down the steps.

He drove around for twenty minutes just to unwind and picked up two Big Macs before heading to his house. It was going to take half the day to clean up the mess there, so he needed some energy.

As he turned into his driveway, finishing off the last of his second Big Mac, his heart sank. A mob of reporters stood on his front lawn, and they'd already spotted the truck. Mick groaned, hopping out of Aaron's vehicle and holding out a hand while they rushed toward him. It brought him back to his football days. Except they tackled him with words.

"Are you innocent?"

"What do you have to say?"

"How well did you know Taylor Franks?"

The questions screamed past him, and Mick felt dizzy as the reporters pushed their microphones in his face.

"No comment," he mumbled, making his way around them, trying to avoid the cameras that were shoved in his face. He wanted to turn around and clobber all of them, but he knew how that would play out on the ten-o'clock news.

He finally made it to the porch. As quickly as he could, he unlocked the door and slipped inside, turning to close it and locking the dead bolt. He rested his head against the door, out of breath and trying to come off the shock of it all. His life was not going to be even close to normal any time soon. He squeezed his eyes shut, keeping the emotions at bay.

With a deep breath, listening carefully, Mick could not hear the racket of the reporters any longer. He dared not peek out the window for fear of his picture being taken. He was glad the blinds were pulled. He always left them open and figured Aaron had closed them.

Mick turned, irritated at the mess he needed to clean up. But what he saw caused him to gasp.

The house was back to perfect order, as if not a single thing had ever been touched.

chapter fourteen

Crawford watched out the second-story window of the DA's office. A group of reporters, the Sunday crew no less, stood chattering away in hopes of learning some gruesome details about a kidnapped woman.

"We're going to need more evidence for the grand jury indictment," Sandy said. The police chief was lounging on the DA's sofa, his arms sprawled across the top of it. "It's all circumstantial right now. We need that smoking gun, Shep."

Shep turned to Sandy, folding his arms against his chest. "It's a mistake."

"I know you think that. And for crying out loud, Shep, I have supported you on nearly every call you've made since you've been working for

me. That's why I made you head over the division. But we have a man seen leaving a bar with her and leaving her apartment the next morning. Drunk out of his mind, by all accounts, including his own."

"That doesn't make for a kidnapper."

"I made the call; that's final. Now go find the evidence that will put our suspect behind bars." Sandy pulled his large frame off the couch and stood next to Shep at the window. "You should've been down there making the announcement. You shouldn't shy away from the attention. You're good at what you do. People should know the brains behind it all. It ain't Fiscall."

Sandy left the room and Shep watched Fiscall approach the reporters, his nose hung in the air with great importance. He buttoned his suit in a gentlemanly manner. Shep couldn't hear what he was saying, but he watched his mouth move.

Fiscall was behind all of this. He knew it. Fiscall had called Sandy over the weekend, pressuring him to make an arrest. Fiscall had decided what the public wanted, and he was going to hand it to them on a silver platter.

And who knew what kinds of strings Sammy Earle was pulling. The man knew a lot of powerful people.

Shep watched as the red dots glowed on the tops of the cameras all at once. It would be breaking news on TV.

And the start of a whole new kind of war.

Aaron hung up the phone and flipped on the television, watching Stephen Fiscall announce they had issued an arrest warrant for Mick Kline, believed to be the man behind the disappearance of Taylor Franks.

He quickly dialed Fred's home phone number. "Captain, it's Aaron."

"Aaron, I'm sorry. I don't know what to say."

"Can you give us some time? Can we set up a time and a location?"

"They're headed over to his house now."

"Just have them wait outside, okay? Give us some time and Mick will come out quietly."

"Forty minutes."

Aaron hung up and dialed Mick's number. When he didn't answer, Aaron slammed down the phone and raced past Jenny. "I'm going over there. Call Bill and tell him to meet me there. Mick's going to need a lawyer whether he likes it or not."

In Jenny's car, Aaron drove to Mick's house as fast as he could, hoping he would be there. He didn't want the police to have to track him down.

Within fifteen minutes, he was there. Reporters' vans lined the streets, and Aaron spotted two detectives' cars in the driveway. Aaron got out and tried to walk calmly toward them.

Detective Monty Wailes was standing by his car when Aaron approached. "Hey, Monty."

Monty shook his hand. "I'm sorry, man."

"I can't believe this has turned into such a circus," Aaron growled, glancing at all the reporters who had their cameras aimed at him.

"Fred said to give you some time. Mick knows we're here. He's in there waiting for you."

Aaron nodded, feeling a tinge of relief. His attorney friend from church, Bill Cassavo, arrived, pulling next to one of the news vans. Bill didn't represent many criminal cases, but he would be fine for now.

"Aaron," Bill said, approaching, "ready to go in?"

Aaron led Bill to the front porch. Knocking twice, he heard Mick come to the door. Aaron and Bill slipped inside quickly, trying not to allow any more photo ops. The first thing Aaron noticed was that the living room was back to normal. Aaron walked over to where the TV and stereo had been. They were put back into place and, oddly, dusted. Mick had never been one to dust.

Mick looked like he didn't want to talk about it, so Aaron let it go. "You okay?" Aaron threw his wallet, badge, and keys on the coffee table, then placed his hand on his brother's shoulder.

Mick shook his head. His eyes were sunken, his face drawn tight. "I can't believe this."

Bill introduced himself and asked if they could sit down together.

Mick looked like he was in a trance.

"Here's what's going to happen. They're going to come in, read you your rights. My advice to you is to say nothing. I'll be with you once you're arrested, all the way through the process. I know you want to proclaim your innocence, and there will be time for that, but I don't think it's smart for even me to make a comment to the media at this time. They'll dissect everything I say. We'll make our battle inside the court of law." Bill continued, explaining that a grand jury would have to hand down the indictment separately from the arrest warrant.

Aaron examined Mick's panicked face. He moved over to where his brother sat. "Everything's going to be okay."

"No, this isn't right. I didn't do this. I didn't take her. The whole world is going to think I did."

"We'll prove them wrong."

"We'll get you the best criminal defense attorneys," Bill said. "I've got friends in high places."

"The evidence is circumstantial at best," Aaron added.

Mick stared at the front door. "I've got to do something." He stood. "I've got to find Taylor. Something terrible has happened to her."

"You need to worry about yourself right now," Bill said as they both watched Mick pace the room.

"No, you don't understand." Mick turned to them. "I should've done something to stop whoever did this. I should've helped her. I could have if I hadn't been so drunk." He slapped his hands over his face in anguish.

Aaron stood, grabbed him, and pulled him to himself, wrapping his arms around his back. "It's all right. This isn't your fault."

Mick stepped back and looked at him. "You do believe it."

"Believe what?"

"That I'm innocent. I can tell. I can see it in your eyes."

"Of course I do."

Mick nodded, glancing at Bill, looking embarrassed by his emotions. "How long do we have?"

"About fifteen minutes or so."

Mick rubbed his face, his hair, exhaustion striking a hard edge onto his expression. "God knows the truth."

Aaron smiled. "Yeah, buddy. He does."

Mick looked worried, his gaze circling the room, a complex mixture of emotions setting into his eyes. "There's more to this than it seems."

"More to what?"

"Too many things don't make sense." Mick sighed off his last comment and turned his attention back to Aaron and Bill. "Okay, well, I guess I better get some things in order here."

"You won't need anything at the jail," Bill said.

"I know. But maybe I should shower. It may be my last hot one." Mick smiled mildly. "Call Mom and Dad for me, okay?"

"Sure."

"All right. Give me five minutes, and I'll be ready to go."

Aaron and Bill watched Mick slack down the hall. Aaron gently slapped his own cheek, trying to knock away the emotions that swelled in his throat.

Bill clapped his shoulder. "It's going to be okay. Faith, my friend. Faith."

Aaron walked outside. A few law-enforcement personnel mingled on the front lawn, including his partner, Jarrod, who acknowledged him, remorse in his eyes. Halloway and Martin walked up to Aaron. "Tell them five minutes. Mick's showering and getting ready."

"No problem," Halloway said. "You okay?"

Aaron tried to smile. "They've got the wrong guy. I can't believe it, but they've got the wrong guy."

Martin stared at his feet. Halloway glanced at Bill, who looked like he really wanted to go tell the media what was on his mind.

Next to the police cars Aaron spotted Shep Crawford, several feet away from the other detectives, staring at him in a way that sent a chill down his spine. Crawford didn't look happy, which baffled Aaron. He was getting his arrest. What else did he want?

Detective Prescott approached Aaron. "It's about time."

"Okay." Aaron told Bill to wait outside and went in to get Mick. The shower was still running, and steam floated all the way down the hall. Aaron laughed. They had always fought about showers when they were teens. Mick loved an hour's worth of hot water, never caring that anybody else had to bathe. Still seemed to be true.

Aaron lingered around the living room for a moment, waiting for the shower to turn off. It amazed him how quickly Mick had put everything into place. Aaron walked around the room for a moment. It had been months since he'd been in his brother's house. Pulling out a couple of drawers out of curiosity, he picked up a stack of pictures. Pictures of Jenny and Mick. Looked like they were at the new Hawaiian restaurant. Aaron threw them back in the drawer. He got the girl, but it didn't always feel good. It was hard seeing pictures of the two of them in better days. There had been something between them, even though in the end Jenny knew Mick wasn't right for her.

Aaron checked his watch and then the hallway. He noticed the absence of steam, but the shower was still running. Aaron walked toward the bathroom, but not before stealing a glance out the window, where things looked to be getting a little restless outside.

138

Aaron knuckled the door. "Mick, come on. They're waiting."

There was no reply.

He gave the door a firm rap. "I know this is tough, but we gotta get out there."

Running water was the only reply.

Pounding, he called Mick's name again, then rattled the door, which was locked. "Mick!"

Without further hesitation, Aaron stood back and kicked the flimsy wooden door in. The shower curtain was flapping ever so slightly . . . in the breeze? He yanked the curtain to the side. In front of him was an empty tub with ice-cold water running out of the showerhead.

And a square window opened above it.

———

Sammy Earle could not hold his liquor tonight. Stumbling toward his bedroom, he was half laughing, half snorting, the television remote in one hand and in the other a bottle of cognac, though he'd have preferred to be at Tiki Bob's having a White Russian. But his publicist had told him to keep a low profile, so he was keeping one between the dark walls of his two-million-dollar home.

"What a doll," Sammy said, slobbering out his words as he thought of the pretty boy whose picture was now posted by the word *fugitive* on all the channels. There was scarcely a mention of Taylor. All the better. He hated her name. It gave him hives.

"Mickey, Mickey," Sammy said, dancing across the Spanish tile. He needed a cigar. A cigar, a cigar. Cause for celebration. All the sweating for nothing. His name wasn't even mentioned in the press! For once, that was a good thing.

"Shouldn't have gotten yourself involved with a woman named Taylor. And I use the word *woman* very loosely."

Sammy snickered, burping and then nearly vomiting before he fell into his feather bed. He managed to kick his slippers off, hitting his French poodle in the head. A long blink indicated she disapproved of his antics, and she curled up in the corner of the room in her dog bed.

"Mutt," Sammy said, but he wasn't talking about the dog. He rolled over onto his back, tugging at his silk robe that tangled itself between his legs. Staring out his bedroom window, he smiled, musing at the events that had unfolded over the past twenty-four hours. How differently things could've turned out. After all, he was in a business where justice mattered little but perception meant the world. And perception could be bought.

The irony was not lost on Sammy that this Mick Kline character could have very well been one of his clients, had he had a little higher status in life.

Sammy chuckled and coddled his bottle of brandy, stroking its long neck with his fingers. Taylor Franks had been bad news since the day he met her, and maybe now she'd be out of his life forever. Kidnapped. Ha. That woman was as tough as a bull. She'd have to be tranquilized first.

Sammy thirsted for more liquor, but he was too tired to lift the bottle. With blurry vision and a mellow head, he smiled out his last conscious thought and drifted into slumber, rolling to his side, barely aware that his brandy was spilling onto his arm.

Thump.

Sammy's bloodshot eyes flew open. Stared into Taylor's face.

She was looking through the window at him, her hair tousled over her face, her eyes glowing with rage. Her hands were plastered against the glass.

A gurgle rose from his throat, and he twisted himself the other direction, trying to scramble off the bed. He landed on the other side, unable to catch his breath, smelling like he'd bathed in cognac.

Closing his eyes and clasping his mouth with a trembling hand, Sammy willed himself awake. He'd had nightmares before. From Vietnam. Which was why he'd started drinking in the first place. Usually hard liquor put him out of any misery that wanted his attention.

He talked himself back to sanity. He would open his eyes again and be staring at the ceiling and an empty window, where the rain had begun to mist down from the sky. Yes, it was just a dream.

But when he opened his eyes, he was on the floor next to his bed, half his body drenched with a wretched, wet odor. Sammy staggered to his knees, peering over his bed.

A black, lightless window stared back.

chapter fifteen

at 4 a.m., Aaron's head bobbed and he startled himself awake, blinking at a fuzzy television screen. He'd fallen asleep? In his lap was his phone, still silent. He'd prayed all night that Mick would call.

He pulled an afghan that Jenny had brought over a few weeks ago around his shoulder and gazed out at the pitch-black night. His emotions had finally settled into a somewhat comforting numbness.

He still couldn't believe it.

His brother had run.

Knock, knock.

Aaron jumped to his feet, bolting for the door. Without even looking through the peephole, he swung the door open.

"Hi," Jenny said softly, her eyes swollen.

"Jenny," Aaron said, unable to hide his surprise. "Come in." He ushered her inside, his arm around her shoulders. "I thought you might be Mick."

"No word?"

Aaron shook his head. "What are you doing here? You should be asleep."

Jenny set a box of donuts on the table. "I can't sleep." She glanced toward the front window where the curtains were drawn. "You know they got a car out there?"

He nodded, going back to the living room and sitting on the couch. His eyes stung from fatigue.

"Are you okay?" She joined him on the couch, touching his arm and folding her fingers into his.

"I don't know what's more insulting: Mick taking off on me, using me like he did; or my department not trusting me enough that they send a car out here to watch the house. Of course I'd turn Mick in if he showed up."

Jenny studied him. "Are you sure?"

Aaron's gaze darted to hers. "Of course I'm sure."

Jenny sighed. "Look, Aaron . . ."

Aaron watched her struggle for words. "What?"

"He's innocent."

Aaron looked away.

"He's innocent," she repeated.

Aaron could say nothing.

"Don't you believe that?" Jenny asked.

"I thought I did," Aaron said angrily, fleeing her embrace and walking to the fireplace, leaning on the mantel and looking into its black, ash-covered hole.

"I'm not saying it's right," Jenny said, sitting cross-legged on the couch, the way she did when she was up for a long, friendly debate. "But your brother has never been conventional, and he's always balked at authority, ever since he was young, as you tell it."

Aaron smiled as a memory floated through his mind of Mick sticking his tongue out at a police officer while the two boys walked by. As he recalled, the police officer followed them, grabbed Aaron, and lectured him, even though it was Mick who'd done it. "Control your kid brother," the officer had huffed.

Aaron had tried his whole life, but it had backfired at every turn.

"But what a stupid thing to do!" Aaron said. "Now he's a fugitive. They're going to hunt him down like an animal. He had a chance to prove his innocence and now it's gone."

"I think Mick is a pretty smart guy, Aaron. And I think he sensed there would be some injustices done."

Aaron crossed his arms as he leaned against the wall next to the fireplace. "You know, he's the only one I've heard show any concern for that lady. Everybody else is treating this like a crime that needs to be solved. Mick still thinks there's a woman out there to save."

"He has a good heart, though sometimes he doesn't use his head."

"I'm scared that somebody will get hurt, Jenny. They're going to consider him armed and dangerous. I have no idea if he has a weapon or not. Surely he wouldn't be that stupid."

"Mick's got a plan." Aaron looked up at her. Her always-positive face glowed with a shade of enthusiasm. "He didn't just bolt to run from the police."

Aaron sighed and rejoined her on the couch. "I pray that Mick knows what he's doing. Because I sure don't." He pulled her into a hug. "I'm sorry I didn't call last night. I was under interrogation for nearly the whole evening."

She sat up. "Really?"

"I think they believed me in the end, but it looked pretty bad because I asked for extra time and met Mick at his house; then he disappeared. Anyway, I'm on paid leave."

"Oh, Aaron. I'm so sorry."

"I don't know how long it will be. Captain Bellows knows me. I'm sure he believes me, but I understand why he's doing it."

"You want some coffee?" Jenny asked.

Aaron nodded and she went quietly to the kitchen to make it. He found himself staring out the window. The only thing staring back was his somnolent face.

He wondered if he should tell Jenny. It was probably better that she didn't know. It was better that no one knew.

Mick had taken his badge.

Assistant DA Stephen Fiscall had slept soundly and was now enjoying a double caramel mocha as he drove to work. The radio waves were filled with alerts that a fugitive was on the run, and the DJs were talking about it as if it were sport. Some stations were placing bets. Others were issuing overly dramatic warnings about what you should do if you see this "very dangerous man."

It all massaged his ego, because he knew he'd been right. Shep Crawford and his amour propre had done nothing but make himself look foolish. Maybe Chief Howard would see Crawford for what he really was this time. The department could live without his maniacal tendencies, regardless of his proclivity toward brilliance.

Last night before he'd turned in, Fiscall heard the police helicopters overhead, the thumping of the blades at times shaking the glass of his house.

The man had run. Fiscall couldn't have orchestrated anything better. Secretly he'd had doubts about being able to prosecute either suspect. There simply wasn't enough hard evidence, especially with no true validation of a murder and barely validation of a kidnapping. But now he had a fugitive.

As he rode the shiny gold elevator up one floor to his office, he turned toward the mirror, mindless of the others in the elevator, and adjusted his tie. He'd picked his best suit, the one he wore for press conferences. He suspected he'd be on television at least twice today. As he got off the elevator, his prosecutors and fellow employees grinned and shot thumbs-up.

Fiscall nodded humbly, smiling cordially and shaking the hands that were offered.

District Attorney Willie Blazedell, his boss, caught him as he rounded the corner toward his office. "Stephen," he said with a lazy accent, "my goodness. What a day. Good job. Not bad for a Yankee." He offered his large hand and winked.

"Thank you, sir."

"Sandy called, said they picked up Kline's scent but lost it across the highway."

"They'll find him. Nothing like a good manhunt to get the police fired up."

Willie laughed but then turned serious. "Good call, by the way. I looked over the evidence. Not enough against Sam Earle."

"Not the kind of mess we want right now anyway."

"I agree. The flowers made me hesitate, though. We're going to have to figure out what to do with those."

"Hmm."

"But in the end, it was this Kline guy who was at the scene of the crime."

"Can't say I'm a big fan of an attorney like Sammy Earle, but we got the right guy."

Willie smiled. "Would've been something. Taking down one of the most despised attorneys in Dallas."

"Ever been up against him?"

"No. But feel like I have, as much press as that guy gets. I just hope he never sets foot in Irving." Willie checked his watch. "Well, don't let me stop you. You've got things to do. Heard there's a press conference called for 2 p.m."

"Hope I have some news to report."

"If not, play the other coin. Try to avoid mentioning his brother. Let's keep that out of the news as much as possible. Want to make this about the man and the evidence. Just be careful what you say."

"Yeah." Fiscall held back a smile. It was nice to have his boss trust him with a press conference.

He tried to receive the slap on the back with grace, though he still wasn't used to all the slapping and hee-hawing that went on in this part of the country.

In his office, he set his briefcase and mocha down and stretched, releasing a tired yawn that the mocha had yet to remedy. He slipped off his jacket and hung it on the back of his door. He buzzed his secretary. "I want all calls pertaining to the Kline case passed to me."

He had a lot to do this morning. But he always allowed himself to enjoy his mocha. So he took it off the edge of his desk and turned, ready to relish the warm sunshine that filtered through his second-story window at this time of the morning.

He stopped.

Smeared across the outside of his window was . . . was . . . what *was* that?

He stepped toward it, leaning in and squinting. He grimaced and stumbled backward.

Blood.

Splattered in every direction across his window.

He lost his taste for the mocha, setting it down on his desk, nearly spilling it. Shaking his head, he turned from the sight.

A bird had probably flown into the window. He buzzed his secretary. "I need somebody in here from maintenance. Now."

Dumb Texas birds.

"Baaahhhaaaa."

Mick jolted upward, causing the sheep to stir. They eyed him nervously. He was hunched in one corner of an open-air barn, leaning against a dusty wall. The sheep were roaming around freely near the barn. Mick suspected they were probably waiting for food, which meant somebody would be arriving soon.

He checked his watch. It was a little after nine. He'd been asleep for two hours. Exhausted from the night of fleeing in the darkness, he had trouble standing. His legs ached and his toes were sore.

He coughed and sneezed, his allergies hitting high gear. Dusting himself off, he stepped forward, causing the sheep to scramble nervously toward the sheepcote. He grabbed the small, black duffel bag he'd managed to get out his bathroom window. Aaron had given it to him a while back, something he'd won in some church marathon. Mick had never used it, but inside he knew it had a few items from sponsors, such as a toothbrush, toothpaste, a religious T-shirt, a candle, wind pants with a logo on them, and restaurant coupons. He'd added to that the money he'd taken from his home.

And Aaron's badge.

He held it up and carefully looked at it, then stuck it in his pocket, biting his lip at the thought of what his intentions were for using it. Running his hands through his tangled hair, he tried to focus on what he needed to do.

He tried to remember all the information about Taylor he'd gleaned from the news and from his brother. She had worked for Delta Airlines, and her friend Liz Lane was the one who'd first talked to the police. The police had interviewed Taylor's mother, who lived in a trailer park outside Irving.

Aaron had told him that Taylor had dated Sammy Earle, a well-known defense attorney from Dallas. The relationship had broken up a year ago from what Aaron heard. But he said the day before Taylor disappeared she received a bouquet of flowers from Sammy. That was the only evidence they had that he'd been in contact with her.

Mick processed all this, storing it away in his mind, and then tried to figure out what he was going to do. He wasn't sure where he was, somewhere about ten miles north of Irving, he thought. Last night he'd made his way to a grouping of trees and had darted around avoiding the helicopter's spotlight for thirty minutes before finally shifting directions and leaving the search behind.

He'd even heard the dogs, though they were far enough away he didn't think they'd be able to find him.

Mick fingered his three-day stubble and realized if he was going to go back into town, he needed to look different. He imagined that the picture floating all over the airwaves was his mug shot from seven years ago, when he'd been arrested on a DUI he was later cleared for.

He could grow a beard in four days, his stubble grew so fast. He had to shave every morning to even look presentable. By tomorrow, his entire chin and jaw would be darkened by hair.

He glanced around the barn, looking for anything that might come in handy. Walking the dusty path inside, he was starting to get sick of the heavy farm smells that lingered despite the open-air barn. Parked in the corner was a John Deere tractor. Stacked in the other corner were bags of feed for a variety of animals. An assortment of tires and wires and junk lined the closed wall of the barn.

Over by the tractor was a workspace of some sort, and as he approached he saw miscellaneous tools and farm equipment. He picked through some nails on a workbench, but avoided a variety of prods, a box of horseshoes, three dirty syringes with four-inch needles, and a long extension cord. He followed the trail of the cord over to a small secluded area and discovered what the cord was plugged into.

Electric shears.

Mick scratched the back of his head, his mind hurrying through possibilities. He looked at the large razor attached to the end of the shears, powerful enough to remove a sheep's thick coat. He reached down, clutched the shears, and turned them on. They vibrated wildly in his hands, and at the sound, the sheep who'd gathered in a little closer to observe him sprinted away.

Mick started at his forehead and worked backward, clamping his teeth together as the shears tugged and ripped at his hair. He wished he had a mirror, but feeling with his hands, he managed to shear himself in about five minutes.

He rubbed his hand in circles around his scalp, feeling for any missed hair. There was nothing but nearly smooth skin. He'd need a razor to go completely bald, but he figured this was enough of a change.

He set the shears down and scooped as much of the hair up as possible. He didn't want to leave a trail. He wrapped the hair in some discarded newspaper and threw it in the barrel of garbage just outside the barn.

When he stepped outside, he was surprised to see another barn, not as big but closed and newer looking, about twenty-five yards away. He hadn't noticed it last night in the dark, but he'd been so weary he hardly remembered collapsing into the hay.

Making sure there was nobody nearby, Mick hurried over to the small, red barn. The two large doors were padlocked. Mick went around the corner and found two windows. Deciding to try one, he slid it open easily. With one jump, he managed to pull himself up to the window and fall in on the other side, landing on a pile of grain and causing a huge cloud of dust to drift up.

Coughing and waving his hand, Mick looked around. This place was much more organized than the other barn.

A shiny four-wheeler sat in the middle, as though the barn had been built specifically to house it. Mick guessed the guy used the vehicle to get around his land. On the far wall, tools hung in an orderly fashion, and two large shelves held bottles of medicine, hoses, and other items. Hanging above all that was a shotgun.

Mick noticed a wall of keys and walked over to it. Right in the middle, on a bright red key chain, hung a padlock key. But he wondered what all the other keys were for. There were at least twenty. Some looked like house keys. Others looked like car keys.

Mick turned to scope out the rest of the barn. In the opposite corner looked to be a pile of junk. But as he got closer, he noticed three dirt bikes, all fairly old and run-down. He pushed some sheet metal out of the way and lifted the motorcycles off one another. The one leaning against the wall of the barn didn't look as beat-up as the other two. He pressed on the tires, which were both full of air. Pushing as much junk as he could out of the way, he rolled the bike out into the open, next to the four-wheeler, and kicked the stand out. Mick wiped the seat free of dust. By the mud caked to it, it looked like an amateur racing bike.

Mick returned to the wall of keys and studied each one. He grabbed six that looked like they could fit a motorcycle. He tried the first three and had no luck. On the fourth try, though, the key slipped into the ignition and turned easily. Mick swung his leg over the bike, prepared to give it a good kick start. He tried it once, but nothing happened. A second time, the bike sputtered but died. Mick stood, ready to use his entire weight for the kick start when he heard the sound of an engine.

Hopping off the bike, he ran to the window. Coming toward the barn was an old Ford pickup, bouncing along the dirt path, the trail of dust behind it looking like the bushy tail of a wild animal.

chapter sixteen

mick watched the tall, elderly man carefully ease out of his pickup, one foot at a time. He plopped a large cowboy hat on his fuzzy head and looked around, arms stretching in a lazy yawn. The man noticed the sheep nearby and walked to the open-air barn.

Mick's heart stopped.

The duffel bag was still over there!

Where? He thought he might have set it over by the shears, which would be hidden behind a small table but easily seen if the man went over there.

Mick watched cautiously as the farmer grabbed three large feed bags and threw them into the dirt, slicing them open with the knife from his pocket. The sheep eagerly huddled around. Then the farmer started dawdling toward the red barn.

Mick turned and, as quickly and quietly as he could, seized the bike and rolled it back to the corner. He knew if he moved the sheet metal, it would make too much noise, so he tried to lean it against the other bikes. It didn't look at all like it had before, but it was a start.

Outside, the farmer was singing a familiar hymn. He heard the chain against the metal door clang as he unlocked the padlock.

Then Mick realized he still had the six keys in his hand!

He looked up at the key wall and wondered if the farmer would realize they were missing. There was no time to think about it. He had to find a place to hide.

There were three closed, closet-looking doors at the end of the barn. Mick could make it over there, but there wouldn't be enough time to do anything else if they were locked. He heard the chain fall as the padlock was opened. The farmer was starting to pull one of the heavy doors open. Mick dived behind a large piece of wood, twice as big as a door, that leaned against the wall near the window.

The window was still open!

Mick started to step out from behind the wood plank to shut it, but a long block of sunlight stretched itself across the barn floor as the farmer pulled the first door open. Mick slid back into the shadows.

Holding his breath, he listened as the man sang his way into the barn and messed with a few things over on the shelves. Mick noticed a small crack in the wood plank. With one eye, he peered through it and had a good view of the wall of keys, the four-wheeler, and now the farmer, who had stepped into his line of sight.

He watched the man take a spray bottle, open another bottle, pour it in the first one, and then close it, shaking it vigorously. Next he stepped over to the wall of keys.

The man took off one of the keys and turned, his eye on the four-wheeler. Mick let out a gentle, quiet sigh. But as he observed the man, he saw something cloud his expression. The farmer stopped and stared back at the keys. Walking over to the board the keys were hanging on, he was just about to reach up toward the places where the keys were missing.

Mick kicked the board.

The farmer whirled around, looking for the origin of the sound. Mick stood still, watching carefully through the small crack.

Without another second's hesitation, the farmer grabbed the shotgun off the wall. "You stinking racoons!" he blasted. "Get outta here! Get outta here before I make you into soup tonight!" He swiveled the shotgun around, balancing the butt on his shoulder. "Come on, you two-bit rascals. Show your ugly faces!"

The barn remained quiet, and the farmer moved about, searching the dark places against the walls and corners. His gaze met the wooden plank, and he studied it for a moment before moving on. But then he noticed the open window. "What the—?"

He examined the window carefully before pulling it shut. The farmer was no more than seven feet away from Mick.

"You're opening windows now, are you, you little rodents?" He locked the window. Grumbling something about mating season, he looked at his watch. Walking to the other wall, he hung his shotgun up and slowly made his way onto his four-wheeler. He turned the key and revved the engine, then drove the vehicle out of the barn.

Mick waited a few seconds before stepping out from behind the wood. He looked out the window and saw the farmer racing toward a distant pasture.

Mick quickly pushed the bike to the center of the barn. He tried a few more times to start it before realizing it was out of gas. He scanned the barn for a gasoline container. He checked the closets, but there was nothing but junk.

Outside the barn, Mick scratched his nearly bald head and tried to figure out what to do. He immediately noticed the man's truck sitting with its windows down. Could he really steal a truck?

He walked over to it. The keys dangled from the ignition. A nervous itch tickled his neck. He knew that the police would be paying special attention to any reports of stolen vehicles. He could get into the city with the truck, but then he'd have to dump it. And he'd leave the poor farmer stuck with only a four-wheeler.

From the corner of his eye, he spotted a red plastic gasoline container in the bed of the pickup. Mick picked it up. Full!

He ran back to the barn and filled the bike's tank. Climbing onto the bike, he cranked the engine again. It roared, rumbling and lurching like it'd been waiting for years to be brought back to life. Mick laughed and oriented himself with the clutches and brake. It had been a while since he'd ridden a motorcycle, but he didn't have much choice now.

He gripped the gas container, and, using his feet, rolled the bike slowly out of the small barn over to the open-air barn and hopped off the bike to grab his duffel bag. He pushed the bike to the pickup and replaced the container, about a third less full now. Mick noticed a pair of old, dusty sunglasses on the dashboard of the truck. He snagged them, threw them into his duffel bag, settled himself on the bike, and took off.

He made his way slowly down the dirt-and-grass path that the farmer had driven on. He didn't want his bike noise to draw the farmer's attention, wherever he was.

After about two minutes, Mick hit a paved road. He stopped the bike and studied his surroundings. His first task would be to find out where in the world he was.

And then he would try to find a hat. His head was cold.

Mick drove toward Irving, taking as many back roads as he could. A dirt bike would draw way too much attention on a highway. The ride was smooth and calming, though he did miss the wind whipping through his hair.

As he trailed a slow-moving combine, Mick's thoughts tangled with one another, and he tried as best he could to sort through them in a coherent fashion. The first thought to detach itself from the sticky web in his brain was his house: put back together as if nothing had happened.

Aaron had been at his house, had taken pictures, but did not put his things back. At least he didn't mention it. And he would've told him had he done that.

Somebody was playing mind games with him. Not only was his house in perfect order, but it was in better order than before. It was part of the reason he'd decided to run. This was not a simple police investigation about a missing woman. Things ran much deeper. The net was cast wider than what was being reported in the news.

His thoughts turned to Shep Crawford. The man seemed to know more than he said, but strangely he'd also indicated he was an ally. Was it a trick, meant to draw him in and make him trust the detective? There was certainly nothing to confess, but the man had an edge about him.

Mick wished he'd been able to say more to his brother before bolting. He couldn't imagine what Aaron must be feeling or thinking right now. Probably feeling betrayed and condemning him for another stupid move. He knew Aaron was being watched, maybe interrogated. It was better that Aaron hadn't known anything beforehand.

Coming into the city limits, Mick pulled into the parking lot of a small diner and sat on the bike, trying to devise a plan. Ultimately it was Coach Rynde's words that had made him believe in himself enough to go find the truth on his own. But he was sure the truth would not easily be found.

First, though, he needed a test.

Climbing off the bike, Mick took the sunglasses out of his duffel bag and put them on. His hand self-consciously glided over his nearly bald head.

When he entered the diner, he was barely noticed by the small number of customers eating a late breakfast. Mick scanned the room. Two elderly men sat near the back, sipping coffee and playing dominoes. A truck driver read a newspaper at the counter. On the front page was his mug shot staring back at him.

Hanging above the counter was a small, fuzzy television. *The Price Is Right* boasted an earful of excited cheers. This was a place that watched the news. He was sure that television was never turned off.

Breathe, dude. He wasn't going to look inconspicuous with a nervous tick to him. Shaking out his hands, he walked toward the counter, where an impassive-looking waitress was circling a wet rag over the top. He popped the sunglasses on top of his head.

She glanced up at him, giving him a much-needed polite smile. "Hi there," she said, wiping her wet hands on her apron. "Coffee?"

"Sure. That would be great."

The trucker sitting four seats over looked at him and went back to reading the paper.

Mick stared at his picture for a moment.

The waitress poured him a cup of coffee and offered sugar and cream. "What can I get you today?"

Mick figured he'd better be careful with his money. "Just some toast. With jelly."

"A big, good-looking man like yourself surely eats more than toast for breakfast." She smiled.

Mick smiled back. "Not feeling all that well this morning."

She went to prepare his toast.

Mick stared up at the television, where a *Breaking News Flash* sign was preceded by a news anchor's face. But Mick couldn't hear. The waitress returned with his toast and noticed the anchor. She reached up and turned up the volume.

"*. . . in the next few minutes we expect Assistant District Attorney Stephen Fiscall to explain the charges that are being brought against the man they say is responsible for the kidnapping of twenty-seven-year-old Taylor Beatrice Franks.*" Mick's picture flashed across the screen.

Sweat trickled down his backbone, but he tried to take a bite of toast anyway. He attempted to seem only mildly interested, like everyone else in the diner.

"*. . . and here he is now, Assistant District Attorney Stephen Fiscall.*"

The scene cut from inside the newsroom to outside the Irving courthouse. Mick watched the DA approach the podium of microphones. Behind him was Chief Sandy Howard and Captain Fred Bellows. Next to him stood two homicide detectives whom Mick recognized from the first day Taylor was missing.

Noticeably missing was Shep Crawford.

"Poor woman," the waitress mumbled, serving Mick a selection of jellies and butters. "My goodness, you are fast."

Mick looked up at her. "Excuse me?"

She nodded toward his empty coffee cup. "You want a refill?"

Mick declined. He was jittery enough as it was.

Looking back at the television, the news station was running some apparently pretaped footage of Taylor's mother addressing the media. "*. . . and please, please let Taylor go if you have her. Please. She's the nicest girl and I just want my baby home. . . .*" The downtrodden woman fussed with her worn and dirty blouse. Her hair, loosely pinned to the top of her head, looked as if it received little care.

The mystery of Taylor Franks grew.

An urge to talk to her mother swelled inside Mick. He

reached in his duffel bag and pulled out a twenty, sliding it over to the waitress. While she was making change, Mick continued to watch the news, wondering how he would be able to talk to her. It would be a tremendous risk but could provide invaluable information.

Mick noticed the base of a water tower behind her trailer. A blue marking showed just above the base. Royal blue markings.

He knew the water tower. It was about fifteen minutes from his home. His football team's mascot was painted on the side.

The waitress handed him his change, but the look on her face made his stomach lurch. It was the look of recognition.

"You from around here?" she asked.

Mick forced a kind smile. "Just passing through."

"Huh. You look familiar. You ain't never been in here before?"

"First time. But it was a great experience." He winked at her.

She blushed, waving her hand at him. "Well, you bring your pretty little self back in here soon, you hear?"

"I will." Mick zipped up his duffel bag and turned to leave.

A man stepped in his way. He was large and gruff, with a John Deere hat perched on the very top of his head, the bill tipped upward. A pack of Marlboros peeked out of his flannel shirt pocket.

Mick felt his knees weaken. He was going to have to make a run for it.

"That your bike out there?" the man said.

Mick shifted his eyes out the window where the bike sat. "Yeah."

"You interested in sellin' it?"

"Larry, for crying out loud, let our customers be!" the waitress said as she returned from the kitchen. "Don't you got enough junk around that house of yours!"

A grin eased over Larry's weathered face when he looked at Mick. "Crabby today, ain't she?"

Mick smiled. "Sorry, it's not for sale."

"It's a piece of junk. Surely want to get yourself a better bike. I'd pay two hundred bucks for it."

"Actually, I'm saving up for a car."

"A pickup, you mean?"

"Yeah. A pickup."

Larry nodded and stepped to the side. "Well, hope that thing doesn't bust up on you."

"Thanks." He slid the glasses over his eyes.

The man tipped his hat as Mick headed to the door. Outside, he let out a long groan. Stress twisted the muscles in his neck. He hopped on the bike, and after three tries, got it started.

He didn't mean to peel out.

Fiscall, Captain Bellows, and Detectives Prescott and Wailes huddled outside at the corner of the county courthouse. Bellows was watching in the distance as Chief Howard was giving a statement to a few lingering reporters.

Fiscall noticed the window washers had finished spraying down his office window. Thank goodness. Even though his back was to the window most of the morning, it was as if the blood were shouting his name. Chills kept running over his body. One of the two washers was stuffing a rag in his back pocket and heading around the corner where they were standing.

Fiscall caught his attention. "Thanks for the wash."

"Sure." The man shrugged.

"You picked up the dead bird too?"

"Didn't find a bird."

"On the grass below?"

The man shook his head. "Naw. Didn't find nothing like that. Maybe a cat had a good lunch."

Fiscall nodded and let the man pass by. He tuned into the conversation Wailes and Prescott were having.

". . . probably the biggest mystery of this case."

"What's that?" Fiscall said.

"Those flowers." Prescott sighed. "We can't trace the payment of them to Kline, Earle, or anybody else involved in this case. Looks like the man's credit-card number may have been stolen, though he doesn't report anything else strange on his statement."

"We're sure this man isn't connected?"

"He's sixty years old and wheelchair bound, according to the Maine police," Prescott said. "Was in Irving about a month ago."

"What was his business here?"

"Came to bury a friend or something. Said he was here for less than twenty-four hours."

"Okay, well, let's keep working that angle."

Bellows stepped back into the conversation. "Kline hasn't been spotted yet. We sent out a citywide 'attempt to locate' message on him that's been read at all the shift briefings. Pictures were sent along too. The warrant has been entered into NCIC. I also sent some of the flyers over to Dallas PD asking for assistance in the search. They'll hand them out at their briefings."

"What about the search for Franks?" Fiscall asked.

"Still cold. Right now, unfortunately, our best bet is what Kline can give us when we get him," Bellows said. "We should've arrested the guy the day we had him. I don't know why Crawford didn't at least bring him in."

Prescott and Wailes didn't have an answer.

"Speaking of Crawford, where is he? I was surprised not to see the lead detective standing in support," Fiscall said bitterly.

Bellows said, "Crawford isn't one for media attention."

"I took it to mean that Crawford isn't on board here."

"Look, Stephen, Crawford is his own man. Always has been. But the department is backing the Kline angle. I think it's as solid as we've got. Crawford will continue to work the case. His objective is to find this woman—dead or alive—and bring evidence against whoever did it."

Fiscall stared out across the street. "Crawford is a bad seed, Bellows." He glanced at the captain. "He's a rogue."

The other two detectives shifted and watched silently.

Bellows looked at them and then at Fiscall. "He's the best homicide detective I've ever seen. He has solved unsolvable cases."

"That may be true. But he's as weird as they come. And I don't trust him."

"You have no reason to fear him." Bellows smiled. "Some people do."

"And who is that?"

"Criminals, of course," Bellows said.

Wailes and Prescott chuckled.

Fiscall shook his head, hardly smiling, and he smoothed his tie. "So what do you suppose Crawford is doing right now?"

"Finding clues that nobody else sees."

Fiscall found it odd, because he felt like somewhere nearby, Crawford was watching him.

chapter seventeen

ick had parked the bike at a dilapidated tire shop, where two mechanics didn't bother to notice. He figured he was about a mile from the water tower. He dropped his bag behind some bushes and began to walk.

He had no trouble finding Mrs. Franks's trailer near the water tower. He could see the news vans and their antennas easily.

He walked down Bellmont Avenue, noticing from a distance the cluster of news reporters gathered in the street waiting around for something big to happen. Mick didn't see any government vehicles or patrol cars. How was he going to get into the house? He saw no way, even posing as a reporter.

Mick fingered the badge in his pocket. Was it worth the risk of getting caught to find out perhaps nothing more than how Taylor grew up? Mick bit his lip as he stood behind a large oak, glancing around it now and then at the commotion down the street of trailers.

He studied the trailer park, noticing the chain-link fences around some of the yards. He wondered how easy it would be to get to the backyard. He could walk one street over, and if he could clear the first yard, he'd be in hers.

But then what?

As he thought this out, Mick decided to go ahead and

walk one street over. He didn't need to be seen loitering. In four blocks he was in front of the larger trailer whose yard backed up to Mrs. Franks's.

He wiped the sweat off his upper lip with his thumb and forefinger. Perspiration, along with a thumping heart, warned him how bad an idea this was.

But so far it was his only idea. And the only way he was going to get himself out of this mess was to prove that he didn't do it.

A picture of Coach Rynde hiding in a closet flashed through his mind, and determination built up inside him. Nobody ever got anywhere amazing by not taking risks. Mick just hoped a stubbly head, a prickly face, and a pair of round sunglasses were enough to hide his identity.

He would knock on the back door, flash his badge, and pose as a detective. He'd ask a few questions and then get out of there as quickly as he could before some real cop showed up.

It was a flimsy plan, but it was the best he had. First of all, he had to explain why he was coming to the back door. How in the world was he going to sell that plan? Doubt nudged itself forward.

Mick quietly walked alongside the trailer. A dog two houses down barked at him, causing him to pick up his pace.

He immediately noticed that her backyard could not be seen from the front yard, thanks to the long angle of the trailer. Several large trees also proved to be a good shield from the crowd in the street.

Mick jumped the chain-link fence that separated the two lines of trailers and walked into her backyard. What if she was watching him out the window?

Mick walked onto the covered patio, complete with fake turf and real dog dung. He stepped over everything care-fully, climbed up the creaky wooden steps that met the back door, and found himself staring at a screenless screen door, loose at one hinge.

Behind it was a white wooden door. Mick opened the screen door cautiously and then, with bated breath, knocked.

She must've been standing two feet away, because the door swung open immediately. The woman whom he'd seen on television looked even more worn in real life. Her face was crinkled and strained.

But Mick recognized Taylor's dark eyes in hers. And these dark eyes were beginning to fill with fear.

"Ma'am," Mick said, "it's okay." He flashed his badge. "I'm with the police department."

"Why are you at my back door?"

"I didn't want all the media making a big fuss, as I'm sure you don't."

She frowned, but Mick couldn't read her expression very well. "Well, your other two detectives just left five minutes ago."

Mick felt his chest constrict. "Oh. Yeah. Right." He willed himself not to say *um* but to think very quickly. "I'm actually the department chaplain."

"A chaplain?"

"Yes. And I offer counseling to families with whom we have an open investigation."

"Oh. I didn't realize they did that."

Mick looked behind her. A few people, apparently relatives and neighbors, mingled in the small living room, stealing glances at them. "Listen, why don't you step outside here, and we'll sit for a moment on your back porch. I won't take up much of your time."

Mrs. Franks hesitated, studying him. Mick was just about to open his mouth to say who-knew-what, when Mrs. Franks said, "But I ain't religious."

Mick closed his mouth and drew in a mild breath

through his nose. "That's fine, Mrs. Franks. We'll just talk, and maybe I can offer some consoling words." That sounded like something Aaron's pastor might say.

Mrs. Franks sighed and stepped outside, leaving the door open but letting the screen door shut. "I doubt that. I can't sleep a wink. Got to use them pills."

There was no place to sit except on two rickety old lawn chairs that looked like they'd been folded against the house for twenty years. Mrs. Franks grabbed one in each hand, and with a mighty flick of her wrists, they opened. She set one in front of Mick and sat down on the other.

Mick hooked the badge on his shirt and sat down, trying to remember that he wasn't a detective here to question her. He was going to have to be careful with how he approached this.

"Look, mister . . . what's your name again?"

Mick grinned, using the pause to come up with something quick. "Chaplain Goode."

"Okay. What I was saying is that I feel so desperate. I can't imagine what I'm gonna do if they find her body. I just can't imagine."

Mick nodded, a thousand thoughts and questions spiking in his mind. "I understand." He tried to sound very pastorlike. He blinked slowly and tilted his head ever so slightly.

"I been feeling so much guilt," she said through watery eyes.

"Guilt? What for?"

The woman used cusswords like adjectives, but she finally got around to saying that she and Taylor had not spoken in a year because of her breakup with a boyfriend.

"What is the boyfriend's name?"

"Sammy Earle," she said. "I told all this to the detective, but I could see the judgment in his eyes. Like I was a horrible monster for trying to tell the girl she didn't know what she had. She had so much! More than I could've ever dreamed about."

"And that's why you two don't speak?"

"I got knocked around a few times myself before the husband died. You live with it. You figure, what am I gonna do by myself? Starve to death! And the man bought her lots of things. Clothes, jewelry. She was living a good life."

"So Sammy Earle hit her?"

"Just said that, didn't I?" she snapped.

Mick nodded, backing off his intense need to find out more.

"I done the wrong thing. I don't doubt that now. But I was just trying to help her. And now look. She probably got killed by some psychopath anyway."

"Do you believe she's dead, Mrs. Franks?"

"What kinda question is that?"

Mick tried not to flinch. "I only want to know if you're prepared for whatever kind of news you might get."

"Don't think I can be prepared." Mrs. Franks sighed. "I don't feel like she's dead. Surely a mother would know that kinda thing. Feel it here." She pounded her chest. "Surely I'd know if her soul flew off to heaven."

"Tell me a little more about your daughter," Mick said. "Sometimes it helps people to just talk about their loved ones."

Mrs. Franks eyed him and then gazed out into her small backyard. "Well, what can I say? Taylor was the kind of girl who was always into trouble. Not bad trouble. She was just a little wily. Okay, a lot wily. She had this thing about her since she was a young'un. Don't know if it was 'cause her daddy was on the bottle or what. But it was like she had this instinct to want to survive on her own."

"How so?" Perspiration trickled down Mick's nose, and he had to keep pushing his glasses up his face.

"Always staying out late, like she had to show me she could do it. And she got picked up for shoplifting a good time or two. They never pressed charges. Saw what kind of life she came from; guess they felt sorry for her. I dunno. She managed to get into trouble at every turn."

"But it seems from all accounts that she's a regular, productive citizen."

"Guess you could say that, yeah. She grew out of it, from what I could tell. Got herself a job when she was sixteen. Liked making that money. Thought she'd go to college, but then she went to work for the airline and done real well there."

"What kind of person is Mr. Earle?"

She waved her hand at him. "Don't know him really. Never met him. Didn't want him to see where she came from."

Mick felt sad for the woman. In her own desperate way, she was trying to do a good thing for her daughter. But hearing this about Taylor was hardly believable. He would have never guessed she was from a poor family with an alcoholic father. Yet there was a mystery about her that he never could put his finger on in the short time he'd known her.

"You think God'll forgive me?"

"What? I'm sorry?" Mick blinked away his own thoughts.

"God. Will He forgive me?"

"Umm . . ."

"I mean, I made some bad choices in my life. I guess I'm here because of those choices. Been a bad mother. Probably should've left the drunk and taken my daughter, though I don't know what we'd have done."

Mick scratched his head. Aaron's words about forgiveness flooded his mind. He smiled at Mrs. Franks, who was looking at him curiously. "Yes, He will."

"Are you sure? Because you took an awfully long time answering that." She frowned.

"It's sometimes hard to believe, isn't it?"

She nodded solemnly.

"I have a hard time with it myself."

"You?" She laughed. "My goodness, the sins of a chaplain. You didn't share your bologna sandwich with a street bum or something?"

Mick laughed a little.

"I been prayin'. I said I ain't religious, and I ain't. But you know when you get to those desperate times in your life that there's nothing else to do than fall on your old, worn-out knees and pray *something*."

Mick nodded. "What did you pray?"

Mrs. Franks stared at the plastic grass beneath her house shoes. "I prayed . . ." She choked on her words. And then she whispered, "I prayed God would have mercy on me and my family. If there was a God and there was such a thing as mercy."

Mick looked into her despondent eyes. "Don't you believe there is a God?"

"I guess it's harder not to believe it. I been a bitter woman. I been mad at a lot of things. So I said I didn't believe in God. But I never really could say it and mean it. Because somewhere inside me I know it ain't true."

"Hope is all we have sometimes. Hope. And the truth."

She looked up at him. "You think God hears the prayers of sinners?"

Mick nodded. *So my brother says.*

In the spare bedroom of his house, Aaron lifted dumbbells, trying to work out all the nervous energy that had taken his appetite and replaced it with an intense headache.

The doorbell rang, and Aaron wiped the sweat from his face as he walked to the front door and opened it. Shep Crawford and Detective Prescott were standing on his porch. He wrapped the towel around his neck and grasped the ends of it with his hands.

Crawford's intensely wild eyes narrowed in scrutiny. "Can we come in?"

Aaron opened the door farther and led the two into his living room, gesturing for them to sit wherever they wanted. Aaron sat on the brick hearth in front of the fireplace. He was still breathing hard.

"You heard from him?" Crawford asked, sitting on the edge of the couch, his hands clasped together, his forearms propped on his knees.

"Nope."

"Any idea where he might go, Aaron?"

He didn't like the way Crawford used his first name. It was deliberate and patronizing. "I have no idea," Aaron said firmly. "He could be in Texas, Mexico, or three houses down. I don't know why he ran. I know he was concerned about Taylor, felt guilty for not being able to help her that night." He blinked tiredly. He didn't mean to, but he was beyond exhaustion. The words were hard to drag out of his mouth.

"Okay if we look around?"

"Fine. He's not here, Crawford. Give me a break. You've had a car out there night and day. He wouldn't be stupid enough to come here anyway."

"Mind if we check your truck out there?"

Aaron hung his head. This was impossible. "Whatever. It's unlocked. Go ahead."

Crawford nodded toward Prescott, who rose and went outside.

"Should lock your truck, you know," Crawford mumbled.

Aaron stood, his legs restless with anxiety.

Crawford stood as well, glancing out the front window toward Prescott before he said, "I don't think he did it."

"What are you talking about?"

"What else? Your brother. I've looked over all the evidence from the crime scene. I think there are things pointing to the fact that your brother *didn't* do it. Like leaving his phone number."

"Nobody else is seeing it that way."

"It's because he's an easy target. He was there, and he's had problems in the past."

Aaron watched Prescott rummage through his pickup. He looked at Crawford. "What's going on here?"

Crawford sighed, scratching at his messy hair. "Look, Kline, the best thing your brother could do is turn himself in so I can use my manpower to figure out what really happened. Instead, I've got everybody looking for him. And as you're well aware, we never had this conversation."

"I don't know where he is."

"If he contacts you, urge him to turn himself in."

"He won't contact me."

"How can you be so sure?"

Aaron looked away from Crawford's concentrated stare. "We don't see eye to eye on things. We don't speak much anymore."

"Is that so?" Crawford's fidgety mannerisms were making Aaron nervous. He'd never seen a man with more tics.

"I don't know what kind of game you're playing here," Aaron said, "but I don't like it."

"You think this is a game?" Crawford stared at Aaron in the most uncanny way.

Aaron forced himself to stare back.

"I am trying to help you out here." Crawford was nearly

shouting. "I am trying to tell you that I may be the only one who can help your brother!"

"Nobody is helping my brother! You issued an arrest warrant! What is he supposed to think about that? Why didn't you sit on this a little longer, investigate Earle more?"

At Earle's name, Crawford's entire expression changed. The intensity froze on his face. His fire-flashing eyes turned ice-cold. And then in a rare self-conscious manner, Crawford swallowed and glanced at Aaron. "That man . . ."

Aaron waited for more, studying Crawford's telling eyes.

". . . beat Taylor Franks, played emotional mind games with her. Used her." He rattled off these facts quietly.

"So why aren't they arresting him? He seems a much better suspect."

"He wasn't there," Crawford said. "Your brother was."

"What about the flowers?"

"Not enough."

"Not enough? They show Earle had her on his mind the day before she was kidnapped!"

Crawford took a step closer to Aaron, sticking his neck out in a socially awkward manner that nearly invaded Aaron's space. Aaron didn't budge. "But you've been snooping around, haven't you, Kline? And you know that there are some discrepancies about who actually sent those flowers. You traced it up to Maine, just like we did."

Aaron wordlessly acknowledged it with a long blink.

Crawford's eyes shifted again, but this time impassively scanning the room.

Aaron shut his eyes and rubbed his forehead, trying to get ahold of the situation . . . and what Crawford's intentions were.

Crawford was back to acknowledging Aaron. "My superiors bought into Fiscall's idea that justice for the people was more important than justice for the victim."

"The town wanted an arrest so he gave them one."

Crawford said, "I've got a hard enough job solving a murder case without all this other mess. I'm telling you that the more you get in the way, the worse off your brother is going to be. The whole town and every law-enforcement officer this city's got think he's at the very least a kidnapper."

"There's always hope. And truth."

"Truth." Crawford carved out a laugh from the disdain in his voice. "Yeah. Truth. I hope your brother makes a smart decision and turns himself in. And I hope you figure out that the more you interfere, the better chance your brother has of spending the rest of his life in jail. That's simply if the body doesn't turn up. If it does, he's looking at the death penalty. But, of course, you already know all of this."

Prescott walked in, hands on his hips in an authoritative manner. He was about to say something when Aaron asked, "You find him hiding out in my cab?"

Prescott smirked, noticed Crawford, and dropped the grin.

A mix of mustered cordialness and intense scrutiny read like a warning sign on Crawford's face.

Aaron held his own expression steady until the detectives left.

It amazed him how freely he could move. For two hours, completely unnoticed, Mick had been at the library, going through archives, trying to find as much information on Sammy Earle as he could, resisting the urge to repeatedly rub his bald head.

Earle was in the headlines frequently, and Mick sorted through the various cases and suspects he'd defended. By all appearances, he was a smooth-talking, sharp-dressing Southerner, whose thick accent was mentioned in the press nearly as much as his victories.

Prosecutors referred to him in media-acceptable derogatory language, citing his promiscuous tendencies toward cheating in the courtroom. Once, in a rape case against a well-known area CFO, Earle had leaked the victim's name by an "accidental" slip of the tongue.

His tactics were shady, but his success rate was high. And rumor had it that the Kellan Johannsen case had brought him at least a two-million-dollar paycheck.

Mick had even found several society-page pictures in which Taylor was on his arm, looking charmingly rich but decidedly out of place.

What interested Mick the most was a small article in which Earle's name appeared concerning local Vietnam veterans. It showed Earle looking particularly uncomfortable among the three other vets who were being photographed, his crooked, insincere smile offered to the camera lens.

The local vets met for coffee on Monday nights at seven at an old-timer café between Irving and Fort Worth. Mick wondered if Sammy still attended. To get an up-close look at him might be worth something.

Inside the library bathroom, Mick splashed his face and took wet paper towels, bathing his torso with them inside one of the stalls. It was a little before five. He knew his destination for this evening, at least partly. But the question was where he would sleep. *If* he could sleep.

A man who had come in the bathroom finished washing his hands and left. Mick opened the stall door, listening for signs of another person. The bathroom was quiet, so Mick went to the mirror again, gazing at his new appearance. With the shaved hair, he really did look amazingly different.

Dark eyebrows still framed his eyes, and there was no getting around his distinct blue eyes, but most people hardly looked you in the eye anymore.

Mick folded the notes he'd taken about the vets' meeting and shoved them in his duffel bag. He opened the door and stepped out before he saw the two police officers. Mick retreated into the bathroom, cracking the door enough so he could watch them. They were at the front desk talking to a librarian. She was pointing in the direction he'd been sitting earlier.

And now a man was walking toward the bathroom. Mick swung the door open and acted like he was walking out, allowing for the man to come in. Mick grabbed the pay phone next to the bathroom and pretended to dial a number, his back turned to the officers.

Glancing over his shoulder, he watched the two cops smile and joke with one another while the librarian disappeared momentarily. When she returned with a book in her hand, Mick relaxed. He hung up the phone as the officers left the library.

He waited five minutes, then left as well.

Now he would have to figure out how to get all the way across Irving on a dirt bike.

chapter eighteen

the diner was nostalgic, a modern restaurant with a fifties theme. Elvis bellowed through a state-of-the-art jukebox that flipped CDs rather than records. The waitresses wore wireless mics, communicating through them to the kitchen.

Relieved to find the Seat Yourself sign greeting him, Mick took a corner booth. He was about ten minutes early. His stomach grumbled, but he ordered only a basket of fries for three dollars. And a water.

He was beginning to feel the fatigue of sleeping only two hours and most of that lightly. He sat in the booth, his body hunched over his water, keeping an eye on the customer activity while fighting menacing thoughts. Without much to do other than wait for his French fries, his mind drifted to Taylor, and soon her voice uttered words in his mind.

> *"I guess nobody is really who they seem to be, when you come down to it."*
> *"Why do you say that?"*
> *"Who do you think I am?"*
> *"A beautiful woman. You have a kind spirit. You're bold and I sense a toughness about you."*
> *"Like a boxer?"*
> *"Not enough muscles."*

"*A lot of cowards look tough. But they'll always be cowards. And eventually somebody will find out.*"

"*You're not a coward.*"

"*I've known a few. Who are you?*"

"*Football coach, former part-time accountant, lover of storms.*"

"*Storms?*"

"*Don't you love them?*"

"*I don't think about them too much.*"

"*I think about them all the time. A perfect mix of power and beauty. Like you.*"

"*I'm not powerful.*"

"*You got my attention, didn't you?*"

"*Hmm. I'm only surviving.*"

"*Surviving what?*"

"*Life. It's all about survival.*"

"*Don't you think there's more?*"

"*No. I want there to be more, but in the end, there isn't anything more.*"

"*How can you believe that?*"

"*You're telling me you believe there's more?*"

"*I believe we all have a special identity, something we're supposed to fulfill, some reason we were created.*"

"*Created. Sounds like the alcohol talking. I didn't realize you were religious.*"

"*I'm not.*"

"*Sounds like it to me.*"

"*I guess I believe there are no accidents.*"

"*Right. No accidents. Only purpose in everything.*"

"*You think it's all arbitrary?*"

"*I think it's what you make it to be.*"

Her voice faded, her eyes diminishing in his mind. He noticed three men walking in together, each dressed casually, looking between fifty and sixty years old. They waved at a nearby waitress and crowded two tables together. Two more men arrived, jovial and chatty. And then a sixth straggled in. There were places for three more people, but ten minutes went by without anyone else joining them.

The waitress arrived at his booth carrying French fries glowing with grease. A thick ribbon of steam climbed the air in front of his face, and Mick thought twice before touching them. "Right out of the fryer. That all you want?"

Mick pointed to the pad in her hand. "Can I borrow that? And your pencil too?"

"I don't know. Do you tip 10 or 15 percent?" She offered a smoker's grin.

"Twenty."

"Keep 'em," she said and walked off.

Mick flipped open the small notepad and let his fries cool. Outside, the streetlights blinked on, and daylight dimmed.

The men were engaged in their conversation, oblivious to staring eyes. With every fry, Mick found a bit more inspiration, a slightly greater urge, and an increasing resoluteness that created a strange boldness inside.

Soon, greasy, salted wax paper was all that was left of his dinner. Mick wiped his fingers on his napkin and observed the men individually. He wondered if Earle would be coming in. Should he go talk to these men or wait for Earle to show up?

Mick fingered the notepad and tapped the pencil, wondering how to engage in a useful conversation with them. There was no time like the present.

He paid for his dinner, leaving a nice tip for the waitress, then approached the men, none of whom had noticed him amongst the increasing dinner crowd.

A short, stubby man spotted him first, stopping his

conversation and making the others look in Mick's direction.

Mick smiled. "Hi there."

The men nodded, curiosity sweeping their faces.

"I'm Trent," Mick said.

The stubby man said, "Hi, Trent. What can we do for you?" There was a bit of a sarcastic edge to his voice, a simulated congeniality.

"I'm with *Time* magazine, and I read in the paper that you all meet here every Monday night."

"What? You doin' a story on a bunch of middle-aged men teetering on the edge of divorce and financial bankruptcy?"

The crowd laughed nervously at the self-deprecating, tall, bald man with the short list of personal problems.

"Actually," Mick said, portraying himself as self-important, "I'm writing an article on Sammy Earle, the attorney."

The laughter died down a little, and the men glanced around the table at each other.

"I'm doing a piece on the Kellan Johannsen trial, and my editors wanted more insight into the attorney who made the magic happen. You soldiers up for answering a few questions?"

A few shrugged.

Mick sat down, already forgetting what he'd called himself. Brent? Trent? He was not a man used to disguises. Not of this nature, anyway.

When he pulled out the notepad, a large man with curly, bushy hair said, "Don't you all have those fancy computers you use these days?"

"Or a tape recorder?" Pudgy asked.

Mick smiled. "I come from a long line of journalists who believe shorthand is the way to go. Now why don't you six introduce yourselves?"

They went around the table, giving their name, rank, serial number, and their current occupation. There seemed to be some excitement building as they realized they were going to be quoted. If they only knew.

"So," Mick said after the introductions, "does Earle come meet you here anymore?"

They shook their heads. Horton, the financial adviser, said, "Hasn't been here in several years. Maybe four or so."

"Why'd he stop coming?"

"Who knows. We've had as many as twenty-five and as few as four. We just keep meeting. Whoever wants to come can come, as long as they served in Vietnam and live in the great city of Irving."

"There's not an organized local chapter?"

"Yeah, but we like to just chew the fat," said Arnie, the oldest-looking member. "We like gettin' together and talkin'. And not about the war. Though we've done that too."

"What kind of man is Sammy Earle?"

The group hesitated, and Mick watched their eyes carefully avoid his. Mick cleared his throat. "Look, this is off the record, okay?"

Worried glances subsided. The pudgy man, Lenny, said, "Sammy was a soldier just like the rest of us."

"What kind of soldier?"

"The kind that goes and risks his life fighting a war none of us should've been in," Lenny said. His eyes told an unvoiced story.

Mick scribbled down notes. "He's a high-profile attorney now. What kind of man was he to be around?"

Again, the apprehension. Mick tried to look at each of them, unscrambling the code of honor they surely upheld for one another. But nobody had to tell Mick that there was something else going on.

"You know," Mick began, after nobody answered, "there's a lot of rumors that float around, and many times these rumors are reported as fact and believed as fact. If there's something you can do to set the record straight about Mr. Earle, I'm sure he would appreciate it."

Arnie spoke up. "Are you talking about what happened to him over in—?"

Mick kept a steady eye on the notes he wasn't really writing. "Is there something more I need to know?" he asked when Arnie didn't finish.

"Shut up, Arnie," Horton said. "It's nobody's business."

Mick glanced up. "It'll be reported, regardless of what is said here. You'd be able to make a difference in how it is reported."

Horton didn't look like he was buying it, but the man sitting next to Lenny, who had introduced himself as George, a helicopter pilot, said, "Why are we protecting him?" He looked around the bunch. "You all know as well as I do that Sammy Earle would sell us out in a heartbeat if it meant he might get some extra television exposure."

A few agreed.

Horton stayed his ground. "What happened over there doesn't have anything to do with what happens here."

Lenny said, "You all are acting like it's something he should hide. It's nothing to be ashamed of. It's something he wanted to forget, that's all." He cast his eyes down.

After a few moments of silence, Mick said, "I'm sensing some of you aren't fond of Earle."

"He's a loudmouth know-it-all," said Arnie. "But that's just me. Maybe some of the other fellas were impressed with his expensive suits and elaborate language."

"He never fit in," Horton explained mildly, eyeing the others in an attempt to take control of the conversation. As he continued, he looked at Mick. "He tried, I guess. But he always had that better-than-you attitude. Just rubbed some of us the wrong way. But we didn't think too much about it. He wasn't a regular, came every once in a while, and we haven't seen him in years except on the television."

"Big case he won," Mick said.

Horton sighed, fingering his coffee cup. "Sure. Big case. But that's the kind of guy Earle is. He's going to go for the big guns, and morals aren't necessarily his main objective."

"You believe this is because of what happened over there in Vietnam?"

The others waited for Horton to respond. He took his time thinking over his answer. "I don't know. He talked about it in very vague terms."

"How vague?"

"You know, sort of treated it as no big deal. He'd talk about the court case a little, mostly from the point of view of a haughty lawyer."

"What'd he say about it?"

Horton hesitated. "He said he believes in the court system. Even the military court system."

"I always thought it was strange," said Lenny. "I had some buddies die over there. And I can hardly talk about them without choking up. I hardly talk about it anyway. But Earle, he'd tell the story like he was recounting a scene from a movie."

"In what way?"

"You know, something like, 'I was under the bushes, saw Matty get shot. Tried to revive him.'"

Mick tried to be patient with his questions, but he couldn't understand what a trial had to do with all of this.

Arnie soon answered his question. "Well, I'd say it could mess you up going through all that. I mean, a fellow soldier shooting your best friend. That's crazy."

185

"How'd it happen?" Mick asked, forgetting he was supposed to know the story.

"According to Sammy, he was under some brush, hiding out from 'the enemy.' That's what he called them. Always. Never used another name. Anyway, he heard somebody behind him, rolled around, heard a shot, and his buddy, Matty Lasatter, I think was his name, was shot dead."

Mick was writing real notes now. The men forgot their apprehension, relishing a good war story. "By another American soldier."

They all nodded, as if they were hardly able to fathom the scene. "The other soldier . . . what was his name again?" asked George.

"Delano, wasn't it?" Lenny asked. The others nodded. "Yeah, that's right. Patrick Delano."

"Staff sergeant. Shot another soldier," Horton said in nearly a whisper.

"It was an accident, I'm assuming?" Mick asked.

Horton shook his head. "This was no accident. Delano shot Lasatter on purpose, claiming he was about to shoot Earle."

Mick looked up from his notes. "I'm sorry. I'm not following."

"According to Earle, Delano said that it looked as if Matty Lassater had mistaken Earle for the enemy in the bushes. Lassater was getting ready to shoot Earle when Delano took him out."

"Saving one soldier's life by killing another," Mick said.

Horton nodded. "At trial, Delano claimed he made a split-second decision and had not intended to kill Lassater. But when he raised his gun to shoot, his arm hit the tree next to him, and it bumped his aim up, hitting Lassater in the chest."

"And Delano probably would've gotten off if it hadn't been for his mouth," added George.

"Oh?"

Arnie said, "Earle says that Delano pontificated himself to death on the stand, claiming Lassater was a useless soldier anyway. Earle said it was horrifying to hear. Basically Delano claimed he saved the better soldier, which meant he made a more deliberate choice than he originally admitted. And then he kept going, telling Earle that he wasn't being appreciative of Delano's sacrifice for him."

"Earle tells it like the guy turned on a gigantic messiah complex," said Lenny. "I guess nobody had ever seen anything like that. Earle said it was like the guy went insane right on the stand. Shouting. Screaming at Earle, asking him why he wasn't standing up for the man who saved his life."

"Said it was like everything from the war culminated right there in the courtroom."

George snickered. "It's really something else to hear Sammy tell it, though. He sort of ruffles up his hair and makes his eyes all wide and crazy, pretending to be this Delano fellow."

"Sammy can do some pontificating himself," Horton mused.

"So what happened?" Mick asked.

"Delano got court-martialed," Horton said quietly, and the men settled down their laughter. Horton, in practiced dramatic fashion, added, "And then he disappeared."

Mick laughed out of shock. "Delano disappeared?"

Horton nodded. "According to Earle, he escaped custody and nobody has heard from him since."

"No idea what happened to the guy?"

"Earle always jokes that he's out there somewhere preaching the gospel of justice," Horton said. "Of course Earle would be doing the exact opposite."

"The guy has seriously never been found?"

"Most likely dead," said Lenny. "Or a street bum some-where."

"War can make you go crazy," said a guy named Mike, who'd yet to speak up. He looked around the room, then back down at his hands. "But you can get past it if you try hard enough."

"Anyway," said Horton, turning his attention back to Mick, "who knows why Earle is the way he is. I mean, the guy's successful, living the American dream, right? He was probably just a snob since he was born."

The men laughed.

Mick smiled, finishing off his notes. He wasn't sure how this information was going to be useful, but he thought it certainly showed some character background for the guy.

"Well," Mick said, sensing the men may have begun regretting all they'd said, "I doubt I'll use too much of this in my article. The focus is really on the Johannsen trial."

The men looked relieved. Horton said, "Are you going to interview Earle?"

"Don't know yet. I have a lot of quotes from him already through the media. You're right. He does like to spout off. But sometimes it's what is *not* said that is most interesting."

"Yeah, well, catch Earle when he's drunk and you may get more than you bargained for," said Horton, as if speak-ing from experience.

"Is that so?"

Horton grinned. "Yeah. The guy can get liquored up. He's sort of famous for it, but he keeps it out of the court-room, I guess."

Mick closed his notebook and stuck the pencil through the spirals. "Well, gentlemen, thanks for letting me take up some of your time this evening. I appreciate the information you gave me. And now I'll let you get back to whatever it is you talk about every Monday night."

They all smiled. "Mostly just what's in the news," said Arnie.

"Oh," Mick said, a spider of apprehension crawling up his back. He grinned. "Murder and mayhem in Irving, and all that, huh?"

Horton shook his head. "Nah. Once you've seen one murderer, you've seen them all."

Mick couldn't help but look down at nothing in particular as his face turned hot.

"We actually like talking about the weather." Lenny laughed. "As crazy as that sounds."

Mick wished he was not a fugitive on the run. How nice it would be to sit and talk about the weather with a group of fine American soldiers. His body longed for that kind of normalcy. "Sounds nice," Mick said gently.

Suddenly the waitress who had helped him was carrying a platter full of food to their table. Mick tried to swing his bag around and make an exit, but she was already addressing him. She looked at his notepad. "That working out for ya?"

Mick nodded, hoping nobody was catching on. "Take good care of these gentlemen. They're a fine group of men."

"Always do," she said.

Arnie stood and shook Mick's hand. "Thanks for making our evening interesting, Trent."

"You're welcome."

Arnie looked at his duffel bag. "They don't pay you enough at *Time* to afford a briefcase?"

Mick smiled. "Always thought they looked pretentious."

Arnie and the rest of the men laughed. "Amen, brother."

chapter nineteen

the ten-o'clock news droned on as Aaron lay on his couch, yet to change out of the tank top and sweatpants he'd been in earlier when he exercised. A flulike ache added to his fatigue.

He'd spent an hour on the phone with his parents in Kansas City, trying to assure them it was going to be okay. They wanted to drive down, but Aaron insisted they wait. It had been only a day. Mick would surely turn up. Somewhere.

Jenny walked through the front door, carrying Chinese food. Aaron's appetite had waned all day, but he knew he needed to eat. She went to the kitchen and slid the food onto a plate, bringing it to him with a warm smile. "Here you go."

He toyed with the fork and listened to the anchor report that the manhunt was still on for the suspected kidnapper Mick Kline. He set the food on the coffee table and rubbed his eyes.

Jenny slipped her arm around his neck.

Aaron said, "I keep thinking of the time Mick disappeared. I think he was about six or seven. It was a Saturday night, and we were all in the house doing our own thing. It was Mom, I think, who realized that Mick was gone. We started looking for him, but we couldn't find him."

"What happened?"

"It was horrible. He was gone for about eight hours. Turns out he'd wandered off while chasing a dog he'd found outside in the backyard. We didn't have a fence or anything, so Mick just followed him into the trees and then couldn't find his way home because it was dark."

"How terrifying!"

"I remember the whole neighborhood was looking for him. The police. The firemen. I had my flashlight, and I was bound and determined to find him. If it was the last thing I did, I was going to find him. I was walking through the woods, crying my eyes out, shouting his name. Anyway, they finally found him, four miles away near the creek bed and the highway."

Jenny fingered through his hair.

"I kind of feel like that right now. He probably is wandering around in some trees somewhere. But his soul has been wandering around for so long too, you know? Just looking for something to attach to, something meaningful . . ." Aaron muffled his words into his hands.

Jenny wrapped her arms around his waist. "It's okay."

"There's a dozen or more law enforcers out there with guns, ready to shoot a man they think has done this horrible crime."

"We trust God to protect him."

Aaron scratched his cheek and shook his head. "You believe so easily."

"No. Not easily. I just believe."

"And trust. I've never met a more trusting person than you. It doesn't come that easy for me. I've built a career on not trusting people. Not trusting people to drive safely, to treat their spouses kindly, to earn a living the honest way."

She laughed. "Well, I'll remember that while I plan this wedding of ours."

"No," he said, "that's all yours. I totally trust you."

"I thought so." She winked. "See, you are trusting! Now trust me, and get some food down you, okay?" She picked up his plate and handed it to him.

"Where's he sleeping? What's he eating?"

"Your brother is very savvy. He's probably found a way to stay at the Hilton!"

Aaron laughed. "Yeah. Right."

Mick had parked the bike behind a crowd of trees, fairly well hidden, at least in the darkness. From the hill, he could see the Heppetons' large, Victorian-style home that sat on fifteen acres of land, its many windows still glowing this late at night. He watched Alice, in her late sixties now, loading the dishwasher. He couldn't see Jack, her husband, but figured he was probably in his study working. The man worked long, hard hours as an architect, he supposed, so they could continue to live like they did.

Mick walked down the hill toward the fishing pond, away from the tiny, little-known road that gave access to the pond area. Moonlight rippled across its murky waters. The fishing dock on the other side of the pond, shadowed by the many trees that hung over it, brought a smile to his weary face. How many days and nights he'd spent at this pond, fishing with Aaron and the Heppetons' two children, Luke and Maggie. The families had been longtime friends, and though Mick had lost touch with the kids, he knew his mom and dad still talked to Alice and Jack regularly.

He wondered if Jack and Alice had heard the news. What they must be thinking. He'd always had great respect for them. As he neared the pond, most of the house went out of view, except the roof and its three towering chimneys. The moonlight sliced a path through the dense brush for him. Looked like there hadn't been much activity down here in a while. Jack had always been good about clearing the brush for ample fishing room. But the water was down, and there was a collection of windblown trash against the southern part of the pond.

Mick wrapped his arms around himself, wishing he'd thought to bring a coat. At this time of year, the temperature at night could range from the sixties to the forties. Mick guessed it was probably around fifty-five. Cool and windy enough to make him tremble. The bike ride alone had chilled him to the bone, even riding the whole way at twenty-five miles an hour.

The water sloshed along the shallow and muddy banks. The sound reminded him of days spent jumping off the dock, fully clothed, enjoying the warm water. He would float on his back and stare up into the blue sky that stretched across the horizon. Those were the memories that grieved him—when life was simple and fun and full of hope, with no real responsibilities. He supposed it was foolish to mourn the fact that he was all grown up. But it came with such burdens. Maybe he'd enjoyed his childhood more than he was supposed to. His actions even baffled himself sometimes.

His thoughts turned to the night he met Taylor and how he'd told himself to go home, to stay out of trouble, yet instead he folded to a simple temptation from a woman offering to chat with him, and now it had turned into the greatest nightmare of his life.

Something told him that Taylor Franks was a woman very much in control of herself. Those dark, smoky eyes of hers told conflicting stories, though. On one hand, they had the pragmatic stare of a woman who knew what she wanted. But flickering through the fortitude was an uneasy ambivalence. He saw in her a longing to connect but a sturdy wall that would not allow it.

And that he could remember, never once did they do more than philosophize about life, in general terms at best.

Mick sighed, throwing a few sticks into the water. He had enough on his own plate. No need to be psychoanalyzing someone else. But even in the drunken stupor he'd been in, he remembered wondering who this woman was and what was behind the mystery. He couldn't shake the feeling that whatever it was, it had something to do with her disappearance.

It took him ten minutes to make his way around the pond, clearing the brush as he went. He didn't bother being extremely quiet. He knew the Heppetons didn't have dogs. Alice was allergic to them, and Jack was good enough with a shotgun not to need one.

The wind carried some of the sounds from the house— a lantern swinging, the door to Alice's gardening shed banging slightly against the doorframe. Something in him wanted to go up to their back porch and knock on the door. He knew they'd take him in, which is why he would never go.

Once on the other side of the pond, Mick stopped near the fishing dock and looked toward a grouping of trees that had once been familiar but had now filled in so much he couldn't decide if that was the right location or not.

This was going to be quite a task, even with ample moonlight.

Mick trudged forward, his arms and legs being scraped with each footstep. About twenty yards ahead, he thought he recognized the area and tried to pick up his pace. When he got there, he knelt down and used his hands to clear away the leaves and limbs. But there was nothing. He moved a few feet over, doing the same thing. But again, he found nothing.

After fifteen minutes, he still had not found it, so he

stood, panting out his aggravation. It was a silly idea to think that it would be here after all these years.

But as he looked to the west, he saw a small blue corner of something. Mick rushed over to it, three tree groupings down. Falling to his knees again, he shuffled his hands through the dirt and leaves until he cleared enough of it that he realized he'd found what he was searching for.

"Hah!" Mick laughed. Taking the edge of it, he pulled it loose from the rest of the dirt.

Their old tent!

It smelled musty, and the royal blue color had faded. The long, narrow bag that held all the equipment to set it up was still tied to the side. Mick quickly unrolled it, fighting the breeze, and dumped the ridgepole and pegs out.

It had been a long time since he'd pitched a tent, and probably the last one he'd pitched was this one. They'd spend long summer nights out here, he and Aaron and Luke. Maggie was never allowed to join in and never wanted to anyway.

When Luke got into high school and lost interest in their friendships, Mick and Aaron still wanted to come out and camp, so they buried their tent here and thought of ways they could sneak out and come over. They did it two or three times, but without Luke, it wasn't nearly as much fun.

He shook off more dirt and crossed the poles, stringing them through the loops. It wasn't fancy, but it would do to block the wind at least. After putting it all together, Mick raised the tent and drove the pegs into the ground.

"Yes!" Mick felt like he'd just won a football game.

He dusted his jeans off and was about to climb inside when the wind picked up and he heard a loud ripping sound. Before he could blink, a large piece of vinyl flapped in the wind, and one entire side of the tent tore away. Mick kicked the rest of it down in anger, stomping it into the soft ground. He should've known a tent's threads would never hold up to years' worth of the elements.

He threw the poles down and turned away, grabbing his duffel bag off the ground.

And then he had another thought.

The tree house.

It was about fifty yards from the old pond. Jack had built it when Maggie was born, and Mick and Aaron had spent plenty of time in it over the years.

Surely it had not survived the fierce Texas storms.

When he'd cleared enough trees to look for it, he was surprised to find it still up in the large oak tree. Mick laughed. Could he still climb a tree?

Walking the length of the yard, the main house came into view again. A few more lights had been turned off. He wished he had a bed.

When he got to the tree, he looked up, wondering how they ever did climb it. Jack had nailed a feeble ladder that was now missing three out of its five rungs. Mick tried a couple of times to use it, but one rung broke off, and the only one left was three inches above his head.

Mick wondered if he could jump high enough to grab the bottom limb, and then hang on to it.

Then he had an idea.

He threw his duffel bag up into the tree house.

That would be incentive to get up there. It contained all the money he had!

After three jumps, he finally caught a large branch, but his hands slipped off. One more time, and he grabbed it, his feet swinging a couple of feet off the ground. He turned his body and tried to use the last wooden rung to get a foot-hold. It teetered but held his weight. With his right hand, he managed to grip a small, healthy, bendable limb. With a lot of muscle, he pulled himself upright and swung a leg over the branch he'd been hanging from.

He was at the front porch of the tree house. Mick used his hands to test the durability of the wood. It looked like it could hold his weight. After all, Jack was an architect. Surely he'd built this to stand the test of time.

Carefully and slowly, Mick crawled in on his hands and knees. How small this place looked now! Years ago it seemed like a mansion in the trees. Now his head nearly hit the ceiling while he sat.

Mick scooted to the corner, trying to see through the dark if there was anything left inside. When his eyes adjusted, he noticed a few metallic candy wrappers and a box of old baseball cards, wet and warped.

Mick leaned against the side that blocked the wind, then lay down, using his duffel bag as a pillow. Without the wind, he'd probably be okay, though it was going to take a good two hours to finally warm up the place so his teeth weren't chattering.

He closed his eyes, but sleep wouldn't come.

Through the small wooden window that was missing two shutters, Mick watched ghostly gray clouds drift over the moon. He rubbed his eyes and suppressed the urge to scream. That's what he wanted to do. Scream bloody murder.

And then he found himself shouting. "God!"

He stared at the moon as if it were the Almighty's face. "God!!"

Only the wind answered, quietly howling through the treetops.

"*God*!"

A furious gnawing inside his chest urged him to punch a hole through something.

"Is this how You want me?" Mick cried out. "A

wandering, homeless fugitive? Does this make You happy? You showed me, didn't You!"

Mick kicked the heel of his shoe into the plank beneath him. "You know I didn't do this!" He rested his head on his knees. "I didn't do this," he mumbled. He was sure God heard mumbling as clearly as shouting. Maybe even better. He closed his eyes and tried to settle himself down.

He began to feel a strange assurance brought about by knowing God was just. It had never brought him any peace before. It was that very attribute that scared him, in fact. But now he could use God's justice.

Use. Mick shook his head. It was just like him to use God when he needed something. A favor. Unfortunately, Mick didn't have any favors to call in with the man upstairs.

He figured God was pretty good at creative punishments as well. Mick's life turned terrible because of the *one* thing he didn't do wrong. How many other times had he not received punishment for all the things he had done wrong?

What a mystery, Mick thought, gazing at the moon again. It was full and round, glowing white-orange, dusted with shadowy designs.

He continued to pore over the odd cliché that was his life.

mick awoke, rolling over onto his stiff and aching back The sun blinded him, and the sweat that had collected under his neck trickled down into his shirt as he sat up. Still, it was a welcome temperature change from the last three cold nights he'd spent here.

On Tuesday morning, after the first night in the tree house, came the sobering realization that he couldn't live like this forever, but there was nothing to show him that anything would change soon. He'd curled up and slept most of the day. That evening, he counted his money. He had only thirty dollars left. It would last a few more days, but that was it. For all he knew, he could be running for the rest of his life.

No. One way or the other, there would be resolution.

On Wednesday, Mick was nearly delirious with hunger. Alice and Jack had left midmorning in their Cadillac, so Mick crossed their large backyard to Alice's garden, where he found a variety of vegetables. He'd munched on tomatoes, tried a pepper but it was too hot, and helped himself to the seeds of the mammoth sunflower garden. The food nourished him but didn't fill him up. He'd been mindful not to take too much for fear that she would notice or that he might not have food for the following days. He'd kept hydrated by drinking from the garden hose.

He didn't know how long he would stay here. Fall temperatures were approaching, and soon enough, he'd have to find better shelter. That morning he'd also discovered a few old towels stuffed into the back of Alice's gardening shed. He'd taken two to use as blankets. It had helped a little. But last night, he was sure the temperature had dropped below fifty. He would not be able to take another night of it.

Putting the sunglasses on, he stuffed the towels into his duffel bag. He'd also found an old cap with a construction company logo on the front, and he took it. It did a lot to keep his head warm.

Through Wednesday, he'd watched with little interest as Alice and Jack came and went from their house, living normal and easy lives. He wondered briefly what Luke and Maggie were up to. Last he'd heard, Luke was in medical school and Maggie had finished West Point.

He'd thought more about Sammy Earle. With the information he had, there really wasn't much he could prove, other than Earle wasn't a likable person. Something told Mick to keep sniffing around.

He wouldn't be able to move about so easily anymore. His five-o'clock shadow had turned into a short beard, and he was looking decidedly homeless. He could use a shower. He was inside Irving city limits, thankfully, but he had no idea where to go or what to do.

Leaving the tree house, he walked the grassy hill toward where he'd parked his bike and wondered about Aaron. For whatever strange reason, it meant something to him for Aaron to know the truth about why he ran. Maybe it was all the memories that danced around him in the tree house. Before Jenny.

Mick was relieved to find his motorcycle still propped against the dense patch of trees. He dusted off some early fall leaves and hopped on, giving it a good revving before circling around and catching the old, dusty path that led out to Peachtree Street, which ran behind the Heppetons'.

It was nice to get on the road again, and Mick took the same back roads into Irving as he had before. When he reached an area with heavier population, Mick pulled into a gas station and used quarters to get a newspaper from an outside machine.

Flipping it over, he was surprised to find that his face was not the largest picture on the front; in fact his face wasn't even on there. There was only a small headline near the bottom: Irving Fugitive May Still Be in Area.

Mick opened the paper to page 4A and read the rest of the article that confirmed his belief: They had no idea where he was. Coach Rynde was quoted as saying he believed in Mick's innocence.

At the end of the article, a small blurb about Sammy Earle said he'd had a previous relationship with the woman but was never considered a suspect. Mick wondered how that was playing out in the media.

Mick noticed a man about his age staring at him. Raising the paper to cover his face, his heart started racing. When he glanced back at the man, he was on a cell phone, pretending Mick was not there.

Mick stuffed the newspaper into his duffel bag and walked as slowly as his adrenaline would let him. He tried to nonchalantly get on the bike, but once he met the man's eyes, he knew he'd been recognized. Throwing his bag over his shoulder, Mick started the bike and sped away, looking over his shoulder to find the man running after him, apparently trying to get a plate number.

As he rushed toward one of the busier roads, indecision caused him to slow down. Everybody would be looking for a dirt bike, and they'd probably be smart enough to look on the back roads. Mick drove on the two-lane street, trying to think logically. But he could barely catch his breath, and his eyes watered enough to blur his vision.

And then he passed a patrol car.

He heard the sirens first. When he looked back, the police cruiser was whipping a U-turn and speeding toward him. Mick crossed a four-way intersection without even knowing it, floating between two passing cars.

Stop it. Stop this insanity! Pull over and turn yourself in!

But Mick knew he couldn't do it. Not after what he'd been through already.

He increased his speed, determined to flee, determined to find out what happened to Taylor. But coming over the hill in the distance was another cruiser, sirens screaming and lights flashing.

He had only a few seconds to make a decision, so he scanned the area quickly. Pastures and farms were scattered among a few houses and businesses. And then he saw his chance: an old farmer out of his truck, opening the gate to his pasture to feed his cattle. About fifty stood on the hilltop in the middle of the pasture, ears twitching with alertness to all the sounds.

A car passed him and then Mick turned, crossing the other lane and bouncing into the ditch. He came up on the other side and made a sharp left turn on the dirt road, the pickup and farmer only fifty feet away. The farmer stepped out of the way just as Mick sped past him and into the field.

Glancing behind him, he could see the cruisers screeching to a stop, trying to maneuver around the truck and through the narrow gateway. Mick zoomed forward, scattering the cattle in his path. Disapproving moos mixed with the sound of his motor as the bike climbed the hill.

He didn't know what was on the other side of the hill. He had little time to prepare, because he was now flying in the air like he'd just launched off a ramp. The bike wheels spun underneath him, reflected in a large, muddy watering hole below.

"Come on!" Mick yelled, urging his bike forward through the air, hoping to clear the water.

The front tire reached land, but the back tire hit the water, flipping him forward, the bike landing on top of him. His hands and feet stuck in the mud and he couldn't get any leverage to lift himself out of the water with the bike on top of him.

Blinded by the swirling mud, he wondered how deep he was. His lungs wilted with every passing second.

With a panicked maneuver, he slid sideways and the bike sank into the mud where he'd lain. He groped for anything nearby, which ended up being the bike, and pulled himself out of the water, gasping for breath, gagging on the water he'd swallowed.

His clothes were soggy and heavy. He was caked with mud, but he spotted his duffel bag a few feet away, completely dry. Crawling toward it with every limb shaking, Mick grabbed it and stumbled to his feet.

The sirens were so loud he couldn't hear himself coughing, and when he turned, he saw the two cruisers had stopped short of plunging into the water. Two cops from the first car and one from the second were opening their doors and drawing their guns at the same time.

To his right were some trees, but only a few, and then another major road. The pasture was a full square mile. In the distance, thick black smoke bellowed like a dangerous thunderhead. Mick wondered what was on fire.

He wiped his eyes clear of mud and started running. Running and praying. *If I can find the truth, let me find the truth.*

It felt as if he were running in slow motion.

The cops were yelling at him to stop, but Mick didn't

look back. If he was going to get shot, he didn't want to see the bullet coming.

Air wanted to stop short of going into his lungs. All the water he'd swallowed was swishing in his stomach, making him nauseous.

He reached the patch of trees in front of the road, navigating through them in a way that could possibly block any bullets. So far he had not heard a shot. He leaped over a barbed-wire fence, catching his leg and ripping his jeans. Blood dripped from his calf down to his ankle, mixing with the muddy water that was already draining from his jeans. Falling into a ditch, he rolled to a stop and scrambled up, trying to reach the road.

Just as he did, the farmer drove his tractor by and Mick jumped on it.

The farmer saw him in his rearview mirror; Mick could see the terror in his eyes. He probably looked like a swamp creature.

Mick motioned for him to keep driving, but he could feel the tractor slow. When the farmer whirled around, his attention turned to the cops who were running after them. The man shifted down, his expression frozen with shock.

Climbing around to the opposite side of the tractor, Mick tried to hide behind some of its metal but remain out of the farmer's reach, in case he decided to give Mick a good punt. The man craned his neck out the cab window and yelled something at Mick, but Mick couldn't hear. When he poked his head up, one of the cops was shouting something into his radio. The other two were still running, pointing their weapons toward Mick.

Mick ducked and looked around. A slow-moving truck crested the hill on the road and rumbled toward the commotion. It pulled over to the side of the road. He could see the silhouettes of two passengers.

Mick hopped off the now stationary tractor and ran toward the truck. The police were still about forty yards away, waving and yelling.

Mick crouched behind the pickup, hidden from the police momentarily, though there was no question about where he was. Everyone had seen him take cover behind the truck. But the cops weren't going to shoot with innocent bystanders nearby.

The woman in the cab was screaming hysterically, her eyes wide with horror as she stared into Mick's face through her passenger window.

Mick could hear sirens wailing again. More cops.

The driver was now reaching for the hunting rifle that hung in the back window of his pickup.

Little did Mick know this was going to be an asset. As he sprinted toward the field, he looked back to see the officers shouting at the man with the shotgun. For now, they had more problems than just him.

He hopped another fence. The country air smelled burned, and Mick noticed the smoke seemed just over the hill, perhaps half a mile away. Immediately in front of him, there wasn't a tree in sight. All he could do was run.

Glancing back, Mick saw the driver of the truck aiming his rifle at him as the police shouted and scrambled toward the man. Nearly giddy with relief, Mick noticed something amazing. The man had only one arm! How good of a shot could he be?

A bullet whizzed past his hand and hit the dirt right in front of him. Mick yelped, losing his foothold and falling to the ground, tumbling forward across the grass. When he looked back, one of the cops was tackling the man with the gun.

A part of him just wanted to play dead.

But he got up and started running again. The other two

cops had jumped the fence and were chasing him, but Mick still had quite a lead.

In the distance, he could hear the quiet thumping of a search helicopter. And something else he couldn't identify. A low roar.

He jumped the far fence, this time clearing the barbed wire. Across the next road, gravel and barely wide enough for a car, a steep hill hid whatever was on fire on the other side. He had run far enough that he was truly in the country, where the square mile no longer existed between paved roads. Climbing a hill this size, rare for the Texas plains, seemed impossible.

Coming to a standstill momentarily, Mick tuned in to another sound in addition to the sirens and the thumping of the helicopter. To the west he saw a train thundering north. If he could get on the other side of that train, the cruisers would be blocked and he would have time to escape. But could he grab hold of a fast-moving train?

Only if this were a movie.

The two cops were now gaining on him. A couple of cruisers were speeding toward him on the road west of the field he was about to clear.

He started running again. Toward the smoky hill.

donning his favorite workout clothes, a worn Dallas Cowboys tank top paired with his gray cotton sweats and Nikes, Aaron walked out the front door of his house and threw his gym bag into the back of his truck, which he never did.

It was all for show.

There wasn't a car in sight, but he figured the police wanted him to think that they'd stopped watching. After Crawford's threats, though, Aaron assumed they were somehow keeping a good eye on him. He didn't doubt his house was bugged either. And Prescott could have easily put a locator device, which the cops called a "bird dog," on the bottom of his truck the other day.

He had spent the entire morning thinking out the plan.

Driving against city traffic, Aaron checked his watch. It was six thirty Thursday evening. He hoped he had this timed right.

Aaron thought he'd seen a tail twice in his rearview mirror, but then the car would disappear into the traffic. He turned on the sports news, trying to drown out the paranoia that was definitely following him.

Ten minutes and a hundred glances back later, Aaron pulled into the crowded parking lot of Gold's Gym. He got out, retrieved his gym bag with great deliberateness, and strolled toward the gym, as if he had nothing better to do.

Once inside, a spandex-clad woman, her blonde hair lusterless and sticky with hair spray, greeted him with a fixed smile.

"I'm interested in joining the gym, but I wanted to see if I could get a pass to try everything out, maybe for a day or two."

She reached under the desk she was standing behind and came up with a red laminated ticket. "Sure. This will get you in three times, and then if you want to join, you'll just need to fill out some paperwork."

"Great." Aaron smiled at her, but his delight was coming from the fact that his plan—so far—was working. He glanced out the front window of the gym, looking for Big Brother. Nothing caught his eye.

She smiled back. "I'm Trisha."

"Aaron."

"I'll show you around."

"Oh . . . that's okay. I'm sure I can figure it out."

"Sorry. Policy. We have to go over all the rules with you or we might get sued," she recited.

Aaron followed her into the gym, where she pointed a perfectly manicured fingernail toward different equipment as she walked him to the locker room. But Aaron was hardly paying attention. He was scanning the gym rats for someone.

"Hello?"

Aaron looked at Trisha. "I'm sorry. What was that?"

Her hands were on her hips. "Gawking is allowed but not preferred," she snapped, her attention on a beautiful woman near the StairMaster. Her gaze cut back to Aaron.

"I'm looking for someone I know," Aaron explained.

Trisha didn't look sold. "Anyway, do you have any questions?" she asked in a tone flat with skepticism.

Aaron shook his head.

"All right. You're welcome to use any open locker to put your bag in. The next two times you come in, you need to have this ticket punched."

"Thanks."

As Trisha walked away, Aaron watched her eye the StairMaster woman, apparently hefty competition with her tighter spandex and silkier hair.

He looked around the gym, trying to form a strategy and hoping it would work. He prayed that Liz Lane's new commitment to a healthier life would get her here.

But in the meantime, he might as well take out some of his frustration on the leg press.

Climbing the hill—which Mick thought of as the Hulk for its patchy green, bulging surface—turned out to be a difficult feat. His legs barely found balance, and as he clawed his way up, grasping at parched grass and unstable dirt, he thought he'd never make it all the way to the top.

The polluted air didn't help. Behind the hill, the fire roared and hissed, and Mick was unsure what he would find once he reached the top. The heat could be felt even on this side of the hill.

The police were more than a hundred yards behind him. The helicopter that had been just a dot in the sky earlier was now lower and crossing the fields behind him like an advancing scorpion.

Insanity. What did he think he was going to do when he got to the top of this hill?

As he clambered upward, the sound of the fire, which he now guessed was either a large grass fire or a controlled burning of the field, swallowed up every other sound, hollering like a rushing wind.

When he finally reached the top, his hair was blown

backward by the thermal wind and his face flushed from the heat. Angry orange flames greeted him below. It was a large fire, stretching at least twenty acres in length, spreading south with the slight wind. Groupings of trees crackled, the smoke intensely building upward, floating from one tree to another, while spreading fluidly across the ground.

But the fire was still in patches, and the black and smutty ground it had already claimed fumed with ghostly smoke trails.

Mick was suddenly glad he was wet. He glanced behind him. The helicopter was gaining, and a cruiser was less than twenty yards away on the gravel road below. Studying the fire, he wondered if he could race around the flames. Hide beneath the dark gray smoke. And not kill himself.

It was his only option now. From the top of the hill, he could see the end of the train rolling away. With a hefty shove, he slid down the grassy hill toward the fire. As he tumbled downward, the heat intensified and he found it even harder to breathe.

Surrender, you fool.

There was no indication of what was ahead. He could see nothing beyond the thick veil of smoke. It was an odd feeling, seeing light from the fire but running completely blind in the dark.

He wondered if hell was like this strange paradox.

Stopping near the bottom, Mick gulped down a breath and ran forward. The sound was like a curtain being whipped and snapped by a stiff breeze through an open window.

Mick dashed around the patches of flames, so far finding it fairly easy to maneuver. Much harder to breathe. His eyes stung, watering so badly he could barely see. Clutching the bottom of his wet and muddy T-shirt, he held it over his mouth, hoping to create a small amount of breathable air.

As he ran farther in, blackness swallowed him. His other hand tried to shield his eyes, but it was worthless. He stumbled forward, stepping over small hot spots, darting flames that shot overhead from one tree to the next.

Choking and gasping, he kept running, sweat pouring down his face. In front of him, a large wall of fire hissed, its flames slithering against the air that fed it.

No longer worried about being caught, Mick fell forward, splashing into the ashes, his face charred by their glowing embers. Crying out, he leaped to his feet, the skin on his hands stinging.

Go back.

He turned, but disorientation swirled around him. Peering through his watering eyes, all he could see were spots of orange, flags of black smoke, snowy gray ashes floating listlessly through the air. The intensity of the fire created its own breeze, but it slapped his face like an angry hand, choking his throat and clawing at his eyes.

"God!" He'd walked straight into hell. He'd delivered himself here. As he turned in circles, fire surrounded him everywhere, and he saw no place where he could break through.

Mick gulped down the air thirstily, drinking in its dusty grit, swelling his lungs with poison. He would suffocate himself so he wouldn't be burned alive.

Then he gasped. And gasped again. He couldn't breathe. Falling to his knees, his senses raged with acuteness. The vinyl fabric of his duffel bag seared his arm. His feet were hot. His tongue stuck to the roof of his mouth.

He was not certain about his state of being, but he found himself standing again and sprinting toward the fire in front of him, as if two hands were gripping him under each arm and dragging his cautious feet toward his own death.

Right as he confronted the wall of flames, he jumped higher than he ever thought he could, trying to clear it like a hurdle.

Pain shot through his calves and knees. And then he felt cold, as though his body were being lowered into the icy earth, and the images around him contorted like a reflection in a warped mirror.

His eyes, wide-open, stared toward a skyless horizon. He felt weightless but not free. An invisible heaviness closed in around him, and his hands reached upward, trying to find something to hold, but there was nothing.

It had been forty-five minutes, and though Aaron had worked up a sweat, he had not found whom he was looking for. He leaned against a nearby wall, next to a poster of a man with rippling muscles. He dried his face with his white towel, scanning all those around him, looking for Liz Lane.

His mind wandered to Mick, his thoughts uttering desperate, wordless prayers energized by fear but filled with little hope. He couldn't imagine where his brother might be. The next state over? Two miles away? It sickened him to have no control. For so long, he'd tried to control Mick, tried to push him in the right direction. Mick always pushed back.

Aaron broke from his thoughts when he saw Liz Lane toting a large workout bag over her shoulder, looking decidedly out of place while managing to hold her head high. She eyed a skinny brunette working two dumbbells, rolled her eyes, and journeyed forward with a heavy sigh. Aaron watched her drag into the women's locker room, and a minute later return with a fluffy white towel around her neck and her frizzy blonde hair in a high ponytail. Scratching her face nervously, she looked like she didn't know what to do next.

After several seconds of deliberation, she decided on the leg press, and Aaron trailed her from a distance until she got situated. She did a rigorous set. When she stopped to rest, Aaron approached her. Her attention was on a woman whose bones were protruding from her overly tanned skin.

"She could use a trip to KFC, eh?" Aaron said.

Liz looked at him, chuckled, and then recognition lit her eyes. "You're the—"

"Yes. Aaron. How are you?"

Her expression turned disturbed. "You work out here?"

Aaron maintained a smile. "Just finished." He wiped his forehead for effect.

"You're the guy's brother," she said suddenly. "The cop."

Aaron tried to play it as casually as he could. "I am. My brother is Mick."

"You didn't tell me that," she said, "when you came to interview me."

Aaron sat on the bench next to her. "My brother wasn't a suspect then."

"What do you want from me?"

"Liz, my brother didn't do what they are accusing him of. But I think you may know who did."

"Why would I know?"

"I think Taylor Franks told you more than you told me."

"I don't know anything about her disappearance."

"I believe that. But I think Taylor may have indicated more about Sammy Earle than you said earlier. Maybe you were trying to protect your friend. She may have told you some things in confidence."

Liz shook her head. "I told you all I know."

"You mentioned she was on antidepressants. What was the reason for that?"

"You already know everything I know about her boyfriend. Yeah, the relationship hit her hard. Breakups hit a lot of people hard." Her expression told him she wasn't pleased with the questions. "This isn't official police business?"

"No."

"Then I don't have to answer any of your questions."

"No, you don't."

Liz licked her lips. "If you don't mind, I'd like to get on with my workout, which should tell you something, since this is my least favorite thing to do." An unkind smile swept her lips.

"So you're okay if the wrong guy goes to jail?"

"I just want Taylor back, and it doesn't sound like that will happen," Liz said, pumping her legs back and forth on the press. Sweat trickled down her temple, but Aaron suspected it wasn't from the workout.

"That's not going to happen if the police are focused on Mick. If you can tell me anything that might help the police look in a different direction . . ."

"Maybe you just want your brother off. Who cares if he did it, right?"

"That's not true. If I thought Mick did this, I'd be out there helping them hunt him down."

Liz studied his eyes carefully, then looked away. "All I know," she finally said, "is that this Sammy Earle made her life miserable. And Taylor was a woman who hated who she was."

"Really?"

Liz nodded. "Yeah, I mean, she's beautiful, but she never saw herself that way. She always seemed like she needed someone to affirm that. I tried to do that for her, and I think I accomplished it in a way. As we grew to know each other, I saw this quiet strength in her, growing day by day, you know? I can't comment on Sammy Earle. Taylor never talked specifically about him very much. She tended to talk in more general terms. Really, the only thing I do know about him is that, though he was really rich, when it came to her, he was cheap."

"Cheap?"

"From what I understood, he would buy her things in such a way that it made her feel really bad. Like he would never buy her anything nice, as if she wasn't worth it. Maybe he'd buy her jewelry, but he'd go to Sears and get it at 75 percent off, always making sure she knew he bought it at a discount."

Liz swiped the towel across her forehead, then blotted her face, as if trying to hide something revealing in her eyes. After a moment, she reemerged and looked at Aaron. "Something happened."

"What?"

"I don't know specifics. I swear she never told me. But one day, a month or so after they broke up, Taylor came to work, and there was just something different about her. Something in her eyes. I'm not sure I can describe it. I asked her about it, and at first she shrugged it off. But then she said something." Liz bit her lip, shaking her head at the thought. "She said that she'd been reading about revenge in the Bible."

"Revenge?"

"Yeah, it was strange. I asked her what she meant. She said she thought it was really interesting what God did to evil people in the Old Testament."

"Did she happen to give details about that?"

Liz shrugged. "I don't know my Bible all that well, to tell you the truth, and I never thought Taylor was the churchgoing type. So I was trying to follow. I got this odd feeling that maybe her boyfriend had done something really bad to her."

"Who broke off the relationship?"

"She never would say. She was just very weird about it. I guess this guy was a big society guy, so maybe she didn't want gossip to start. I don't know."

"Did she seem happy after the relationship was over?"

"Sort of. She seemed heartbroken for a while, probably when she was on the antidepressants. She seemed to take a liking to a guy in accounting. Joe, I think his name is. But it didn't really go anywhere. She suddenly stopped taking the antidepressants, which I hear is pretty dangerous. Anyway, over the past few months, I thought she was doing much better. But then last month that changed."

"How?"

"Taylor was becoming more and more distant. I asked her if she had gotten back on the antidepressants, and she'd answer very vaguely. I had no idea what was going on with her. I'll admit I was worried."

"What do you make of her disappearance, Liz? Do you think all of this is connected?"

"I don't know. A random act seems to make more sense, you know? I just keep thinking something horrible has happened to her."

"Did Taylor happen to mention which book of the Bible she was reading?"

Liz thought for a moment. "The book of Easter."

"Esther?"

"That's it." Liz smiled slightly. "Sorry . . . I don't own a Bible."

"Esther is a fascinating book."

"You go to church, huh?"

Just then, Aaron felt someone hovering over him. He looked up at Trisha, her noodle-thin arms flopped across one another. "You're not going to lose flab sitting around talking to beautiful women." She looked at Liz. "I'm sorry

218

about that, ma'am." She snapped her fingers at Aaron, indicating he should stand. He did. "Apparently you're going to have to learn more than one discipline at this gym, sir." Trisha pointed a strict finger away from Liz.

Aaron smiled sheepishly, glanced back at Liz with an embarrassed grin, and walked away.

He could hear Liz laughing.

chapter twenty-two

Choking and gagging, completely disoriented and as cold as if he were dead, Mick paddled toward a thick and muddy embankment. Air tried again and again to squeeze into his lungs, but it was useless. His rigid fingers found a stable root, and he pulled himself upward, his arms trembling ferociously, his body depleted of oxygen.

With his feet still dangling against what he perceived to be water, Mick laid his cheek in the mud and vomited. Rolling over onto his back, he sucked in air as fast as he could, but it was too quickly, and he vomited again. With slow and deliberate breaths, he cautiously refilled his lungs with air.

After a few moments, Mick opened his eyes. Everything around him blurred, and dizziness nauseated his stomach again. Closing his eyes, he coughed and spewed, then managed to sit up. He raised his hands high over his head.

"I give up." It was barely a whisper, raspy and hoarse. "Don't shoot. I give up." He tried to keep his arms up, his voice louder this time. "Please don't shoot. I give up."

He thought he heard guns being cocked, and his body shivered from head to toe. Maybe they couldn't hear him. "I give up!" This time his voice cracked, and his words were louder. "I give up!" he tried again, and now he was shouting loud enough that he knew they could hear him. He half expected a shower of bullets to race toward him.

High above, a breeze swished the treetops, and the leaves applauded his efforts. Mick fell backward onto the embankment, using it like a recliner. *Shoot me dead now. I don't care.*

He waited for gruff hands to yank him to his feet and clasp handcuffs around his wrists. But after a few moments, he heard nothing but the sound of water. He tried to open his eyes again as slowly as he could. A sharp pain stabbed behind his left eye, so he kept that one closed.

A gurgling and foamy creek, swollen from rain waters, rushed by him. The creek looked to be about ten feet across at its narrowest point and up to twenty feet wide downstream. Thick groupings of trees lined both sides of the creek, which Mick thought probably flowed much more lazily on normal days.

He took note of his surroundings and realized he was totally alone. Listening, he could hear the sound of a helicopter very far away. And when he gazed above the trees, a plume of smoke clouded the distant horizon.

Another breeze made him shiver; he desperately needed to get out of the water that had somehow carried him to safety. He rolled over and grabbed a thick tree root, pulling his feet out of the water and climbing up the embankment toward the wooded area. His teeth chattered violently enough that he thought he was going to inadvertently bite his tongue.

At the top of the four-foot embankment, Mick rolled to his back, took a few more deep breaths, and then sat up.

His duffel bag.

Across the creek, he saw it caught on a bobbing log at the water's edge. If he wanted it, he was going to have to wade across the creek to get it.

Right now, he wasn't even sure if he could stand.

Pressing his hands into the ground, he steadied himself

and tried, but as he did, sharp claws of pain scraped up the back of his calves and he yelped, collapsing to the ground. Situating himself, he turned and looked behind him, trying to figure out what was wrong.

Huge white blisters bubbled up from fire red skin. His jeans were singed and burned away. On his right leg, the burns were confined to the back of his calf, but on the left leg, they wrapped around his shin too.

Though painful, the blisters were signs that it was probably a severe second-degree burn. His entire body shook violently, protesting the pain and the cold it was being forced to endure. Mick looked again at the duffel bag dancing in the water.

He tried to remember how much money he had left. Twenty-five dollars or so? Plus he had a change of clothes in there too.

He managed to stand on trembling legs. As his body adjusted to the pain, he took a few careful steps, then used a tree that was growing horizontally across the water to help him down the embankment. He was just about to step into the water when he heard them.

Dogs.

Their hollow, frenzied barks carried through the windswept trees. Had the police discovered he'd made it out of the fire? It had stretched on both sides of the creek, swallowing up any good visuals for a while, he imagined. Were they now catching on that he'd escaped through the creek? The dogs wouldn't find a scent in the water.

Mick trudged forward, his shins pressing against the fast-moving water that rushed around his body. As he made his way toward his bag, the creek bed plunged, and the water now rose to his waist.

Even though his body was probably suffering from hypothermia, the pain in his legs slowly dulled. After a minute or so, he reached his duffel bag. He clasped his arms around the log and unhooked the bag, throwing it over his shoulder. Underneath him, the water swept his legs free from the bed, and Mick felt weightless and comfortable.

A water moccasin on a log that rested halfway out of the water greeted him with a forked tongue. It uncoiled and slithered into the water.

Mick swallowed hard. He hated snakes. Especially water snakes. Still gripping the log, he wondered what he should do now. His body wouldn't take much more of this abuse.

He laid his head on the log, his legs swinging weightlessly beneath him. The fact that he had been ready to give up caused him to rethink running again. Did he have any more energy left? any will to find what he was looking for? What *was* he looking for?

A delirious energy swarmed his mind. He felt half dead anyway. Why not go for it? If he got shot down, he'd be out of his misery. If he succeeded, in whatever he was supposed to be succeeding at, he'd be set free. At least in one sense.

He bobbed up and down in the water like a fishing cork, his stomach scraping against the log with each surge of frothy, reddish brown water. It lulled him but with the bite of a cold, uncaring mother.

With dull resignation, he stared downstream, unable to deny his own mortal shortcomings that had led him into this predicament. His tide had come in. He always knew it would. In every part of his life where he'd strayed from what he knew to be right, fear of the consequences diminished his gratification.

Ahead, the swollen creek wound around the trees and through the land, narrowing in the distance and curving so that Mick couldn't see where it headed. Feeling an unexplainable peace flood his insides, he allowed himself to breathe normally. He stopped trembling, like somebody had robed him with a heavy blanket. Perhaps God's gentle hand did reach down to hell after all.

He closed his eyes, holding back hopeless tears.

He was tired of running.

But he needed to find the truth.

Then a coarse but slimy ropelike sensation tickled his skin, and he felt something wrap around his ankle and climb up his leg. Thrashing in the water, Mick tried to pull up onto the log but couldn't grasp it tightly enough. With legs kicking, he tried to untangle himself out of its grip, but it wrapped tighter.

Mick's body went rigid with fear.

Punching his hand down into the water, Mick grabbed the snake, squeezing its body, attempting to pull it up out of the water and away from his leg, but it wasn't an easy task. The snake's tail clung to his ankle. With a mighty yank, he ripped half its body out of the water, his fingers squeezing mercilessly around it.

Holding it high over his head, shouting out his rage toward it, Mick stared into its face only to frown in disbelief.

This was no snake. It was a soggy, scummy tree limb, dripping water, not blood, from its mangled body. With a cynical laugh, Mick threw the limb into the water and rubbed his eyes. All he wanted was a warm bed. A jail bed would do nicely. At least he'd have dry clothes.

And then he heard the dogs again. The pitch of their bark was higher, and he could tell that their yelping pleas were advancing at a faster pace through the trees.

Gripping his bag, Mick released himself from the log. The fast-moving water carried him easily, and he paddled around obstacles. It was not an easy ride. He'd lose his footing against the creek bed and have to swim with all his might to try to stay above the water.

Something he couldn't identify kept him from releasing control and letting himself drown.

So he kept swimming.

———

After assuring Trisha he was not hitting on Liz, Aaron received his three-day pass back from the Gatekeeper of Flirtation with a careful smile. He took it, placed it in his bag, and left the gym through the front doors.

"Kline."

Whirling around, he spotted Shep Crawford leaning against the brick building like one might do while enjoying a smoke. But he wasn't smoking. His casual demeanor contrasted with his sharp eyes.

"Lieutenant."

Shep pitched a thumb to the door as he approached Aaron. "Good workout?"

"Sure."

A knowing smile put a small curve into the straight line of his lips. "Uh-huh."

"Why are you here?" Aaron asked.

"We found Mick."

The words punched his stomach. "You caught him?"

"I didn't say that."

"Then what?"

"He was spotted on the southwestern edge of Irving, riding a dirt bike. The chase is still on. We've got the chopper in the air, dogs on the ground."

"Is he armed?"

"Don't know."

"So he hasn't fired off a shot."

"No."

Aaron ran his fingers through his hair. "I pray they don't kill him."

Crawford said, "Looks like he was in to kill himself. He ran straight into an uncontrolled burn. They think he might still be in there somewhere. The fire's at least fifteen acres wide. I thought you should know."

"Know what?"

Crawford's expression didn't budge. "Your brother has messed a lot of things up by running."

"I have a feeling Mick's running for more than the reasons you think."

"Oh?"

"Mick's not a guy who scares easily. But he knows something. He senses there is more to this case than meets the eye."

"What has he told you?"

"I haven't seen or talked to him since he ran, if that's what you mean. But I agree with him. There's something more to this case." Aaron looked at Crawford. "Don't you agree?"

Crawford's eyes glazed with displeasure. "Rethink getting involved, Kline. I'm warning you. The consequences you could face for doing so aren't worth it."

"Is that a threat?"

Crawford didn't blink. "Some things that are put into motion cannot be stopped."

Aaron narrowed his eyes. "You're a man who likes justice, aren't you?"

Crawford's words were held back by an intensely drawn mouth. He seemed somewhat flustered by the comment, and Aaron had never known Crawford to be flustered. Anger flashed through Crawford's eyes. But it was followed by something else, something deeper.

"Just stay out the way," Crawford mumbled, then walked toward the parking lot, his body thrust forward as if his legs couldn't keep up.

Aaron looked around, still not spotting a tail. He watched Crawford speed away in his sedan.

Dropping his bag to the ground, he leaned onto the brick that had supported Crawford moments before. "Mick . . ." Part of him wanted them to catch Mick. But something urged him toward a prayer that was quite different from capture.

"Don't let them get you," he said aloud. "Keep running, brother. I'm close to the truth."

But in his mind's eye, he could only see a blazing fire consuming Mick.

chapter twenty-three

mick's skin felt thick and heavy and completely numb. The dark sky glowed faintly from the fire. Mick trudged to the littered embankment, where beer cans, fast-food cartons, paper, and oily residue piled along the banks.

All around him, shiny metal buildings reflected the dusky moon's timid light. He'd climbed out into a seemingly abandoned industrial park. Large cranes, motionless like fossilized dinosaurs, cast monstrous shadows across the gravel roads that wound around the quiet buildings. But there wasn't a car in sight, except the stream of headlights to the north. Loop 12?

He stumbled across the gravel, nauseous and hungry. When he reached a stretch of buildings, he tried a few doors, but they were all locked. A musty, pungent smell swept past his nostrils. He needed food soon.

Through the darkness, Mick wandered around, finding everything securely locked up. Then he spotted an open window, three stories high in what looked to be a large warehouse.

Small, metal rungs protruded from the west side of the building, which was not as tall as the rest of the warehouse. From the roof of that part of the building, he felt sure he could reach the open window.

Hoisting the bag over his shoulder, he feebly climbed

upward, breathing hard and shivering with each burst of wind. With an awkward roll over the top of the two-foot wall, Mick landed on his back with a thud.

It was colder up here.

Without wasting time, he made his way over to the window. He was high enough that he could see in the window, but it was so black inside he couldn't tell what was in there. He wondered if he had enough energy to lift himself up through it. With both hands, he grabbed the bottom of the window and pulled, hoping his feet could get a grip on the side of the metal warehouse. But his shoes, still soggy, slipped right out from under him, and he couldn't do much more than hang there.

Letting go, he kicked his shoes and socks off his shriveled feet. After airing them out a bit, he tried again. This time his sticky skin proved enough to give him leverage, and within seconds his waist was hanging over the windowsill and he was peering into a gigantic black hole. Clenching his teeth to manage the pain in his legs, he awkwardly scooted through the window onto a metal platform that he could see extended several feet each way. Beyond that, the warehouse was completely dark. Later in the night, as the moon moved across the sky, he might be able to see more, but for now he was next to blind.

He sat down, pulling his knees in. He immediately felt warmer. Looking around, he noticed a few cigarette butts. He hoped he was the only homeless person around tonight. Distant scratching sounds and high-pitched squeaking rose from behind nearby walls.

He had enough light to see his duffel bag, so he unzipped it and pulled out the contents. They dripped with creek water, and he laid everything out to dry. Then he fumbled around inside for his money. All that emerged was three dollars.

Frantically, he searched the bottom of the bag. The rest of the money must have fallen out somewhere along the creek. In a fit of rage, Mick threw the money back into the bag, zipped it up, and threw it down. He curled into a ball.

"I've done a lot of things I'm not proud of."

"You, Mick? You seem like such an outstanding citizen."

"Don't I? Hanging out at the bars at all hours of the night?"

"I'm serious. I see compassion in your eyes. A certain warm light."

"Sounds poetic."

"I should look hard into people's eyes more often. The window to the soul, right?"

"That's what they say."

"We all have our pasts, you know. They're not easy to shake."

"Sounds like you're talking from experience."

"We all try to reinvent ourselves, don't we? In some way. But that person we know ourselves to be continues to follow us. It spies on us, doesn't it? And reports everything it sees."

"I don't think too much about it."

"You live in the moment."

"I try to."

"So the woman you loved so much, you've forgotten her?"

"There are some things that will always stay in your heart."

"If only money could buy new hearts."

"Money can't buy a whole lot."

"I think it can. I think it can buy newness. And newness will go a long way."

"What does that mean?"

"It's not permanent. The real person always comes back.

> *But for a while, it is a certain kind of shelter from the world."*

"Haaa haaaaa!" A wide grin stretched across Mick's face as he lay on top of the roof, basking in the midmorning sun. Lying spread eagle, he felt warmth on his skin, through his bones, and into his blood for the first time in hours. The humid air meant thunderstorms would probably arrive later.

But right now, it never felt better to be warm. His nose tickled with the first indication of a cold, his eyes stung with fatigue, and the backs of his legs still gnawed with pain, but he wasn't wet and he wasn't chilled.

He didn't think it was possible, but two hours later, he felt hot. Drowsy but hungry, he was motivated to do more than sit there.

He donned another white T-shirt—the one from the bag—and the wind pants. The new T-shirt had a large cross on the front, and Aaron's church's logo and "Running for Jesus" printed across the back. Couldn't it have at least been another color? The appearance of his clothing had hardly changed, except now he looked like a priest. He'd put his shoes on without socks. While the creek was pretty muddy, it had actually washed him of the caked-on dirt, and it was probably the closest thing to a shower he was going to get.

Climbing down the ladder, he walked toward the sounds of traffic, wondering how far out of Irving he really was. If that was Loop 12, he was going to have to hitch a ride if he wanted to get anywhere fast.

He followed the road for about an hour but knew he was a long way from Irving. He wasn't really a man of prayer, but he was becoming one, and he didn't even care that it was because of desperation. He just knew he was out of options.

Mick entered the first parking lot he'd seen. It was attached to a large building with a computer-sounding name on the front. But apparently, whatever the business, it had been overly ambitious in its perceived need of parking space. Only about a fourth of the lot was full.

It was slightly elevated, and when Mick reached the top, he could see the swarming madness of Irving in the distance—perhaps ten or twelve miles away. Nothing to it in a car, but on foot, it would be a day's journey.

He heard laughter and turned. About thirty yards away, some junior-high-aged boys were doing acrobatics with their skateboards, bicycles, and scooters down a small entry ramp. He watched them for a few moments, and then a tall kid with spiky hair spotted him and yelled an obscenity at him. The other boys laughed.

Mick walked at a brisk pace toward them. A few other boys piped in their thoughts, though with a little less confidence than Spiky. As Mick approached, three or four of the eight boys looked nervous. The others folded their arms in front of their chests.

Standing about ten yards away, Mick looked at Spiky. "What'd you say to me?"

"What do you think I said?" Spiky laughed, and the other boys joined in.

"What in the world would make you say that?" Mick asked.

Spiky looked ready to fight as long as he had his gang behind him. "What are you doing out here?" Spiky asked, left hand on his hip, right arm embracing his skull skateboard.

Mick noticed his black T-shirt said "I'd Rather Be Dead."

"Aren't you all supposed to be in school?" Mick scanned each of them as guilt betrayed their faces. Mick thought this would be a good time to pull out Aaron's badge.

Spiky was just about to come up with some unclever way to use another profanity when a small boy with large brown freckles across his face gasped. Everyone turned to him, but he was staring at Mick.

"What is it, Bobby?" Spiky asked. Bobby's mouth was hanging open. "Bobby!"

Bobby glanced at Spiky, then back at Mick. "I-I know who you are," Bobby stammered.

The others turned their curious stares toward Mick.

"Is he famous?" another kid asked.

Bobby shook his head; then his eyes fell to Mick's duffel bag.

Mick wasn't sure what the boy's intentions were, but he knew one thing: He'd fight to the death to save the three bucks he had. He drew the bag toward himself, unzipping it slightly and sliding his hand in, hoping he could feel where the money was.

Bobby yelled, "He's got a gun!"

The other boys yelled too and started to run.

Mick shouted, "Stop! Don't any of you move!"

Bobby looked like he was about to hyperventilate. Stuttering, he said, "T-that's the guy!"

"What guy?" Spiky asked.

"The guy the police are after! He kidnapped a woman or something! He's a murderer!"

Mick swallowed as the boys' eyes grew large and round. A short, large kid in the back was trembling uncontrollably. Spiky's confidence had disappeared as his complexion grew pale.

"I didn't kill anybody," Mick said with what he'd intended to be a casual gesture. But his hand was still in the duffel bag, and when he moved it, all the kids hollered. "Settle down; settle down!" Mick yelled over the chaos.

Whimpering ensued.

Mick tried to think quickly. He'd been recognized, so that was going to be a problem. But he'd survived a raging fire. Surely he could survive a few bratty kids.

He turned his attention to a skinny kid in the back who was clutching his bicycle as if it were a limb. "You," Mick said, pointing to him, "come here. Bring the bike."

On shaking legs, the kid stepped forward, stopping about eight feet from Mick.

"Give me the bike," Mick said.

The kid complied, rolling it toward him. Mick noticed his name and phone number written on the side of the bike, and the kid noticed him notice.

Then Mick looked at a tall kid who was holding a Taco Bell sack. "What's in there?" he asked him.

"A b-b-bean b-burrito."

"Onions?"

"No."

"Hand it over."

The kid threw it to Mick, who caught it with one hand. "Anybody else got any snacks they want to tell me about?"

The big kid in the back mentioned he had gum.

Mick figured he'd better wrap this thing up before the kids figured out the weapon he was clutching in his bag was a soggy dollar bill. He looked at Spiky. "Give me your shirt."

Spiky's hands crawled up his chest as if Mick had just asked him for a vital organ. "My shirt?"

"You heard me."

Spiky glanced around at the other kids. A few still stared in dazed silence, but a couple had amused looks on their faces. Spiky slowly peeled off his shirt, revealing a bony, white torso. A few kids snickered in the back. Spiky shot them a look, then threw the shirt to Mick.

Mick took off his shirt, and to everyone's great surprise, threw it to Spiky, who couldn't have looked more stunned.

"Put it on," Mick said, suppressing a smile.

Spiky eyed the duffel bag, looked around at his cohorts, and then slowly put the shirt on.

"Running for Jesus!" one kid howled, reading the back of the shirt.

"Shut up!" Spiky yelled.

"All of you, listen up," Mick said, after putting on Spiky's shirt. Maybe they wouldn't be looking for a fugitive with the words *I'd Rather Be Dead* on his black shirt. Then again, if the kids talked, they could describe exactly what he was wearing. "Here's the deal. If any of you say a word about seeing me, I'm going to call each and every one of your mothers and tell them that you ditched school today." He looked each of them in the eye. A few looked like they'd rather be shot dead right then and there. "And you know what I'd do if I were you?"

They all shook their heads.

No, Mick imagined they had no idea. "I'd go back home and find a local church, and I'd go in and get down on my knees and pray for forgiveness for using such awful cusswords."

Spiky, in particular, looked perplexed.

"And you, my friend, do not take that shirt off until you get home." Mick swung his leg over the bike and said, "Now, if I were you, I'd run and run fast. *Go!*"

The boys shouted and turned, clutching whatever they could carry and racing down the entrance ramp into a nearby, grassy stretch of land that led to a viaduct.

Mick ripped open the Taco Bell sack.

After that episode, Mick realized he was probably more delirious than he wanted to acknowledge. Fatigue and pain were making him bolder than he really should be, and the fact that he was peddling along a service road in the middle of the day wearing a T-shirt saying he'd rather be dead was proof enough.

He headed toward Irving with burning legs, sporting old-man sunglasses, a young man's smelly T-shirt, and an attitude that was something akin to suicidal.

But what did he have to lose?

Shep Crawford scrawled with permanent marker as fast as he could. The words came faster than he could write. But he tried. After ten minutes, he backed away from the large wall on which he'd scribbled and stared at it. The wall stretched twenty feet wide and was about eight feet tall. It once held a mural in the old firehouse. Now it held Crawford's sanity.

Like unraveling yarn, a black mess of scribbles captured years of journal-like thoughts onto drywall, hiding the incoherent thoughts of a madman.

Crawford clicked the lid back onto the red marker and placed it in the drawer that held the rest of his various-colored Sharpies. In all the years he'd lived in this firehouse, he'd used red only four times. Amidst the dark colors, the red lines bled through, catching the eye quite majestically, he thought.

Moving to the open second-story window, Crawford gazed out at the sky, drawing in fresh air through his nostrils. As much as he tried not to think about the runt, Crawford could not shake Fiscall out of his mind. He simply could not understand, for any reason, a man who would lose his soul for political gain.

Rubbing his eyes and stretching his arms upward in a relieving yawn, Crawford made his way downstairs, where his teapot was screaming. Taking it off the stove, he poured himself a cup of hot water and steeped a green-tea bag, bobbing it up and down for several minutes, unaware that the liquid in his cup was nearly black now.

His thoughts continued to consume him.

But what comforted Crawford was the fact that he was totally in control. Despite the chaos that had erupted because of those who were incompetent, Crawford knew that things would be as they should. He smiled at that thought, lifted the tea bag out of the mug, and placed it in his mouth, sucking out the flavor. Then he spit it in the trash.

Sipping his tea as he leaned against the wooden island in the middle of the large kitchen, Crawford stared at the American flag that covered the wall near the stairs.

He hummed "The Star-Spangled Banner," watching the flag as if it were on a pole, flapping its glory in the wind. The hum turned into a recital of the third verse. Hardly anyone knew it, but it was seared onto his heart.

"'And where is that band who so vauntingly swore that the havoc of war and the battle's confusion, a home and a country should leave us no more?'" Crawford gestured upward, as if he had an entire choir singing behind him. "'Their blood has wash'd out their foul footsteps' pollution. No refuge could save the hireling and slave from the terror of flight or the gloom of the grave.'" He walked to his front door, carefully watching the street as he said, "'And the star-spangled banner in triumph doth wave, o'er the land of the free and the home of the brave.'"

chapter twenty-four

With each mile, Mick's resolve built. He peddled rhythmically, never looking around, never worried he would be seen. He simply pressed forward.

A cooling breeze tore through his stubbly hair, but the wind would not erase the unbelievable stench coming from the shirt he'd traded. Part of him wanted to jump in a river to try to wash away all the grime. But he couldn't afford the time to dry out again. So he pedaled on, trying to forget what now cloaked him. Why would anybody in their right mind trade a nearly clean white shirt for this rag?

Above him, the highway roared, and Mick wound his way through an old commercial district. Generations-old businesses, like tire stores and donut shops, lined the streets. Elderly people sat in chairs and talked or played dominoes. Large oak trees on the corners told of how long this area had been around. How many times had he seen new developments, with skinny, sickly trees everywhere, their roots as feeble as white string? Yes, this place had roots. Deep roots.

Mick sighed as he sped through a four-way stop. Roots. He'd managed to cut his off. His parents still loved him and of course talked to him, but Mick had wanted separation from their old-time ideals. The final blow of the ax had been Aaron's decision to take Jenny, but he knew deep in his heart that he'd been separated from his brother long before that.

Mick had never really understood Aaron's religious fervor. His parents, though always religious, were much quieter about their faith. They'd raised Mick in church, but once he was on his own, they let him make his own choices. Aaron, on the other hand, could never let things rest.

Yet there was something oddly endearing about his dogmatic tendencies. Mick hated to admit it, but the way Aaron chased him, like one of the hounds from heaven, was strangely comforting. It was as if Mick knew he couldn't run too far away. But now he had. He'd outrun the hounds. He'd fled to the dark side of the mountain.

Mick wiped the sweat from his brow and continued toward downtown Irving. He looked to be only three miles away.

He turned onto Las Colinas Boulevard and rode his bike onto the sidewalk, where he hopped off and walked it toward the Irving Convention and Visitors Bureau. Pressing his lips together in hopeful determination, he looked for a large bus across the street in the parking lot. Five years ago, Mick had met a woman at a club who was from out of town. She had said she'd love to get to know Dallas better, so Mick found out that Irving offered visitors a tour from Irving to the Dallas/Fort Worth area.

Mick parked his bike on the rack bolted into the sidewalk next to the Visitors Bureau. Inside, an elderly woman greeted him from behind a plastic ticket-booth window.

"Do you still offer the visitors' tour?"

The woman looked at the schedule on the wall. "Yes, we do."

"What time does it run?"

"Only on the weekends."

Mick sighed.

The woman studied him. "You really want to go?"

"Yeah."

She looked around and said, "Well, in an hour there's a special seniors' trip going."

"Really?" Mick's eyes widened with hope.

She nodded. "I'll have to get special permission, but we'd hate to turn down somebody who wants to see our great cities!"

"I would be so grateful." Mick smiled. A fleeting flash of fear told him that at any moment this woman could recognize him, but he kept his smile steady and his eyes locked to hers.

"Hold on. Let me see what I can do."

Mick waited, and after a few minutes the woman returned with a guest pass in her hand. "It leaves from across the parking lot in an hour." She gave a playful wink. Apparently she couldn't smell him from the other side of the window.

"Thanks," Mick said, taking the pass.

"That'll be five dollars."

Mick grimaced. "I don't have five dollars."

She looked at him curiously. "Really?"

"Yeah."

"Well, don't worry about it, okay? Go on, enjoy yourself. You look like you could use some relaxation." She was reading his T-shirt.

Mick laughed. "That's the truth." He met her eyes. "Thank you."

"You're very welcome, young man," she said. "Every once in a while, we all need a little grace."

Aaron hung up the phone and sat down at his kitchen table. The flowers that Taylor had received before she disappeared struck him as odd, and now he knew why. After an hour's worth of investigation, Aaron found out that the bouquet had cost over a hundred dollars. At first he didn't think much about it. He was actually calling to see if anybody at the flower shop remembered the voice of the person who had ordered them or anything at all about the phone call. Nobody did. As an afterthought, Aaron had asked about the cost.

A hundred dollars seemed like an awful lot of money for a man who, according to Liz Lane, was as cheap as they come. Aaron tried to connect the dots, but right now the picture being drawn was only a jagged, uninterpretable line.

He'd also found out a little more information about Taylor Franks, though it didn't seem immediately helpful. She'd worked for a while at the front ticket counter before moving to the gate. So she sold people airline tickets. Right now that did nothing to explain her disappearance.

Aaron had every reason to believe that Sammy Earle was involved, but he had no way to prove it. And little room to maneuver to try to. Shep Crawford and his maniacal tactics didn't scare him. But he knew if he made the wrong move, he could permanently end his career in law enforcement, not to mention hurt the case against his brother.

His doorbell rang and Aaron rose, hopeful and fearful at the same time.

When he opened the door, his partner, Jarrod, greeted him with a smile atop a worried expression. "Hey, Aaron."

"Jarrod. Hey. Come in."

Jarrod walked in and held out his hand to Aaron. "How are you?"

Aaron shook it. Jarrod's depressive tone worried him. "I'm okay. What are you doing here?"

"Just came to check on you."

Aaron guided him to the living room, where they sat down. "How's work?"

Jarrod shrugged. "It's okay. They've got me with Jay Caroll now. Not a bad cop, just sort of stiff. Hard to talk to."

"Yeah. Doesn't have much to say unless it concerns baseball, from what I've found. But he'll teach you a lot. He's a great guy."

Jarrod nodded, staring at the beige carpet under his feet. "There's news?"

"Not really. Nothing more on the evidence that I've heard. But I know that the DA is going to step it up a notch in the hunt for Mick. He wants him."

"What, another news conference?"

"Probably. The guy likes to see his ugly mug on TV."

"So it's Fiscall behind all this?"

Jarrod nodded. "From what I can tell. Rumor has it that Lieutenant Crawford disagreed with the decision to name Mick as the suspect."

"He wanted Earle?"

"Didn't say. I just think the evidence was too ambiguous. If Mick hadn't been there the night before . . ."

"I know, I know." Aaron sighed, standing and walking to the back window, gazing out at nothing but bad memories. "I know."

"Any idea where Mick might be?" Jarrod asked.

Aaron hesitated. Was that an innocent question, or had Jarrod been sent? He knew Jarrod could be impressionable and easily influenced. His brown eyes stared vigorously at everything but Aaron.

"No idea," Aaron said, continuing to look at his green yard. How much time he'd spent making his lawn perfect. But as fall arrived, the grass was fading, dying with the season. He wondered why he spent so much time making everything around him look perfect. Why did he strive for things that weren't attainable or attain things that would eventually die?

"Aaron?"

Aaron turned. "Sorry. Deep in thought."

"You have a lot on your mind." Jarrod offered a smile, but Aaron's suspicions rejected the sentiment.

"Yeah, sorry; probably not good company right now."

Jarrod took the hint and stood. "Right." He stuffed his hands in his jeans pockets and made his way to the front door. Aaron opened it for him.

Jarrod was about to say something that was sure to be cordial, but Aaron cut him off. "You should know, Jarrod, that Mick is innocent."

"Sure, Aaron."

"I would bet my life on it."

"No kidding. Don't you think that's misplaced confidence? Your brother has done nothing but mess up his whole life. And I believe I'm using your words. *Innocent* is overstating it a little, isn't it?"

"He doesn't have to earn the right to innocence in this situation," Aaron said. "He's innocent until proven guilty."

Jarrod agreed. "Yeah. Too bad most of us are guilty of much more than our crimes." He patted Aaron on the shoulder. "Have a good day. I'll let you know if anything breaks."

Aaron watched him walk off the front porch to his car. He couldn't return the short wave Jarrod gave as he drove off.

What was it going to take to clear the name of a man whose name was synonymous with wrongdoing?

The tour guide, a middle-aged man who looked like he'd rather be doing anything but showing out-of-towners around the city, handed Mick his guest pass. "Sure, whatever Nowella says. I swear she'd let every street person on the bus if she could."

Mick managed to smile. "I'm not a street person."

The man, whose name tag read Simon, sniffed. "No kidding."

"Just had a hard day's work, that's all."

"Ah." The man eyed the skull and crossbones on Mick's shirt. "Mind sitting in the back?"

"No." Mick got on the bus. As he walked toward the rear, he heard a few of the seniors mumble. What'd he give for his brother's Running for Jesus shirt right now.

He sat in the very back, his least-favorite seat when he was a kid. He had always liked to be in the center of the action, mostly around the cheerleaders.

Simon was the last on the bus, and he greeted the seniors with a nod and a forced smile. "Who's ready to see the Metroplex?"

Fanciful cheers erupted and Simon's glassy eyes tried to acknowledge the crowd with a bit of enthusiasm. He asked a few people about where they were from. Mick couldn't have orchestrated this better. Since no one was from around here, he had much less of a chance of being recognized.

And Simon looked like if he did recognize him, he wouldn't have the energy to do anything about it.

Leaning on the pole at the front of the bus and grabbing a microphone, Simon introduced the driver and the tour began. Mick stared out the window. At some point, he was going to have to find a way to get off.

Thanks to the common condition of overactive bladders that often plagues seniors, Mick had no trouble finding a time to get off the bus. It stopped every thirty minutes for a bathroom break.

When they stopped near downtown Dallas, Mick decided this was probably going to be his best bet. He was unsure if they would stop again inside the downtown area.

After everyone was off the bus and headed into the gas station, Mick circled to the back of the bus and wandered off. Simon, who was at the espresso machine, wouldn't notice he was gone.

Mick walked toward the skyscrapers, and before he knew it, their shadows loomed over him. He'd grown used to the hot, throbbing pain at the bottom of his legs, the result of treading through fire and living to tell about it.

The search for the truth had filled his soul with an urgency, an appreciation for life, an acknowledgment of mortality. For once in his life, he had not done anything wrong, but it was his past sins that now haunted him into this present, hanging over him like the shadows of skyscrapers. He would have to walk long and hard to get out from under them. But he knew as the sun moved, the shadows only grew longer.

A phone booth across the street caught Mick's attention, and he crossed at the light. Inside, he opened up the chained phone book and turned to the yellow pages. After a few moments, he found it: Sammy Earle, Attorney-at-Law. Mick ripped out the page and stuffed it in his pocket.

chapter twenty-five

Stephen Fiscall laid his hand casually next to his phone, never taking his eyes off the man who stood over him at the edge of his desk. In one sense, Fiscall had every right to call the man's captain. But something told him that Fred Bellows was another puppet on Shep Crawford's stage of theatrics.

And besides, if he called Bellows it would seem like Fiscall couldn't handle Crawford, and that was the last impression he wanted to give. His ambitions in life called for him to rise to the occasion. Though he doubted he would have to face many more Shep Crawfords in his career.

This guy was one in a million.

Fiscall waited for him to finish, then offered a polite but pugnacious smile. If he needed to, he could call security very quickly. His fingers twitched beside the number pad.

"Look, Lieutenant," Fiscall said carefully, hoping the use of his rank would help stroke the ego that apparently felt neglected. "I can understand your frustration. I hope you know that."

Crawford cocked his head.

Fiscall had no idea what that meant, so he continued. "But the facts speak for themselves. It surprises me that you are not acknowledging this."

"The facts."

"Sammy Earle wasn't there. Sammy Earle hasn't seen the woman in months. And before you mention the flowers," Fiscall said, raising a finger to cut him off, "we cannot find any evidence linking him to those flowers. It's an odd occurrence; I'll grant you that. But right now, it does more to prove Earle wasn't involved."

Fiscall glanced at Crawford, then casually looked away, as if something more interesting lay at the corner of the room. "They call you the Blood Man, and I understand your love for it as evidence. Granted, we have traces of blood. The only other evidence we have that something bad has happened to Miss Franks is her attempted 911 call and a cut window screen. A man was seen leaving her apartment. A man who was so drunk he 'doesn't remember' the night before. Now I'm not sure why you're so adamant against Mick Kline being our man, but I think you're mistaken." The word *mistaken* rolled off Fiscall's tongue with trepidation.

"Fiscall, you are a snake. The only reason you're after Kline is because a successful prosecution of a cop's brother would bring you more publicity. Frankly, I think you're scared to death that you couldn't prosecute a savvy lawyer like Earle."

"Your finely minced words are not going to do anything to change my mind. What I'd like you to be doing—instead of badgering me about how smart you are and how dumb I am—is to be out there hunting Kline down so I can prosecute him for kidnapping. And if you have some extra time on your hands, it'd be nice to find a body in a nearby lake." Fiscall stood, though he still remained a foot shorter than Crawford, and smiled.

Crawford did not smile back. "And what happens to Earle? We just leave him alone; is that it?"

"Earle is not our suspect, for the hundreth time. Mick

Kline is. And in case you've forgotten, your superiors agree with me and disagree with you. I know this has been hard for you to get used to, Crawford. Normally you're the one calling all the shots. Unfortunately, this time it's me."

Fiscall observed a purple darkness encircle Crawford's raging eyes, as if all the blood in his body were surfacing just beneath the skin of his bottom lid. But then he seemed to gather himself, and Fiscall felt the air clear a little.

Crawford smirked and lazily ran a hand through his rumpled hair. "There once was a man, many years ago, who folded to political pressure."

"I'm not folding to anything," Fiscall snapped.

"He may have cared about innocence and guilt. But at the end of the day, it was politics that caused him to betray his convictions." Crawford stared at him. "And I can't say that you care about either of those things."

Fiscall sneered. "To whomever you're referring, I don't know. But you obviously have no sense of the office I hold, Lieutenant. Nor any respect for it. I have not gotten to where I am today by folding to pressures, sir. Yours or anybody else's. Stick to what you do best, Crawford. Follow the blood trail."

Then Crawford did something completely unexpected, causing Fiscall to nearly gasp. He stuck out his hand for Fiscall to shake.

Fiscall looked at it as if it were a weapon. In order to shake it, Fiscall's hand would have to leave the security of the phone behind, if only for a few seconds. The absurdity of fearing a homicide detective danced across Fiscall's intellect. Crawford was quirky and egotistical. But that was it, right? Fiscall licked his lips and offered his hand, trying to keep it from shaking.

Crawford squeezed it, holding it hostage for several uncomfortable seconds.

Fiscall gazed into the abyss of his eyes.

"You do what you have to do," Crawford said and then let go of his hand.

Fiscall took a step backward, though his desk was between them. He tried to project confidence, holding his head up and swelling his chest with a deep breath.

Crawford had turned and walked to the door. Before leaving, he glanced back at Fiscall and said, "Pilate."

"Excuse me?"

"Pontius Pilate. That's who I was referring to."

Fiscall shook his head. "I didn't realize you were a religious man, Crawford."

"I'm not."

Mick walked through the revolving door of the plaza building and entered an overly air-conditioned lobby sparkling with gold decor and shiny white marble.

Across the room two security guards chatted, watching an attractive woman shuffle through her briefcase. To one side of the lobby were four elevators surrounded by floor-to-ceiling mirrors. Among the business professionals Mick stood out, but he knew not too badly. He was sure there were many lawyers in the building with clients who looked worse than he did.

He waited around until he could grab an elevator by himself. One opened up, several people rushed out, and Mick slipped in, double punching the Close Door button, though he never thought those buttons ever worked very well.

The elevator swiftly lifted him to his eleventh-floor destination. In the hallway, Mick noticed three different suites, but there was no question which was Earle's. A large, gold-plated sign, with letters about two feet high, read

Earle, Jacobs, and Welleston. All big-name attorneys in one of the best-known law firms in Dallas.

Mick had no game plan, just determination. He wasn't even sure what he was going to say once he got to Earle . . . if he got to him. And he knew there was probably little chance of his leaving this building without handcuffs around his wrists or bullets through his gut.

But sometimes the truth was worth a high cost.

He opened the glass door. A large, gaudy reception area greeted him, minus the receptionist. Mick noted that the office seemed unusually quiet. A large silver digital clock read 12:22. Lunchtime.

Two hallways led in opposite directions from the reception area, and Mick had no choice but to guess. He turned right and passed a small office, where a man was eating a sandwich, oblivious to anything other than his bologna. A woman approached him, but her nose was buried in a folder, and she never looked up as she passed him.

He came to a door with Earle's name on it. A medium-sized reception area was to the right, apparently for his secretary. Her computer was on, with a word-processing document on the screen. To his surprise, Earle's door was open. Mick walked straight in, his fists clutched and his teeth grinding.

The office was empty. Earle's laptop sat on his desk, closed, and his chair was swiveled toward the window. A small cabinet sat nearby, and on top of it was a McDonald's Monopoly game, pieces neatly glued in place. For as garish as the letters were that announced his name on his door, Earle's office was comparatively reserved, with second-hand-looking furniture and mediocre office equipment. The aqua-colored wall art looked to be purchased from a hotel auction.

Mick quietly shut the door, then went to Earle's desk,

trying to find some kind of link to Taylor Franks. He opened desk drawers, sifting through papers and junk, but nothing caught his eye. Mick thought it odd that the man didn't even have any photographs in his office. In fact, he saw nothing at all personal about Sammy Earle here. The office was frighteningly void of any human touch.

Mick doubted he would find any evidence here anyway. A slick lawyer like Earle wasn't going to leave anything lying around. Mick sat in Earle's chair and stared at the laptop, his fingers playing with the Release button on its edge.

Maybe a letter? Mick glanced at the closed door, then without further hesitation, snapped open the laptop. The screen blinked to life and was open to some legal form in WordPerfect. Mick opened the folders and scanned through them, but they all seemed to be business related.

And then he heard the doorknob click.

Mick slammed the laptop shut and shot to his feet.

Even after eating brunch with Jenny, Aaron still couldn't shake the restless, simmering anger. Things were not adding up, questions were being raised that had no answers, and yet the prosecutors and detectives seemed to indicate they had all the evidence they needed.

Aaron's confidence about Mick had wavered, especially after he ran. But the more questions that opened up, the more Aaron began to suspect that something strange was going on. What that was, he didn't know. But after talking with Liz, Aaron's suspicions were quickly falling on Sammy Earle. How was he going to get everybody else to pay attention, though?

Aaron had paced the halls of his home long enough. If the cops were going to tail him, then so be it. He didn't have anything to hide, and Crawford's threats didn't scare him. Nobody else was looking under rocks. Aaron decided it was his time to play the snake.

Getting in his pickup, he drove to Taylor Franks' apartment. The yellow tape had been taken down, probably at the request of the apartment manager. Aaron walked to the manager's office, who luckily recognized him and agreed to open the apartment for him.

As he unlocked the door, Chuck asked, "Any word on Miss Franks?"

Aaron shook his head. "Unfortunately, no."

"This world, it's so nuts." He opened the door. "Here you go. Just let me know before you leave so I can lock it."

"Thanks, Chuck." Aaron entered the apartment and looked around. Nothing had been touched. He coughed just to clear the eerie silence.

He wandered around the edges of the living room, then found a collection of photo albums in a small chest near the television. Sitting on the floor, he flipped through the first one, looking at pictures of Taylor's childhood, many taken in front of a trailer home. Her mother's eyes, narrow with tiredness, made her smile looked forced. Taylor, if he guessed correctly who she was from the photos, looked like an energetic kid whom nobody had told she was starting out rough. A wide smile brightened her torn and dirty clothes. Her hair was stuck into a tangled ponytail.

In the next photo album, apparently from Taylor's high school years, her cheery eyes were sparked by something else . . . defiance? In many of the pictures beer cans and cigarettes were in plain view.

The third photo album looked to be the most recent. Only about ten pages were filled. There was a picture with Liz Lane and another one with what might have been her coworkers.

Aaron started to close the album when a picture fell

out the back. It was a picture of Taylor with Sammy. They were at a party, and he was smiling casually at the camera. Just behind him, but definitely in the background, was Taylor, who was staring at the camera awkwardly, smiling timidly. Sammy Earle didn't even seem to know she was there.

Aaron remembered the framed photograph of the couple, which had been knocked over by the window in Taylor's apartment. It had been taken as evidence. Why would she keep a photograph out after they broke it off?

Aaron closed the albums and put them back in the chest. He walked to the kitchen, looked around, and then headed down the hallway. As he did, he tried to imagine what might have happened. He envisioned the woman being dragged down the hallway. Did she scream? Did she struggle? Was she forced? or tricked?

Aaron observed her bedroom, trying to see if anything seemed out of place. But after fifteen minutes, still nothing significant.

He sat on her bed, pulling out the small bedside drawer. Inside was a Bible, looking nearly brand-new. Aaron picked it up and flipped through it. Most of the pages were still crisp, unread, but there was a bookmark in Esther. Immediately Aaron noticed that passages and verses were underlined, highlighted, starred. He could hardly believe it. Not a single page in the rest of the Bible looked to be touched, but Esther had been well-read.

Aaron focused on what Taylor had underlined, various seemingly unrelated verses in the first chapter of Esther.

"On the seventh day of the feast, when King Xerxes was half drunk with wine, he told Mehuman, Biztha, Harbona, Bigtha, Abagtha, Zethar, and Carcas, the seven eunuchs who attended him, to bring Queen

Vashti to him with the royal crown on her head. He wanted all the men to gaze on her beauty, for she was a very beautiful woman. But when they conveyed the king's order to Queen Vashti, she refused to come."

Refused to come was underlined twice.

"Women everywhere will begin to despise their husbands when they learn that Queen Vashti has refused to appear before the king. Before this day is out, the wife of every one of us, your officials throughout the empire, will hear what the queen did and will start talking to their husbands the same way.

"One day as Mordecai was on duty at the palace, two of the king's eunuchs, Bigthana and Teresh—who were guards at the door of the king's private quarters—became angry at King Xerxes and plotted to assassinate him."

Taylor's attention seemed to be on King Xerxes and his relationship with Queen Vashti, but it seemed she had missed the forest for the trees. What exactly was she searching for from God's Word? An answer? A solution? And why the book of Esther?

For Aaron, the book's theme showed Esther's bravery when one of the king's men decided to plot to annihilate all the Jews and her and Mordecai's ingenuity in exposing the man for who he was.

Aaron wasn't sure if Taylor had read the rest of the book. Flipping through it, he didn't see anything else that was underlined. If Taylor had read the rest of the book, she would know that King Xerxes became a hero to the Jews and a friend to them. But what Taylor was underlining didn't make sense in the context of the story.

Flipping back through the pages, Aaron found one more set of verses underlined with a light blue pen in chapter 4. He'd almost missed it.

"Mordecai sent back this reply to Esther: 'Don't think for a moment that you will escape there in the palace when all other Jews are killed. If you keep quiet at a time like this, deliverance for the Jews will arise from some other place, but you and your relatives will die. What's more, who can say but that you have been elevated to the palace for such a time as this?'"

The very end was underlined:

"Then Esther sent this reply to Mordecai: 'Go and gather together all the Jews of Susa and fast for me. Do not eat or drink for three days, night or day. My maids and I will do the same. And then, though it is against the law, I will go in to see the king. If I must die, I am willing to die.'"

Aaron shook his head, riffled through the rest of the Bible one more time, and closed it, putting it gently back in the drawer. This woman was becoming more and more of an enigma. Something told him he wasn't seeing the forest for the trees either.

———

The door swung open and a woman with large glasses and curly hair walked inside, sifting through some papers. "Jim says he needs this signed today, and Rick Stanley called, said that the meeting is on for tomorrow at two—" She looked up, stopped, and stared at Mick. The papers fell out of the folder and slid across the floor.

Mick reached in his back pocket and pulled out Aaron's badge. "Don't be scared, ma'am. I'm with the police."

She glanced at his clothes, her face still bright with fear.

"Undercover," Mick added quickly.

"What are you doing here?" she breathed, uncertainty building with each drawled word she spoke.

"We're still investigating the disappearance of Taylor Franks. What is your name, ma'am?"

The woman's eyes widened. "Uh-uh . . . JoAnne."

"JoAnne what?" Mick tried his best to get the attention off him.

"Meeler. JoAnne Meeler."

"And what is your relationship with Taylor Franks?" Mick lowered his voice, trying to sound authoritative. Apparently it was working. JoAnne looked like she'd been caught red-handed.

"Nothing. No. Don't know her."

Mick went to the door and shut it, gesturing toward a chair that JoAnne should sit in, which she did. While her back was turned, Mick quietly turned the lock. "You're telling me you don't know Taylor Franks?"

JoAnne stuttered through a difficult sentence until it finally came out. "N-no. Yes. I-I mean, I don't know her. I've t-talked to her a couple of times on the phone, but—"

"A couple of times on the phone?"

"She was calling for Mr Earle." JoAnne looked like she was about to hyperventilate. "I don't know the woman. She called for him all the time."

"So you talked to her more than twice?"

JoAnne's face flushed. "Yes, of course I talked to her, but nothing more than saying, 'Hold on; let me see if he's in.' There were two times that I can remember that I had a longer conversation with her."

"About?"

"Once she was very upset, crying hysterically, as I recall. I never could quite understand what the matter was, but at the end of it, I gathered they'd had some sort of fight."

"And the other time?"

"It was shortly before they broke up. She called, was real curt. Snapped at me, said some things about Sammy."

"What kinds of things?"

"Well, I don't cuss so I couldn't say, but I'm sure you can figure it out."

"So she was mad at him."

"You could say that."

"Do you know why?"

JoAnne was staring at Mick, pushing her glasses up her nose with a shaking hand.

"Ma'am? Do you know why she was mad at Mr. Earle?"

JoAnn didn't answer and Mick grew hopeful. The woman knew something. Something very important. "Ma'am? I'm asking if you knew why she was mad. If you know something, you need to say it."

JoAnne stood up suddenly, backing away, trembling from head to toe.

"Ma'am?"

She stumbled over a rug, catching herself on the side of Earle's desk. "Stop it! Right there! Stay where you are!"

Mick squeezed the badge in his hand. "Ms. Meeler, you—"

"You're him!" she said frantically. "You're the—you're Mick Kline!"

chapter twenty-six

mick held out his hands, trying to calm JoAnne down. But the color had drained from her face, and she was now backed up against the far wall of the office.

"Don't scream," Mick said.

JoAnne opened her mouth like she intended to do just that, but all that came out were strange gurgling noises. One hand was patting her chest as if she were trying to restart her heart, and the other was pointing and waving at him as if she were hoping it would turn into a gun.

"Ma'am!" Mick said, his tone cautious but stern. "Calm down! I'm not going to hurt you!"

JoAnne swallowed, her hands dropping to her sides, then flat against the wall behind her. "Wh-what are you doing here?" Tears brimmed.

"I'm not going to hurt you," Mick reiterated. "I'm just here to find out what happened to Taylor. The police want to pin this on me, but I didn't do it. All I want to know is what happened to Taylor and who's behind it. That's all." He studied JoAnne's face, and some of what he was saying seemed to register. But she still looked scared.

Mick continued. "I think Sammy Earle could be behind this. I've done some research on him, and the fact of the matter is, he's not the most compassionate guy around. Heard he's not very nice."

"It's true," JoAnne agreed. "He's not a very nice man." Her body relaxed a little, though she was still so flat against the wall she looked like part of the wallpaper.

"Sounds like you have firsthand knowledge of this," Mick said. He put his hands in his pockets, trying to look casual. JoAnne looked away. "It's okay. You can tell me. Anything you tell me could help."

JoAnne's nostrils flared, and her expression clouded. "He's the definition of *jerk*."

"What does he do?"

"Thinks he rules the world. No respect. No kindness. I don't know that he's ever said a nice thing to me, to tell you the truth. Most of the time he complains about my hair or what I wear. It's like he's embarrassed that I work for him, but I'm probably the only person who will put up with his ego. I've noticed he only treats women this way. He treats me like I'm trash, and I serve him like he's some king." She glanced at Mick with shame. "I'm not proud of it."

"So why do you work for him?"

"I probably should tell him where to shove it, but I need this job. It's got benefits and pays well. So I put up with it. He probably knows that too."

"What do his coworkers think of him?"

"As long as he's bringing in the big dough and the big clients, what do they care?" JoAnne folded her arms against her chest.

Mick stepped closer. She hardly seemed to notice. She was thinking something troubling by the way her eyebrows folded inward. "What do you know about his relationship with Taylor?"

"Not much," JoAnne said.

Mick sensed she wasn't telling everything she knew. "When she disappeared, did people call here, wondering if Sammy was okay or upset?"

"Naw. Nobody really knew Taylor's name. I mean, he'd take her to parties and stuff but wouldn't introduce her to many people. She'd sit in a corner by herself. If a man came up to talk with her, then Sammy would be right there. But other than that, she was expected to just stay out of the way. It was like Sammy wanted a beautiful woman on his arm but didn't want to deal with caring about her."

"He's a cold man."

JoAnne didn't respond.

"Look, I need information, and I have a feeling that if roles were reversed, Sammy Earle would have no qualms about digging up dirt on you and sharing it with the world. Now is your chance to give information to somebody who could set things straight. Maybe even save someone's life."

"You think Sammy Earle could murder somebody? or kidnap them?" JoAnne asked.

"Sounds like he would have no problem getting rid of something that's in his way, even if it was a human being."

JoAnne looked sideways, her eyes cast away in deep thought. Then she looked at Mick. "I'll tell you this, but I swear I'll deny it if anybody asks me. Sammy would kill me if he knew I knew. And he doesn't know I know, so I would rather it stay that way."

"Okay."

She took a deep breath. "This is all I know. One day— it's been a year or so ago—Taylor came up here and broke up with Sammy. I think Sammy was pretty shocked. He thought she was totally dependent on him, you know? I guess he didn't realize there's only so much a woman can take. So she was really bold, came here to do it in person and give him a piece of her mind. There was a lot of shouting, I know that. And after about fifteen minutes, Taylor left. She looked pretty calm. But Sammy was beside himself. He had to leave the office."

"Interesting."

JoAnne nodded. "But here's what I wanted to say. I think this will tell you what kind of person Sammy Earle really is. A couple of weeks after they broke up, he ruined her credit."

"How?"

"Somehow he got ahold of some documents and falsified information, from what I could tell. Anyway, her credit is completely ruined, and she can't get a credit card or a loan or anything. It will probably take her years to get it straightened out, and of course Sammy covered his tracks really well, I'm assuming. He's pretty slick."

"How do you know this?"

"I heard most of it through the door. Sammy talks really loud, especially when he's mad. Taylor called as soon as she figured out what he did, and Sammy just laughed and told her she had it coming."

Mick shook his head. "That's unbelievable. I don't understand why the police aren't looking at this angle."

"One cop came by not long after it happened. But he's the only one who's been here. I guess he was just confirming that Sammy had an alibi. I don't know what that alibi is, though."

Mick scratched his head and leaned on Sammy's desk. "JoAnne, is there anything else you can tell me that would help?"

"There's really not. That's all I know."

Mick sighed.

The doorknob rattled on Earle's office door. Mick spun toward the door. JoAnne covered her mouth.

Outside, they could hear Sammy swearing. "JoAnne! Where are you? My door's locked! Why is my door locked?!"

JoAnne stared at Mick, who gestured with his hands to

stay calm. He moved closer to her and whispered, "He doesn't have a key?"

"No," she whispered back. "He never locks it."

Mick looked out the window. "No fire escape?"

"Not through this office." JoAnne was trembling again.

Mick put a gentle hand on her shoulder while they listened to Sammy curse and call JoAnne all kinds of despicable names. JoAnne's eyes reflected the lacerating effects of his words.

"Don't listen to that nonsense," Mick said to her, and she looked at him right as Sammy was calling her the dumbest person on earth. "It's not true. He's a liar."

JoAnne smiled a little. "Thanks."

"What do you think he'll do?"

JoAnne looked back at the now silent door. "Come on," she said, pulling at his shirt as she walked toward it. She put her ear to the door and listened. "He's gone. I'm sure he went to get the janitor." She cracked the door open and peeked out. Then she pulled Mick out of the office and shoved him toward the door. "Go! Hurry! Get out of here before he comes back!" She grinned, like this was the most excitement she'd had in her life in a long time.

Mick looked at her. "What about you?"

Confidence calmed her eyes. "I'll be fine."

"You're sure?"

"Yeah. Good luck. Now go! And try to find a shower, will you?"

Mick smiled and raced down the hallway.

Aaron returned to Taylor's living room. He couldn't get himself to leave. Not quite yet. He sat on the couch, trying to imagine what Mick's time here was like, trying to imagine who this Taylor Franks was. His mind wandered to his worries about Mick and where he might be. Was he even still alive? A detective had called late last night to tell him that they had not found Mick's body in the fire. But was he hurt? And how in the world did he escape all that? Endless questions. No control.

All he could do was pray, and so he did. In the home of the stranger whose disappearance had led to this mess, Aaron prayed for Taylor, for Mick, for the police. Once there were clear definitions for everybody in his life. Now the lines were blurred. All the boundaries had folded in on top of one another.

Aaron shook his head. His prayers hit the ceiling and fell flat onto the floor in a smoking heap at his feet.

Aaron's stomach grumbled, and he realized he had not eaten anything all day. *"Do not eat or drink for three days, night or day."* Aaron sat up on the couch. A fast! Yes, just like Esther and Mordecai. He would fast for three days and three nights. He had nearly completed one day already.

He knew that the weak body fell easier to the knees than the strong one.

chapter twenty-seven

even over the buzzing sound of the sharpener, Crawford could hear the birds chirping their delight at the spectacular sunset outside. On this Saturday evening in autumn, Crawford's firehouse was ablaze. The curtains flapped delicately in the slight breeze through the open windows.

But as peaceful as the environment was, Crawford's unsettled spirit gnawed at him, though in a quite innocuous way. He was not one to be torn into pieces on the inside. Merely nibbled at. He'd learned long ago to save himself. At all costs, save himself.

So, basking in the warm and final light of the day, Crawford mused over the fact that it had been about forty-eight hours since they'd almost captured Mick Kline. How he'd escaped was anybody's guess, but the theory was that he'd swum downstream. Of course, nobody had known there was even a streambed there, or they might have thought about that. The farmer who owned the land said normally the bed is close to dry, but the wet season had caused it to swell.

Lucky for Mick Kline.

Crawford was formulating a plan. Deep in his mind, in a nearly unreachable place that had formed years ago, churned a desire to see things as they should be. And Crawford, long ago, had decided to let that part of himself remain untouched, to rise to be unequal, to play as though there were no boundaries. Oh, it was such a small part of who he was! But powerful. And intelligent. And passionate.

Crawford smiled at the thought, but the bliss was interrupted. He glanced to his front door where Sandy Howard stood, dressed in a floral Hawaiian shirt and khaki shorts. His ugly feet were adorned in black, dusty flip-flops.

"Hey there, Shep."

Crawford went to the screen door and opened it for him. "Chief."

Sandy smiled and offered a hand. "You were pretty deep in thought there. I knocked twice."

Crawford stared at Sandy. He felt violated.

Sandy didn't seem to notice. He was looking around the house. "I've heard about this place," he said, inviting himself in farther. "Refurbished firehouse. What a thought."

"I like it here," Crawford mumbled.

"You've done a nice job with it," Sandy said.

"Give yourself a tour. Bottom level only, though. Top level's my private quarters."

Was Sandy a man who could understand that it was the spirits of heroes that dwelled here, creating the ambience everybody loved so much?

Sandy stared at the pile of No. 2 pencils on the kitchen counter, but he remained silent. He walked around the bottom floor, peeking into a few rooms. "You have a lot of books," Sandy called from the small library in the back wing of the house.

Crawford joined him there.

Sandy pulled out a book on the Vietnam War. "You served, right?"

Crawford nodded.

Sandy smiled a little as he flipped through the book.

"My brother did too. He never liked to talk about it much either." He placed the book back on the shelf with a respectful tenderness.

Sandy scanned the rest of the books, but Crawford kept a protective eye on the well-worn pages of one particular book that had carved his soul as much as his life experiences had. He thought he had probably owned ten or more copies in his lifetime. The words were the same in each one, but as if they were alive, each book spoke something more and more profound.

Sandy's fingers climbed its spine. *The Count of Monte Cristo.* His finger and thumb tugged at it, right over the smudge of blood Crawford had marked it with.

"Leave it," Crawford said.

Sandy turned, an eyebrow raised.

"It's just really old. It's a family treasure."

"Oh," Sandy said, "I understand. I did love that book." His fingers dropped from the spine.

"Don't ever remember you dropping by my house in all the years we've worked together," Crawford said, walking back into the kitchen and standing on one side of the long island in the middle of the large room.

Sandy followed and slid onto one of the four barstools. "Don't believe I have, Shep, but I wanted to talk to you." He seemed to have trouble starting his next sentence. "It was close the other day. Almost got him."

Crawford nodded but said nothing.

Sandy licked his lips. "Some of the guys have indicated you're not too happy. I'm here because I want to hear what you have to say. Nobody else agrees with you—"

"Everyone does as they are expected to."

"I've always respected your opinion."

"The man who deserves to go down for this crime will go down, Sandy. I believe in justice and its system."

"As do I." Sandy nodded. "But you don't think it's Kline."

"It doesn't really matter what I think. I'm still doing my best to catch him."

"I wish we could find Taylor Franks," Sandy grumbled. "The woman has seemed to vanish. It keeps me awake at night."

"We may never find the body."

"You're sure she's dead?"

Crawford fiddled with one of his newly sharpened pencils. "It's my instinct you rely on so heavily, isn't it, Sandy?"

"It makes you one of the best detectives I've ever seen. Too bad we have to back it up with evidence." An edge chimed in Sandy's statement.

"Maybe if Kline hadn't run, we could spend our time finding out the truth rather than hunting him down," Crawford said after a brief silence.

Sandy nodded. "True. But the fact that he did run makes me wonder if he hasn't got something to hide, you know?"

"Everybody pays for their crimes eventually," Crawford said, staring out his window at the line of crows on the large limb of the oak tree. "It always catches up to you, no matter who you are or what you've done."

"I guess that's true."

"It doesn't make the world go around. It just keeps the world from stopping."

"People would disagree with you, Shep. There are a lot of people who have been victims of injustice."

"Their justice is coming."

Sandy let out a nervous laugh. "Sounds like an apocalyptic prophecy."

"Sometimes you have to make justice happen. If you sit

back and wait for a benevolent higher being to do it for you, you'll never get it."

"I guess you're in the right business then." Sandy smiled; then his expression turned serious. "Shep, my opinion aside, the judge wouldn't have issued the arrest warrant if he didn't think it was Mick Kline."

"Why do you care what I think about it?"

"Because you're my best detective, and we've always seen eye to eye on things. This is an exception, but it's not the rule. And it shouldn't put a wedge between us. We have to trust each other to work like we do. And the same goes for Fred. He's your captain, Shep."

"Have I done anything to indicate I'm working less than I would if I agreed?"

"Not at all. But I wanted you to know that. And be at peace with the outcome."

"You also don't want this to leak to the press because then I could be fodder for the defense in cross-examination."

Sandy shook his head. "That's not my fear."

"True colors will show, my friend." Crawford glanced into Sandy's eyes. "A killer, a kidnapper . . . can't hide behind himself very long."

"You have a strange belief system, Shep, but it works for you. It lets you sleep at night, I guess." Sandy rose from the barstool, using his two hands to push his heavy body off. He walked to the door, his flip-flops dragging across the floor in a shuffling manner. "I think we'll get Kline. He's been a little too bold. Don't know why in the world he's hanging around here anyway. Suppose 'cause he's got family. We still got a tail on Aaron?"

"Off and on. I don't think Aaron knows where he is. Sometimes tailing a less-obvious person pays off anyway."

"All right. Well, let's try to hit the news this weekend. I want this guy's photo all over the place."

Crawford nodded.

Sandy shook his hand again. "Have a good evening."

Two knee-replacement surgeries caused Sandy to take the porch steps slowly, and he waddled his way to his sedan. He waved before driving off.

The vanishing sun left the air cold.

"This was nice." Jenny smiled at Aaron as they headed back from Grapevine, where they'd taken an evening drive. "It's been a while since we just drove around. Like teenagers do."

Aaron laughed. "How come I don't feel like a teenager?"

She stroked his arm and looked out the windshield of the pickup. "The sunset was beautiful tonight."

Aaron nodded. "What do you say we go by Mick's house? Make sure it's in order and everything. We're only a couple of minutes away."

"Sure. Whatever you want to do."

After a few moments of silence, Jenny asked, "So what do you think now that a few days have passed? Do you think he's innocent? Deep in your heart?"

"I know he's innocent of this crime. I know it. I just hate that his life has had to fall apart like this. I always expected it would happen, you know? Eventually you hit bottom. But I hoped that he wouldn't have to go so low that he might not get back out."

"Have faith that God knows what He's doing."

"Don't you think, though, Jenny, that eventually God turns us over to the devil if we deny Him enough times?"

Jenny sighed. "I don't know, but don't you think God is capable of handling your brother better than you are?"

Aaron glanced at her. "Are you saying I've done something wrong?"

"I'm saying that you've planted a lot of seeds along the way. Maybe it's time to let God water them."

Aaron sighed, leaning his head against his hand, which was propped up against the driver's-side window. "There's a calm about you. It's a little uncanny, to tell you the truth."

Jenny shrugged. "I guess I just believe that this isn't an accident and that God is using this in some way. That's all."

"No accidents." He shook his head. "I don't know that I can believe that. Do you know how many car wrecks I've worked? Drunk teenager hits a family of five head-on? The blood and carnage I see just on the roads make me wonder."

"Aaron, your faith is being challenged. Let it be challenged. Don't fight it. Let God show you what He can do."

"Would you be saying the same thing if we're putting my brother's body in the grave next week because he was shot to death by the police?"

"Don't you have enough to worry about today?"

Aaron pulled into Mick's driveway and stopped the truck. "I'll be right back. I'm going to check around the house, make sure everything's intact."

Aaron hopped out and checked the front door, which was still locked. He peeked through the windows, then went around back where past memories snapped at him like a vicious dog.

Aaron sat on the back-porch steps, holding his head, heavy with despair, in his hands. "Mick," Aaron whispered, "I'm sorry. I'm so sorry for all those times I never gave you the benefit of the doubt. I think I'm most scared of never seeing you again and you not knowing how much I love you. That's all. We all mess up, bro. I think I became a self-righteous pig and didn't see . . . I should've looked deeper."

Aaron stared at the dirty cement under his feet. How much he longed for the simpler days of their childhood, when they played and laughed and had few cares. Life was real now, and somehow Aaron had taken the right track. *By the grace of God*, he reminded himself. *I was one beaten path away from the wide road too.*

Standing, he checked the back door, peered into the still and somber house, and returned to the truck.

"You okay?" Jenny asked.

Aaron nodded.

"Why don't we get his mail?" she suggested.

"Good idea." It would make it seem as if Mick were just on a long vacation and returning soon.

The mailbox boasted a wide mouth crammed full of junk. Aaron attempted, unsuccessfully, to pull it all out without dropping it, but several letters fell onto the ground. Pushing the rest of the mail under his armpit, he bent to retrieve the others. As he straightened, one envelope stood out among the junk mail and bills.

Walking back to the truck, he studied it. It was a hand-written envelope, with no return address.

"Here, Jen, hold these," Aaron said, standing at the passenger's side and handing the mail to her through the window.

"What is it?"

The postmark was from Irving, mailed the day after this whole fiasco started. Aaron flipped the envelope over, deciding whether or not he should open it. Now he was snooping through his brother's mail? Biting his lip, the indecision caused several seconds to drift by. He could feel Jenny staring at him.

"Okay, just do it," he mumbled to himself. He ripped the envelope open. Inside was sixty-two dollars—three twenties and a couple of ones.

"What, Aaron?" Jenny asked.

Aaron got back into the truck, still holding the envelope. He handed it to Jenny. "I don't know what this means, but hardly anybody sends cash through the mail, with no note and no return address. Think it's weird?"

Jenny fingered through the cash. "Yeah."

"I don't know." Aaron sighed, backing out of the driveway. "Maybe I'm grasping at straws."

"What do you think it means?"

"I have no idea, really. It just seems weird, and at this point I'll look to anything if I think it could lead me to Mick."

"Do you think he'll contact you?"

Aaron snorted. "Doubtful. He hardly wanted anything to do with me when his life was going fine. I think I'm the last person on the face of the earth he would turn to right now."

"If he did turn to you, what would you do?"

"He won't."

chapter twenty-eight

You need to go."

"I don't want to go. Aren't you enjoying the company?"

"I'm not joking. You need to get out of here."

"What? Did I say sommmething?"

"You're slurring your words. Don't you know when to stop drinking?"

"I don't remember you telling me to stop as you brought me out these beers."

"Look, just forget it. I'll call you a cab . . . hello?"

"Don't . . . don't . . ."

"Hey, wake up. Come on, please, don't do this to me. Wake up. Come on. There you go, open your eyes."

"Arrre you slllapping me?"

"I just really need you to wake up. Now. Please. Pleassse wake up."

"I . . . I'm soo . . ."

"Please don't do this. I need you to . . ."

Mick opened his eyes. Darkness swaddled him, but above a white light burned an outline around something. His head throbbed, and even the tiniest move caused him to moan in pain. After a few tries, he finally managed to sit up. His limbs shook from horrible hunger. His tongue stuck to the roof of his mouth.

Looking around, he remembered. He'd crawled into this abandoned apartment last night through a window that had been boarded up. Above him were other windows that were covered with plywood, but the daylight was seeping through.

His eyes were adjusting to the darkness now. An old, stained couch had been left, but to him the soft cushions had looked luxurious last night. Even with the dirty stuffing poking out the sides, he'd crawled onto it with little hesitation and fallen asleep.

But this morning his nose was stuffy from the mildewy air. Through the streaming daylight he could see dust particles swimming above him.

He was going to have to get something to eat very soon. Making his way out the same window he'd crawled in, the bright light assaulted his senses. Thankfully, his bike was still where he'd parked it.

He needed to find out what time it was. Midmorning, he assumed.

Several things had clicked for him last night, though perhaps not as consciously as he would like to take credit for. One, he knew he was going to need help. He had a lot of information but no way of implementing what he knew. If someone else had the information, they could take it to the authorities, perhaps change their mind. Two, he knew the only person he really trusted was Aaron.

The trick was going to be contacting Aaron without anybody seeing him. But he thought he had a good plan.

He also had a strange feeling that Taylor Franks had known something was going to happen to her the night she disappeared. As his memory surfaced, her words became pieces to a wide and difficult puzzle, but nevertheless, they were beginning to form more of a picture.

If he had any chance of not being a fugitive forever, it

would be to find out what all this meant. And somehow make sure Sammy Earle got what was coming to him.

Mick peddled the back streets, his duffel bag across his shoulder. He had to get food.

And go see Aaron.

In that order.

━━━━━━

A gothic-looking but gateless iron fence guarded the two-story home, one of the smaller ones in the Cottonwood Valley neighborhood of Irving. Rumor had it that his wife had left him and taken his children to Florida. The lawn, as green as a crayon and as flat as the end of one, had perfectly squared edges and uniform bushes, a sure sign that no children lived there. Half a dozen inground sprinklers sprayed the ground simultaneously. Heavy white curtains hung in all the windows, looking as if nobody ever peeked out of them.

Aaron suspected that on this Sunday afternoon he would find Stephen Fiscall at home. From across the street he watched Fiscall's two black Labradors stare distrustfully at him from near the end of the drive.

He contemplated how he was going to convince the prosecutor to allow him to argue his brother's case. If he could just say a few words, put doubt into Fiscall's mind about his decision to pursue Mick, maybe it would make a difference. He would try to convince him to take another look at Sammy Earle.

It seemed to be the only thing he could do.

Now sitting stoically, the dogs waited for Aaron to make a move. Aaron put his truck in gear and began to turn down Fiscall's driveway.

No.

Braking, Aaron turned around, sensing someone behind him, but there was nobody. The word was spoken firmly, like a father scolding a young child. He was sure he heard it, as clear as if someone had whispered it in his ear. His pounding heart offered evidence that he had heard something.

He turned back around, facing the large white driveway that traced itself through the green lawn. Had he just imagined the word? What harm was there in talking with Fiscall? Yet that small part of his conscience, where he'd doubted this decision and found himself contemplating his trust in God, grew ever larger.

The two dogs' ears perked, and low growls vibrated in their throats.

He wanted to speak a few brief words to Fiscall. Perhaps Fiscall would sense somebody outside and come out. Aaron's fingers twitched against the steering wheel, fighting the basic urge to obey.

Backing up, he turned his truck and sped back down the quiet residential street.

Anger grappled him. He was sure God had spoken to him, but He wasn't making sense. He was scolding him, controlling him. Yet nothing was being done to save his brother. He pounded the steering wheel as he swung out into traffic, heading home.

"Answer me!" Aaron yelled.

A stern horn blistered his ears as he almost crossed the double yellow line.

Mick parked his bike between some trees near the back of the church. It took him until early evening to ride there, as he'd gotten lost twice on the back roads and had needed to stop and rest several times. Muffled organ music pushed through the white wooden walls of the historic Methodist church. Its gleaming gold steeple spiked toward the fading blue, dusky sky.

The humidity was high, the temperature still well into the seventies. To the northwest, Mick could see clouds gathering toward a thunderhead, which was pulling energy into itself from the unstable atmosphere.

Stumbling forward, he grabbed for a tree to keep himself from falling to the ground. Famished and fatigued, it was all he could do to stand. On the way to Aaron's church, he'd thought of several different options on how he might get food, but nothing seemed feasible. The boldness that had directed him into Earle's office had faded.

Hanging on the tree, he stared at the Dumpster parked directly behind the church, an eyesore hidden from the parishioners. Church was in session. Maybe he could climb in there . . . find some food. . . .

He thought the idea would sicken him. Groping through garbage for food? But instead, his body urged him onward. With heavy feet, he dragged his stricken body toward the Dumpster, his shoes inching against the gravel of the empty back parking lot.

Never in his life had he wanted to stand in a shower of rain more than he did now. His sweaty and smelly body needed to be drenched.

Finally reaching the Dumpster, the wretched smell made his overloaded senses come to life, and he bent over, intending to vomit. He'd never known hunger this severe. What could make a man climb into maggot-infested garbage for food? He gripped a bar that stuck out from the top, pulled himself up with shaking arms, and rolled over into the Dumpster, which was about half full. Flies swarmed and buzzed, unhappy with their new visitor. Mick covered his mouth and nose with the bottom of his T-shirt. Even the smell of sweat beat the pungent odor of sour milk that rose from one of the bags.

Wasting no time, he began ripping open garbage sacks,

tearing his way through the insides, trying to find something he could eat. There were a few half-full cans of soda, a container of juice, fried chicken, and rolls. His mouth salivated while his stomach churned.

He found an uneaten chicken leg, which he threw into his duffel bag. Then he found an open bag of Lay's potato chips, crammed three into his mouth, then threw the rest into his bag.

And then, to his delight, he found a ham sandwich completely sealed in a Ziploc bag. He grabbed it and half of a Diet Dr Pepper and climbed out of the bin. He wanted to sit and eat, but he knew his time was short. He devoured the rest of the potato chips and managed three large bites of the sandwich.

Setting his duffel bag down at the corner of the church, Mick peeked around the side. Nobody was in sight. He hurried toward the front parking lot, probably three hundred cars full, and tried to spot the top of Aaron's black truck.

The music had stopped for a while, but now he heard it again. Running through the parked cars, he finally hopped onto the bed of a pickup and looked around.

"There!" It was on the other side of the parking lot. Jumping off the pickup bed, he carried himself swiftly through the lines of cars.

But then Mick heard voices. He stopped and turned back toward the church, glancing around a large SUV he was standing behind.

A stream of people flowed down the front steps of the church.

Hand in hand, Aaron and Jenny made their way out of the crowded church. Jenny was talking with one of her friends, but Aaron didn't feel much like chatting. Jenny had insisted they go to Sunday night church since he missed this morning. He'd gone, but not happily.

"Babe . . ." Jenny was looking at him. Her friend was gone.

"What?"

"My hand. You're squeezing it to death."

"Sorry." Aaron released her hand and guided her down the steps with his hand on her back.

"Where'd you park?"

Aaron pointed toward the back of the lot, where he'd found one of the last spots. He'd dropped Jenny off to find them a seat since they were running late. As they walked, Aaron noticed a large thunderhead to the northwest. The sun glowed around it, creating a majestic throne of clouds with faintly rumbling thunder through the thick air. Jenny's heels clicked alongside him, and she pulled him to a stop.

"What?" he asked.

"You're walking like we're in a marathon."

Aaron shook his head and laughed. "I'm so sorry."

Aaron fumbled with his keys as they reached his truck. He could sense Jenny studying him as she went around the other side. He tried to look casual and normal, just the opposite of what he was feeling. "Jenny! Come here!"

"What is it?"

"Look!" He pointed to the side of his vehicle as she came around to him. The magnetic fish symbol that was always on his tailgate was now just below the door handle.

"A prank?" Jenny asked, though her eyes told him that she knew what he was thinking.

"Mick always hated this fish," Aaron said quietly, looking around to make sure he couldn't be heard. "I know he did this."

"But why?"

"Get in the truck," Aaron said; when they were both inside, he continued. "Maybe to tell me he's alive. Maybe he's trying to let me know."

"By moving your fish?"

Aaron glanced around, trying to spot Mick's face through all the people coming out of the church. Opening his hand, he looked at the fish he'd peeled off the side of the truck. "I think he's trying to tell me something."

Shep Crawford stood on the fourth stair of his home and ran his fingers along the red stripes of the American flag that he proudly displayed on the wall. It was like tracing blood.

His thumb gently touched the pure white stripe below it. Blood and purity. He thought it appropriate that the two, the blood and the purity, didn't mix. How could they? Perhaps they could run alongside each other, complement each other like a fine wine to a good steak. But never mix. Because to mix would be to perfectly sacrifice. And as far as Shep Crawford was concerned, there was no such thing. So the white would remain white, and the red would remain red.

His fingers grabbed the red stripe, and it bunched inside his hand.

Today he would choose red.

mick staggered, clutching his ever faithful duffel bag. The zipper looked like a smile. Well, more of a grimace. Sweat poured from his face and his legs shook with each step he took, while waves of chills prickled his body.

Death walked next to him in the woods, snickering. Whispering. The only part of him that felt alive was a restless, provoking fear.

Across the treetops to the north, a mighty storm crawled, lightning spidering through the towers of clouds, thunder shaking the ground underneath him. In about thirty minutes, the storm would be here. Darkness had settled itself across the sky. The warm and wet wind that pulled the storm brushed the trees like the fingertips of ghosts.

Falling forward, Mick collapsed into a bed of leaves, his eyes rolling back into his head. Food poisoning.

He was sure this would be his end. If he could only make it to the pond, maybe Aaron would at least find his body. If Aaron understood the clue he'd left him, that is. It was a long shot. Perhaps Aaron didn't even remember the days they'd spent here together fishing.

With his hands, he clawed at the dirt, inching his way ahead. When he got to a small hill above the pond, he let gravity roll him downward. He hit a log and lurched to a stop. Lying on his back, he stared upward. Black clouds swam swiftly against the sky.

Breathing shallowly, Mick lay still. Pain stabbed through his stomach in predictable waves. His mouth hung open wide, as if beckoning his spirit to escape through the hole. His eyes were open, but he couldn't see anything.

A large raindrop splashed against his face, bringing his senses to life momentarily. And then another. The wind picked up, whistling above him. The sky groaned.

God. The name tingled his lips like salty water.

Beneath him, his fingers scratched the muddy ground, the ground he would be lowered into one day. Probably very soon.

I don't want to die.

As his T-shirt became wet, the stench grew more caustic, as if he could smell himself dying, his skin rotting, his blood draining.

"Aaron," he groaned.

Squeezing his eyes shut, he tried to bear the hot pain that clamped around his intestines.

"If you could become anybody else in the world, Mick,
who would you become?"

"I've never thought about it."

"You like who you are?"

"Yeah, I guess."

"There's nobody else you'd want to be like?"

"I don't know. My brother, I guess, though he can be a
real pain."

"This is the same brother who stole the woman of your
dreams?"

"Yeah. Same brother."

"That's weird."

"You don't know him."

"All I've heard about him is what you've said. Sounds like you hate his guts. Why would you want to be like him?"

"Maybe that's why I hate him so much. Because I've always wanted to be like him. I was never able to, though. He was born with a good heart."

"I think people can create whoever they want to be."

"I disagree. I think people are who they are, and they can only improve upon that."

"I'm going to become the person I always wanted to be."

"And who is that?"

"A woman who can tell a man no and defy him and an entire kingdom if she has to. A strong and courageous woman."

"Who are you now?"

"I'm still the caterpillar."

Sammy Earle whirled around, dropping his glass of whiskey to the kitchen counter in his Dallas home. It splashed and spilled over the top, its liquid sliding across the shiny counter.

Thump.

He swallowed, backing up against the refrigerator, panting. Was it the liquor talking? He was hearing things now too?

Earle rubbed his eyes, trying to get a grip. He hadn't slept well. Nightmares had haunted him from the moment his head had rested on the pillow last night. Everything from Vietnam to Taylor Franks. Each night they'd gotten worse. Last night they were nearly unbearable.

Thump.

Gasping, Earle looked toward his front door, from where the sound had come. Outside, weather as wicked as devils crossed the sky and blew the leaves off the trees. Still, he'd heard a noise. He knew it. Maybe the wind was blowing something against the door. Rain splashed against the windows in fierce waves, and in the background he could hear the weather alert beeping on the television. But right now a tornado was the least of his worries.

Creeping forward, he tiptoed out of the kitchen and toward the door and listened. There, a faint sound—something he couldn't identify—rattled right outside. A crack of thunder caused Earle to jump backward, and then another loud crack made him look out the front window. A large tree limb had snapped and was dangling high above his lawn.

All Earle could see out his peephole was rain splashing against the concrete of his driveway, creating a white, hovering mist. The front door was bolted shut, so Earle slowly unlocked it, pressing his weight against the door, afraid as soon as he heard the click something might shove the door inward.

But the click did nothing more than accelerate his heartbeat. Earle shut his eyes and mumbled, "Get a grip, soldier." He used the word loosely. He'd never thought of himself as a soldier, even when he was in combat. He'd never felt like a killer. He'd never felt brave. His mind and his charm were the weapons he used these days. But when swimming in alcohol, neither proved to be too effective. He'd tried to stop drinking, but the nightmares kept driving him back.

With a swift pull, Earle opened his front door. A warm breeze blew his hair back, and the pouring rain was deafening. He looked around but saw nothing.

Then he heard that rattling noise again, and when he looked down he saw it. Near his doorway, by a flowerless pot, was a white piece of paper, flapping in the wind, held down by a smooth, round stone. The rain had not reached it, as it was under the protection of the porch. Earle looked around again, stunned.

Thunder clapped and without further hesitation, Earle picked up the stone and grabbed the paper with his other hand before the wind carried it off. He tried to hold the paper upright so he could read the typed note:

> *Mr. Earle,*
>
> *I have some information about you concerning the Taylor Franks case. Information that is neither helpful to you nor to me in my prosecution of the suspect of this case. I need to meet with you privately. Do not bring any lawyers or anybody else. This stays between you and me. Come to my house tonight between 10:30 and 11:00. 11898 Blaine Street. And whatever you do, destroy this letter.*
>
> *S. Fiscall*

The rock rolled out of Earle's trembling hand, landing on the porch with a loud thump. He stared at the note in disbelief. Backing up through his doorway, he slammed the door shut and took a loud, wheezing gulp of air. This was no alcoholic mirage. Stumbling into the kitchen, he scrounged around for another bottle, all the while holding the paper delicately, as if it held the very power of life in it.

Drinking straight from a bottle of chardonnay he reserved for special guests, Earle tried to get a grip. He studied the paper, examining every word. But with each passing minute, he grew more and more anxious. What information did Fiscall have? Why did he want to see him?

Earle gripped the bottle in one hand and the letter in the other. He looked at the kitchen clock. It was a little after seven.

Holding the letter over his stove top, he turned on the gas flame. The paper ignited, and a hot orange flame climbed its fibers. White smoke twirled toward the ceiling as gracefully as a ballerina. Earle stared at it, memorizing the address. Neither fire nor alcohol could kill the demons. Wherever he went, they followed.

He dropped the letter into the sink and pounded the small fire out, leaving crispy edges but the letter intact. His gut told him to keep it.

chapter thirty

Sammy Earle stood under the cold water of the showerhead, slapping his hands against his cheeks. He managed to bathe before grabbing a towel and stepping onto a small, round red carpet.

Scrubbing his head with the towel, he then pulled on a purple silk shirt and black slacks but no tie. The crumpled note held down by a stone was indication enough that this meeting wasn't going to be formal.

He was feeling sick. Fiscall knew enough information that he was certain Earle would show up. But it also sounded like if Earle would cooperate, this information might be gladly swept under the rug.

He combed his hair and smothered his cheeks in aftershave, then went to his closet and put on a black raincoat. As he buttoned it up, he stared out the window at the storm. White light cut into the dark, and Earle sighed. There was hardly a good reason to go out into weather like this.

Hardly a good reason. But this was a good reason.

He pulled up the collar on his coat and found his keys. Taking another swig of chardonnay, he headed to his garage, cursing the day he ever met Taylor Franks.

Gripping the steering wheel, Aaron navigated through the torrential rain, leaning toward the windshield, wishing the wipers on Jenny's Honda would swipe twice as fast. Next to him, Jenny gripped the door with her right hand and with her left held two sacks of groceries on her lap.

The lightning gave them some needed light on this dark country road. They'd been traveling on what they thought and hoped was Agriculture Road for about twenty minutes, but this far out, road signs were nonexistent. The only thing that told them they were on the right road was all the agriculture.

"Please let us be right," Aaron mumbled.

Jenny touched his arm. "It's a long shot."

Aaron squinted through the foggy windshield. It *was* a long shot. Connecting a fish on his truck to a fishing pond he and Mick had played at as kids. But it was a perfect hideout, if that's where Mick had been all this time.

They'd decided to take Jenny's car out of simple paranoia. Though there wasn't a car in sight at Aaron's house and hadn't been for days, the thought of a bird dog being attached to his truck caused him to think out his plan further. He'd checked underneath his truck twice, but the thing could be well hidden.

He hated to drag Jenny into this, but so far the detectives had shown little interest in her. Besides, she insisted on coming and was tough and stubborn—two of the qualities that had initially drawn him to her. Jenny had even thought of going to the grocery store to pick up food for Mick . . . and make it look like an innocent trip.

"Should I get the map out again?"

"No. There's only one Agriculture Road and only one Peachtree Street." A bright light flashed in the rearview mirror, and in the distance, two foggy headlights glowed. Soon enough, the lights faded into the rain, and they were alone on the bumpy paved road again.

The headlights caught a shimmering, rectangular green sign: Peachtree Street.

"Yes!" Jenny cried.

They turned right and the car climbed a steep hill, the wind rattling the windows and the loose metal on the bottom of the car. This was the worst storm Aaron had seen in a long time. Ironically, it had always been these kinds of storms that Mick loved.

As the car topped the hill, Aaron saw a blurry white box on the top of the next hill. The wipers struggled to keep up with the sheets of rain rolling against the windshield.

"There," Aaron said, pulling to the side of the road. He turned off the headlights. "I think that's the Heppetons' house."

Checking the rearview mirror, he found nothing behind them but a black, lightless tunnel of rain.

"Where's the pond?" Jenny asked.

Aaron studied the fields and trees. "I'm not sure. I can't remember which side of the house it was on. All these groupings of trees look alike. But there's only one pond here. I think the property's about fifteen acres."

"What should we do?" Jenny was nearly shouting over the noise of the storm.

"Stay here. I'm going to see if I can find it."

"No!" Jenny grabbed his arm. "If Mick's out here, we've got to find him fast. We'll split up."

"I don't want you out in this storm!"

"I'll be fine. We can't sit here arguing. We have to go—and now!"

Aaron stared forward.

Jenny opened the car door.

"Wait!"

"What?"

"All right, listen. See that group of trees over there?" Aaron said, pointing near the house. "You go and look and come right back. *Right back.* Do you hear me? I'm going to check the other side of the house. I'll have to walk this ditch and cross the road up ahead. I doubt anybody would be looking outside, but just in case, I have to be careful."

Jenny nodded.

"Promise me you'll come right back," Aaron said.

"I promise."

"Leave the groceries here. We can come back and get them if we find him."

"What if he's there?"

"Stand at the edge of the trees and flag me down when I come back."

A gust of wind pushed Jenny forward as she stepped out of the car, and she stumbled, almost falling. The flimsy material of her Windbreaker did little to shield her from the storm, and though she tried to pull her hood up, the wind blew it quickly off her head.

"Hurry!" Aaron yelled at her from across the top of the car. It was only fifty yards to her destination. He knew she could get there and be back quickly. It would be several more minutes for him, even running.

Jenny walked toward the trees. Whirling around, Aaron thought he heard the sound of tires on pavement only a few yards away, yet there was nothing but a dark road behind him.

The clouds were the darkest he'd ever seen them, and the thunder was consistent and deafening. Jenny was walking quickly; she was a small white image against the dark green land now. Aaron hurried along the side of the road, studying the two-story house ahead. Warm, orange light glowed from a few of the windows, but nobody passed in front of them.

Glancing back, he could barely see Jenny. She was only a few yards from the trees. He picked up his pace and ran for the larger grouping of trees on the other side of the house, about a hundred yards away.

Thunder clapped overhead. Aaron could no longer see Jenny. An uneasy feeling settled in his gut. He kept running, but his feet were heavy with indecision. Something kept making him look back for her. Was it the storm? or something else?

He sprinted down into the ditch as he crossed in front of the Heppetons' home so he wouldn't be seen. He whirled and looked for Jenny again, but all he saw was a black hole where the dark trees stood against the slightly lighter sky.

"Jenny . . ."

He turned and raced back toward the trees. He couldn't leave her alone out here. No matter how tough she thought she was.

Earle cursed the rain and the weather as he drove down the tree-lined street in the Cottonwood Valley neighborhood to Irving. It had taken him an hour to drive from Dallas. Squinting through the blurry glass of his windshield, he managed to find Blaine Street. His BMW crawled along the pavement as he read the numbers on each house. Fiscall's turned out to be a gaudy, white house with an overly manicured lawn surrounded by an iron fence.

He pulled into the drive. It seemed the only lights on were glowing from the porch. But as he got closer, he could see faint light from one of the windows. Earle turned off his car and smoothed his hands across his chest, pulling the wrinkles out of the silk shirt. He fingered the twenty-four-carat gold buckle that held the quill ostrich leather strap around his Milano El Jefe. Running his fingers through his hair, he plopped the two-hundred-dollar Western hat onto his head. One of the few things worth spending money on.

Setting his jaw, he sniffed the air, jutting his head upward. He opened his car door and walked quickly toward the covered front porch, where he would at last be free from the annoying wetness.

Skipping three steps, he bounded onto the porch and noticed that a large clay flowerpot had apparently blown over, scattering a mess of moist soil across the pathway to the door. There was no way around it, so Earle gently stepped into it, then wiped his feet on the welcome mat.

Taking a deep breath, he geared himself up for whatever was on the other side of the heavy wooden door that towered before him. He glanced at the front windows, sure he'd see Fiscall peeking out at him. But the white curtains stayed closed.

Earle decided he'd better just get on with it. He hated not knowing things, and the sooner he understood what was going on, the better he could find a way to use it in his favor. Grabbing the knocker, he pounded lightly on the door. After a few moments, he tried again but received no answer.

"Come on, Fiscall, get to the door," Earle grumbled. "I don't have all night." He pressed a firm finger into the small, glowing rectangle, and he heard the faint response of the doorbell inside. He pressed it two more times.

With a flat hand, he pounded against the thick oak. "Fiscall! Open up!" Earle sighed and turned, watching from the covering of the porch as the rain splashed against the ground. The flowers that had been in the pot hung off the side of the porch, their petals flapping in the wind. A strange sense of dread wrapped around Earle, and his body went cold.

Something was wrong.

He walked to the small, long window beside the door and pressed his hands and face against it, trying to see through. He could make out a semidark foyer and a sparkling chandelier, but that was it. Inside it was still.

He tried the doorknob, but it was locked.

He watched as lightning illuminated the front yard. Earle gasped. Near the corner of the yard next to a large tree, he thought he saw something move. As he tried to study it through the flashes of lightning, all he could make out was what looked like two black lumps, slightly moving . . . but maybe it was the wind.

"What *is* that?" Earle whispered, stepping onto the dirt toward the edge of the porch. He glanced back at the door one more time, flared his nostrils, and clenched his fists.

Running into the rain, he got into his BMW and started it. The windshield wipers thumped to life, startling Earle. Peering through the glass, he tried to make out what the two black lumps were, but he couldn't. Circling the drive, he turned back out onto Blaine Street.

Staring out the rearview mirror as much as he was watching the road in front of him, Earle felt dreadfully sick.

He slammed his hands against his steering wheel and cursed. Someone else was in control. Control of what, he didn't know.

"Mick? Are you here?"

A slight breeze rustled the wet leaves above Mick, and droplets splashed against his already drenched face. Was he hallucinating now? Was that Jenny's voice?

He blinked slowly, trying to speak, but all that came out was gurgling.

"Mick? Are you here?" Her voice nearly drowned in the racket of the storm.

He knew anything he attempted to whisper would not be heard. He tried to raise his arm out of the mud.

"Mick?" Her voice sounded more distant.

He turned his head, trying to locate her. *Jenny, I'm here. Come to the other side.*

One more attempt, and his arm was in the air. He waved his fingers into the wind. He could hear nothing but the storm. Jenny's voice was gone.

Come back. Please. I'm here.

He closed his eyes, his arm still in the air.

Come back to me.

And then he felt a hand on his shoulder.

"Mick!"

He turned and looked into her shiny, wet face. He wasn't sure if he was smiling. Her eyes turned worried.

"Jenny . . ."

"Mick, please try to tell me what's wrong. Are you hurt anywhere?"

He mumbled, "No. Food . . ."

"Food? You need food? I brought some! A ton. Here, let me—"

He squeezed her arm. "Poi . . . son . . ."

Jenny knelt beside him. "Food poisoning." Indecision swept over her features, and she glanced toward the trees. "Mick, we have to get you to a hospital. Now."

"No . . ."

"Yes! Yes! You could die out here."

"Where's Aaron?" he whispered.

"He's coming. He couldn't remember where the pond was. He's looking on the other side of the property. I'm going to wave him over."

"Don't leave me," Mick moaned.

"Mick, listen to me . . . ," Jenny started.

Mick shook his head. His attention turned toward the sky. The clouds were low and thick. And rotating. He looked at her. "You need to go. Now. Go up to the Heppetons' house. Hurry, Jenny. This is bad."

"I'm not leaving without you."

"Jenny, go!" He clutched his stomach and squeezed his eyes shut.

Tears streamed down her face. "I can't leave you here. I won't. Come on, I can help you to the car. We can at least get out of this storm."

A showering of hail fell into the pond, like a million pebbles dropping into the water.

Mick seized her forearm. "Tell Aaron that I'm sorry."

Jenny wiped her tears. "You don't have anything to be sorry for."

"I have more regrets than you could possibly imagine," Mick said. His chin quivered with every word. "But I need Aaron to know that I love him."

"Aaron loves you."

"I know that." He looked into the sky. "It's so beautiful, so powerful. I bet the head of this storm is towering above forty-seven thousand feet."

"Look, the storm is passing," Jenny said as the wind suddenly died down. The sky was a milky green.

"No. Go, Jenny. You must go. Please. The storm isn't over."

Aaron was about twenty yards from the trees that Jenny had run into. She hadn't emerged yet. He didn't want to draw any attention from Jack or Alice Heppeton so he'd yet to call out her name.

Pulling to a stop, Aaron tried to catch his breath. He looked down the gravel road, but it remained quiet.

With each step, he became more and more hopeful of seeing his brother. Maybe Jenny had found him. The wet grass was slippery. He approached the woods. There! He could barely see the pond, but he could hear the rain splashing into it and could smell the fish. Smiling, he began to walk into the darkness of the trees. Maybe Mick was waiting for him on the dock.

As he rounded a large tree, someone grabbed his arm.

chapter thirty-one

aron twisted his arm, trying to get loose, but the next thing he knew, his head whipped back, hitting the trunk of the tree so hard that when he opened his eyes, arrows of light shot through his vision. A gloved hand wrapped around his neck.

When the darts of light faded, he stared into two cold, black eyes. He grabbed at the hand around his neck. After a few seconds, the grip relaxed and Aaron swallowed air as fast as he could.

"Don't make a sound," came a whisper.

Shep Crawford's wet and angry face stared at him, his knee jammed between both of Aaron's. Aaron knew if he made a move, he'd pay for it. How did Crawford find him?

"Listen to me and listen to me very carefully," Crawford said. He glanced over Aaron's shoulder, and Aaron knew immediately that Mick was there. "You have two choices. Turn your brother in, or I'll guarantee that he and probably you will get shot." Crawford looked behind his own shoulder, then back at Aaron. "I've got two other agents here, weapons ready. I don't want your brother to get hurt, which is why you're going to go in there, walk him out like there's nothing going on, and hand him over."

"You want me to turn my brother in."

"You better believe it," Crawford snarled. "I'm tired of

chasing that boy around, and as far as all these men around here are concerned, he's armed and dangerous."

"You don't know that."

"Who's to say that he hasn't gotten ahold of a weapon?" Crawford let the words hang in the air. "Now, you can either tip your brother off so he can run right into a spray of gunfire, or you can walk him out peacefully."

"Betray him."

"You know it's for his own good," Crawford said.

Aaron looked away. "I was under the impression you thought he was innocent."

"Doesn't matter what I think. Am I the one in control here?"

Aaron looked at him. It was an odd question, and one that was spoken as more of a statement than a question. A strange twinkle glinted in Crawford's eyes, and he smiled ever so slightly as the rain washed over both their faces.

"That man is innocent."

"Don't you believe, Aaron, that in the end justice will be served?"

"I don't know what to believe."

Crawford pushed his hand off Aaron's chest and stepped back a foot. "You don't know what to believe? You always seemed to me to be a man of belief."

Aaron's nostrils flared. "I believe in God."

Crawford stared at him. "'I have my mode of dispensing justice, silent and sure, without respite or appeal, which condemns or pardons, and which no one sees.' So you must trust me."

"You're quoting from *The Count of Monte Cristo*," Aaron breathed. "'Now the god of vengeance yields to me his power to punish the wicked!'"

Crawford smiled at him. "Good book."

"Haven't read it lately."

Crawford's attention turned toward something behind Aaron. "Now go. Get your brother. Bring him up the hill to me, and I can guarantee his safety. If not, I cannot guarantee anything."

Aaron stared at the muddy ground.

Crawford said, "And in case you decide to do anything crazy, it's not just your life we're talking about. Your girlfriend is down there too."

"Jenny . . . ," Aaron breathed.

"How do you think I found him? You decided to take Jenny's car tonight. Bad choice."

Aaron headed toward the pond. As he cleared the trees, he immediately saw Jenny and Mick. Mick lay on his back about four feet from the edge of the swollen pond. Jenny was tugging at his arm. The wind picked up.

Aaron ran toward them. "Jenny!"

Jenny looked up, surprise lighting her eyes.

Aaron scrambled beside them. Mick looked barely conscious. A dark beard covered his jaw, but his head was nearly bald. Aaron grabbed Jenny's shoulders. "You have to get out of here."

"Don't worry about me," she yelled back. She pointed to Mick. "He's really sick. Food poisoning."

"Aaron . . . ," Mick mumbled. Though the wind was warm, he was shaking.

Taking Mick's hand, Aaron tried to focus, but he thought he could hear guns being cocked all around him. Or limbs snapping. It all sounded the same.

"We have to get you out of here," Aaron said. He glanced through the trees and couldn't see anybody. An eerie silence settled over the water. He pulled his brother to a sitting position, but Mick's head whipped backward and he groaned. "It's okay, it's okay. Just hang with me," Aaron urged.

Aaron tore his raincoat off and said to Jenny, "Help me with his shirt." They peeled it off and Aaron took his own shirt off, mostly dry from the protection of the raincoat. He slid it over Mick's head, and Jenny helped him poke Mick's arms through. "Let's get this coat on him. He's trembling."

After a few seconds, the coat was on and Jenny helped button it up. Aaron held Mick's soggy wet shirt in one arm, his brother's limp body in the other. "Jenny, hold him up for a second." Jenny braced herself against his back, and Aaron slipped on Mick's shirt. Something told him if the police got trigger happy, they were going to go for the man in the black T-shirt, especially under these stormy conditions.

"Where are you going to take him?" Jenny asked as Mick slumped back into Aaron's arms. "He's really sick."

"No . . . no hospital . . . ," Mick groaned.

Aaron grabbed Jenny and caught her attention with stern eyes. "Listen to me," he said quietly. "I want you to stay right here until I come back and get you."

"What? Why?"

"Jenny, you must trust me. You must."

Her eyes shone with fear.

"Do not get up; do not walk anywhere. You sit right here until I come back and get you. Do you understand?"

She nodded but said, "What's going on?"

Aaron didn't answer. He flung Mick's arm around his neck and lifted him up underneath the armpit. Mick cried out in pain. "Stay with me, buddy. You can do it. Gentle steps. We just got to get up this small hill."

With gritted teeth, Aaron carried his brother up the hill toward Crawford. Mick's feet dragged alongside him, his eyes dull and lifeless. Aaron breathed methodically as if he were lifting weights. A few more feet, and they'd be up the hill. Mick tried to help, but his limbs were so weak it ended up making their effort clumsy.

"Come on, brother, come on . . . there!" Both men stood panting. Aaron looked around, trying to identify where the officers were. But at night, all he could see were drifting shadows and dark, lightless corridors. The rain pounded again.

"Where . . . where are we going?"

"Come on," Aaron said, pulling him forward. As they walked toward the black trees, Aaron's mind raced, but he had no options. Mick was too weak to do anything but be carried.

Mick turned his head toward Aaron. "I knew you'd come."

Aaron squeezed his shoulder. "Save your strength."

"No, I mean it. I knew it. I'm sorry, Aaron. . . ." His voice cracked. "For everything. I'm sorry."

"Don't talk." Aaron looked his brother in the eyes and gave him an assuring nod. Mick grinned, a grin that Aaron hadn't seen in years. Aaron plodded through the trees, adrenaline pulsating through his blood. Any moment, he was going to be considered a traitor by his brother, and everything would be back to where it was.

He glanced at Mick. "You must know that everything I've ever done I've thought was in your best interest. But since you've been gone, I've realized that, more than anything, I've judged you instead of loved you. I'm sorry if I've ever made you feel inferior. We're both from the same dust."

Mick smiled as much as he could. Sweat poured from his face, but his bloodshot eyes warmed. "I'm sorry I've been such a disappointment."

"Don't say that—"

"*Freeze!*" Standing at the edge of the trees, Shep Crawford had both hands wrapped around the butt of his gun, one arm braced against the side of a tree.

Mick gasped and started to struggle.

Aaron held him steady against his body. "Crawford, he's sick. He needs medical attention. Tell your guys to call an ambulance."

"What are you doing?" Mick cried.

Crawford stepped forward, ripped Mick's arm away from Aaron's shoulder, and cuffed him, then patted him down. Mick swayed.

Aaron grabbed Crawford's shoulder to steady him. "Did you hear me? He's sick! Have your guys call—"

Distant lightning glinted off Crawford's eyes. "There's nobody here but me." Dragging Mick forward, he turned right, and Aaron could see Crawford's car parked under a tree, hidden by shadows.

Aaron ran up beside them. "Mick, listen to me. He followed us here. We didn't know. I didn't know."

"Shut up," Mick spat.

"Mick, please listen, I had no choice. Besides that, you're sick. You need medical attention—"

"Get outta here," Mick growled as he stumbled alongside Crawford, his hands chained behind his back.

Aaron rushed in front of Crawford, pushing his hand into the detective's chest to stop him. "If you lay a hand on him, you'll be sorry."

"I'm taking him to jail, where he belongs." Crawford looked at Mick. "You should have never run, son."

Mick stared with vacuous eyes.

Crawford knocked Aaron's hand off his chest. "Officer Kline, believe me when I tell you this is the best thing that could have happened to your brother. Now get out of my way."

Aaron swallowed, glanced at Mick, who wouldn't look him in the eye, and stepped aside.

Crawford shoved Mick into the front seat of his car and

strapped the seat belt around him. In the distance, Aaron could see bright flashing lights speeding toward them, their sirens echoing through the countryside. Crawford was on his radio. Mick's head lay against the seat as he gazed out the passenger window.

Looking toward the tree line, he saw Jenny walking out of the shadows. She stood with her arms wrapped around herself, her hair matted against her small face. Betrayal glowed in her eyes too.

In the side mirror, Mick could see two trailing police cars' lights flash exuberantly. The processional announced itself as it flew down the highway toward the Irving jail. Mick sat next to Crawford in the spotless sedan, the metal cuffs grinding against the bones in his wrists. With his hands clasped behind him and the seat belt crossing his chest, Mick sat motionless. He'd listened to Crawford on the radio, but now there was silence.

Then Crawford looked at him sideways, narrowing his eyes. "How'd you like your house?"

"What?"

"Your house. Did I put it all back in order?"

Mick swallowed down the bitter bile that sat in the bottom of his throat.

"You're a bit of a slob, man. But I thought it was the polite thing for me to do. Put all your toys back where they belonged."

"You did that?" Mick could only whisper.

"Nothing personal. Just needed some info about you."

"Bull."

Crawford's eyes smiled. "Well, it was fun too."

Mick closed his eyes, tilting his head against the back of the seat. "Why?"

"Why did I do it?" Crawford laughed. "Why not?" An insidious snicker filled the car. "I like taking these things to the next level; you know what I mean?"

"Mind games."

"Whatever you want to call it. You can tell a lot about a person by how he reacts to certain situations."

"You have me all figured out, don't you?"

"The question is, do you have me figured out?"

chapter thirty-two

bill Cassavo met Aaron at the jail early Monday morning. They walked together toward the room where the guard would bring Mick.

"The fact that he ran is only going to hurt us," Bill said with a heavy sigh. "We had a good shot of proving him not guilty before. But now things have changed."

Aaron glanced at him as they walked. "We'll just have to work with it. It's all we have."

Bill nodded. "It doesn't guarantee defeat. I'm telling you, the prosecution doesn't have a lot to go on here, other than Mick was at her apartment. It's all circumstantial. As long as a body doesn't show up, I think we're in the game."

"What about Sammy Earle?"

"My investigator is already on it. He's definitely got a motive. One can never be sure why they chose Mick over Sammy. But the more we have on Mr. Earle, the better."

A guard unlocked a large metal door for them.

"I just can't get over those flowers, Bill. They mean something, but I don't know what."

"The ones that were signed Sammy but billed to an obsolete credit card? The police are kind of pretending like they don't even exist, aren't they?"

"I don't think they know what to make of it. It doesn't fit into the theory that Mick did it, that's for sure. And if Sammy did it, it seems rather obvious."

Another guard let them into a room full of long metal tables and orange plastic chairs. Bill and Aaron sat facing the door so they could see Mick coming.

"How's he feeling?" Bill asked.

"They released him from the infirmary early this morning. He's going to live, but other than that, I don't know too much. Last night he looked like he was knocking on death's door."

Aaron saw Mick through the small window of the room. The scrubs hung on him. Mick's dreary eyes met Aaron's, then shifted to Bill's as the door to the room opened.

"Sit here," the guard instructed and put a firm hand on Mick's shoulder, pushing him into the seat as if he couldn't do it by himself. The guard chained his leg to the chair but uncuffed his hands.

"Hi," Aaron said gently.

Mick didn't respond.

"Mick," Bill tried, "you should know, the detective followed them to the pond. It wasn't a setup. They had no idea."

Mick's eyes shifted back and forth between the men. Then he stared at the table. "Okay," he murmured.

"How are you feeling?" Aaron asked.

"If I died in the next five minutes, I wouldn't be upset about it."

"We're going to get you out of here," Aaron said.

"I'm not holding my breath."

"Things aren't adding up. There are a lot of things about this case that don't make sense if you're the fall guy," Aaron said.

"I'm confident I can build a good defense case," Bill added. "They don't have a body. They don't have anything other than your admission that you were there."

"That seems to be enough." Mick sighed.

"Do you remember anything from that night? anything more?" Aaron asked.

"Things have become less foggy. But I don't remember anybody coming in and taking her, if that's what you mean."

"What do you remember?"

"Bits and pieces of conversation. Taylor seemed to be searching for who she was. Apparently she came from a pretty rough background."

"Did she say that?" Aaron asked.

"No. I found it out. Talked to her mother."

Aaron and Bill exchanged glances. "When?"

Mick shrugged and smiled. "I've been doing a little investigating in my spare time."

"No kidding. What else did you find out?"

"Sammy Earle's a woman's worst enemy. According to his secretary, he ruined Taylor's credit when they broke up."

Aaron shook his head while Bill feverishly wrote notes down. "Wow. Who else did you talk to? The president?"

"Crawford. According to him, you've been doing some investigating too."

"Finding out everything I can, brother, to prove your innocence."

"I just wish I knew what happened to Taylor. We had this weird connection. Nothing really even romantic. Just two people who could connect."

"My money is on Earle, and I think that's where we need to focus," Bill said. His cell phone rang, and he excused himself from the conversation.

Aaron shook his head and sighed. "He just got that thing, and it rings all the time. I think I liked pagers better."

Mick leaned forward and in a hushed voice said,

"Aaron, I can't afford an attorney like Bill. I'm going to have to have a state defender."

"Don't worry about the cost. I'll take care of it."

"I've gotten myself into a real mess here."

"I've been pray—" Aaron stopped himself. His brother didn't want to hear it.

"You've been praying what?" Mick asked.

"Um . . . praying for you."

"Probably what kept me alive," he said with a boyish grin. "I ran through a fire to escape!"

Aaron laughed. "That's what I heard. Pretty bold move."

"Wouldn't do it again. Lucky for me, there was a stream that ran through the field. I have no hair left on the back of one leg. However, I did learn that it's really not that helpful to be soaking wet, because it causes steam burns. Who knew?"

They both chuckled and Aaron said, "Probably every firefighter in America."

Then Mick said, "I prayed too."

The men smiled at each other.

Aaron said, "Bill and I will get to work on your case. We'll leave no stone unturned. And I called Mom and Dad this morning. They believe in you. Don't doubt that." Aaron reached into his pocket. "I almost forgot. I went by to get your mail, and this was in your mailbox." He handed him the envelope.

"What is it?" Mick looked down and opened it, pulling out cash. Aaron watched as he quickly counted it. "I can't believe this."

"What's wrong?"

"This is the exact amount that was stolen out of my wallet."

"You had money stolen?"

"Yeah. But I couldn't quite figure out when. The only thing that made sense was sometime at Taylor's, but I could never put it all together."

Aaron and Mick stared at each other across the table.

Bill approached. "You're not going to believe this. My investigator just called, and he's pulled up some very interesting information on Sammy Earle."

"What?" Aaron asked.

"Let me guess," Mick said. "Found out that Earle was involved in a controversial shooting in Vietnam."

Bill and Aaron looked at Mick.

Bill's mouth was hanging open. "How'd you know?"

Mick offered a sly grin. "Like I said, I've been poking my nose around."

"What happened?" Aaron asked Bill.

"According to my investigator, Earle witnessed his best friend get shot to death in Vietnam by another U.S. soldier. Earle has sought psychiatric help for it. He's a known alcoholic. Anyway, the soldier who shot Earle's friend was court-martialed. Earle testified against the man, who claimed he was saving Earle's life because his buddy was getting ready to kill him by accident."

"So Earle testified on his dead friend's behalf."

"That's right."

"It certainly gives us a good idea about his past," Aaron said.

"So was he found guilty?"

"Yes," said Bill.

"And then he disappeared," Mick added. Bill and Aaron couldn't hide their astonishment. Mick smiled mildly. "Patrick Delano, right, Bill?"

Bill nodded.

"What do you mean he disappeared?" asked Aaron.

"Disappeared before he was sentenced. Escaped some-

how, but there's not a lot of information on how he did it."
Bill looked at the money on the table. "What's that?"

Mick fingered the bills. "A clue that may lead us to
prove that things aren't always as they seem."

———

It had been over a week since Aaron had put on his
uniform. It felt heavy. He drove toward the police station,
wondering how he would be received. How many people
believed in Mick's innocence? How many in his guilt?
Uncertain about how he would feel seeing Jarrod again, he
tried to sympathize with his situation. Jarrod was young,
impressionable, and easily persuaded.

At the back of the building, Aaron parked his car and
got out, hoisting his belt up and touching his badge. Mick
had used it wisely, but Aaron had been dumb not to report
it stolen. Aaron walked through the back door and down
the long hallway. He noticed a certain empty, eerie silence
through the hallways. Where was everyone?

As he turned the corner, he heard murmuring. His heart
skipped a beat, and he felt unbearably self-conscious.
Nearing the break room, he could hear distinguishable
voices. A large group of people surrounded the small television.

"What's going on?" Aaron asked.

The group jumped and glanced from Aaron to the television.

Captain Bellows was standing near the front, and he
looked uneasy as he approached Aaron. He took Aaron's
elbow and guided him outside the room.

"What's going on?" Aaron demanded again.

"Stephen Fiscall was found dead in his home about
twenty-five minutes ago."

"W-what?" Aaron stammered. "How?"

"Looks like he shot himself in the head."

Aaron shuttered. "Suicide." He turned to walk back down the hallway.

"Kline! Get back here!" Bellows called after him.

"I have to go!" Aaron said, picking up his pace.

"Kline!" Bellows hollered as Aaron pushed the back door open. The bright sun blinded him while he raced to his car.

chapter thirty-three

aron sped toward Cottonwood Valley, his thoughts twisted around in shock. He pulled into the neighborhood, which was barricaded four streets away. Pulling his car to the curb, he flashed his badge and ran toward the amassed cars in front of Fiscall's home.

Yellow tape crisscrossed the porch. Detectives Halloway and Martin stood on the sidewalk by the front door and watched him approach.

"Can you believe this?" Halloway said quietly.

Aaron shook his head. "Crime-scene techs in there?"

"Yeah, along with Crawford and his team."

Martin jabbed his thumb toward the door. "Found him at his desk in a silk robe and slippers, one gunshot through the head."

Halloway studied Aaron. "You okay? Heard they got Mick last night."

Aaron nodded.

"You look beat. Why are you here?"

"I had to come see this for myself. I'm supposed to be at work."

A shadow crossed the doorway, and Aaron glanced in. Shep Crawford was walking across the entryway. He looked directly into Aaron's eyes, held them steady for several seconds, and then walked on.

Aaron, Martin, and Halloway watched a technician lift

fingerprints off the doorknob. Halloway shook his head, staring at the man. Martin was glancing around at the frenzy. All Aaron could hear was the stern *no* that he had heard the day he had come here, intending to knock on Fiscall's door.

A wave of chills raced down his body.

Crawford was kneeling by Fiscall's body, his small flashlight tracing the wood underneath the desk. Fiscall was slumped to the side, purple blood snaking down the left side of his face, his right hand stiffly dangling over the side of the chair. A small pistol lay at Fiscall's foot. A water glass was shattered against the wood floor near where Crawford knelt.

Randy Prescott came up beside him. "What are you looking for?"

Crawford didn't answer but continued to flick his flashlight toward the floor. Then he fell forward, his hand crunching against the broken glass. He cursed and stood up.

"You okay?" Prescott asked.

Blood dripped from a large gash below his thumb. As Crawford held it up to examine it, a stream of blood fell onto Fiscall's forearm. Crawford cursed again, this time loud enough for everyone to hear, and grabbed the bottom of his shirt, wrapping it around his thumb. "Somebody get me a Band-Aid! Prescott, make notes right now. Mark the exact places my blood hit Fiscall." He clasped his hand around the wound and backed up slowly.

The medical examiner, Douglas June, approached and said, "Let's go outside."

In the front yard, Crawford opened his hand, and the ME wrapped his thumb. "You'll need stitches," he said, winding gauze around it. Crawford stood silently as June secured the wrap with tape. "You sensing something here?" June asked, ripping off the tape and patting it into the gauze.

Crawford massaged his thumb. "There's something not right."

"I heard the guy was pretty depressed about his family leaving him."

"Come with me." Crawford led June back inside to Fiscall's body, warning him not to step on the glass. "What's your estimated time of death?"

June shrugged. "I'll know more precisely when I get him back to the lab, but I'd say somewhere between ten and midnight."

"Look at this," Crawford said. He pulled on medical gloves and pointed toward the bloody, matted hair on Fiscall's left side.

"I see a bullet hole."

"Ever so slightly indented?"

June looked closer. "Okay. Yeah."

Crawford stood up. "Correct me if I'm wrong, Dr. June, but isn't it true that the gas from the muzzle of a gun puffs out the skin?"

June glanced back at the wound and nodded slowly. "You're exactly right."

"So why is his skull indented instead?"

"As soon as I can get this body, I'll have a lot more information for you," June said.

"We'll work as fast as we can."

Chief Sandy Howard walked toward them, his face drawn into a professional but stern expression.

Prescott shifted uncomfortably, his eyes wide and set toward Crawford.

"Lieutenant, give me an update. I've got a swarm of reporters out there wondering why someone is dusting for fingerprints inside the home of a DA who killed himself." Sandy's eyes shifted to Fiscall's cold, pale body. He shook his head remorsefully.

"Sir, I think we have a homicide made to look like a suicide," Crawford informed him.

Sandy's bulging eyes widened. "A homicide." He glanced to the gunshot wound on the side of Fiscall's head. "Don't say it flippantly, Shep. If we've got a murdered DA here, things are going to go mad very quickly. You better be sure of what you're saying."

June said, "There is something fishy about the bullet hole. As soon as I get him, I'll be able to confirm it."

Sandy swallowed, glancing around the room. Crawford pointed to an 8-x-10 photograph of two black Labrador retrievers sitting on the edge of Fiscall's desk in front of a picture of his family. "I saw two bowls of dog food and water in the kitchen. Where are those dogs?"

The three other men standing around the body stared at the picture for several seconds.

"Prescott, get another detective, and go search the property. Hurry." Crawford made a strict gesture, and Prescott exited the room.

One of the crime-scene technicians came through the door. "We've got a set of prints off the doorknob and an entire handprint off the front glass window. The rain was so heavy we didn't get any footprints except—" the tech smiled—"across a patch of dirt on the front porch. A perfect imprint of a shoe. Size 12."

"Run the prints," Crawford said.

Sandy was shaking his head. "Our number-one suspect has an alibi."

"Can't get a tighter alibi than being in police custody," Crawford said. "We'll see if the prints tell us anything."

"Do you think this is connected to the Franks case?"

"I think we're getting ready to start a whole new chapter," Crawford said.

Sandy blew out a tense sigh. "Okay. I'm going to put off

the press conference for another hour. Nobody leaks a thing or heads will roll. Understood?" Sandy stared at Fiscall's frozen face, turned, and walked out of the study.

Crawford pointed to Fiscall's arm. "Prescott made note of this. His forearm was marked with my blood when I cut my hand on that glass."

"Okay, I'll make note of it in my files too," June said.

Prescott rushed through the door, his cheeks flushed and his hair tangled from the wind. "We found them."

"The dogs?"

Prescott nodded, catching his breath. "Looks like they were killed near a large tree and then dragged underneath some heavy bushes near the outskirts of the front of the property. Their necks may have been broken."

"Why would someone break their necks instead of shooting them?" June asked.

"To show they had control of the situation, control of the animals meant to guard Mr. Fiscall, I imagine." Crawford rubbed his fingers against the stubble on his face and walked out of the study toward the front door.

Stepping into the bright light, he watched law-enforcement personnel scrambling around the yard in haste. Aaron Kline stood by two other officers near the front porch. Crawford looked at the two uniformed officers and said, "Move the crime-scene tape out to the front-fence line where the dogs are before we lose whatever evidence there is." When the two officers left, Crawford said to Aaron, "Looks like the law was on your brother's side after all."

———

Bill Cassavo sat across from Mick in the early evening of his first day in jail. Mick felt weak but passed on the food offered so far. He doubted his appetite would return for a while. No one expected the judge to grant bail, which was contributing to his appetite loss as well.

Bill was talking about the arraignment hearing, which was set for the end of the week. His words faded in and out as Mick studied the attorney. So much like Aaron. Pulled together, with peaceful, confident eyes. Mick wasn't sure what people saw when they looked in his eyes, but he figured most of the time his eyes betrayed him. If they were indeed a window to his soul, there was no telling what looked back at others.

". . . and I'm keeping a close eye on the Fiscall case," Bill said.

Mick tuned back in. He'd heard the news soon after Aaron left. It was one more bizarre thing trying to insert itself into the mystery that had now overrun his life.

"I'm going to assume it's related, Mick. It's the only thing I can do. Rumors are running rampant that this is not a suicide. I know Aaron will keep us abreast of the situation."

Bill's remarks vied for his attention, but his mind wandered back to Taylor. And the strange envelope of money that had turned up. Add that to the mysterious death of the DA, who was sure Mick had done it . . . it made his head spin.

Aaron had told him of the flowers that were sent to Taylor before she disappeared, signed Sammy, even though Liz claimed he only used his initials and was usually too cheap to spend that kind of money on flowers. The details attached to how the flowers were paid for fascinated him as well.

He tried to match all of Aaron's information with what he knew about Sammy Earle. But there were no real links between the two sets of facts.

He hoped that Fiscall's death was somehow connected. All he could do now was sit. And wait. And think.

And pray.

Another two hours of paperwork begged for attention from
Crawford's desk. Night dissolved into the windows, and the
squad room's fluorescent lights were beginning to strain his
eyes. A rare anxiousness tapped at his insides, causing his
foot to bounce up and down.

His phone rang and Crawford snatched it up.

Prescott and the other detectives at their desks watched.
"Yeah?"

"Lieutenant, it's Dr. June. You were right. The skull
was crushed. Looks to be something smooth and round, but
I can't directly identify it. That didn't kill him, though. It
would've done some brain damage, but he died from the
gunshot wound from his own gun."

Crawford wrote down notes. "When will you
conclude?"

"Probably within the next twenty-four hours, I'll have
my full report. It will take a couple more days to get the
toxicology screen done."

On the television, Crawford watched the governor make
a statement, presumably about what a fine assistant district
attorney Stephen Fiscall had been.

Prescott had answered another phone call and was
nodding.

"Okay. I'll be waiting." Crawford hung up the phone.

Prescott scurried toward him. "They identified the
prints," he said. "They belong to Sammy Earle."

The room hushed.

Crawford didn't hesitate. "Okay. Call the judge; let's
get an arrest warrant and a search warrant. And contact the
Dallas PD."

chapter thirty-four

I'm feeling better . . . ," Sammy managed, pressing his lips into the phone's receiver, rolling each word off his heavy tongue. He was lying on his couch, where he'd managed to crawl after redrowning himself in alcohol late last night. His throat burned like a roasting shish kebab. JoAnne's mousy voice recited the details of his revised schedule for tomorrow. "Stop talking so loud," he barked. He listened for her usual apology, but there was nothing but silence. "You there?"

"Is there anything else you need?" Her tone was flat.

Sammy rolled his bloodshot eyes. "See you tomorrow." He threw the phone down and groaned, reaching for the whiskey bottle that was just a finger's length out of his reach. "Come to Papa," he muttered. Even the slightest movement caused his stomach to lurch.

Something caught his eye out the window. The drapes were barely parted, and he thought he saw something black move against the window. Fright gripped him, and he fell off the couch, crawling to the other side of it, his pajama bottoms ripping at the seams in his haste.

There was a loud thud. Then several in rapid succession, coming from the front door.

"Sam Earle? Open up! It's the police!"

Earle froze, his hands clutching the fibers of the carpet beneath him. Whipping his head around, he could see an officer, dressed in black, sliding himself along the outside wall, toward the back door, a rifle standing straight up against his arm.

Earle yelped, shivering as if he'd fallen into snow. Then gunfire. Tearing into his skin. He clutched his chest, his rib cage, his arms. Looking down, he expected to see himself settled into a pool of blood. Nothing.

But he could hear the jungle. The hissing of animals that lived high in trees and deep in the earth. And the language of the devil. Chattering in his ear. He squeezed his eyes shut.

A loud bang caused him to gasp, and he watched his back door slam open. Men paraded in, yelling at him to stay on the floor.

Everything in the room spun, and Sammy's head slammed against the floor. "I'm an American soldier. . . ." He felt his arms being stretched behind him and then cold metal against his wrists.

He was yanked to his feet in a matter of seconds, and he threw up. Collective groans filled his ears, then an unfamiliar male voice. "Mr. Earle, you are under arrest for the murder of Stephen Fiscall. You have the right to remain silent. . . ."

"No, no, no, no . . ." Sammy tried other words, but nothing else would come out. Two strong arms ushered him through his front door, where he was met by a dark night. Bright, flashing police lights assaulted his eyes, and he looked away, squinting. "No . . . no . . . this is a mistake. . . ."

Running down the front porch steps, Sammy felt like he wasn't even in control of his own feet. He turned his head to the right, trying to shield his face and eyes. Near a tree at the corner of his yard, a man stood, silhouetted by street-lights, his face darkened in places by shadows. When

Sammy was whisked toward a patrol car, he could swear he saw the man smile at him.

"Watch your head," an officer said, pushing him down and into the backseat.

Sammy looked back to where the man was standing, but he had vanished. Blinking rapidly, he tried to decide what part of all this was real.

Surely any moment he would wake up screaming like he did from all his other nightmares.

"Wake up . . . please. . . ."

At four in the morning, Aaron's shift ended. Back at the police station, he and Jarrod continued on in silence, as they had for most of their shift. Jarrod had tried to make small talk, but Aaron's mind was too full to have room for it.

Jarrod grabbed his things from his locker and left, giving Aaron a short, apprehensive wave. Aaron waved back.

Forty minutes later, Aaron still couldn't leave. He'd sat at his desk, filling out the final paperwork, his mind drenched in the chaos of all that had transpired.

"Hey, Aaron." Ian Lewis, an investigative assistant, a short man with youthful eyes and thick glasses, smiled down at him.

"It's kind of late for you, isn't it?"

"This bank-scam deal is killing me." Ian sighed. "I can't wait for them to catch this guy so I can get some sleep. Here." Ian handed him three papers.

"What's this?"

"That information you requested."

"What information?"

"You wanted me to print out all the credit-card activity on a Mr. Peter Walker?"

"Oh yeah, right. The guy from Maine." Aaron took the pages from Ian.

"That's just a few days' worth of purchases," Ian said, shaking his head. "Looks like the guy travels a lot."

Aaron scanned the papers. "Puts all his business expenses on here." He raised an eyebrow. "Including some interesting hotel television-viewing habits."

Ian made a face. "Anyway, sorry about the delay."

"No problem." Aaron put the papers on his desk and methodically went through each line. Peter Walker was a frequent traveler; his credit card was filled with purchases from airlines, hotels, and restaurants. In the past seven days, the man had traveled to Chicago, San Jose, Phoenix, and Detroit.

Then something caught his eye. A bus ticket. From Irving to Wichita. Aaron stood up. The dates matched the dates that Mr. Walker was obviously in Chicago!

Aaron circled the line and gathered his things.

Two hours into the search of Sammy Earle's house, Crawford stood outside on the porch with his favorite flashlight.

Detective Mitchell walked out the front door. "Lieutenant, you better look at this." He handed Crawford a crumpled white note that looked to be partially burned. "We found it at the back of one of the drawers in his bedroom."

Crawford stepped into the light of the doorway.

Mr. Earle,

I have some information about you concerning the Taylor Franks case. Information that is neither helpful to you nor to me in my prosecution of the suspect of this case. I need to meet with you privately. Do not bring any lawyers or anybody else. This stays between you and me. Come to my house tonight between 10:30 and 11:00. 11898 Blaine Street. And whatever you do, destroy this letter.

S. Fiscall

"Bag it," Crawford said, and the detective nodded. Crawford smiled. "Guess you should've destroyed it, Mr. Earle."

Chief Howard came up beside him. "If that's not a motive, I don't know what is."

Crawford nodded, his flashlight scanning the rock bed next to the porch.

Sandy continued. "But what in the world did Fiscall have on Earle? Nothing was said to me about it. As far as I knew, the prosecutor's office was solely focused on Mick Kline."

Crawford shrugged. "Fiscall never said anything to me about it, and he had ample opportunity."

"We're going to have to get into some deep investigation on this one."

"Whatever Fiscall had on Earle, Earle felt it was worth killing for."

Sandy shook his head. "Sloppy murder. 'Course, Sammy was so drunk he didn't know which end was up."

Crawford squatted and pulled on a latex glove.

"What is it?" Sandy asked.

Carefully, Crawford reached for a smooth, oval stone, a little smaller than his hand. He held it up in the light and shone his flashlight on it.

"Whatcha got?"

Crawford turned the stone over and held it toward Sandy. "Do you see what I see?"

Sandy squinted, and then his eyes lit up. "That looks like blood."

"With two strands of hair matted to it. Prescott! Bring me a bag!"

Sandy's face showed nothing less than shock. "You probably just found the other half of the murder weapon."

Crawford smiled. "That's why you pay me the big bucks."

"Kline! Wake up!"

Mick turned over, sat up, and grabbed at the pain stabbing through his back. His body had not gotten used to the sleeping conditions here.

"You have a visitor," the guard said.

"What time is it?" Mick asked as the guard opened the door.

"Just after five."

"In the morning? Is it my attorney?"

The guard didn't answer. He led Mick down the corridor to a small conference-like room, identical to the one he'd met his brother and Bill in yesterday. As another guard opened the door, Bill Cassova stood and greeted Mick.

"What's going on?" Mick asked, his eyes still swollen from fitful sleep.

"They arrested Sammy Earle, Mick. For Fiscall's murder."

"You're kidding!"

Bill shook his head, a grin sweeping across his tired face. "Aaron said they found a note, a note that gives a motive and proves a lot more."

"A motive? Why would Sammy Earle kill the prosecutor who thinks he didn't do it?"

"It's unclear right now. Aaron doesn't know the entire content of the note, as it is being kept under tight wraps. But apparently Fiscall had some bit of information on Sammy. One can only guess that it's damaging. Tried to pass it off as a suicide while leaving two dead dogs in the yard. Sammy was drunk out of his mind, from reports."

Mick swept his hand over his face. "This is unbeliev-able."

"And that's not even why I'm here."

"You have something else?"

Bill nodded eagerly. "Your brother thinks Taylor Franks might still be alive."

"Alive?"

"Yes. On the same credit card that bought those flowers that she received is a purchase for a ticket from Irving to Wichita."

Mick fell back into his chair, shaking his head. "What's he going to do?"

"He wants to know if you have a credit card."

Mick frowned. "Um . . . yeah. One. But it's maxed out right now."

Bill was nodding and dialing his phone at the same time.

As fast as his fingers could flip through the envelopes, Aaron raced through the stack of mail that he'd gotten out of Mick's mailbox. The morning sun was just peeking over the horizon, but the sky was still dark and the air cold.

"There," Aaron said, pulling an envelope out of the stack. He thought he'd seen this when he'd quickly rummaged through the mail on Saturday. There was a Visa logo on the envelope, but it didn't look like a credit-card statement, as a computer-typed label addressed the outside.

Tearing open the envelope, he pulled out what looked like a form letter that had parts filled in with darker ink.

Dear Mr. Michael Kline,
This letter is to inform you that you have reached your credit limit
with this account. Unfortunately, we were unable to process the

request from Beauveaux Furniture on 9-14-95. We thank you for your business and if you have any questions, please feel free to call our customer service number.

Aaron snatched his telephone and dialed information.

"What city please?"

"Wichita, Kansas."

"Hold, please."

"Information, what city?"

"Wichita."

"Yes?"

"Beauveaux Furniture."

He heard typing in the background. "Yes, please hold for the number."

Aaron grabbed a pen.

chapter thirty-five

Wichita, Kansas, was a straight shot up I-35. The truck's wheels spun against the flat pavement of the interstate, windows rattling from the high speed. It was a six-hour trip that Aaron made in five.

He pulled into a gas station to fill up and used his calling card at the pay phone.

"Captain Bellows."

"It's Aaron."

"Kline, where are you?" Anger chased away the grogginess in Fred's voice.

"I'm in Wichita."

"Kansas?"

"Yes."

"What's going on? For crying out loud, I have a dead DA and now an officer who got lost on his way to work."

"Fred, I'm almost certain Taylor Franks is alive."

A pause was followed by, "What are you talking about?"

"I'll explain it later. Time is critical, sir. I need our contact at the Wichita Police Department."

"Kline! What in heaven's name are you doing? What in the world makes you think this woman is alive or in Wichita, for that matter?"

"I'm asking for your trust. I just need clearance to investigate this."

Another pause. "Why not? Like there's not enough going on around here."

"If I find her, a lot of questions will be answered."

"All right. I'll call a buddy I went to the FBI National Academy with and tell him to expect you. Are you going there now?"

"First I have to go to a furniture store."

Bellows growled, "Well, pick me up a La-Z-Boy while you're there, won't you?"

Aaron and Detectives Boyd and Shall from the Wichita Police Department stood at the front counter of Beaudeaux Furniture Store while a wispy woman went to get the manager.

An older, professional-looking woman appeared and asked how she could help them. Detective Boyd explained they were with the police and needed some information. After inspecting their IDs, the woman complied.

Aaron handed her the credit-card number. "Someone attempted to order furniture off this credit card, and the card was declined. Would you still keep all the information in the computer?"

She nodded. "Certainly. We take all the information down first before asking for payment. If the card was declined, we would save the information in the computer in case the customer wanted to use another source of payment." The woman read off the number and typed it into her computer. "Yes, here it is. Michael Kline."

"Yes, that's it."

"Okay, looks like the billing and shipping addresses are different."

Aaron held his breath. "The shipping address is in Wichita?"

"Yes, it is."

"What was ordered?"

Interest flashed across the woman's face. "Looks like a clearanced couch."

"We need the shipping address," Aaron said and turned to the two Wichita detectives. "I'd bet all I own that Taylor Franks needed a couch."

Two backup units were called in at the Rose Creek Apartments on the north side of Wichita. The apartment was on the third floor. The two detectives followed Aaron up the stairs. The other two units stayed a few feet back.

"Your call, Officer," Detective Shall said. His hand was near his holster.

Aaron nodded, turned to the door, and knocked. "Maintenance. Here about your toilet."

At first there was silence, but then Aaron heard footsteps coming toward the door. He looked down at his jeans. Boyd and Shall were on either side of the door, out of view from the peephole.

When the door opened, Aaron stared into the eyes of a beautiful woman with dark hair. "Taylor Franks?" he asked.

The two detectives stepped into view.

Color drained from her face. She couldn't answer.

"A lot of people have been looking for you," Aaron said.

A deep swallow triggered tears, and Taylor Franks covered her face with shaking hands.

Aaron helped her back inside, and the detectives followed. The other officers stood in the doorway. Aaron noticed the apartment was nearly empty. A small chair and a TV were all that was in the living room. "Sit down," he instructed.

Taylor wiped the tears from her face, terror flashing through her eyes.

"Why don't you tell me what's going on?" Aaron asked, controlling the anger that made him want to grab the woman by the shoulders and shake some sense into her.

Taylor looked at the other detectives and broke down crying again. Finally regaining her composure, she said, "I'm running from the most despicable man you could ever imagine."

"Let me guess. Sammy Earle."

She nodded slowly.

"But you're not just running from him, are you? You set him up, to make him look like he kidnapped you."

Taylor nodded, tears splashing from her eyes. She covered them and shook her head. "You don't understand. I had to make sure he wouldn't chase me." She cried harder. "He took everything from me. My life. My dignity. My money. My home."

"It's okay, ma'am."

"No, it's not okay. It will never be okay again."

"What did you plan on doing here in Wichita?"

Her teary eyes met Aaron's. "Try to start a new life, I guess. I'm starting poor. But I can live poor. I just can't live as a captive."

Aaron bit his lip, emotions split between anger for the woman who nearly wrecked his brother's life and sympathy for her troubles.

"A well-thought-out plan," Aaron said to her. She stared at him with startled and fearful eyes. "Sent flowers to yourself, right? Made sure to use his name instead of his initials, so the police would have an immediate suspect. Dialed nine and one on your phone. Tilted a few pictures. Put a picture of you and Sammy near the open window. And sprinkled blood in the bathroom."

"Blood in the bathroom?"

"The drops of blood? Very clever."

"But I didn't . . . wait a minute . . ."

"What?"

Taylor smiled slightly and with a bit of amusement in her eyes, she hiked her pant leg up and showed a nearly healed wound about an inch across. "I nicked myself good with my razor that morning. Nothing bleeds longer or faster than a razor cut." Then her smile faded. "But everything else you said was right."

"You know, this was a good plan, except Sammy Earle didn't go down for your kidnapping. My brother did."

Taylor's eyes widened. "Your brother? Who's your . . . wait." She studied Aaron's face. "Mick."

Aaron nodded. "Yeah. He almost got killed over it."

Taylor's lip trembled. "I'm sorry. It wasn't supposed to be like that. I mean, I wasn't supposed to meet Mick, you know? I should've never gone to the bar that night. Right when that guy bumped my fender in the parking lot and yelled at me that it was my fault, I should've just left."

Aaron almost laughed. "So that's the mysterious man you had an altercation with."

"What?"

"Nothing."

"I tried to get Mick to leave, but he was too . . . he was too drunk."

"He left his phone number for you, which linked him to your house."

"I just thought he'd get up and leave the next morning."

Taylor's gaze encompassed the officers around the room. "Am I going to jail for this?"

"Believe it or not, Miss Franks, faking your own kidnapping is not a crime. However, you'll be charged on one count of credit-card fraud and one count of attempted credit-card fraud. We'll see what the DA does with the fact that you tried to set Sammy up for this, especially in light of Sammy's current circumstances."

Boyd gently placed the handcuffs around her wrists. He looked at Aaron. "We'll take a statement and then have her transferred back to Irving."

Aaron nodded and they started to lead Taylor away when she cried out, "No! Please! I can't go back! He'll find me! He'll hurt me!"

Aaron walked to her side. "Taylor, I don't think Sammy Earle is ever going to be able to hurt you again. He was arrested this morning for the murder of our assistant district attorney."

Taylor's face froze in shock. She opened her mouth but couldn't speak.

"I guess Sammy proved what he was capable of after all," Aaron said. "Proved what you knew to be true all along."

The detectives took Taylor away, and Aaron stepped to a nearby window, watching them lead her down the steps.

chapter thirty-six

through the overly bright, musty concrete hall of the jail, Mick trailed a slow-moving guard. A hint of apprehension tickled at his heart. The smell reminded him of the worst days of his life.

Metal clanging against metal rang in his ear; and every sound seemed to vibrate off his memory. The guard smiled as he unlocked the visitors' room door. Mick smiled back. It was only a few days ago that he'd been the one here in chains.

Taylor Franks sat in the far corner of the room, her fingers twisting around one another. She reluctantly smiled at him as the door opened, but a worried expression intruded.

Mick walked through the room and sat across from her. "Hi," he said, smiling.

"I can't believe you came to see me." Tears welded in her eyes. "After all the trouble I caused you."

"By trouble, you mean the fact that I was nearly burned alive? or that I almost drowned? or died from food poisoning?" He waved his hand in the air. "No big deal."

A smile broke onto her face. "Yes, I heard all the details. I can't believe you did all that just to try to find me."

"Maybe I could live in prison, but I don't know that I could've lived thinking I hadn't done anything to protect you."

"We hardly knew each other. Most strangers don't care about one another."

"I thought you were special from the moment I met you."

Taylor looked down. "I'm a crook. A petty thief. And a liar. That's what I am. I was getting my life together, though. Had a steady job, making sure I was always on time and responsible. Things were looking up for me."

"You've come from some tough times. I don't think less of you. I've made a billion mistakes in my life too."

Taylor studied him. "You seemed at the end of your rope when I met you."

"Hanging by a thread," Mick admitted.

"And now?"

"Believe it or not, all this has changed my life for the better."

Taylor nodded, looking unsure if she could believe it.

"What about you? Are you okay?"

"My lawyer says I may not even have to do jail time. But if I do, it'll be for three months or so. The credit-card thing is going to be the biggest problem. I was always good at that, stealing credit cards. It was so easy to do when I worked the ticket counter. These guys fly, charge things, never look at their statements. That's how I got my bus ticket to Wichita and the flowers."

"At least Sammy's out of your life for good now. By the way, why did you send the money back?"

"I took the money, but then a few days later I found out your card was maxed out. So I sent the money back. I wasn't trying to steal; I was just surviving. Sammy took everything from me. But you were so kind, I wanted to give it back. I had no idea you were even involved in the case. I thought you'd get up and leave that morning and I'd never hear from you again."

"It's okay."

"I'm so sorry for all that's happened."

"It worked out. Somebody other than us was in control. That's what I've found out through all this. God loves sinners."

"I'm not sure I can believe that. There are some sins worse than others."

"And there is a forgiveness that's divine."

"What are you going to do with your new life?"

Mick smiled at the thought. "I don't know. I still love to coach football. Or maybe there is another purpose for me to step into."

"That's great. I'm happy for you. Maybe you'll find true love soon too."

He squeezed her hand. "I wish you the best, Taylor. I don't know why our paths crossed. I'm so glad you're okay. I think you'll find your life amazing someday."

Taylor shrugged but smiled and squeezed his hand back. "Thanks. Mick," she said with hesitation. "You don't . . . you don't know what you saved me from."

Mick held her eyes and then stood and walked across the room to the door. As the guard let him out, Mick looked back once and waved. "Good-bye," he said quietly.

She nodded and smiled. "Good-bye."

***

Aaron stood outside next to a dogwood meant to add some serenity to the stale jailhouse landscape. The doors pushed open, and Mick strolled out. "How'd it go?" Aaron asked.

Mick nodded, coming alongside him and walking a little farther until they were out from underneath the shadow of the building. "I think she's going to be okay. I'm glad I came to see her. I assured her I'm fine, and I think I assured her she's going to be fine too."

Aaron smiled at him. "You're looking better, man."

"Why do you say that?"

"I don't know. I think I see hope in your eyes."

A sloppy grin crossed his face. "The eyes are the window to the soul, so they say."

Aaron clapped Mick's shoulder. "I'm so glad I have you back."

"Yeah, that was a long ten days."

"No, I mean *back*. In my life. In my world."

Mick traced lines in the cement with his shoe. "Me too."

"I think it was a journey we were meant to take. Both of us." Aaron looked out across the parking lot. A flock of birds had gathered around a McDonald's sack. "Does this mean you'll be the best man at my wedding?" He glanced at Mick, who was also watching the birds.

"Yeah, but you better marry her quick." He smiled. "The new and improved Mick might catch her eye."

Aaron laughed and smacked him on the back. Mick laughed too. Aaron said, "You know, bro, with all that detective work you did on this case, you might think about going into law enforcement."

Mick howled. "Oh yeah, that would be something, wouldn't it? They have a lot of need for football coaches?"

Aaron grinned. "The FBI hires accountants all the time."

Mick raised his eyebrows. "No kidding?"

"No kidding. They dropped all the charges against you. There's a chance it could work."

"Me in the FBI. And the walls came tumbling down."

Aaron put his arm around Mick and led him down the final cement steps toward the parking lot. "Let me buy you lunch."

"For sure. And please tell me you're going to buy my tuxedo. I'm totally broke, man."

Aaron laughed. "Of course."

"And one more thing."

"What?"

"At your wedding reception, promise me you won't serve any food that can spoil."

It was nearing the end of the day when Aaron pulled into the driveway of Shep Crawford's firehouse. The man stood looking at a small flower garden as if wondering what made the things grow.

Aaron got out of his truck and approached Crawford, who stuck his hands in his pockets and casually observed him as if they'd never spoken. Aaron stuck out his hand.

Crawford shook it firmly, but his eyes were cold. "Kline, what are you doing here?"

Aaron wasn't sure. He glanced at the flowers for something to do with his eyes and to avoid Crawford's uncanny stare. "Look, I just wanted to come and say . . . I don't know . . . I guess, thank you."

"Thank you?" Crawford sniffed. "Interesting."

Aaron finally looked at him. "I never understood if you were a friend or foe."

A twinkle came into his eyes. "Sometimes I'm both."

"Whatever the case, if you hadn't caught Mick, things could have been a lot different. Sammy might not be the lead suspect in Fiscall's murder. Mick would've had motive and no alibi."

Crawford looked bored and unimpressed with the conversation. He suddenly took a shovel that leaned against the side of the house and beckoned Aaron to follow him.

Aaron followed uneasily. Around the corner of the house, he watched Crawford kneel beside a small dark object covered with buzzing flies. Taking a closer look, he realized it was a dead bird.

Crawford pushed his shovel under its decaying body and lifted it off the ground. "Been meaning to get rid of this." He smiled.

"A dead bird."

"Probably met its death splattered against a window."

Aaron glanced up. There were no windows on this side of the firehouse. He took a couple of steps back. "Anyway, I'm not sure why I'm here. It just seemed like I needed to be."

Crawford tilted his head. "Kind of like this bird, your brother was in the wrong place at the wrong time, mostly due to his lifestyle choices. I hope he learned a lesson."

"Mick found his peace with God."

A joyless smile spread across Crawford's lips. "Well, then, Kline, 'tell the angel who will watch over your future destiny to pray sometimes for a man, who like Satan, thought himself for an instant equal to God.'"

Aaron shook his head, laughing a little at Crawford's absurdity. "You seem to live and die by *The Count of Monte Cristo*, don't you?" Aaron met his eyes carefully. "But you didn't finish the quote. It continues: 'but who now acknowledges with Christian humility that God alone possesses supreme power and infinite wisdom.'"

The smile remained steady across Crawford's face. "I'm glad you know your literature so well."

"You seem to know it better than I," Aaron said. He stared at the bird on the shovel. "For many of us, the last few days have brought us to hell and back. I'm better for it. Mick's better for it. Taylor Franks will get a new life. Seems like things worked out for the better. Except for Earle and Fiscall."

Then, to Aaron's surprise, Crawford broke into insidious laughter. Aaron stood there, feeling like he wanted to leave, but curiosity kept him planted.

Crawford's laughter faded. He walked toward his garbage can, and without wrapping the bird up, dumped it in. Then, as casually as if he were talking about a storm gathering in the distance, said, "Well, to quote a book *you're* fond of, Aaron: 'an eye for an eye.'"

Shep Crawford walked up the stairs of his porch and, opening the screen door, turned back to Aaron and winked before disappearing inside.

acknowledgments

the writing of this book presented many challenges and caused me a lot of long and late nights! But the end result could not have been achieved without the help of my ever loyal technical advisor, Ron Wheatley, whom I thank from the bottom of my heart for your never ending charisma and enthusiasm for my projects.

I'd also like to thank Bill Engleking for a lot of good feedback, and Terry Phelps for your meticulous and thorough readthrough. Also, much thanks to Dave Schill, Steve Blake, and Andrea Wood for research help.

Thanks also to Don Gutteridge, my father-in-law and brilliant attorney, who helped with much of the technical advice on the book.

Many thanks to my editor, Lorie Popp, who patiently worked with me through the trials and tribulations of this novel. And thanks also to Jan and Becky and the always supportive Tyndale team.

Special thanks to my prayer team, whose prayers sustained me, and to my agent, Janet Kobobel Grant, whose calm and encouraging voice on the other end of the phone kept me afloat on more than one occasion.

My husband, Sean, sacrificed many hours in order for me to write this book . . . more hours than a husband should have to. Thank you so much for working so hard to help me.

And thank You, Lord, for another chance to get to do what I love. To God be the glory!